A Throne of Blood and Vengeance

Lunaria Realms
Book 3

Alex Frost

GREYMALKIN

Published by Greymalkin Press
www.greymalkinpress.com

Dev & Line Editing by Proofs by Polly
Copy-editing and Proofreading by Rachels Top Edits
Cover Design by Cover by Jules

Ebook ISBN - 978-1-963368-06-2
Paperback ISBN - 978-1-963368-10-9

The Lunaria Realms Series

A House of Fangs & Deceit

A Court of Bones & Sorrow

A Throne of Blood & Vengeance

Note From Author

A gentle reminder that this is a why choose romantasy, which means there are going to be multiple love interests. And our dear, sweet Samara will not be choosing between any of them.

You can still pick a favorite though. I won't tell.

Let's chat real quick about what to expect in this book. This is a fantasy novel that contains adult content and situations. If it was a movie, it would probably be rated "R" for violence, language, and sexual content. If you want to go into this book completely blind and prefer not to read content warnings, you can skip on ahead, my friend.

If there are certain topics that you need to avoid for the sake of your own mental health, or that you simply don't like, please take a look at the list below for some things you will find in this book.

- Explicit consensual sex scenes (there is no dub-con or non-con)
- Blood drinking
- References to parental death

Also… quick little note on language. I am a strange, strange person, and I've lived a bit of an odd life. I was born and raised in California, but was mostly raised by my Canadian grandmother and was then unofficially adopted by an Irish family in my late teens. You might be wondering why I'm mentioning this, and the reason is that I have a bit of a magpie approach when it comes to the English language.

Sometimes I like the American English spelling… sometimes I'm really attached to that extra "u" and go for the non-American version. Variety is the spice of life y'all.

Bless the soul of my copy-editor because she just sighs heavily at the start of each manuscript and deals with my eccentricities. So if you're an American and looking at a word and thinking it's not spelt right… it is most likely the non-American version of the word.

LU
Lake Sp
Alph
A
VELE
Lake Turoth
ORDER OF
FERVIS TERRITORY
Lake Aridesh
FURIE
REALM
Fae Temp
Ruins
The
Badlands
Furie Stronghold
N
W
E
S

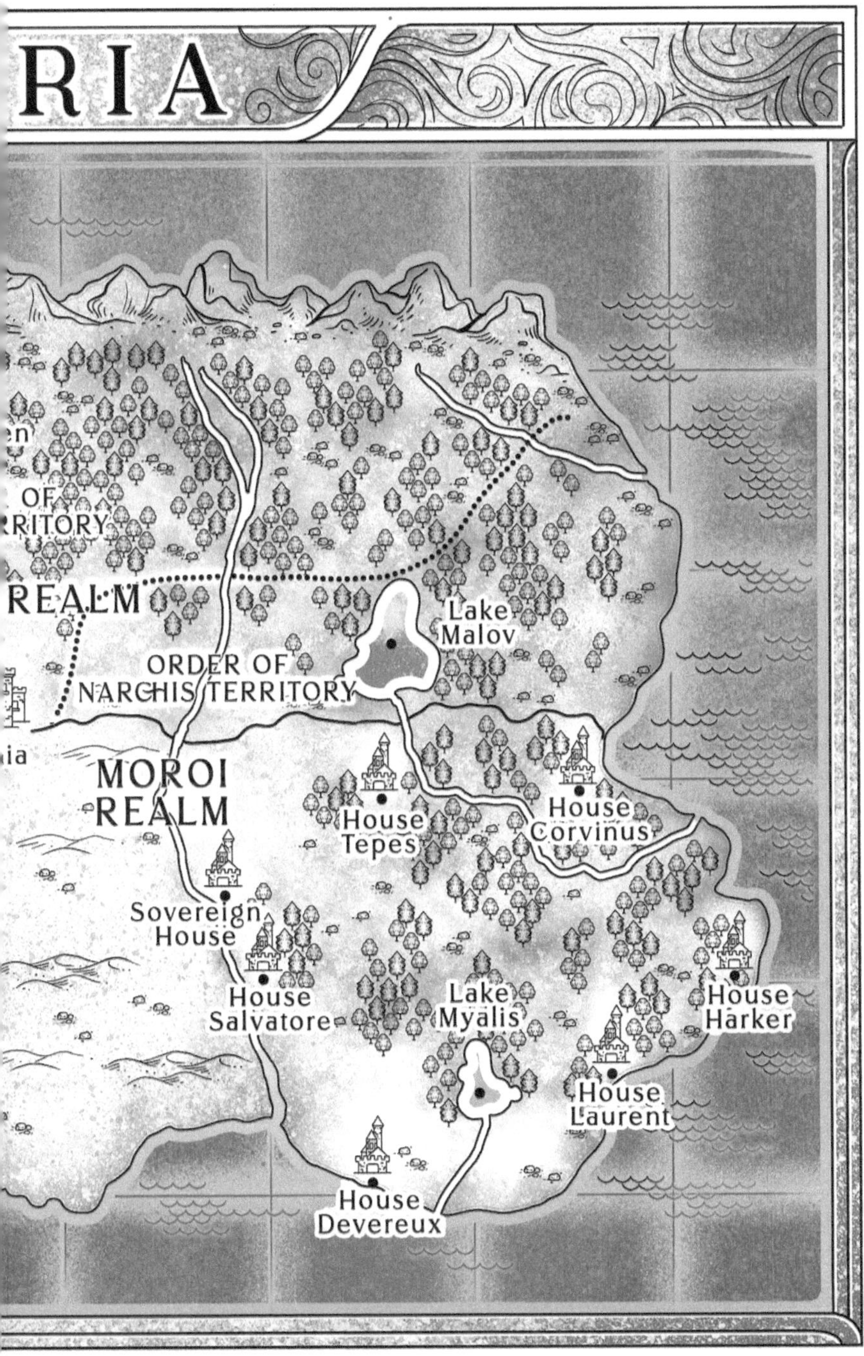
RIA
REALM
OF
RITORY
REALM
ORDER OF
NARCHIS TERRITORY
Lake Malov
MOROI REALM
House Tepes
House Corvinus
Sovereign House
House Salvatore
Lake Myalis
House Harker
House Laurent
House Devereux

*Need a reminder of who is who and what freaking House they belong to?
Or what the hell I mean by House? There is a character and world guide
in the back of the book!*

For every person who read a love triangle and thought…there's another solution to this problem…

CHAPTER ONE

—

Alaric

I was always in control. Every word I spoke. Every move I made. Controlled.

Even when I allowed my bloodlust to come out and play, I did it carefully and in situations where I'd mitigated the risks.

Most Moroi viewed the tight control I kept over myself as a disadvantage. We lived in a world of predators, and our bloodlust was what gave us enough of an edge to survive. By letting it rise, we became just that much faster and stronger.

Of course, if we let it out too much, we might never be able to pull it back. Some Moroi were willing to risk that. I was not.

But as I looked around the meadow that I'd turned into a sea of blood, a cruel smile spread across my lips. I'd pit my controlled brand of violence against their bloodlust any day.

My eyes scanned the tall grass, looking for any other threats, but only the broken bodies of howlers—canine-like beasts—littered the ground. With nothing left to vent my rage on, the desolation I'd been feeling all week started to creep back in.

"Bit much, don't you think?" Samara's voice said dryly in the

1

back of my mind. I could practically envision her toeing one of the corpses with a smirk on her face. *"You could have just gotten me flowers."*

But Samara wasn't here. She hadn't been for almost two weeks, and we only had rumors to go on for where she was.

Hence the carnage.

Several shadows moved from a patch of the meadow where the grass had grown over six feet tall, the tips ending in seed pods. *Looks like I missed a few.* Exhilaration replaced the despair as three howlers crept closer.

The howlers didn't make a sound. Even if I hadn't known they were sick, that would have been a clue. Normally, the beasts were loud, letting out excited yips and howls as they closed in on their prey, but these ones—like the ones I'd already killed—were rabid and not acting normal.

I watched them draw closer, fighting the revulsion as I slowly slid my sword back into its sheath and drew the bow from my back. Howlers were always a little freaky looking, having only a passing resemblance to the canines I was familiar with—mostly the lycanthropes. There were a few Fae murals that depicted domesticated dogs that, apparently, they'd kept as pets once upon a time.

"Can you imagine?" Samara's voice once again spoke to me. Maybe I was finally losing it. *"Keeping cute little dogs as pets? Such luxury."* She'd have drawn out that last word in a way that would've made me instantly hard. I still didn't know how she did it. Somehow, she could make any word sound obscene.

Gripping my bow with one hand, I pulled an arrow from the quiver.

The largest of the three split off, and I adjusted my stance as I aimed the tip of the arrow towards it. Two pairs of eyes, one stacked on top of the other, watched me from a long, narrow head. The madness that rotted their minds did the same to their flesh. Its sleek black coat was missing large patches of fur in places, and its ribs were starting to show. Howlers were built with speed in mind—a lean body that cinched and narrowed at the hips sat on long legs. Once they got going, they could almost outrun a horse, their stamina definitely better.

Bits of rotting flesh hung from its teeth as its mouth gaped open. The other fun part about howlers was they could open their jaw almost to a perfect hundred eighty degrees. Their teeth curved backwards, and their favorite way of bringing down large prey was for several of them to latch onto it, slowing it down, while others in the pack did their best to trip the panicked prey. Once the prey was on the ground, the pack wouldn't bother to kill it, they'd just start feasting.

I couldn't fall. Howlers might be low on the food chain, but it was still three against one. A little of my bloodlust rose, and I let some remain while pushing most of it back down. It wasn't enough to actually do anything other than change my eye color, but I found it easier to control if I let a small amount linger.

It would've been smarter to let more of it come to the surface. I was bleeding from at least half a dozen wounds that I hadn't healed yet. Plus, I'd need every inch of speed I could muster up for this fight.

But I couldn't bring myself to trust the bloodlust that hummed in my soul, begging to be set free.

Samara was confident that I would never turn Strigoi, especially if I continued to drink from her regularly. But it'd been weeks since I'd sunk my fangs into her soft flesh and swallowed the sweet elixir that was her blood.

As much as I wanted to share her faith in me, I'd seen my cousin turn Strigoi. The funny boy I'd grown up with was gone, and all that had remained was a monster that'd tried to rip out my throat. And he wasn't the only one in our family who had been lost.

I wouldn't risk it.

Besides, I was looking forward to more physical pain. Anything was better than the sharp, bitter feeling of loss and failure that I felt every waking moment.

I focused on everything Samara had taught me about shooting. Exhale when you draw the string and keep that exhale slow and steady through the release.

The sound of the bow string snapping echoed across the meadow, followed by the thunk of it sinking into the neck of the large howler.

Damn it. Missed. I'd been aiming for its fucking eye, but instead, I'd hit the meaty part of it's neck. So all I'd done was piss it off.

Samara wouldn't have missed.

One of the smaller howler's heads swung away from me and towards the larger one, its nostrils flaring at the scent of fresh blood. Usually, they weren't cannibalistic, but when they were this far gone, they'd go after anything that was potentially food—even each other.

The beast launched itself at its larger packmate and the two of them tumbled across the ground. I tossed the bow aside and pulled my sword free. It didn't take long for the larger beast to overpower the smaller one, gripping it by the neck and shaking vigorously. I heard the telltale snap of a neck, but the beast didn't halt its assault.

My instincts screamed at me to move, and I barely managed to step to the side as the third howler lunged for my throat. I brought my sword down on its neck, severing its spine with one stroke.

Pain lanced up my right leg as the large howler clamped down on my thigh. Flesh tore and bone snapped, forcing a scream from my throat. The howler shook its head back and forth, trying to tear my leg away, and my vision darkened for a second, the bloodlust trying to surge forward.

No.

My back hit the ground, and I dropped my sword. Shoving the pain into the same box I locked my bloodlust in, cool metal met my bloodsoaked fingers as I reached for the dagger holstered on my hip. The howler opened its jaws and bit down again, shattering the bone it'd already broken.

With a guttural yell, I slammed the blade into its eye.

The blow didn't slow the beast down at all; instead, it just started shaking its head again, slamming me into the earth. I gripped its head with my other hand and drew the dagger out.

Stab. *Die.* Stab. *Fucking die already*!

Its jaws finally loosened and the howler collapsed partway on top of me. I shoved it off with a groan and left the dagger buried in its flesh.

I needed to heal the wounds—rationally, I knew this; aside from the pain, I was losing too much blood. Moroi were hard to kill, but I'd been a little reckless in this fight, and I was fairly certain one of my arteries had been hit during that last round.

That explained the lightheadedness and my darkening vision.

"Yep. You're the epitome of control," the imaginary Samara teased. But as amazing as she was, Samara didn't have telepathy.

She wasn't here.

I was definitely losing it, but I couldn't bring myself to care. "I miss you. Please be safe."

My body protested as I forced myself to sit up and draw the glyph for healing on my leg with shaking fingers. I panted through the pain of bone fragments piecing themselves back together along with my torn flesh. Once that was done, I set to fixing the other wounds, and twenty minutes later, my body was healed but my soul was still aching.

The sound of hoofbeats drifted to me, and I turned to watch three rangers approach. I was surprised but glad that it'd taken them this long to get here. A few rangers had seen me leave alone earlier, and I had no doubt they had reported that to their superiors—who, in this case, were the rangers before me.

"Damn it, Alaric." The lead ranger glared at me, her blonde hair shining brightly in the afternoon sunlight. "I told you we would handle this."

I shrugged, picked my sword up off the ground, and swung it into the sheath on my back, ignoring the reproachful look the oldest of the rangers gave me over not cleaning it first. There wasn't a patch of my clothing that wasn't coated in blood—mine or the howlers'—and I hadn't bothered to bring a pack of supplies with me since I wasn't far from House Harker.

"Adrienne. Emil," I said in greeting before glancing at the third ranger, who had dismounted and was surveying my work close up. "Nyx."

The young ranger glanced up at me. "Nice work."

I grunted. Howlers were some of the least dangerous of the monsters that prowled the forests. They were pack hunters and really only posed a problem if the pack got particularly large. Occasionally, some type of madness would infect them. We didn't know what caused it, but if one of them got it, the entire pack would and, worse still, would transfer it to any other pack they came into contact with.

They'd turn highly aggressive and would attack anything, even if they had no chance of winning, leaving a trail of corpses behind them until they eventually starved to death. Rabid howlers didn't eat, only slaughtered. This sick pack had been reported a week ago with a warning that they were slowly moving closer to House Harker territory. I'd been sparring with the rangers when the report had come in.

Emil had specifically told me to stay out of it when he'd caught my interest in the news. But the daily sparring hadn't been cutting it anymore, and I needed an outlet to vent my frustrations on.

For a few moments, I'd managed to forget that my world was on fire. The fight had given me some clarity, and even though I felt the embers burning again, I knew I'd be able to concentrate better for at least a day or two.

Then I'd need to find something to kill again.

Emil gave me an understanding look. Everyone at House Harker was feeling the strain. The Head of the House, the Heir, and the Marshal were all gone. Everyone knew Carmilla was at the Sovereign House, but no one had seen Samara or Vail.

Neither of them, or Carmilla for that matter, had sent any messages to clear up the confusion.

Something was very wrong. We all knew it, and we all had different ways of coping while we tried to figure it out.

Adrienne was staring daggers at me from atop her enormous chestnut stallion. Her way of coping had me grinding my teeth on most days. She was second-in-command with Vail being gone and had a tendency to be overprotective of everyone, like she alone could keep us all safe through sheer force of will.

Before, it had been Nyx who had borne the brunt of Adrienne's obsessive protective inclinations, but that had now been extended to me, Roth, and Kieran.

Roth rolled with it, mostly because it was hard to get them out of the library, so the only thing they fought with Adrienne about was eating regularly. Aside from that, they were able to handle Adrienne's constant hovering.

Kieran and I did not handle it well.

Emil sighed, likely sensing the brewing fight between me and Adrienne. He'd been the one to break up the fight between her and Kieran, though not before Kieran got a split lip and a black eye. Adrienne might have been the protective sort, but she also had a wicked temper—and if she thought knocking us out was the best way for her to achieve her goals, she'd absolutely do it.

"Do you need a ride back?" Emil asked. "We should get out of here. The blood is going to attract all kinds of nasty things."

"Which is why we planned to draw the pack farther from the House," Adrienne growled.

I winced. It had actually been my intention to do just that, but I'd underestimated just how good the creatures' sense of smell was. The howlers had been on me before I could attempt to get them farther away . . . which was no doubt one of the reasons Emil had ordered me to not go after them. Not just for my own safety, but because this was what the rangers did. None of them would have made the mistake I had.

"We can send extra patrols this way." Nyx mounted their bay gelding. "Just to keep an eye on things. I'll make sure it gets done."

"You will not be on those patrols." Adrienne finally stopped glaring at me to give Nyx a sharp look.

"Wouldn't dream of it," Nyx replied smoothly.

I was pretty sure they were lying, and based on how Adrienne narrowed her eyes at the young ranger, she clearly thought the same. Good. Maybe Nyx could draw her ire for a while.

"Ride?" Emil repeated calmly.

I raised my fingers to my lips and whistled. Moments later, a dark grey mare came charging past the tree line at the other end of the meadow, where she'd been munching on grass like she didn't have a care in the world while I'd been fighting for my life. She didn't bother dodging the howler corpses on the ground; if anything, she purposely went out of her way to stomp on them.

"Brave of you." Emil's brows rose. "That horse is evil incarnate."

Zosa slid to a stop in front of me, howler blood smeared across her legs and stomach, and her dark eyes were full of a fire and rage that echoed my own soul.

"We have an understanding." I stroked the mare's nose. "She'll take me where I need to go, and I'll kill anything that stands between me and the woman who owns both our souls."

"STILL NO MESSAGES from her or the Sovereign House." My fingers tightened on the stone wall of the balcony just off the aviary where we kept the strikers.

"Told you we wouldn't hear anything." Roth gave me a flat look. "Can I return to the library now, or would you prefer to waste my time further?"

This was exactly why I'd snuck out this morning to hunt down the rabid howlers. I'd needed something to take the edge off so I could deal with Roth.

I'd gotten used to their taciturn personality since Roth had moved to House Harker, but it'd been different ever since Samara—along with Vail and Draven—had vanished. Thanks to Kieran's connections, we were pretty certain they were all at the Sovereign House, but the other information we'd received was confusing . . . and disturbing.

Supposedly, Carmilla had overthrown Queen Velika with the help of Velika's consort, Samara's ex-husband Demetri . . . and Vail. What had happened to Samara and Draven after that was a little harder to determine. There were rumors that the prince was dead, something that didn't bother me all that much but had sent Kieran spiraling. Nobody had seen Samara recently, but one guard who was loyal to Kieran said she was in the dungeon.

That couldn't be right though. If Carmilla had truly overthrown the Sovereign Queen—something that was hard to come to terms with because we all thought they'd been friends despite Velika's ill intentions—why would she throw her niece into the dungeon? Carmilla had helped raise Samara after her parents had been killed and had always been fiercely protective of her, and Samara was completely loyal to her aunt.

None of this made sense. It had been almost two weeks since Samara and Vail had left on their mission to find the other half of the lost Fae crown that supposedly could override the free will of others. Velika had the other half, and those two had raced off to make sure she didn't get the second piece. Against my better judgment, we'd told Draven where they'd been heading when he'd demanded to know, and he'd gone after them.

I glanced at Kieran, who hadn't even acknowledged us when Roth and I had barged up here. Even now, all his attention was on the letter he was composing.

He loved Samara . . . and Draven. Both of the people who mattered to him more than anyone else—vanished. Samara, I understood. She and Kier had been in love the moment they'd laid eyes on each other. The prince . . . *that* I was still having a hard time wrapping my head around.

I hadn't even known Kieran and the prince had been involved until recently, which was something I was still a little pissed off about. Kieran had been my best friend for well over a decade, and he'd kept something major from me.

Despite Draven's declarations about caring for Samara, I still didn't trust the Moroi Prince. Velika was his mother, and we knew he was working for the wraiths and had helped them slaughter several of our outposts in recent years. Despite that, Kieran loved him, and Roth, of all people, backed Kieran up when he suggested we tell Draven. I was the odd person out, but even I had gone along with it because, despite my feelings about Draven, I did believe there was something between not only him and Kieran but Samara too.

And it wasn't a minor something. Not with the fierce and possessive look he'd had in his eyes that day.

"Apologies, Roth." I spun around and leaned against the stone wall, crossing my arms over my chest. "Do you have something useful to add? By all means, speak up and let us know what you've found in the library that will answer what the fuck is going on right now."

Fiery orange flecks burned in Roth's hazel eyes as their bloodlust rose. They'd barely left the library for the past two weeks, but after I'd returned and cleaned myself off, I'd gone there to find them waging war on the books. Several of them had pages torn out, and Roth was cursing in languages I didn't even recognize. I'd tried to calm them down, but they'd only stormed out, as if the books had betrayed them in failing to provide an answer.

It'd taken some doing, but I'd convinced them to come up here for some fresh air. I'd had no idea if it would help, but I needed Roth to keep it together because I barely was . . . and Kieran definitely wasn't.

Given Roth's current mood, I kept one eye on their fore-arms, where bloodred ropes were looped. They used to be flat ribbons, but now the fabric was thicker and looked like three pieces braided together, making it more rope-like.

The only place Roth had spent any time besides the library was the target range in the training yard. On particularly bad days, they'd trash a dozen targets. With half a thought, they'd have their ropes unwinding from their arms and shooting towards the wood targets we used for archery, and blood-colored protrusions would jut out seconds before the ropes made contact, slicing through the wood.

Roth had always been a bit grumpy and standoffish, but

this viciousness was something new that we were all getting used to.

At the rate Roth and I kept going at each other, I knew my blood would be dripping from those ropes sooner rather than later.

Clearly, Kieran felt a fight between Roth and I was imminent because he looked up from the letters he was rapidly churning out to give both of us an annoyed look. "If the two of you are going to bicker, go somewhere else." His eyes, which had been more gold than brown lately, dropped back to the note he was writing. Normally, Kieran kept himself clean-shaven and his hair neatly styled, but he was sporting a week's worth of stubble, and his blond hair looked like it hadn't been brushed in days.

"Are you reaching out to the same people?" I asked tiredly. "I don't see why they'd tell you anything different than they did two days ago."

"Maybe don't tell me how to interact with people." His words were clipped, and there was an edge to his voice I'd never heard from him before. His eyes dropped back to the letters. "Roth is supposed to be good at research, although that's been an epic fail. I'm good at gathering gossip and cashing in on favors, which is why we have any information at all right now. What the fuck do you do, Alaric? Other than going traipsing off into the woods and leaving all the work to us? Do you even give a shit about getting her back? Or does this make you happy?"

I swallowed back my growl. Thank fuck I'd gone out this morning; otherwise, I definitely would have ripped his head off —best friend or not.

"Sorry," Kieran said tightly without looking up.

Roth and I shared a look. We might constantly fight with each other, but that was mostly because we were too similar in a lot of ways. As pissed off as we'd get, neither of us ever held a grudge—at least not for long. Kieran was the peacekeeper in our group, and neither of us knew how to roll with the changes in his behavior.

Roth and I were good at a lot of things, but emotional comfort was not one of them. I cared about Kieran because he was my best friend, and I thought Roth had grown to like Kieran despite themself. Kier was just so . . . Kier. He was honest, loyal, and always willing to help everyone.

Now he was hurting and neither of us knew what to do because we were trying to keep from spiraling into panic and despair ourselves. Samara would have known what to do. She always did.

I missed her so much, it hurt. Up until recently, we'd been adversaries, but even then, I'd been obsessed with her. Samara had consumed my soul long before I'd ever tasted her lips against mine, and now she was missing and I had no fucking answers as to why or how to help her.

She was counting on me—on us—and we were failing her. I found everything about that unacceptable.

I took a deep breath. Letting myself unravel into despair wouldn't help.

The absence of both Carmilla and Samara hadn't exactly gone unnoticed. There was a quiet tension in House Harker, and the other advisors had been looking to me for answers. I'd been Carmilla's top advisor, and since returning, I hadn't exactly hidden that things between Samara and I had changed.

Everyone was aware of her relationship with Roth and Kieran. I hadn't stood in the center of the courtyard and dramatically declared my feelings, but I hadn't needed to. I spent every waking moment trying to figure out what had happened to Samara. And even though we were biting each other's heads off constantly, Roth, Kieran, and I were often together.

It didn't take a genius to figure out that Samara had

claimed another lover—just the gossip mill that was the House Harker court.

I was trying to figure out how to suggest to Kieran that maybe he should try some new contacts without setting him off when the doors to the rooftop burst open.

Adrienne stalked out onto the stone balcony, Emil and Nyx right behind her. A few of the strikers flapped their wings in unease at the sudden intrusion, their brightly colored scales glistening in the sunlight.

"I take it from your grim faces that you don't have any news—good or bad—to share?" Adrienne asked. Like Kieran, Adrienne was usually perpetually full of joy, but recently, the ranger, who was only a decade older than us, looked tired and drained. The other two rangers—Nyx and Emil—didn't look any better.

All of the rangers were feeling a little uneasy about Vail's absence. But Adrienne, Emil, and Nyx were part of Vail's personal squad—more than that, they were friends.

The fact that they hadn't heard anything from him either had only increased everyone's concerns.

"No," Kieran replied without looking up from his letter. "Nothing today. You?"

Adrienne didn't answer, and it was then that I noticed the letter she clenched at her side.

"What did you learn?" It took every ounce of my self-control not to close the distance between us and rip that piece of paper out of her hand. But I knew Adrienne would tell us— we'd been sharing information all week—and she could absolutely kick my ass. So I stayed where I was and forced myself to be patient.

"It's not good." Her expression was pinched, and when she opened her mouth to say more, it was like the words escaped her. Finally, she just held the letter out, and I quickly walked over and grabbed it, eyes skimming the words. There wasn't much written, as if the person had only had a small opportunity to send the message and had hastily slapped it together. I'd expected it to be from Vail, but this wasn't his handwriting.

"Well?" Roth pushed. Even Kieran had stopped writing and was completely focused on me.

I swallowed. "It says Carmilla has been seen walking around the Sovereign House . . . with a crown of silver and gold on her head. Vail is often at her side."

Kieran slammed his palm down on the table he'd dragged up here, sending some of the paper flying and several strikers to take off in the air. Then he rose and stalked to the other side of the balcony.

"Anything about Samara . . . or Draven?" Roth asked.

"No." I shook my head and stared at the short note, as if some further insight would magically appear. Based on all the information we'd been able to piece together, it wasn't a surprise that Carmilla was walking around free. Confusing, absolutely, because I didn't understand why she hadn't reached out to us. Queen Velika being dead had been reported by enough sources that we'd all accepted that as well—shocking as it may have been.

But the crown . . . that was new. We'd been so worried about Velika getting her hands on both pieces that it had never occurred to us that someone else might not only know of its existence but would be vying for it as well. And definitely not Carmilla.

As unbelievable as it seemed, if Kieran's informant was telling the truth, Samara wasn't simply missing—she was imprisoned in the Sovereign House. And Carmilla now possessed the whole crown . . . and Vail wasn't sharing a cell next to Samara.

"Did Vail betray us?" I half whisper the accusation. On one hand, it didn't seem possible . . . but then Vail might not have seen it as betrayal, at least not to House Harker. He was loyal to Carmilla, almost fanatically, and his dislike of Samara wasn't exactly a secret, but it'd seemed like things had been changing between them. Had he deceived all of us? A humorless laugh flowed from me. "We were so concerned about the wicked prince that we didn't see the devil already walking amongst us."

"We don't know that Vail betrayed Samara," Nyx snapped. They were the youngest of the rangers and held Vail up on a pedestal, more so than even Adrienne and Emil. "Maybe Carmilla used the crown on him. We know it can force anyone to obey the person wearing it. He may be just as trapped as Samara, even if there are no visible bars around him."

Roth shook their head. "She still would have had to get the crown, and Vail was with Samara. If they found the other half, it's not that big of a stretch to think he stabbed Samara in the back and gave it to Carmilla."

"Vail must have had his reasons," Emil said evenly, which seemed to soothe Nyx somewhat. I could see the doubt in the older Moroi's eyes though. Despite his words, Emil clearly had some concerns about what Vail was up to.

"So what do we do now?" Adrienne asked. "Keep waiting for more information to trickle in? Or go to the Sovereign House to see for ourselves?"

"If that crown truly does everything we think it's capable of, then our free will could be taken away as soon as we walk through those gates." Emil's dark bushy brows creased in concern. It didn't escape my attention that he hadn't said Carmilla's name. We were all having a hard time coming to terms with the fact that the House Leader we'd served our entire lives—someone we'd thought had been just and fair— would be okay with enslaving her own people like that.

I glanced at the letter again. *Carmilla wears a crown of silver and gold.* If my parents had been here, I'd have asked them— they knew Carmilla well since they'd served her for over a century before semi-retiring—but lately they'd been foregoing the safety of the Harker fortress to spend time helping in the outposts. No amount of pleading on my part about the dangers facing our outposts had convinced them to return. Now, I was a little thankful, because if Carmilla truly was seizing power over the Moroi, it would be the Houses she targeted first.

"Roth," I said slowly, my gaze flicking briefly to Kieran, who had silently joined us again, a storm brewing in his eyes. "Do we have any books or documents that show the interior layout of the Sovereign House?"

"No." Eyes that burned like fire looked at me. "But I know where we can get some."

CHAPTER TWO

—

Samara

"HAVE YOU RECONSIDERED YOUR ANSWER YET?" My ex-husband smiled down at me through the bars of my cell, where I was leaning against the back wall. There'd been a time when I would have found that smile appealing. It had a charming, sly quality to it, like he was thinking of something amusing and couldn't wait to share it with you. With his perfectly tousled chestnut hair and stunning hazel eyes, Demetri was quite the looker, and he knew it, but I wasn't a sixteen-year-old girl anymore who could be dazzled by easy grins and pretty eyes.

Actually, even at sixteen, I hadn't been that gullible. Just a little more willing to put aside my happiness for the sake of my House.

That was no longer who I was. At twenty-four, I knew exactly what and who I wanted, and I did want Demetri.

I wanted him bleeding out on the floor at my feet.

"Have you considered shutting the fuck up?" I gave Demetri a smile that showed way too much fang to be considered anything friendly. "Or better yet, slitting your own throat?"

The grin slipped as the muscles along Demetri's jaw tight-

18

ened. He'd come down here every day to ask if I'd reconsidered his offer of marriage. Because being married to that worthless piece of shit hadn't been bad enough the first time—he actually thought I'd willingly sign up for round two.

I had a feeling he'd love nothing more than to open the door to my cell, step inside, and throttle me for all the insults I'd hurled his way over the past week. That would be a nice change of pace. I wasn't particularly good at hand-to-hand combat—knives and bows were my thing—but with how wrathful I was feeling, I had no doubt I could rip out Demetri's throat faster than he could blink.

Alas, the hulking brute standing directly opposite me on the other side of the dungeon kept Demetri from trying anything devious. Well . . . more devious than going along with having your ex-wife thrown into a prison cell while you tried to strong-arm her into marrying you again.

So far, my aunt—the real reason I was in this fucked-up situation—had kept her word about not forcing me to marry Demetri. Although she'd also made it clear that she thought the marriage would be in the best interest of everyone.

Everyone clearly did not include me.

There had to be a reason. Neither of them were the sentimental type. There was some political gain to me being married to Demetri that I wasn't seeing, and they must have discovered it recently because they'd both allowed my divorce to go through, and that had only been a couple of months ago.

But since I was locked in this fucking cell, I had no way of finding out the reason behind all of this. I needed to get out of here. I had to make sure Kieran, Roth, and Alaric were alright. Plus check in with Cali and Rynn, who were no doubt losing their minds over my lack of communication. Draven was alive—for now—but I refused to leave him behind, so I had to devise a plan that got him out too.

There was another complication to all of this. A ticking

clock, so to speak. Cramps tore through my lower abdomen, taking my breath away and sending a fresh bolt of pain every minute. I felt like I was dying.

The hulking brute, Vail—also known as the lying sack of shit—glanced at me with a frown. His grey eyes scrutinized me as if he could sense the pain I was in.

I ignored him and tried to will the cramps away. And the Marshal while I was at it. Tragically, they both remained.

When the humans had cast the spell to turn themselves into Moroi, it'd led to a fucked-up reproductive cycle. Every four months, anyone with a uterus would experience the joy of excruciating pain and bleeding. It only lasted for two or three days, but those days were absolute agony. Once that funness was over, my sex drive would go wild. That part *was* usually fun —almost made up for the three days of suffering—but given my current situation, it was a problem.

I wouldn't be completely out of my mind with lust, but thinking coherently would be difficult. So I was basically looking at almost a week of limited cognitive function. Wonderful. As if my situation weren't fucked enough already.

It wasn't as if the woman that I'd respected, looked up to, and absolutely idolized had betrayed me. And not a little betrayal. A *lied to me and manipulated me for years, tortured and impris- oned the man I loved, and had me thrown in a moonsdamned dungeon* type of betrayal.

I rubbed the empty space on my finger where the ring Cali had gifted me should've been. Demetri had been the one to take it off—gleefully. When we'd been married, I'd regularly used it to communicate with Cali and Rynn. He probably knew how much my two best friends didn't like him and took great joy in making sure I couldn't reach out to them.

Rynn was with the Alpha Pack now. No doubt she wasn't happy about that, but at least she was safe. Those assholes would protect her—whether she wanted that protection or not.

It was Cali I was worried about. All Furies had a bit of a short fuse. Cali was pretty good about controlling her temper —unless Rynn or I were threatened, then all bets were off.

The fact that she wasn't already here raining down blood and fury had me worried. My fingers curled inwards until my claws pressed into my skin just shy of drawing blood. I hated Carmilla for imprisoning me and keeping me from helping my friends put out the fires that seemed to be popping up everywhere.

The only person I hated more than her right now was Vail, because he was the reason I was in this mess. When I wasn't trading barbs with Demetri, I was screaming at him. At least, I had been for the first five days. Lately, I'd switched to ignoring his presence because that seemed to hurt him more, based on how his eyes would bleed silver after a few minutes.

I didn't give the slightest fuck about Vail's feelings right now though. He'd betrayed me—after he'd fucked me.

He could rot in a shallow grave right next to Demetri for all I cared.

Demetri's hazel eyes hardened the longer he looked at me, light green flecks starting to expand into the brown as his temper and bloodlust rose. For a second, another pair of hazel eyes surfaced in my mind. But Roth's eyes were far prettier. Their secondary eye color was more of a burnt orange, like little sparks that would flare in their eyes. Compared to my sharp-tongued love, Demetri was nothing.

Less than nothing.

I'd find a way out of here. Back to all of them. Ideally before my lovers tried something insane like breaking into the Sovereign House.

Yeah, because breaking out is a much saner idea.

Shut up, brain. Nobody asked you.

Fuck. *I might be losing it.*

My stomach churned as the pain of my cramps reached a

new level. I was going to hurl up my meager breakfast all over this floor if I didn't lie down soon. A bead of sweat formed at my hairline. It was bad enough that I was sitting while he was here, but standing wasn't an option. I settled for keeping my spine ramrod straight while I sat and didn't let my feral smile falter.

"Fine," Demetri finally said, brushing a hand through his hair as if he weren't monumentally frustrated with me. "I'll take my leave for now." His eyes glinted with a slyness I didn't like one bit. "Perhaps I'll pay the fallen prince a visit and test out my new iron-tipped spear. Maybe I'll get him to scream loud enough that you'll be able to hear him all the way up here."

My mask cracked and then shattered into a thousand pieces. In a second, I was on my feet at the front of the cell, wrapping my fingers around the bars that separated us.

"Touch him, and I'll rip out your spine and beat you to death with it!" I snarled and shook the bars even as they burned my skin. All of the bars in the dungeon had a high level of iron because they'd been built by the Fae. Why the Fae had felt the need to imprison their own kind, I had no idea.

Just like I had no idea why I had a reaction to the iron. It felt revolting against my skin.

"Pretty sure he'd already be dead at that point," Vail said from where he still casually leaned against the wall, sharpening one of his knives. "But I've never really tested Moroi healing abilities in that way. Could be a fun little experiment."

"Nobody fucking asked you," I snapped at Vail before mentally slapping myself. Well, he'd finally gotten me to speak to him.

Demetri gave Vail a cool look. "You were told to stay away. I'll be informing Carmilla of this."

Vail shrugged, eying his dagger for a moment before continuing to sharpen it. "Seems like a poor choice."

"And why is that?"

The Marshal of House Harker finally looked up to meet Demetri's gaze, thick silver cracks weaving through his dark grey eyes. "Because then I'd be forced to rip out your tongue for being a sniveling little tattletale."

Demetri's eyes flashed green for a moment before his cool and collected facade snapped back into place. There was a conniving wickedness to Demetri that I'd never seen in all the years we'd been married. Either it was new or he'd done an excellent job of hiding it. I suspected the latter, which irked me because I hadn't seen through his *lazy but mostly harmless* act for all that time.

"Fine. Stay here as long as you want." A knowing smile spread across his lips. "She'll never forgive you. Samara never loved me, but the way she stares at you when you're not look-ing"—he sucked in a harsh breath—"that's definitely love. The fallout of it anyway. Did you know, Vail? When you agreed to betray her, did you know she loved you? What about when you parted those deliciously thick thighs and fu—"

Faster than I could track, Vail had his hand wrapped around Demetri's throat as he slammed him against the bars of my cell, causing me to jump back. He flung the other Moroi to the floor and took one step towards him before halting and spinning around to pace to the other side of the dungeon.

Demetri had succeeded in getting both Vail and me to lose our tempers.

Instead of being upset, my ex-husband just let out a hoarse laugh as he rose to his feet, brushing away the dirt from his clothes and swiping his hair back. "You're both so touchy." He straightened the collar of his dark red shirt. "See you tomor-row, Samara. I'll tell the prince you said hello."

"Fucker!" I screamed as the heavy wood door closed behind him. A second later, I was bending over and heaving up my breakfast. Then I straightened and wiped my mouth with the back of my hand. It took me a minute to realize Vail had moved over to my cell and was holding a canteen through the bars. I snatched it from him and rinsed out my mouth, then walked as far away from the vomit as possible.

"He's bluffing," Vail said quietly. "Draven scares the shit out of him. He's only been to that level once, and he ran out the door like wraiths were chasing him."

I didn't say anything. Partly to annoy Vail, but mostly because the pain had reached a new level and it was taking all my concentration to stay upright and conscious. A sharp gasp exploded from my lips, and I decided that if I wanted to stay awake, I needed to sit down.

"What's wrong?" Vail crouched outside my cell. Some of the silver had faded from his eyes, but they were still intense as he examined me, trying to find why I looked like a strong wind would blow me over. "Quit being fucking stubborn, Samara, and tell me what the fuck is wrong with you."

"My cycle is here," I ground out. It wasn't like he wouldn't figure it out once the blood started flowing, which would be any minute now, considering how bad the pain was.

"Shit." His eyes widened. "What can I do?"

"Go back in time to when the humans were crafting the spell to turn us into Moroi and maybe tell them to tweak it a little bit so we don't have to suffer through this bullshit every few months?"

"Samara," he growled.

I rolled my eyes. "Just ask the kitchen staff. They'll have some tea that will help with the pain."

He rose without a word and headed towards the door.

"And Vail?" I waited until he looked over his shoulder at me. "Make sure I get some contraceptive tea in three days."

His expression darkened, but he jerked his head in a tight nod before leaving me alone once more. The timing of my cycle was unfortunate for all kinds of reasons. I needed to be sharp right now, and that was hard to do while I was in constant pain. And what came next wouldn't be much better.

Moroi were the most fertile in the weeks after our cycle. Demetri didn't want to marry me because he loved me; I suspected part of it was injured pride over how easily I had left him, but maybe he wanted an Heir—one that came from my bloodline and his. I wouldn't be marrying Demetri again, and I certainly wouldn't be having a child with him. He was too scared to step in the cell with me, but I still wanted to have the contraceptive tea just in case. It would prevent all pregnancies until my next cycle.

And fuck, I better be out of here before then.

When the door opened half an hour later, I raised my head from where it had been hanging between my knees, expecting to see Vail. Instead, my body went still as I took in another familiar face.

"Hello, dear," my aunt said politely. "I think we're overdue for a chat."

A collision of emotions slammed through me like a whirlwind. Hurt and confusion from the betrayal. Embarrassment and frustration for never having suspected her. And a boiling rage beneath all of that.

"Are we?" I fixed my features into a calm but distant expression. Ideally, I would have casually risen to my feet and stood before my aunt, but there was zero chance of that happening. Blood was seeping through my undergarments, and the cramps had shifted to a dull but constant pain.

I wouldn't be moving anytime soon.

Carmilla's dark green eyes swept over me, but whatever she was thinking was hidden behind her own mask. So much of my own tactics when it came to political conversations were based on what I had learned from her. I'd been a constant shadow in her presence growing up—sitting in on meetings and reading the letters she would send to other Houses—I'd absorbed every bit of knowledge and insight she'd been willing to bestow.

And she knew it.

I had never once doubted my aunt. Instead, I'd taken everything she'd told me at face value, whereas if another had spoken similar words, I would have looked closer. And none of that had been by accident on her part. I'd had plenty of time to reflect on my relationship with my aunt the past week, and I didn't like what I'd seen.

How gullible I'd been.

"Don't give me that look, Samara." Carmilla waved a hand as she moved to stand in front of my cell, keeping just out of my reach. "It's not as if I planned on putting you here." She gestured at the dungeon walls.

"But it was *one* of the plans, wasn't it?" I raised a dark eyebrow at her. "'*If you only have one plan, you've already failed…*'" I impersonated her deep, throaty voice. "You might be a traitorous bitch, but I still remember the lessons."

"I haven't betrayed anyone," she said in a calm, even tone that made me want to scream in her face. For a second, my indifferent expression wavered before I wrestled my emotions back under control. "Velika betrayed us all when she started dealing with the wraiths. When she lay with one of them and bore them a child."

My mask shattered.

"So you blame Draven for the sins of his parents?" My voice vibrated with anger. "Do you know? Do you know what Velika did to him as a child? What that fucking crown is capable of?" I flicked my gaze up to the crown made of silver and gold that rested on my aunt's dark hair.

Something tickled the back of my mind. It felt like standing alone in a forest when a predator was stalking you from the shadows.

Was she trying to use the crown on me?

A painful cramp flared, but I hid it behind the rage I was feeling as I tried to guard my thoughts. Although, based on what Draven had said, the crown didn't work well on the House bloodlines, so I should be somewhat protected.

But then again . . . he'd been basing that on only half of the crown. Now that Carmilla had both pieces, could she control me? Was that why she wore it today?

"You truly are remarkable." Carmilla tilted her head as she studied me. "I know you're frightened right now. Probably about this"—she raised her hand and touched the crown—"but you hide it well. Your temper was always your greatest weakness though. I never could break you of that. Something you inherited from your mother, unfortunately."

"Did you ever care for me?" I held my chin high. "Or have I always been nothing but a political pawn for you to groom? The way you did Vail?"

During the long hours I'd had down here to myself, I'd alternated between plotting different ways out and thinking about my childhood after my parents had died. Vail and I had been friends prior to the death of our parents. He'd been enraged at me for my actions the night they'd died—my decision to stop him from going out in a doomed attempt to save them—but we could have recovered from that given time. We could have worked through our grief together. Instead, it had torn us apart.

And Carmilla had played a role in that. She'd been the stand-in parental figure for both of us. It'd given her the opportunity to whisper just the right words in our ears to create a divide in our friendship. She'd fanned the flames of Vail's anger, while at the same time hammering into me how important it was to be strong and not show any signs of weakness. To be the perfect Heir the way my parents would have wanted.

Vail and I had both been too close to her to see it then, and he was clearly still blind to it, but I saw things clearly now.

She could take her pretty lies and manipulative compliments and choke on them.

"Don't be so melodramatic." A half smirk curled up at the corners of her lips as she dropped her hand from the crown. "I only wanted what was best for you, and look how far the two of you rose! If I'd allowed you to remain friends, you wouldn't have reached down deep to find the motivation necessary to recover from a loss like that."

"Did you play a role in the death of our parents?" I pushed.

"Velika ordered it." She shrugged and absently studied her nails. "My sister had been a thorn in her side for too long. Mariona never told me what precisely she was looking for," Carmilla mused. "As much as my sister loved me, she didn't entirely trust me." Those calculating eyes slid to me. "Your sweet, trusting nature, you inherited from your father."

The coppery taste of blood filled my mouth as I bit down hard to keep a torrent of swear words from tumbling out. Apparently, Carmilla was testing for all the sore spots tonight. The question was . . . why? My aunt didn't have casual conversations. I understood that now better than ever before. She'd come down here for a specific purpose, and all her words were crafted to achieve it.

It also didn't escape my attention that she hadn't answered the question about if she'd played a role in my and Vail's parents' deaths. She'd only said Velika had ordered it, but that left plenty of room for her to still be involved. It made me suspect that she had at the very least known about the order . . . and done nothing to stop it. But I dropped it for now. Let her believe I thought Velika was solely responsible. I might be able to use it later.

I knew how to play the long game too.

"Perhaps we can continue this conversation under better . . . circumstances." She walked forward and brushed her fingers against my cell. "I would have come down here sooner, but I've been busy getting this House in order." Once again, my eyes flicked up to the crown.

A crown of two parts. Glittering gold and frosted silver.
One half to see a soul. Another half to bind it.

Those were the words Roth had found in their research. Velika had only possessed the half that bound souls, which meant she'd had to use blood magic to get the binding to settle —something about the ability to see souls made the bindings work better. There was so much we didn't understand about the crown, but clearly, Carmilla wasn't wasting any time testing it out.

I had to warn House Harker and the other Houses; otherwise, my aunt could stroll through their doors and enslave them all within an afternoon. I couldn't pull a complete about-face and suddenly give in to her demands, but getting out of this cell, even under supervision, would help me gather information and improve my odds of escaping.

"And what exactly are these *better circumstances*?" I drawled, my voice deepening towards the end when the muscles in my lower abdomen painfully clenched again. I once again cursed the poor timing of my cycle.

"A dinner." Carmilla smiled. "In three days, when you're feeling better."

I matched her polite smile. "Wonderful. Can't wait."

It wasn't surprising that Carmilla knew I was on my cycle. I had no open wounds, and she could no doubt smell the blood. Plus, my aunt had known me my entire life, so she knew what it looked like when I was trying to hide my pain. The fact that she knew it had just started was interesting. Had Vail told her? Or had she seen him collecting supplies for me and inferred what was going on from that?

"Demetri will be delighted to see you."

My smile turned sharp. So that's what she wanted. Me to

be around Demetri when my cycle had just ended, when I'd be in a lust-filled haze.

"I'll be happy to see him again too." I let my bloodlust rise until I knew my eyes had turned black. "Perhaps I can finish what I started in that throne room."

When I'd done my best to cut his dick off.

Carmilla laughed and touched the crown again. I tensed. Would I know if the crown's magic was working on me? Would I feel my free will slipping away? I didn't feel any different, but the fear that I wouldn't know was almost too much to bear.

That alien presence brushed against my mind again, and I felt the hairs on the back of my neck stand up.

"I have much to attend to over the next couple of days." Carmilla's hands fell from the crown as the corners of her mouth pinched slightly, fighting a frown. "I'll have servants come down for you in two days so you can get cleaned up. Perhaps afterwards, we can see about keeping you somewhere else—under supervision of course—depending on how dinner goes."

Then she launched into a speech about how she truly did care about the Moroi. That she was doing what had to be done for the survival of all, and if I'd just see that, I could be of help to her. It wasn't my aunt's speech I was paying attention to though. It was the other voice drifting through my mind. One that felt ancient and devious.

Hello, my little forgotten one.

CHAPTER THREE

—

Vail

SAMARA WAS in so much pain, she was delirious. I knew this because she was currently curled up on my lap—a place she would never have been if she weren't out of it. It was the second day of her cycle. The first hadn't seemed too bad, although that was most likely due to the fact that she'd chugged the tea I'd brought her like it had been the answer to all her problems before asking for more.

I'd traumatized the kitchen staff with the way I'd barged in there repeatedly throughout the day, demanding more of the tea brewed specifically to dull cramps and help with pain.

When Samara had thanked me after the fourth cup instead of threatening to cut my balls off, I'd known things were about to get bad.

But bad had been an understatement.

Samara had barely moved all day. She'd just curled up in the corner of her cell on the pile of blankets I'd stolen from every vacant bedroom I could find. She'd practically bitten my head off when I'd suggested she ask to be moved to a bedroom just until this was over.

"I'm a prisoner," she'd spat. "Carmilla will want something

if I make such a request." Then her eyes had flashed black. "She will get *nothing* from me."

I thought about going behind her back and asking Carmilla directly, but she had to know the state her niece was in. Even if she hadn't been to see Samara herself, Carmilla was the type of leader who always knew everything that was going on under her roof, and given how I'd stormed into the kitchen demanding the tea . . .

If Carmilla wanted to ease her niece's suffering, she could have done it at any time, which meant Samara was right. If she asked for a room and a more comfortable setting, she would have to agree to something.

Samara was frustratingly stubborn but not without reason. If the situation were reversed, I would have remained in the cell too.

Which was why I was sitting here with Samara wrapped in several blankets and tucked against my chest. She'd been drifting in and out of sleep, mumbling something about a crown that I couldn't quite make out. My arms tightened around her soft body.

This was the first time she'd allowed me to touch her since everything that had gone down in the throne room. Since I'd chosen Carmilla over her. At least, that was the way Samara viewed it.

I hadn't known this was how things were going to go though. I'd thought that once Carmilla and Samara spoke, everything would be okay. That they'd work it out and everything would go back to how it had been—the two of them working together. I mean, they both wanted the same thing— for the Moroi to survive.

It was Draven's fault. Samara had fucking lost it when that prick, Lucian, had stabbed him through the chest, and now it felt like there was a growing divide. Carmilla and her followers

—myself included—on one side. Samara with her lot on the other.

I didn't know what Kieran, Alaric, and Roth had been told, and Carmilla requested that I not inform them of anything for now because she wanted to manage what information got back to House Harker. But the rumors about Velika's downfall and Carmilla's rise had to be spreading throughout the Moroi realm, so I wasn't really sure how well her plan would work.

Nobody was better at collecting rumors than Kieran, and he would have shared whatever he'd discovered with Alaric and Roth. I would've thought they would have been here already, demanding her release. But then . . . they knew about the crown. Surely Carmilla wouldn't use it on them though? Roth was a bit of an unknown, but Carmilla had known Alaric his entire life, and she liked Kieran. Maybe if they were here, they could talk some sense into Samara.

Because she sure as shit wasn't listening to me.

She let out a pained whimper, and I slipped one of my hands beneath the blankets to rub her back. "It's okay, Samara," I said roughly. "I got you."

"Vail," she murmured, turning her face into me to inhale my scent.

I bent my head down to nuzzle her hair. She'd be back to either ignoring me or trying to stab me in a couple of days, so I had to take what I could get. I hoped she'd go for my throat honestly. When she'd looked at me with hate in her eyes after everything that had gone down in the throne room, it'd hurt, but that was nothing compared to when she'd coldly blocked me out.

The violence, I could handle, because at least I knew she was feeling *something* towards me. I'd happily take that over pretending I didn't exist.

Samara had always consumed my soul. Love or hate, it had always been her.

I spent every waking moment thinking about her, and the fact that she could so easily cast me away pissed me off beyond reason. It was exactly why she'd done it. Samara could be a vicious fucking cunt.

And gods, I loved that about her.

My body went still as I heard someone coming down the stairwell. The guards did regular sweeps of the dungeon levels, but they never stepped foot inside this one if I was here.

They never went into the room where Draven's cell was either, just looked through the small window in the door to make sure he was still there. Even imprisoned, the Moroi Prince was feared.

Aside from me, the prince's only visitor was Lucian. I hadn't told Samara that though. While I didn't approve of her devotion to that half-Fae bastard, I wasn't going to tell her that the man who had tortured him for most of his life paid him regular visits. He currently wasn't able to do him any physical harm, but Lucian did enjoy bringing a bottle of wine down to Draven's cell and recounting the many ways he had tormented the fallen prince over the years.

It was fucked up. I didn't understand what Carmilla saw in him. It was on my growing list of things that just didn't add up.

It wasn't Lucian who walked through the door though—it was Demetri.

Another mystery I didn't fucking get. Why was Carmilla working with him? And why was she so keen on Samara marrying him again? She'd never mentioned that to me, and when I'd asked her about it days ago, she'd just brushed me off.

"Is there a reason you're groping my wife?" he asked idly as his sharp hazel eyes scrutinized the blankets covering Samara, as if he was trying to figure out where exactly my hands were.

A warning growl rumbled from me. Samara was half delirious. What type of person would take advantage of her in a situation like this? Even when I'd been moving her around,

I'd been careful to keep my hands over her clothes They were currently resting around her lower back and ribs, but he couldn't see that.

"Ex-wife." I gave him a cold look.

"Not for much longer. She'll be mine again soon." He shrugged and moved closer to the cell. I'd closed it when I'd stepped inside to be with Samara, and despite how much Carmilla wanted Demetri around, she hadn't given him the ability to open Samara's cell. Which told me, at least on some level, she didn't trust the Laurent Heir either.

"She was never yours to begin with." Tension coiled within me. I wanted nothing more than to rip out Demetri's throat. He was a threat to Samara, and despite how much she currently hated me, I *would* protect her. Unfortunately, Carmilla had been quite clear that I wasn't to lay a finger on him again. The little prick had mentioned me losing my temper and slamming him into the wall days ago. "Your marriage to her was nothing but a political move to strengthen the alliance between our Houses. Samara *never* belonged to you."

"And you think she belongs to you now?" Demetri skimmed his fingers across the bars of the cage. "Do you really think you'll get her in the end? After everything you've done to her?" He gave me a knowing glance. "She'll *never* choose you. Not now."

The deep pit that had opened up in my soul when I'd handed over that cursed crown cracked open a little more. Demetri's eyes glinted in the dim lighting of the dungeon, and he smiled at seeing his barbed remark strike true.

Samara hissed and tensed in my arms. Another cramp must have been hitting her. The tea that dulled the pain was also a light sedative, and she'd practically chugged the kettle earlier. Her eyelids fluttered for a second, and she turned her head away from my chest, inhaling deeply. She started to settle back down, but then she abruptly went completely still in my arms.

"Samara's a smart girl. She'll eventually come to realize that marrying me again is in not only her best interest, but that of our Houses—and the Moroi realm as a whole."

I stared at him. Moroi tended to be arrogant, but Demetri was taking it to a whole other level.

Samara started to shift her position, her movements slow enough and hidden by the blanket that I didn't think Demetri noticed as he paced on the other side of the bars.

"You cheated on her," I said flatly. "All you had to do was not be an asshole and she'd still be married to you right now."

Because Samara always did right by the House. I'd doubted her for a long time, but I knew that now. Carmilla wanted what was best too. They just needed more time to come to an agreement, but Demetri would not be part of that agreement. That was a line in the sand I knew Samara wouldn't cross. She might hate me, but she loved Kieran, Alaric, and Roth—and Draven, but I was ignoring that for now. She would never leave them.

And they'd slit Demetri's throat before they ever let him lay a finger on her again. If I didn't do it first.

"That was a misunderstanding." Demetri waved a hand dismissively.

"She walked in on you fucking someone else after she'd been loyal to you that entire time." I bared my fangs at him. Everyone at House Harker had known how much Samara and Kieran had wanted each other, but he'd never pushed and she'd never crossed that line. When Samara gave someone her loyalty, she meant it—whether they deserved it or not.

Suddenly, the dagger on my thigh smoothly slid free from the sheath. I should probably be concerned about Samara having a blade so close to my cock—not to mention a lot of vital organs—but I couldn't bring myself to stop her. Or warn Demetri that he might want to step away from the cell.

"It's not like I expect either of us to be monogamous," Demetri continued. "Although I won't allow her to see that courtier she's so obsessed with or that asshole advisor. There are rumors of another lover my beautiful wife has collected as well—that will have to end too. Anyone on the side must be casual. I'll give her some options to choose fr—"

In a heartbeat, Samara was on her feet and across the cell. She'd timed it perfectly, waiting until Demetri reached the cell wall and had begun to turn away to walk in the other direction. Her arm was through the bars and wrapped around his chest before he even knew what was happening. She pulled him back hard and pressed the dagger she'd stolen from me against his throat.

"Not your wife, asshole," Samara spat, her voice low and dangerous.

"Samara! Don't—" Demetri yelped, and a second later, the scent of his blood filled the air. Not much, but more than just a scratch's worth.

I rose to my feet and strolled over to the cell door. Tremors ran through Samara's body. From pain or rage, I didn't know. Probably both.

She didn't say anything as I leaned against the bars, making no move to help Demetri or get the dagger away from her.

"Do something," he ground out before flinching when Samara dug the blade in a little deeper. Nothing vital had been hit, but she was real close to the artery, and blood was steadily dripping from where she'd broken the skin.

I ignored him and looked at Samara. Her black hair was stuck to the sides of her face thanks to the sweat practically pouring off her. Normally, Samara's rich brown skin had a golden undertone to it, but she looked pale now, and her dark eyes stood out starkly on her face.

She glanced at me, eyes burning with fury.

"I'm not going to stop you," I told her. "Personally, I'm sick of hearing his voice, so his death is very appealing to me."

Demetri started to protest but went still when Samara adjusted the blade so it was resting right over his pulse. One move from her, and his lifeblood would be pouring out. He'd survive—if he got help immediately—which was unlikely, given that we were three floors down and he wouldn't be able to call for the guards with a slit throat.

"There will be consequences if you do this." My voice was calm, not giving a hint as to what outcome I preferred. Mostly because I didn't know. I wanted Demetri dead; every time he opened his mouth and made a claim on Samara, it took all my willpower not to slam his head repeatedly into a wall until it was nothing but a bloody mess.

But I wasn't lying. If Samara killed Demetri, she would be punished.

"I don't care," she half growled at me.

Logically, I knew I should stop her or at least try to talk her down, but it wasn't like she'd listen to me. If anything, my apparent disapproval would spur her on. There was also the fact that I *liked* seeing Samara like this. Most of the time, she floated around in her pretty dresses and perfectly brushed hair, but I remembered the Samara who had thrown a dagger across a courtyard to land between my fingers. The one who had taken out a howler with a crossbow shot most of my rangers wouldn't have been able to manage.

Beneath her beautiful exterior, Samara was a ruthless and cunning predator. It was one of the many things I loved about her.

"Vail will be punished," Demetri said carefully. "He's responsible for you."

Something dark and dangerous flickered in her gaze before she looked away from me. "I don't care," she repeated before digging the blade in a little more. Blood started to drip from the new cut.

She might as well have taken that knife and stabbed me. It certainly felt like she had.

"Draven!" Demetri rasped. "She'll hurt him to hurt you."

Samara froze and slowly turned her head to look at me for confirmation.

"You've made it quite clear how you feel about me." I held her unflinching gaze. "I'll be punished because I allowed it to happen, but Carmilla will have to punish you as well. She wouldn't want to cause you any lasting harm . . . so it makes sense she'd use Draven."

I didn't mention that there were many calling for the prince's public execution within the walls of the Sovereign House. Now that Queen Velika was dead, some of her enemies who had been too scared to speak out while she was alive were targeting her son.

My feelings about Draven were complicated. He was half Fae and his father was the leader of the bloody wraiths. Now that we knew the wraiths were just Seelie Fae fucked-up by shadow magic, it made me even more wary of the Fae in general. It felt like nothing good could come of them, so part of me was inclined to agree that Draven should be . . . eliminated.

But I'd also seen the way he looked at Samara. Oddly, it didn't make me jealous. Just grateful that she had another ruthless bastard in her life who loved her and would do anything to keep her safe.

Moons fucking damn me. How had everything gotten so fucking complicated?

The hand Samara had on Demetri's chest slipped down a

little, and she leaned forward until her chest was pressed against the bars, her mouth inches from his ear.

"Next time I have a blade in my hand, I'm going to cut off your fucking head. Remember that. In the meantime"—she pulled the dagger away from his throat, flipping it in her hand and stabbing it down all in one smooth motion—"*crawl.*"

Demetri released a strangled scream as Samara buried the dagger in his heart, holding it in place for a few seconds before releasing it and stepping back.

I wasn't the least bit ashamed to say the whole thing made me hard as a rock. Gods, she was such a vicious little cunt.

"Help," Demetri panted as he slid to the ground, his hands holding the blade securely against his chest. If he removed it, he'd probably bleed to death before he made it up the stairs. I glanced at the door and calculated the steps. He might make it. Moroi could recover from quite a bit. It would depend on how fast the guards reacted too.

I gave him a bored look. "You heard what the Heir said. I'd hold that dagger still and get to crawling."

Demetri glared at me. I knew I'd get in trouble for this. Carmilla had . . . concerns . . . about how close I was with Samara, but I couldn't bring myself to give a shit. Samara and I watched as Demetri tried to rise to his feet, only to let out a hiss of pain, and then proceeded to stumble to the door. He opened it and staggered outside to the stairs, where he gave up all pretense and proceeded to crawl up.

The heavy dungeon door slowly swung closed, and as soon as it clicked shut, Samara collapsed. I barely caught her before she hit the ground.

"Don't touch me," she growled. It was kind of a pathetic growl though, so I ignored it and picked her up, cradling her against myself. Then I walked to the same spot on the back wall of her cell where we'd been resting earlier and settled back down. Samara remained stiff in my arms, but she didn't fight to get free. I didn't have any delusions about that being because she liked being close to me. Violent shivers were running through her body, and she kept jerking in my grip and sucking in harsh breaths.

"Do you need more tea?" I asked quietly, even though I really didn't like the thought of leaving her. She'd made a good show of things with Demetri, but it was clear it had taken a lot out of her. I was the only ally she had here—other than Draven, but he was locked in a cell several floors below us.

"Won't help," she ground out.

Wordlessly, I reached out and gathered up the blankets she'd cast aside earlier to toss them over her. Samara shuddered but remained stiff against me. Then I adjusted the blankets until I was satisfied. Demetri would be reaching the guards soon, which meant, in an hour or less, Carmilla would likely be summoning me.

I wanted to enjoy the time I had left before I had to go and explain myself to the person who held my loyalty.

Does she though? a voice whispered in my mind.

"Why, Vail?" Samara's question was so faint, I barely heard it as she finally gave up resisting and sank into me. It was only because of the pain she was in, I knew that, but it still had to mean something, right? That, on at least some level, she trusted me enough to be vulnerable like this.

I knew what she was asking. After everything between us, the things we'd done, why had I betrayed her?

My arms wrapped tighter around her as I rested my head against hers, breathing in her scent. At that moment, all my reasoning about how I thought I'd chosen the best option for all of us didn't seem to matter. So I remained silent. And Samara didn't ask again.

"Ah. The enormity of what you've done and just how much you've fucked up has finally hit you," the fallen Moroi Prince said with a cold chuckle. Draven's bright blue eyes were threaded with bloodred cracks. He'd kept his bloodlust at this level all week. Not fully risen, but not completely suppressed either.

It unnerved me a little because he didn't act any differently. I knew, based on how wary others were around me when I let my bloodlust rise, that my behavior changed. It wasn't just that my temper got a little hotter. There was just something *more* to me, like the beast I kept chained down was gazing out into the world and thought everything would look better drowned in blood.

But if it weren't for his eyes and the claws on his fingers, I'd never know Draven's bloodlust was out as much as it was. Samara was the same. Something about them was different from other Moroi.

Draven had been damn near death when he'd been dragged down here, but he'd lain on the ground and bounced back within hours. I suspected it had something to do with his Fae heritage. His father was the Seelie King, after all.

A memory of chains disintegrating to dust flashed through my mind. That day, when everything had gone to hell, Samara had reached for Draven in that throne room, trying to free him. Everything had been so chaotic, but I could have sworn I'd seen the chains disintegrate. Draven had barely been alive —if magic had been used, he hadn't been the source. There was also the fact that she was sensitive to iron, something she'd been trying to hide, but I'd seen the way she'd grimace ever so slightly whenever she made contact with the bars.

Those two things had caused suspicion about Samara's heritage to form in the back of my mind, even if it didn't seem possible. I'd known both of her parents—neither of them had been Fae—but could one of them have been part Fae like

Draven? I mean, the prince *looked* like a Moroi. It stood to reason that one or both of Samara's parents could have had Fae blood running through their veins. Most likely her father because if Samara's mother was part Fae, then so was Carmilla. And given the way Carmilla talked about the Fae as a blight that needed to be destroyed, I didn't think she had any Fae blood.

I hadn't spoken my suspicions to anyone. And if anybody else had noticed some of the odd things that had happened around Samara lately, they hadn't mentioned them in front of me.

The question was . . . did Carmilla have similar suspicions? She hadn't been spending much time around her niece since seizing the throne, but she still knew Samara well. Maybe there had been other clues earlier in Samara's life that we'd all missed but she'd seen.

But why not be open about it? Why all the secrecy? My parents had loyally served House Harker and it had never occurred to me to not be the same—until the past couple of weeks.

I'd never questioned Carmilla's tactics before, but now there were children locked in the dungeon. Fucking *children*. I'd brought this up to Carmilla the day they'd been thrown in cells with their families, but she'd reasoned that it was impossible to know where their loyalties stood because Velika could have used the crown on them. We didn't know if Velika's death had voided all the forced blood bonds. Maybe they were loyal to her even in death.

But we did know that the bonds Velika had created would fade with time. So Carmilla had assured me that everyone would have access to food and water while in the dungeons and would be well taken care of.

It still didn't sit right with me.

Nor did watching some of the people—particularly those

of high rankings who had important knowledge locked away in their minds—be led out of the dungeon to where Carmilla would meet with them. Behind closed doors. While she wore the crown.

I'd done that. It had been me who had handed over the second half of the crown to her, which meant I'd played a direct role in taking away the free will of Moroi.

Carmilla's reasoning had seemed so sound on paper. The wraiths were chipping away at our protections. Velika—and Draven—had been working with them.

Although Carmilla had left out the fact that Draven hadn't had a choice.

It was possible she hadn't known . . . but even I knew that was me being hopeful and only wanting to see the good in her. Carmilla had been sleeping with Velika's consort, and Lucian hated Draven. He also knew a lot about him. It seemed highly unlikely he hadn't shared some of that knowledge with Carmilla.

I didn't want to believe that Carmilla was manipulating me. Both because I loved her as if she were family and because it meant I was a fool.

A fool who had betrayed the woman who *did* love me. The thought jolted me back to the present and Draven's words. Uneasy dread coiled in my gut.

Did I fuck up? Maybe I should have held onto the crown and tried to have Samara and Carmilla negotiate without either of them possessing it.

"Don't recall asking for your opinion." I chucked a canteen through the bars. While Carmilla made sure food and water were brought to Samara and the other Moroi detained in the dungeon, she'd made no such orders for Draven. As far as I knew, I was the only one bringing him sustenance.

Not that he acted the least bit grateful. He did talk to me

during these visits though, which was more than I could say about Samara until recently.

I should have stayed away from her. I knew Carmilla wanted me to. She hadn't specifically forbidden me from seeing Samara, but she had strongly hinted at it. I couldn't stay away though. There was this odd pull inside my chest that I couldn't explain. It was like I was always aware of Samara's existence. Her location—not that she was moving anywhere—her emotions, and just . . . her.

In what was rapidly becoming a habit, I rubbed the spot over my heart where I felt the tightness. It was a weird sensation that I was noticing more and more, but I had no idea what it meant. At first, I thought it was stress, but occasionally, I noticed Samara placing a hand over the exact same place on her chest when I felt it.

There was no point in asking her about it. She'd either lie or spit in my face.

And when she did, that awareness between us ached like a wound that had begun to fester.

It wasn't like Samara and I didn't have a history of hostility and distrust, but even during those tumultuous years, Samara had never ignored me.

She'd never loathed my existence.

"How is she?" Draven asked. His tone was even, but a little more red bled into his eyes.

I rubbed my face. "Her cycle started a few days ago and ended last night. She's due to have dinner with Carmilla, Lucian, and Demetri in an hour."

Understanding dawned on Draven's face, and his eyes turned a deep solid red. "And this is the woman you willingly serve? Samara's blood is still running through your veins. That crown isn't forcing your loyalty."

"You're the son of the Seelie King." I bared my teeth. "Don't lecture me about conflicting loyalties when the blood that runs through *your* veins is the same as the man who's slaughtered thousands of us."

He fell silent for a moment, and I started to leave.

"Velika was never a mother to me." I stopped and turned back to face the prince. "She always hated me. I never understood why . . . and now that she's dead, I suppose I never will, but for a while, I thought Erendriel might actually act like a loving parent. Unlike my mother, he did have my loyalty—for a brief amount of time anyway."

"What happened?"

Draven hadn't talked about Erendriel since telling me who he truly was. Whatever spell had been cast on the Moroi Prince to keep him from talking had clearly been broken. Or maybe he'd been lying about that all along. Samara might have trusted him, but I still didn't.

But do you still trust Carmilla? a voice whispered in the back of my mind. I didn't have an answer.

A humorless smile stretched across Draven's face. "I learned that the Fae King does not love—only uses—and one can either volunteer to be of use . . . or be forced to be."

Guilt and unease rose, but I kept it off my face. Carmilla had made it clear that Draven was the enemy. She claimed she was only keeping him alive to use against his father, but I suspected the real reason was because she saw Draven as a way to control Samara.

It seemed like one way or another, the Moroi Prince had been a pawn for most of his life. His mother had controlled him with her half of the crown, and his father had used Fae magic to bind him. Carmilla condemned Draven because he was half Fae . . . but he hadn't had a choice in any of it. Now, she was going to use that crown to manipulate and bind other Moroi . . . the same way Draven's parents had done to him.

Her intentions might be good, but that didn't make it right . . . did it?

"When I was twelve, Erendriel took me away from Velika," Draven continued. "I lived with the wraiths for a while. Up until that point, he hadn't taken much of an interest in me. I didn't want to be anywhere near Velika, so I did my best to prove my worth."

"What were they like?"

Until recently, we'd thought the wraiths were just strange shadow monsters that plagued our lands. There had been some speculation that they were related to the disappearance of the Fae, but not that the Seelie had turned into the wraiths. It still seemed strange to me because it had been the Unseelie who'd had shadow magic. So how had it been that Seelie were the ones turned into nothing but shadows?

I thought of that hideaway we'd found near the lake in the Velesian territory. So many answers could lie there, or in the journals we'd found in the cave near House Harker. I hadn't mentioned either of those things to Carmilla. It felt like my loyalty was being pulled in multiple directions, and I no longer knew which way was right.

Draven flinched and rubbed his forehead. "There are still some things I cannot speak of." A look of concentration fell over the prince's face, as if he was piecing his thoughts together. "I do not know the specifics of the spell that was cast over my tongue, but I've been able to piece some things together over the years. When something I am forbidden to say becomes open knowledge, it seems to fall out of the scope of the spell."

"Like when Carmilla announced your lineage," I said, following his logic.

"Yes." He nodded. "It's happened for other things too. However, every time a new secret is revealed, it's as if the spell reworks itself and I have to figure out what I can and cannot say again." He paused—another wince of pain—then shook his head. "I cannot say anything more on the matter."

"Convenient," I muttered.

His eyes full of fire snapped to me. "You don't know what it's like to not be in control of your own mind. But don't worry—as soon as the strength of Samara's blood runs out, I have no doubt Carmilla will give you a taste."

It was my turn to flinch as his words struck at exactly what I feared.

"If anything happens to Samara while I'm locked up down here, nothing will stop me from getting to you." Draven leaned forward, something feral swirling in his eyes. "I'll make you suffer in ways you can't even dream of."

"Save your threats for someone else. I won't allow any harm to come to her."

Draven laughed darkly. "You already have."

Again, I flinched.

"Samara won't allow her lust to rule her, no matter how hard her body is pushing it," I swallowed and tried to add some confidence into my voice. "And despite what you think, Carmilla won't allow anyone to take advantage of her that way."

"Your precious Carmilla is trying to force her niece back into a marriage she doesn't want, and she's arranged for this dinner to occur on the night when the lust haze will be hitting Samara the hardest." Draven gave me an almost pitying look. "You really don't see her true intentions, do you?"

"So I'll attend the dinner." I snapped. "You're wrong, but I'll be there anyway to make sure nothing happens."

Samara wouldn't touch that piece of shit, even with the intense desire that hit all Moroi who went through the reproductive cycle. And while my faith in Carmilla was waning, it hadn't faded enough that I believed she'd allow someone to force themselves on Samara.

Still . . . nothing in Lunaria would keep me from that room. I didn't know Lucian well, but from what I'd seen this week, he was a cruel piece of shit, and Demetri was an opportunist prick. Carmilla was likely hoping to wear Samara down, plant a seed of doubt during this dinner that Demetri could jump on while Samara would be using every ounce of her unbending willpower to hold the lust at bay.

She needed a friend in that room. I would be that friend. Even if she wanted nothing more than to bury a dagger in my chest.

"You will keep her safe." The dust seemed to tremble at Draven's feet as he spoke, his words somewhere between an order and a plea.

I held his bloodred gaze that promised death to anyone who harmed Samara and said the only thing I could. "With my life."

CHAPTER FOUR

—

Vail

I STOOD near the doors of the grand dining hall, where Carmilla, Lucian, Demetri, and Samara were having dinner. This space had clearly been built to host at least sixty people back in the day when the Fae had lived here. Most of the murals painted on the walls of the Houses were of pretty landscapes, but occasionally, they'd depict the Fae themselves. Usually dancing in fancy clothing with masks on their faces and crystal glasses in their hands.

It was those paintings that had inspired Velika's ridiculous parties. But even she hadn't been able to justify having food at them because there simply wasn't enough to spare.

Moroi numbers had grown considerably over the last two decades, thanks to the security of the Houses and the wards we'd learned to place around the outposts. But the crops had to be grown outside those wards, and it was a dangerous task, even during the day.

On top of that, all it took was one night for a herd of deer or a pack of boars to bulldoze through an outpost's food supply. The wraiths had also wiped out several high-producing outposts in the last year. We could survive one bad harvest . . . but any more than that, and we would be in serious trouble.

Carmilla had never been one to throw fancy dinners, not even back at House Harker. Some of the other Houses would, the Heads or Heirs enjoying their little pretend world where they could spoil themselves in such a way, as if we still didn't dwell in a land crawling with monsters or weren't two bad growing seasons away from starvation.

But tonight, there was enough food for easily double the people here. It was Lucian's doing. One of the many things I'd learned about him this past week was that he enjoyed the finer things in life and didn't give a shit about anyone but himself. What I didn't know was why the fuck Carmilla was working with him.

Maybe she had needed him to take out Velika, but that didn't explain why she was *still* allied with him, and why she hadn't stopped him from wasting all this food. My lips twisted into a grimace, and my gaze slid down the table to Samara, who had an identical look of disgust on her face. She hid it quickly when Carmilla glanced at her though and instead pasted a beatific smile on her face.

I hated that smile. It was a lie. Her real one was usually close-lipped, the corners of her lips tilted up with a sly but content type of amusement. I hadn't seen that one in a while.

Granted, Samara had been a wreck the past three days. I knew she'd been in considerable pain because she'd voluntarily spoken to me, asking me to bring her more tea. I'd brought everything she'd asked for and then some, as if that would help make everything right between us.

I didn't even know what I wanted to do at this point. There was no undoing that I'd betrayed Samara to be loyal to Carmilla, I couldn't fix that, but with every day that dragged on, it felt more and more obvious that I'd made the wrong choice. If I betrayed Carmilla to ally with Samara, would she even accept my help? Or would that only result in both of them wanting me dead?

Moonsdamn it. How had I fucked everything up so badly?

"You're looking much better today, my love." Demetri smiled at Samara, who was sitting to his left. "If you need help with *anything*, do let me know."

"I have not nor have I ever been your love," Samara replied smoothly as she gave Demetri a cutting look before picking up her glass of wine and taking a delicate sip.

This was one of the smaller tables in the room but was still meant to sit eight people. Carmilla sat at the head of the table with Lucian to her right. She'd had her niece sit at the opposite end of the table, which was considered a seat of respect; if an Heir from another House were visiting Sovereign House, it was where they would have been seated. Considering Carmilla had let her niece suffer in the dungeon for the last few days I was a little surprised. I'd have guessed that Lucian would have sat there, but he seemed perfectly content to be playing the part of Carmilla's consort.

I didn't understand any of this. When Carmilla had told me to bring Samara to dinner, I'd expected armed guards to be standing next to her. Instead, Carmilla had dismissed all of them from the room and had been having—what seemed on the surface to be—a pleasant conversation with her niece.

Their words were like hidden daggers volleyed back and forth. Seemingly polite, but both were bleeding from the double-edged meanings. I was so far out of my depth.

I knew how to track and hunt down any type of monster. There wasn't a weapon I didn't know my way around. But I knew fuck all about politics, and suddenly, I'd found myself swimming it.

Whatever game Carmilla was playing, I didn't understand. Just like I was struggling to comprehend Samara's motivations.

If the lust haze was riding her hard, she wasn't letting an

ounce of it show. She looked as cool and composed as ever, which I knew was annoying Demetri, based on how rigid his smile was.

The idiot had probably thought Samara would jump into his lap out of desperation to get herself off. My lips curled up into the barest hint of a smile. He'd been married to Samara for years but obviously didn't know her at all. For all her polished exterior and determination to never fail as the House Harker Heir, Samara ran on fucking spite.

Dark purple eyes flecked with black locked on to me from across the room. Samara had been allowed to clean up earlier today and change into clean clothing. When I'd arrived to escort her from the guest room, I hadn't been ready for the sight. She wore a dress made of a deep purple that clung to every one of her curves; the neckline was low enough to show off her ample cleavage, and two slits ran up the sides of the flowing skirt. Every step flashed an obscene amount of thigh.

Samara was the one at war with her body's biology, yet it had been me suffering on that walk to the dining hall. All I could think about was what it felt like to have my hands on her soft flesh. To hear her scream my name as I thrust into her dripping wet cunt.

I knew she had sensed my arousal because she had taken two deliberate steps farther away from me as we'd walked. It'd hurt, but I couldn't blame her for it.

Now, her gaze dropped to my lips and the barest smile on them before jumping to the pulse in my neck. Black widened in her eyes, and my own heartbeat picked up as I saw the lust in them. The moment only lasted a few seconds before she snapped her gaze away, the darkness fading from her eyes until they were mostly purple again.

"Messages from Mora and Dominique arrived this morning." Carmilla swirled her glass of wine. "Both will be coming next week to meet with us."

"Pray tell, what did you say in the letter to the Heads of House Corvinus and Salvatore?" Samara arched a dark brow at her aunt. "'Queen Velika lost her head, I'm afraid, but no worries, the crown landed on mine. Please join me for a cup of tea?'"

"That was more or less the gist of it." Carmilla mimicked her niece and raised a brow back at her. "Despite what you think of my actions of late, I am trying to do what's best for the Moroi, and I'm being as truthful as possible."

"Leaving out the fact that if they walk into this House, they'll leave without their free will seems to be *a bit* of a big omission." Samara's eyes flicked to the crown resting on Carmilla's head. Faint creases formed between her brows and at the corners of her lips.

"That all depends on them. The crown will tell me what their intentions are. If they willingly kneel, then they will leave with their minds intact." Carmilla shrugged.

"So you'll be a generous tyrant." Samara smiled wide enough to display her fangs. "What a relief."

What would Carmilla do if the other Houses didn't voluntarily kneel and fought back against the crown's control? Velika hadn't been able to control House bloodlines, but she'd only had half of the crown. What if, even united, it wasn't enough?

I might have been daft at House politics, but even I knew there were some who would never willingly kneel. Like House Tepes and House Devereux. Surely she had some sort of plan for that? Aside from House Harker, they were the two most powerful Houses when it came to rangers. We needed their support if we were to stand against the wraiths and whatever Erendriel was plotting.

"Don't be so dramatic, dear," Carmilla gave Samara a chiding look before focusing on Demetri. "Have you heard anything from your mother?"

Everyone continued on with the conversation, and I

remained in the background, listening. Apparently, Demetri's mother, Marvina, hadn't replied to any of his messages. Not surprising, since she knew he was here and allied with Carmilla. She was technically in charge of House Laurent . . . and she'd always disliked Carmilla for reasons nobody really understood.

For all appearances, Samara looked engaged and contributed to the talks, often coming up with ways to cleverly insult Demetri, who was growing more and more frustrated as dinner went on. Lucian had refrained from saying anything, just leaned back in his chair sipping his wine and letting the barbed words flow around him.

But Samara's gaze kept slipping to the crown. I glanced at it. It was a strange creation. I could feel the Fae magic radiating off it, but as far as I knew, Carmilla hadn't used it on me. At least, I didn't think she had.

It was more than a little unnerving to think that I wouldn't know if my mind had been tampered with, but the crown didn't work as well on those from House bloodlines—or from people who drank from them—and I'd drunk a lot of Samara's blood recently. I was fairly sure I'd be safe from the crown's magic if Carmilla tried to use it on me, but for how long, I didn't know. Something told me Samara wouldn't be opening up a vein for me anytime soon, so it wasn't like I could refill my immunity.

Not for the first time, I wondered why the Fae had made the crown. Had they used it against their own people? We knew there'd been a divide between the Unseelie and Seelie, maybe things like the crown were part of the reason why.

Samara had dropped all pretenses and was staring at the crown now, her expression one of concentration. Suddenly, she jolted in her seat, and the chair creaked. The conversation stopped, and all eyes fell on her.

"Apologies." She reached for her wineglass again. "In the

months since our divorce, I forgot how grating it is to listen to Demetri drone on and on about his mommy issues."

Lucian barked a laugh. "I like her."

Even Carmilla cracked a smile.

Demetri glowered. "If you keep it up, I won't bother hate fucking you later when you're begging for it."

I took a step forward before I caught myself and moved back. Earlier, I'd spoken with Carmilla and claimed I wanted to be here tonight because I was concerned Samara might do something rash.

Carmilla wasn't born yesterday, but she'd acquiesced to my request, though she'd made it clear I was not to interfere with the conversations no matter how heated they got. My fingers curled as I imagined wrapping them around Demetri's neck and snapping it. If he laid one hand on Samara, I'd do it, but when it came to verbal sparring, there was no one better than my dark-haired and clever-tongued beauty.

"Demetri, dear . . ." Samara gave her ex-husband a placating smile. "You're saying your inside thoughts out loud again. Nobody wants to hear about the fantasies you have while getting yourself off."

"That's not what—" Demetri's face burned red, but he was cut off by Lucian, who cocked his head as his eyes glinted at Samara.

"What if he was the last person in Lunaria? Would you hate fuck him then?"

Samara tapped a finger against her bottom lip like she was pondering some great mystery. I chuckled under my breath, earning me a death glare from Demetri. I smiled at him. *Try something, asshole. I fucking dare you.*

He looked away from me and went back to fuming in Samara's direction.

"Depends . . ." she finally said and held her right hand up, wiggling several fingers in the air. "In this scenario, do I still have my fingers?"

"What do your fingers have to do with anything?" Demetri snarled.

"Oh." Lucian laughed and gave Samara a nod of acknowledgment. "I see why you don't want to marry him again. Anyone who doesn't understand why fingers are useful probably has no business fucking anyone."

"I think that's enough for tonight." Carmilla gave Lucian a mildly chiding look before giving Samara a much sterner one. "If you promise to behave and not leave without guards, you may stay in one of the guest quarters."

Any amusement she'd felt at putting Demetri in his place slid off Samara's face. "Either way, I'm a prisoner. I'll stick with the dungeons."

Carmilla eyed her niece, clearly trying to figure out why she had chosen a hard floor over a soft bed, but Carmilla knew the politically savvy side of Samara while I knew the side that was survival first. This was enemy territory to Samara, and the dungeons were less guarded in a lot of ways. Only the door in and out had guards posted. If she stayed in the main house, she'd have no idea where the guards were, and she'd be farther away from Draven.

Samara was plotting something, and I needed to convince her to tell me so she didn't get herself killed.

CHAPTER FIVE

—

Samara

My body felt like it was on fire. I'd never denied my needs like this before. In fact, usually the days after my menstruation were *very* fun. It was a perfectly solid excuse to stay in bed and ignore any responsibilities while getting fucked into oblivion.

When I was at Drudonia, I'd often find another scholar, or several, to keep me entertained. After my marriage to Demetri, I'd been a little more limited. He'd been adequate in bed, not the most creative, but I tended to get a little . . . aggressive . . . when I was like this and made it work.

But now, I'd sooner cut off my arm then let him touch me, even if I had no other options. My fingers were going to be fucking aching by the time this was over.

Vail was a silent presence at my side as we made our way back to the dungeon. It'd been difficult, but I'd managed to mostly concentrate during dinner, and I'd been rewarded with lots of useful information between things both spoken and unspoken.

Carmilla was keeping her coup quiet. She couldn't completely control the flow of information from the Sovereign House—there were almost a thousand Moroi living here on a permanent basis and another thousand rangers who regularly rotated in and out.

But she'd been busy these past couple of weeks, ensuring that the key players were loyal to her and her alone. On my way to dinner, we'd passed several advisors who hadn't batted an eye at me being led through the halls with guards in front and Vail at my side.

The other Houses had no doubt heard rumors, but Carmilla Harker had a reputation as being an honest and respectable House Leader. They would give her the benefit of the doubt.

And their Houses would fall because of it.

Lucian was a bit of a mystery to me. He hadn't spoken enough to suss out his motivation or wants. That worried me. I didn't like having such an unknown adversary.

We passed a hallway that I knew led to some living quarters, and briefly, I regretted not taking Carmilla up on her offer —just so I'd have better access to the rest of the House and therefore a greater chance at escape. But I dismissed that notion a second later. Carmilla would have put guards on me at all times, and I wasn't going anywhere without Draven.

Aside from Vail watching over me directly, the guards were only stationed at the entrance to the dungeons. They did periodic checks of the levels, but there would still be less eyes on me down there. I was sure Draven and I could come up with something—once I made it to him.

That would have to wait another couple of days though because despite my belief that I could work through my stupid horny thoughts, that seemed to be growing more unlikely by the second.

More than once, my gaze had drifted back to Vail during that dinner, and I'd remembered everything he'd done to me in that cave . . . and then the cabin. My thoughts had scattered, and I'd lost track of the conversation.

I couldn't afford to slip up like that during an escape, and based on the way I was feeling, it seemed likely that I'd throw rationality out the window and just jump Draven as soon as I saw him, caring way more about getting his cock inside me than getting the fuck out of here.

My core tightened at the thought, and I knew if I reached beneath my dress, I'd find myself hot and wet.

"Fuck," Vail cursed under his breath and started walking faster.

I had to lengthen my stride to keep up with him, which meant even more of my skin showed with every step. Based on the way Vail's jaw was tightening, I knew he was seeing the flashes of my golden brown skin out of the corner of his eye and it was getting to him.

I should hate him—and I did. He'd betrayed me after everything we'd gone through. After everything we'd done. I'd thought we'd finally gotten past all our bullshit, only to find out it'd all been a lie. My brain and heart were very much on Team Vail Can Eat Dirt and Die.

My traitorous pussy, on the other hand, was very much Team Vail Can Eat Us Out And Then Die.

"Fuck," I muttered and picked up my pace. I needed to get back to my cell and away from Vail, because while Demetri had zero chance of me hate fucking him, I wasn't entirely sure I had the willpower to resist Vail for much longer.

Why did he have to smell so delicious? Like the forest after a thunderstorm. That thread linking me to him practically purred as I breathed in more of his scent, though it felt more faint than it had a few weeks ago. Like it was fraying at the edges.

Good. I hoped it fucking vanished entirely.

Two guards stood on either side of the iron and wood door at the end of the hall. The one on the left nodded at Vail and opened the door. But the one on right openly leered at me.

Dark brown eyes with cracks of green running through them darkened as he inhaled sharply, and I knew he was smelling my arousal.

Not for you asshole. I'd fuck a pine cone right now.

"Grigor, if you want to keep your head on your shoulders, I suggest you look the fuck away right now and keep your mouth shut," Vail said in a low, dangerous tone.

The pervy guard—Grigor, apparently—jerked his gaze away from me, but not before sneering first.

Vail waved me forward, and I entered the narrow stairwell that wound down to the dungeon levels, Vail following behind me. Fae lanterns gave off a pale yellow light as we made our descent.

I hadn't ever gone past my cell, so I had no idea how much farther down Draven was, but I *did* know he was on the bottom level, thanks to information I'd gleaned from conversations over the past couple of weeks. There were three levels above me, and considering this was built underground, it didn't seem possible that it went that much farther.

At least that was what I hoped, because I really didn't want to run down hundreds of stairs and then have to turn around and go back up.

Fuck. Stairs.

We walked past the first level, and I heard several conversations filtering through the door, but the words were too muffled to make out. It was the same on the next floor. When we reached the door that led to the room that contained my cell, I almost shoved Vail out of the way to race inside and lock the cell door between us.

I was practically panting, and it had nothing to do with all the steps we'd just walked down. My body was keyed up, and every part of my skin felt hot, and this was only day one. Tomorrow was going to be even more brutal.

Vail opened the door, and I had no choice but to step

inside. *Go to the cell,* I told myself. *He'll lock you in, and then you won't have to worry about climbing the delicious mountain of a man standing before you. You won't have to resist moaning as he shoves his enormous cock into your dripping cunt, stretching you out—*

FUCK. My breathing grew more ragged, and I realized I'd stopped moving.

For a second, Vail and I stood there looking at each other with less than a foot separating us. Silver bled across his dark grey eyes, gleaming slightly from the ever-burning flames of the Fae lanterns. Something about Vail always looked a little wild, like he wasn't meant to be contained behind stone walls but out in the forest with the other beasts.

Betrayed. He'd betrayed me. I hated him.

Why was this dance between us always so fucking complicated?

With just the two of us in this small, dark space, his scent enveloped me. He smelled rich and earthy. More than a little wild.

Emotions raced across Vail's face. Guilt. Lust. Conflict. I understood those last two because they applied to how I was feeling at this very moment. Only, while he felt guilt, I felt rage.

But I still wanted him. And it wasn't just because of the lust haze coursing through my blood. Nor was it the odd magic connecting us, which I still didn't understand.

For all his hateful words, Demetri had been right when he'd declared my feelings for Vail and why the Marshal of House Harker had been in a position to hurt me so badly.

I loved him. Body and soul. And that wasn't something I could just turn off, even if that love was now twisted with hate.

"Fuck it," Vail growled.

We both moved at the same time, crashing into each other. Vail's mouth claimed mine as his strong hands gripped my ass and lifted me up. Instinctively, I wrapped my legs around his waist, and my fingers wound into his hair, pulling him harder against me as he backed me against the dungeon door.

His tongue slipped into my mouth, and I ground myself against him. Everything I'd been keeping pent up all day slipped free, and it felt fucking amazing. Even with the fabric of the dress between my back and the hard wood of the door, I could feel the iron within it seeping into my body. It felt wrong, but I was too concerned with Vail's hands on me to give a shit.

We broke our kiss when Vail thrust with his hips, one of his hands drifting from my ass to squeeze my breast. A frustrated growl slipped from him before he tore the fabric, then his hand was on my bare flesh as he roughly ran a thumb over my taut nipple.

"Fuck!" My head snapped forward, and then my fangs were buried in his throat. The richness of his blood coated my tongue as I drank him down.

"*Sam,*" he groaned as the hand that was still cupping my ass gripped it tighter.

That nickname on his tongue was like an arrow to the heart.

Between one heartbeat and the next, I pulled my fangs out of his throat, gripped the back of his head, and slammed it forward over my shoulder—straight into the door—with every ounce of strength I could muster.

Vail's hands dropped away, and my feet landed on the floor as he stumbled back, a hand clutching his head while blood leaked through his fingers.

I straightened my dress as best as I could, holding up one side of the torn fabric as I calmly walked towards my cell. Once I was inside, I went all the way to the back wall. He'd have to use his blood to lock me in, but I thought I'd gotten my point across loud and clear.

Lust and tension filled the room as I took a seat on the floor. Vail straightened, pulling his hand away and revealing a nasty cut running diagonally from the center of his forehead to just beside his left eye. I tried not to compare it to the scar that traced a path across that eye—the one he'd gotten the night our parents had been killed. It'd been a severe injury, and we'd been too panicked that night to heal it properly, so it'd left a scar.

Panic flared in Vail's eyes as he took a step towards my cell. "I didn't—I'm sorry. I didn't mean to—"

I cut him off. "What just happened was on me. But it won't happen again."

He stopped in his tracks, his expression twisted into one of pain, and something inside my chest wrenched at seeing that look in his eyes, but I didn't let it stop me. He'd made his fucking choice.

"I have given you so many fucking chances. Even when others told me I was a fool to trust you, I still did, at least to do what was best for House Harker, but what Carmilla's doing"—I pointed a finger up to the House that sat above us—"is wrong. I never would have thought you would stand by someone who planned to strip away the free will of our people. I'm pissed at you for betraying me, for letting things progress as far as they did between us, but that's between you and me, and I damn well know how to separate business and pleasure. But you've fucked over all the Moroi with your actions." I leaned forward and bared my teeth at him. "And that, I will *never* forgive you for."

Vail's hands curled into fists at his sides. "I can make this right."

"No." I stepped away and rested my head against the back wall. My body was still keyed up from almost getting what it wanted with Vail. Denying it hurt, and thinking past the lust and pain was hard, so I focused on breathing. "You can't."

I closed my eyes. A few minutes later, Vail left. It was only then that I let the tears fall.

When the door opened half an hour later, I kept my eyes shut. My emotions had devolved into a maelstrom of lust and rage, so the idea of looking at Vail's face right now made me want to scream. I didn't want to hear any of his excuses or pleas for forgiveness either. I just wanted to be left alone for the next forty-eight hours so I could ride this out.

I'd tried getting myself off after he'd left, but it hadn't worked. It'd only made me more frustrated, so I stopped trying. Vail could probably smell my efforts in the air, but I didn't care. If he wanted to stay in here and stew in it, that was his problem. I hoped he fucking suffered.

"Got an itch you can't scratch, love?" a deep, melodious voice asked.

"Draven?" My eyes flew open, and I expected to see only Vail, as if I'd imagined that other voice. While Vail was indeed standing there—so was my prince, wearing only a pair of loose-fitting pants with his black and silver hair wet and clinging to his sculpted body as it fell to his waist. "Am I dreaming?"

Suddenly, I was at the cell door, clutching the bars.

Those deep blue eyes threaded with red softened as Draven stepped past Vail to my cell. "Pretty sure you and I would have dreamed up something better than this," he said in that dry tone of his. Fuck, I'd missed that. His brows furrowed together as he looked me over, his gaze lingering on where my skin was in contact with the iron bars, as if he could sense the discomfort it caused me. "Are you alright?"

"Am I alright?" I barked out a laugh. "The last time I saw you, a fucking sword was sticking through your chest! You looked half dead, and they *dragged you away from me*. All I've gotten since have been assurances that you are still alive but nothing more."

"Remember the deal," Vail said roughly as he shoved his way between Draven and me to open my cell. There was no door, just a hidden glyph on some of the bars that was keyed to his blood and a few other individuals'—something I was keeping in the back of my mind while plotting how to get out of here. "One hour until the guards change. You have to be back in your cell before then. Don't give me any shit. I'll have no problem killing you, prince."

A warning growl vibrated up my throat, and Draven chuckled darkly as enough of the bars disappeared for him to step inside, then reappeared within seconds, locking us in together.

"Don't mind him." Draven grinned at me. "He's just remembering the last time he had to warn me about how much time I had with you—only now, he won't be getting an invite to join."

"Are you truly healed?" I asked in a low, tight voice. Normally, my control over my bloodlust was absolute. I could let it rise or fall as needed, and even when I let it fully rise, all it really did was heighten my instincts and give me fangs and claws. It didn't significantly impact my temperament the way it did for many other Moroi. But now, I could feel my bloodlust rising and mixing with my arousal. The feeling was intoxicating. I had just enough rationality left to make sure Draven was actually up for this. If he was hiding any injuries and I made them worse . . .

Warm fingers touched my chin as Draven tilted my head up until I met his eyes. "You can unravel those chains you're keeping on yourself. I can take anything you throw at me." Then he leaned down and nipped my bottom lip, causing a shiver to run up my spine. "But before we get to that, I need you to tell me you want this and it's not just your body's needs clouding your thoughts."

"I've had no problem turning down previous offers." I

traced several fingers down his chest before toying with the waistband of his pants, right above where his erection was straining to get free. "Before you walked into my little corner of hell, I had accepted I'd be riding this out all by my lonesome. My fingers weren't much help. Think yours will be better?"

Draven's smile was positively sinful, but I caught the calculation in his eyes and suspected he saw the same in mine. We had to make the most of this time. It might be our only chance to plan our escape together. "Challenge accepted."

In a heartbeat, I was pinned against the wall as Draven gripped my wrists with one hand and held them over my head. His other hand slid down my waist to stop on my thigh—right where the slit of the dress opened.

Then his mouth slanted over mine, and I kissed him hungrily before he broke the kiss, his lips brushing down my jaw until they reached my neck. I tilted my head to give him better access.

"Three floors separate us," he breathed into my ear so quietly, I could barely make out the words before he nipped me. "I'm on the bottom level."

He kissed my jawline, trailing down to my neck. I moaned when his fangs grazed my skin before he bit down hard and drank several deep gulps of my blood.

Vail let out a warning growl from outside the cell, and Draven ripped his fangs out before twisting to snarl back at him. I seized the opportunity to slip one hand free from Draven's grasp and wrap it around the silky strands of his hair, then yanked his head down and to the side so I could bury my fangs in his neck.

It was Draven's turn to moan as I drank from him, enjoying the rich and intoxicating taste of his blood. Reluctantly, I pulled back and kissed his skin before whispering in his ear,

"Vail is usually here. Guards check on me every hour, but they don't stay long."

Draven grabbed my hand that was still twisted in his hair and not so gently tugged it back up to where my other hand was still pinned against the wall. He released me for a second to secure both wrists again, and then his free hand dove straight through the slit of my dress he'd been playing with earlier to the aching center between my thighs—where he stopped an inch away from where I wanted him.

The lust I'd barely been holding back shoved every rational thought from my mind. We'd have to share notes about our situation later.

I needed to get fucked. Hard.

"Draven," I said in a low, throaty voice.

"Yes, love?" he asked almost absently as he traced an infuriating circle on my inner thigh.

"If you try to tease me right now, I'll have Vail march your ass back to your own cell." My bloodlust rose with my desire, and I felt my nails shift to claws. Draven's gaze flicked back up to them before dropping back to meet my solid black eyes. "But not before I punish you for your insolence."

"I think I'd like your punishments." He grinned wickedly.

"Drav—fuck!" I screamed, and my eyes rolled into the back of my head as he speared me with two fingers and his thumb teased my clit. My hips rolled in time with each of his thrusts as he roughly fucked me with his fingers.

"Gods, you are wet," he groaned as he curled his fingers inside me. "Although I'm a little annoyed that you're not wearing any panties. I was hoping to rip those off you."

"Apologies, my prince," I panted as I tried to grind down on his hand, but Draven just tightened his grip around my wrists and drew me up another inch, forcing me to stand almost on my tiptoes.

"Not a prince anymore."

"Trust me"—a strangled moan tore from my throat when Draven added a third finger while pushing down on my clit with his thumb—"Kier and I will always consider you our prince."

"Fuck," he growled and ripped his fingers out of me so he could roughly shove down his pants. His cock sprang free at the same moment he released my wrists so he could grip my ass and slam me against the wall—very much like Vail had done earlier. His cock slid in all the way to the hilt, and we both groaned as I stretched around his thick length, then eyes more red than blue met mine. "Take whatever you need, Sam. I'll always be yours. And Kier's."

"Show me," I demanded. "Claim me."

All the blue faded from his eyes as the last of his control snapped.

Draven thrust into me, hard and fast, and my claws tore into his shoulders and back while I held on. The scent of blood filled the air, and he only fucked me harder. Then the orgasm I'd been chasing earlier barreled through me, and I screamed, his pace never slowing. He continued as he snaked a hand between us and started rubbing my clit.

"Oh fuck!" I panted hoarsely.

It was too much. My entire body was trembling while my pussy clenched around his cock and his infernal fingers worked my clit. I pushed on his shoulders in a desperate need to make a little space between us—just to give me a moment so I didn't pass out.

Draven was having none of it. He growled, and then his fangs were in my throat again. Vail let out a string of curses, but I didn't understand a word as another orgasm tore through me. It might be poor timing to be going through lust haze right now, but fucking hell they were fun.

"More," I demanded. "Fuck me more."

Warm blood spilt down my neck as Draven pulled back,

kissing me hard. I could taste my blood on his lips . . . and it made me want his again.

One of my hands slipped into his hair, and I pulled his head to the side, striking fast. He groaned as I swallowed mouthfuls of his blood while he slowed his pace to hard, deliberate thrusts, both of his hands gripping my ass to pull me against him.

"You are glorious," he breathed. "And this pussy is *mine*."

Another growl from Vail echoed across the room.

My fangs popped free, and I looked over Draven's shoulder to where Vail stood against the back wall. His eyes glowed silver, and his hands were curled into fists at his sides, like it was taking all of his willpower not to do something about the erection straining against his pants.

Slowly, I trailed my tongue up Draven's neck, licking the blood clean, and Vail's nostrils flared when I smiled at him, fangs on display. His gaze dropped to them, and I knew he was remembering what it felt like for me to sink my teeth into his flesh.

Suddenly, fingers wrapped around my hair and yanked my head back.

"Eyes on me," Draven demanded. "Not in the mood to share you right now—even if all he gets to do is watch me take this perfect pussy over and over again."

I whimpered as Draven drew his hard length almost all the way out before slowly sliding back in. Obscene sounds filled the cell as my arousal gushed down my thighs. Draven kept one hand on my hair, controlling where I looked, while the other cupped my ass. My legs tightened around his waist, our panting breaths interspersed with groans as he continued the torturously slow pace.

"Tell me what you want, baby." His eyes bored into mine. "Because I can think of all kinds of wicked things."

"Like what?" I rasped as he bottomed out again.

Red eyes dropped to my lips. "That gorgeous mouth wrapped around my cock. I want to watch your eyes water as you take all of me. Swallow every drop when I come down your throat." His gaze dropped to my cleavage. "Or maybe I'd pull out and decorate those wonderful tits of yours."

My mouth watered at the thought, and I almost demanded he let go of me so I could drop to my knees.

He frowned. "No. I want to save that for when Kieran is with us."

I pouted, and he chuckled darkly before leaning forward to whisper in my ear, "So I can watch him lick my seed off you."

"Oh fuck." My thighs clenched as a slow, delicious need started to build again.

A breathy laugh tickled my ear before Draven straightened. "Maybe you should show me what it is you want right now."

He thrust into me one more time before withdrawing. I hissed my frustration, and he just laughed again as he dragged me down with him. Draven stretched out on the floor and maneuvered me until I straddled him, facing his legs. One hand gripped the rise of my hip, digging into the soft flesh, and the other wrapped around my hair and yanked my head back.

"Maybe you should take pity on him and tug your dress down a bit," he purred slyly. "I think Vail has at least earned a good show. Although, maybe it's more of a *punishment* to be able to see you"—his thick cock slowly pushed inside me again, and I moaned—"hear you, and not be able to do anything about it."

I looked through the bars of my cell to where Vail was still rigidly standing. His eyes tracked my fingers as they tugged at the front of my dress, pulling it down so that my breasts almost spilt out—but then stopped.

My hand snapped up, and I flashed him an obscene gesture.

"Fuck. You're so mean," Draven groaned as he sank in

another inch. "I love it. Now show me how much you want my cock, love."

I closed my eyes, forgetting about Vail. He didn't fucking exist in this moment. All I wanted was to feel Draven moving inside me again. The need to feel his cock stretching me out was all I could think about. I dropped all the way down, and Draven swore, his claws digging into my soft flesh.

Fuck, he felt amazing. This angle was *everything.*

My hips rolled forward, and his grip on my hair tightened, forcing me to arch my back more. I leaned back enough so that my hands could grip his sides. This time, it was *my* claws sinking into flesh.

A husky laugh poured from my lips when he moaned. My prince liked a little pain with his pleasure too.

I ground against him, quickening my pace as I rode him hard, and Draven moved his body to perfectly match my thrusts. Something about this angle made him feel like he was reaching even deeper. I lost myself in the intensity. In him. Everything was too much and yet not enough. Pleasure rippled just out of reach as my body keyed up with the building orgasm.

Almost there.

The world tilted, and I had to quickly pull my claws from Draven's flesh as he pivoted us up until I was on all fours and he was thrusting wildly behind me. His hand was still wrapped in my hair, the other gripping my hip.

"Come for me again." He slammed into me so hard, it almost hurt.

"Make me," I half moaned.

Hot pain flared where Draven's claws tore through the soft flesh of my hip, and I gasped at the perfect blend of pleasure and pain.

Everything became a blur. The sound of flesh slapping against flesh. The feel of Draven pulling me harder against himself as he did his best to go deeper with every thrust. The scent of blood filling the air. Mine and Draven's.

Silver eyes held me captive as strangled cries of pleasure tore from my throat. Draven's breathing grew more ragged, his movements harsher until he finally let out a deep groan. Then heat filled me before spilling down my thighs.

My mind floated, and I barely noticed the sting of Draven pulling his claws from my hips and tugging me upright. A small protest escaped me when he withdrew his cock and some of his seed slid down my legs. Draven growled, and then I felt his fingers reach between my thighs and push it back inside my aching pussy.

I was dimly aware that this was just a side effect of the lust haze and that I had nothing to worry about since I'd drunk the contraceptive tea, which meant I could just enjoy the feeling of being the center of Draven's attention. My eyes drifted shut, and I basked in the pleasure of it all as strong arms pulled me back against a warm chest.

"Mine." Draven nuzzled the side of my neck.

"Yours," I agreed.

I drifted off for a bit but was woken up by a tight exchange between Vail and Draven.

"—proven myself."

Draven let out a harsh laugh. "Is that what this was?"

"I didn't have to bring you here," Vail growled. "I could have—"

"You could have what, Vail?" Draven challenged. "Pretty sure she would have fucked Demetri before you."

Vail's growl gained a sharp edge. "Do not speak his name."

"Oh, so now you get protective?"

"Enough," I snapped, opening my eyes and blinking slightly to shrug off the last of the blissful peace I'd found. I was in Draven's lap with his arms wrapped around my waist and chest while Vail stood on the other side of the cell, blood dripping from his fingers like he was about to open it.

"You want to prove yourself, Vail?" My expression hardened. "Get the fuck out and give us five minutes alone."

"You don't think straight around him." Vail stubbornly clenched his jaw. "He's half Fae, Samara. There's nothing about him that's safe."

I shot him an incredulous look. "You're the reason I'm in this fucking cell, Vail!"

"And it's not like she thinks straight around you either," Draven pointed out. "As far as I'm concerned, you are the greatest threat to Samara, because for some reason, she keeps forgiving you, even when you don't deserve it. If anyone could come back from this epic fuck up, it would be you."

"Unlikely." My annoyed glare slid to Draven. "He doesn't deserve forgiveness."

"What he deserves and what you will do are likely two different things." He shrugged.

The face I'd found so kissable minutes ago, I now wanted to punch. Based on the way he chuckled against my neck as he planted a kiss there, he knew exactly what I was feeling. Gods, I'd forgotten how much of a troublemaker he could be. He and Kieran together would be incredibly aggravating.

And hot.

The lust started to rise again, so I shoved that thought away. My mind was temporarily clear, and I needed to take advantage of that while Draven was here.

"Five minutes, Vail," I said firmly. "You fucking owe me."

"Fine," he ground out. "Not a second more." Vail pointed at Draven. "And you will return to your cell when I get back without any tricks."

"Sure thing, Marshal."

"He will," I promised and twisted enough to give Draven a

warning look. A chastised grin quickly appeared on his face, but it was far too mischievous for it to be convincing.

After a few tension-filled seconds, Vail stalked towards the door that led out to the stairwell.

"Vail."

He stopped and looked over his shoulder at me.

I held a hand against the center of my chest, the place where I always felt this strange connection to him. "I'll know if you linger outside that door and try to listen."

A storm rolled through his grey eyes, but he jerked his head in a sharp nod before leaving and shutting the door behind him. I felt his presence move farther away, like the invisible rope between us was thinning. It was the first time I'd acknowledged its existence to him, but I knew he was aware of it. Occasionally, when he'd be down here with me—usually glowering at the floor—he'd idly rub his chest in the exact same spot where I felt it.

I still had no idea what it was or how to break it. It always gave me an idea of where Vail was and what he was feeling, but it also gave him the same information about me.

Draven gripped my waist and lifted me before turning me and resettling me on his lap so towards him. Then he raised his hands to cup my face before brushing his lips against mine. It was a sweet kiss, and for some reason, it made me want to cry. I kissed him back before leaning my head against his chest, listening to his heartbeat like it had all the answers I needed.

"Do you know of any other exits down here?" I asked, keeping my voice low. Draven had grown up in this House. If anyone knew another way out, it would've been him.

"None that I'm aware of, but that doesn't mean there isn't one." His arms wrapped loosely around my waist, and he rested his head on top of mine. "Prior to our current situation, I haven't spent much time down here. The iron bothers me."

"Because you're half Fae."

"Yes." I could almost hear the question he wanted to ask, but he didn't, so I settled it for both of us.

"And so am I." It felt odd to say that out loud, like I was finally putting away the last of my denial.

"It does seem that way," he said gently. "Maybe not half, but you must have a decent amount of Fae blood for the iron to bother you."

"Has the crown ever spoken to you?"

Draven drew back, and I tilted my head up so I could meet his perplexed gaze. "What do you mean?"

"That crown . . ." I swallowed. "It's spoken to me twice. The first time, it called me 'the forgotten one,' and then, earlier, at dinner, it asked if I was ready to 'take my rightful place.' There was a wraith before . . . he called me *din tros*."

"Forgotten queen," Draven murmured, concern bleeding into his expression. "Are you sure neither of your parents were Fae?"

"My mother was definitely a Harker." I chewed on my bottom lip. "But I don't actually know much about my dad's past. He was born in an outpost. I know his mother died when he was young, and he never spoke of his father. When I was a kid, I just accepted he was my dad and never questioned why he didn't talk about his past."

"We'll escape this place and then find the answers we need." He leaned down and kissed me before pulling back and resting his forehead against mine. "I will always keep you safe, Samara Harker," he swore, "with my life."

"And I will always keep you safe, Draven Nacht," I promised, "with my life."

Suddenly, heat burned inside my chest. I gasped and stumbled back as my fingers gripped the front of my dress and pulled it away, expecting to see burnt flesh, but my skin was perfectly smooth. I looked up to find Draven staring down at his own bare chest, his hand placed on the same spot I'd felt the burn.

He raised his gaze to meet mine. "I'm guessing you felt that?"

I nodded, a suspicion already forming. "Take a few steps back?"

Draven did as I asked, curiosity brimming in his eyes. I also moved back until we were about as far apart as we could get in the cell.

I felt it—the strange awareness of Draven. It was like a piece of his soul had embedded itself inside me.

Draven stared at me in wonder. "What is this?"

"I have no idea," I said honestly. "But you should know, I have the same thing with—"

The door to the dungeon burst open as Vail stormed in. "What the fuck did you two just do?"

CHAPTER SIX

Roth

I GAZED up at the utilitarian fortress before us. Most of the castles left behind by the Fae were architectural wonders that combined beauty and functionality.

The Fae who had built what was now House Devereux had skipped the beauty.

Foreboding, dark grey stone walls stretched towards the sky, while a deep moat curved around the outside of the walls. Its waters were obsidian black, and all kinds of wicked things swam in them. Behind the walls, a singular rectangular structure rose. The windows were hidden by glamour, so it appeared to just be solid walls.

The only break in the uniformity was the occasional turret. But those had none of the whimsical designs like those of House Harker or many of the other Houses. Just more grey stone with no visible windows.

I'd once made a comment to my parents that perhaps the House's appearance wasn't enough and we should hang a sign on the outside that read, "You are not wanted here. Leave or die."

My mother's response had been, "Do you think it will help?"

I hadn't been able to tell if she'd been joking.

Kieran and Alaric stood on either side of me, silently lending their support. We'd all agreed that it would be best if I spoke for the group. It wasn't a position I preferred, but it was my House—my family. Nyx, Adrienne, and Emil were fanned out protectively around us.

My siblings wouldn't be happy about outsider rangers being allowed in, but they'd just have to deal with it. It wasn't like I was happy to be back here after swearing to never return.

"Let's get this over with." I grimaced and strode forward, Alaric and Kieran immediately falling into step with me. It was telling how unlike himself Kieran was at the moment because he had barely asked me about my family and why I'd left in the first place on our way here. He was usually so nosy about everything.

I was pretty sure he was clinging to his rage and channeling that into motivation to get Samara back. Because if he allowed himself to feel the despair and panic that we were all dealing with, he'd fall apart and never put himself back together. I couldn't blame him for that, and personally, I preferred this version of Kieran. I could deal with clipped answers and cutting remarks, but I didn't handle criers well.

Alaric had withdrawn into himself a little more than usual but was otherwise acting the same. If Samara were here, I'm sure she would have picked up on more clues as to how he was truly feeling.

We needed her back. I needed her back.

That was the only reason my steps didn't falter as we moved beyond the tree line and into the view of the two guards posted on this side of the moat. The drawbridge was up, and to lower it, the guards on both this side and inside the fortress had to activate the glyphs.

I had no doubt there were others in the forest who had spotted us miles ago, but it was standard operating procedure for the guards posted in the woods to only observe and not intervene unless necessary. They were meant to be the dagger in your back you never saw coming.

Adrienne and Emil were experienced enough that they probably knew where the rangers were. Nyx was still young and had much to learn. I had no doubt Alaric and Kieran were oblivious.

They were both lucky they were so pretty. Not my cup of tea, but I did have eyes.

The guards watched us approach. Neither of them drew their swords, which made me think they recognized me. Impressive, considering I'd been gone for a long time. I'd left for Drudonia almost eight years ago, and I'd never returned.

It wasn't that I hated my family or that they were unkind to me. I just didn't belong here. Looking at the fortress before me brought back all the memories of growing up as the person out of place. The scholar living amongst warriors.

Paranoid. Violent. Warriors.

The guards scrutinized us from underneath silver visors, their helmets hiding most of their features. Neither of them said anything. Didn't welcome me home or ask what the fuck I was doing in the company of House Harker.

They just waited for me to speak. Argh.

"You know who I am." I raised my chin. "Lower the gate."

"Do we?" The guard on the right cocked their head and looked at the other. "Nothing is jogging my memory. You?"

"Nope. Don't remember a thing," the left guard responded, their pale green eyes mostly focused on the rangers. They sparked with interest as they took in Adrienne. She was quite the looker, but if he didn't drop his gaze soon, she'd have his eyes plucked out of his skull before he could blink.

One of my favorite places to work in House Harker overlooked the training courtyard. I'd seen Adrienne take down just about everyone who challenged her. Only Emil was able to hold his own against the beautiful blonde ranger.

Tension rolled off Kieran, and I didn't miss the way his hand slid to the dagger on his thigh. Based on the way both guards subtly adjusted their stances, I knew they hadn't missed it either. I wasn't a fighter—much to the disappointment of my parents—but I was observant. It was impossible to grow up in House Devereux and not have fighting mechanics and strategies drilled into your head.

It was just, for me, they were all theoretical rather than practical skills. When I'd left here for Drudonia and started going by Roth, it'd had nothing to do with my gender. I'd just needed a way to separate myself from my House. From the legacy of being Astaroth Devereux . . . and just be the scholar Roth for a while.

But I knew who I was now. And I was ready to reclaim the part of me I'd left behind. While I would never be like the fierce warriors behind those walls—I was far from harmless. Something my brothers were well aware of. It was time these guards remembered it too.

"Allow me to properly announce myself."

The guards took a step back and away from each other as the ropes around my forearms unwound. Magic pulsed from me, and the blood magic ropes shot forward. Both guards swung with their swords, trying to cut through the ropes, but the bloodred tendrils snapped out from the ropes and wrapped themselves around the swords, yanking them from the guards' grasps. Before they could take another step, my ropes looped around their necks and pulled them off the ground.

Strangled gasps came from the guards as they clutched at the ropes and tried to stay conscious. Another pulse of magic from me had the ropes lifting them higher off the ground as I stepped closer to the ledge, the drawbridge to my right. The ropes turned the guards so they were facing the House, where I knew we had an audience watching us from the top of the wall, hidden from our sight by glamour.

It was very likely that at least one of my brothers was up there. I bit back a frustrated sigh. Would it have killed them to just let me in?

"I'm Astaroth Devereux," I called out in an even, steady voice. "Open the fucking gate."

"Didn't know you had it in you, Roth," Kieran said in a voice that was almost back to his teasing, light tone. His blue eyes were still strained and tired, but I was glad to see a hint of his old self.

"That was a bit dramatic," Alaric said dryly as we walked across the now-lowered bridge. The guards I'd almost choked out walked behind us. As soon as the bridge had lowered, I'd released them from the ropes. They'd dropped the ten feet to the ground and landed easily on their feet. Instead of being angered or frightened, they'd taken off their helmets and grinned at me before activating the glyphs to lower their side of the bridge.

No doubt they'd be bragging about almost being choked out by the lost child of House Devereux later while they got drinks after their shift.

"Personally I'm disappointed you didn't drop them into the moat." Adrienne glanced over to the dark water. "I've always been curious about what's hiding in there."

"Have dinner with me later and maybe I'll tell you," one of the guards offered.

Adrienne looked over her shoulder, a bright, sunny smile on her lips. "Or I could just throw you in now and find out."

"Marry me." The guard gave her puppy dog eyes, and

Adrienne rolled her eyes, but I caught the hint of a smile on her lips.

Emil and Nyx both zeroed in on the guard and gave him warning looks before returning their focus to the courtyard we were about to walk into. From the outside, it looked like the House went right up to the exterior wall, but there was actually a small space carved out. Lining that small space was a wrap-around balcony, where guards with crossbows would happily point their weapons at any newcomers.

There was a reason other Houses only came here when it was absolutely necessary. More than one House representative had said or done the wrong thing and ended up shot full of bolts and then dumped into the moat. House Devereux was almost entirely self-sufficient and traded very little with the other Houses, and when they did trade, the negotiations were always fraught with tension.

We stopped in the center of the small courtyard while the two guards who had escorted us moved to stand with the others who had lined up on both sides of us. I glanced up to see another dozen guards on the balcony; at least they didn't have their crossbows out. Everyone was just . . . waiting.

I grimaced. This was going to be pure agony.

Adrienne and Emil moved to flank Alaric, Kieran, and me with Nyx guarding our backs. None of the Harker rangers pulled their weapons—as skilled as they were, we were outnumbered, and escalating wasn't in our best interest. Alaric caught my eye and ever so slightly raised his brow in question. I shook my head and mouthed, *Wait.*

Luckily—or perhaps in my case, unluckily—we didn't have to wait long.

Two huge brutes dropped from the second story balcony, landing easily on their feet. They both had the same pale white skin as me and piercing eyes. Unlike me, they had black hair like our father. The one on the left kept his hair long, almost to his waist, with the sides shaved. His eyes were a copy of mine, hazel with orange streaks. The one on the right had always preferred to keep his hair short, only a dark stubble was present, and deep blue eyes flecked with orange stared at me with an intensity that made me want to shift on my feet.

Instead, I raised my chin and gave them both a look of disdain.

Taivan, the long-haired one, broke first. "*Our favorite sibling has returned!*" His voice boomed across the courtyard.

Alaric and Kieran jumped. Even Emil and the other two Harker rangers were surprised, which was probably why they did nothing to help me as my two older brothers charged and swept me up in a crushing hug.

"Gross!" I shrieked. "You're both sweaty and disgusting!" My feet kicked out from where they dangled several feet off the ground. Why did my brothers have to be so freaking tall?

"We missed you, Rothie Bear," Desmond grumbled in a deep, raspy voice. His throat had been mangled in a fight with some wraiths years ago, and while the scar had mostly faded, his voice had been irrevocably damaged.

"Should we . . ." Alaric trailed off. I couldn't see him or the others, thanks to being trapped between the two mountains who were my brothers, but I imagined he had no idea what to do in this situation. Alaric was an only child—something I was very jealous of at this moment.

"No," all three rangers said at once.

"Taivan. Desmond," a clear voice rang out. "Put down your sibling. You know Roth doesn't like hugs."

My feet hit the ground a second later, and a big meaty hand landed on my shoulder to steady me when I stumbled a bit. "Sorry, little sib," Desmond said, looking slightly chagrined.

"I'm not." Taivan ruffled my hair, and I slapped his hand away with a glower. He just laughed at me, the sound threatening to burst my eardrums. Had he seriously gotten louder? "You haven't visited us once since sneaking off in the night. That means you owe me a backlog of hugs."

"That's not how that works!" I snapped. "And you could have visited me!" A small amount of hurt crept into my voice before I could squash it. Nobody in my family had sent me so much as a message since I'd left. I'd always been the odd one out here. They'd likely all sighed a breath of relief when I'd gone to Drudonia—if they'd noticed at all. I wouldn't have been surprised if my parents hadn't realized I'd left for months.

Suddenly, the happy grins on my brothers' faces slid off, and they looked unsure . . . and sad. "We didn't know if you'd want to see us," Desmond said quietly, his eyes on the ground.

What?

Guilt slammed into me. It had never occurred to me that they had stayed away because they'd thought that was what I'd wanted. I mean, it kind of was what I'd wanted at first, but that was just because I'd desperately needed space. But when they'd never come looking for me, I'd just assumed it had been because they had easily wiped me out of their lives.

The air tightened in my lungs. I didn't—

How did I fix this? What was I supposed to say? Fuck! Suddenly, the breaths I hadn't been able to take started coming faster. Oh my gods, I was going to have a panic attack right fucking here in front of everyone.

"It's so wonderful to meet both of you!" Kieran said cheerfully. "I wish we were here under better circumstances, but I am glad that we got Roth here. They've been kind enough to help us with some urgent research over the last couple of months—something they were undertaking at Drudonia—but they've spoken of you often."

Desmond's gaze snapped up to meet mine again, surprise and happiness brimming in them. "You have?"

I hadn't. Kieran was lying his ass off. Sure, I'd talked about my brothers a little bit to Samara, but that was it.

"Of course." I did my best to smile. Both Taivan and Desmond grinned back at me, and the panic I'd been feeling faded. Tension replaced it as I finally looked past my brothers to the woman who had spoken.

In front of the main doors that led inside stood a tall, broad-shouldered woman with the same blue eyes as Desmond. She looked nothing like me—except the hair. We both had the exact shade of deep crimson red. Beside her stood a man who towered over even my brothers. A little surprise ran through me at seeing a few streaks of grey in his black hair. Eyes identical to mine bored into me.

"Hey, Mom." I sighed. "Hi, Dad."

Unlike my brothers—who had always been on the emotional side—my parents gave me nothing in response. Had they missed me? Did they hate me? Were they thinking about what to grab for lunch? Who the fuck knew.

"Astaroth."

My head snapped to the left, towards the woman striding out of the side entrance. Compared to her brother—my father—Thessalia was so dainty. Her hair was almost completely grey, only a few strands of black remaining, but she walked with strength and confidence. All the rangers dipped their heads out of respect and loyalty.

The Head of House Devereux was beloved by her people. And by me.

"Thessalia." Like the rangers, I also nodded deeply in greeting. My aunt was the reason I had stayed sane growing up as I'd tried to devour books while my parents kept trying to shove a sword into my hand. They'd never understood me, but she had, and I had left her behind along with everyone else.

Hazel eyes with burnt orange streaks just like mine and my father's slid to Alaric and Kieran, who had moved a little closer to stand on either side of me. Thessalia's lips curved up ever so slightly at the sight. "Interesting company you're keeping these days."

"They're my . . ." I floundered, searching for the right word to describe what Kieran and Alaric were to me exactly.

"We are theirs," Alaric cut in. "And Roth is ours."

A smile bloomed across Thessalia's face as she looked at me. "My precious child, you finally found your home."

"I did." My voice cracked as heat built behind my eyes. I took a steadying breath as I looked around at the rangers gathered, my thickheaded brothers, my stoic parents, and finally, the woman who had always seen the truth of me. "And I need your help to save it."

CHAPTER SEVEN

—

Samara

I POPPED the last piece of fruit into my mouth and savored the tartness of the coastal berry—and not being in my cell . . . although Draven had definitely made that more bearable over the last forty-eight hours. Vail had snuck him in several times and then waited outside in the stairwell while we'd fucked like animals.

Once Draven had sated my lust haze, he'd remove his scent from my body with his earth magic. As much as I hated the loss of it, I knew it was necessary.

Vail had come back in once we were done, and then we'd gone through different plans for how to get out of this mess.

It hadn't been my idea to involve Vail.

I still didn't trust him and hadn't wanted to include him in any of our plotting, but to my surprise—and frustration— Draven had disagreed. He'd claimed we'd be more successful including him in our plans. I didn't like it, but even I had to acknowledge that having someone who was able to travel around outside the dungeon and get us information improved our odds.

Especially considering none of our plans were great.

Despite being the House Harker Marshal, it was doubtful that Vail would be able to take me past the perimeter wall without someone questioning it and alerting Carmilla—and there was absolutely no way we could walk Draven out with us.

So sneaking out seemed like the best course of action. We just couldn't figure out how. There was one way in and out of the dungeon. The two guards stationed at the top wouldn't be a problem for us, but the entrance was located smack-dab in the center of the Sovereign House, and this fortress was massive.

While being escorted to this dinner, I'd made notes of how many guards were on duty and where they'd been stationed. By the time my count had reached twenty, it had become clear that we wouldn't be escaping this way.

As skilled as Vail and Draven were at sneaking around, we all agreed it was highly unlikely that we'd make it outside the walls without being seen, and as soon as someone sounded the alarm, we would be vastly outnumbered.

Vail had also been able to provide us with the number of rangers stationed on the perimeter walls. Which I hadn't thanked him for—he was the reason we were in this mess—but I had acknowledged that it was useful information. I still fully intended to punch him repeatedly in the face once we were out of here.

Such anger for a young one.

For a second, I froze, but then I forced myself to relax and strike a casual pose. Luckily, Carmilla was deep in conversation with some of her new advisors. They had previously served Velika, and I wasn't familiar with either of them. I also had no idea if Carmilla had used the crown's magic on them or if they had voluntarily switched loyalties.

I'd tried to converse with the crown the night I'd had dinner with Carmilla, but it'd been silent until it'd slithered into my mind with the light reprimand, *I can hear you perfectly fine, little queen. But silence is what I currently seek.*

I'd never been scolded by an inanimate object before, so that had been a fun new experience. But apparently, it was up for chatting tonight.

As much as I wanted to dive into a bunch of questions, I bit my tongue. Maybe this would go better if I thought of it less as a Fae artifact and more as a person?

I'm essentially a prisoner. My gaze flicked to where it rested on my aunt's dark hair. *Don't I have a right to be angry?*

You do . . . as do I, the sly voice replied. *You are my fate. You are mine.*

I wasn't sure what unnerved me more. That the crown could pluck all the thoughts from my mind, or that it believed I belonged to it.

You do.

Great. I now had a possessive Fae artifact in my life. *Not that I'm disagreeing,* I said carefully as I sipped my tea, *but can you elaborate on why you think our fates are linked?*

You are a descendent of the Seelie King.

What? I choked, and the tea went down wrong, causing me to sputter. The conversation died as all eyes fell on me. I ungracefully set my cup down and grabbed a cloth napkin as I tried to get my coughing under control. "Apologies," I rasped. "Swallowed wrong."

Carmilla looked at me with an unreadable expression. "Are you sure you're okay?"

"Yes." I nodded and tossed the napkin down. "Please continue. I believe you were discussing the Houses' inventories of gems to power the wards?"

She studied me for another moment before turning her attention back to the advisors, who had been staring at me wide-eyed before snapping their attention back to Carmilla. I could only imagine the rumors surrounding me right now. The

House Harker Heir locked in the dungeons and trotted out to attend various meals by her aunt, who had deposed the previous Moroi Queen.

You need to work on how you broach topics like that, I thought. *Maybe ease into them a little more.*

A tinge of amusement fluttered across my mind. *I will make a note of that for the next time I need to inform someone of their lost royal heritage.*

Was that sarcasm? Did the Fae seriously make a sentient artifact . . . and give it a dry sense of humor?

The Fae did nothing of the sort. I am this magnificent all on my own.

Well, they definitely passed on their arrogance.

You do realize I can hear all of your thoughts, right? I remember the Seelie royals being smarter.

Can you explain why you believe I'm related to the Seelie King? My stomach churned, and I fought to keep the tea I'd swallowed from coming back up. Draven was the Seelie King's son, and we'd—

Flashbacks of the things we'd been up to the last few days played through my mind. Oh god.

Is there a reason why you just threw a bunch of smutty images at me? the crown asked, sounding puzzled. *You seemed to be enjoying yourself quite thoroughly in them, so I'm not really understanding why you suddenly feel like you're going to spew your tea all over the table.*

I've had—some of the best fucking of my life—*relations with the son of the Seelie King, who you just said I was related to. So, yes. I'm feeling a little freaked out right now.*

Dread coiled in my gut. This couldn't be happening. What were were going to d—

That man is not the son of the Seelie King.

Draven isn't Erendriel's son? How was that possible? Draven seemed so sure . . .

He is.

I inhaled a deep breath, trying to not let the tension

strangle me—or drive me to reach across the table and rip the crown off Carmilla's head.

You should actually do that. I'm meant to be sitting on your head. People should be bowing to us.

What the fuck?

One of the advisor's glanced at me. Whoops. Must have whispered that part out loud. I gave her a polite smile and took another sip of tea. She stared at me a long moment before returning her attention back to Carmilla.

Can you please explain what you mean about Draven not being the Seelie King's son? My smile was so tight on my face, it was causing my jaw to ache. *He is Erendriel's son—and Erendriel is the Seelie King.*

Erendriel is an imposter. Rage flashed through me, and it wasn't mine. *Your paternal grandfather was the true Seelie King. Erendriel betrayed him and has been lying ever since.*

What. In. The. Actual. Fuck.

Did my father know he was the son of the Seelie King? He had to, right? The thoughts fired rapidly in my mind. *At the very least, he had to know he was half Fae. Did my mother know?*

Your thoughts are very loud. And confusing, the crown grumbled. *I only knew your father as a youngling. I do not know if he was aware of his true lineage.*

For a second, it felt like everything in my mind went still. *You met my father?*

Before I was split apart and half of me locked away, yes. He was young. I'm not good with human ages, but all he did was cry. I mostly tuned him out and was happy when he was given to the bloodthirsty woman. Although your grandfather was sad for a long time afterwards.

My grandfather . . . the Seelie King. He'd sent my father away. I wondered if the bloodthirsty woman was Moroi, perhaps my grandmother. My father had never spoken about his parents, and he'd died when I'd barely been a teenager. I'd never had the chance to ask.

And now I never would. The crown might be able to give me a lot of answers, but it had admitted to not knowing my father well. It seemed those secrets had been taken to the grave.

I let the melancholy of a truth I'd never know drift through my mind before fading away. There was no point in dwelling on the secrets of the dead when the living hold just as many.

Who locked you away? I asked. It had to have been referring to the room beneath Lake Malov where we'd found it.

I . . . don't know. When I'm split into two parts, I'm weakened. Whoever did it knew what they were doing because they tore me apart before I knew what was happening. Even though I've been made whole once more, there are large gaps in my memory.

I'm so sorry. That sounds terrible. Sure, the crown was capable of tearing the free will away from people . . . but it was also kind of nice. A nice monster crown.

You cannot leave me behind. This woman . . . she has already made me do terrible things. I'm trying to resist, but I'm technically bound to whoever's head I rest upon, and fighting is exhausting.

The pieces clicked together. *That's why you couldn't talk to me the other day? You were tired?*

Yes.

Guilt nipped at me, but I didn't want to lie. There was no point anyway since the crown could read my mind like an open book.

I have no intention of leaving you in the hands of my aunt for long, but I cannot promise that I will take you with me, I said honestly. *Escaping from here is my priority.*

I am your priority. Its words were tinged with a desperate rage.

Not right now, I told it gently. *There are so many people depending on me. I can't let them down.*

Cold silence reigned through my mind. I must have hurt its feelings. Probably not good to piss off an ancient Fae artifact.

I'm sorry, I tried again. *I have no intention of abandoning you for long, but I will do what I must to get free of this place. Once I'm outside of these walls, I'll be in a better position to plan how to fix all of this.*

More silence.

Before I could make another attempt at soothing the crown—something I hadn't anticipated being on my list of problems to solve—footsteps came from outside the hall. Vail's eyes met mine from across the room. From where he was standing, there was no way he could see who was coming, but he'd likely caught their scent, and he didn't look happy.

A second later, I knew why when a stunning woman with golden blonde hair and tanned skin stepped into the room. At her side was an equally attractive man with light brown hair and chiseled features. I'd had the unpleasant experience of conversing with both of them in the past. They were high-ranking courtiers of House Corvinus. Not advisors exactly but they were close friends of Mora and Darius Corvinus—the Heads of the House.

The two courtiers were also Kieran's parents.

"Davon. Narcisa." My aunt rose and greeted the two newcomers. "We didn't expect you until this afternoon. Please join us."

"I think we have everything we need to get started, Carmilla—I mean, my queen," the fair-haired advisor at the table corrected herself. The other advisor glanced at Carmilla in panic, as if he expected my aunt to lash out.

She just smiled. "Thank you both for meeting with me. If you can have the information to me by tomorrow morning, I would appreciate it."

"O-of course," the woman stammered before both advisors practically ran from the table. Kieran's parents observed everything with amused smiles.

I watched them go and pondered the conversation I'd been trying to keep track of while the crown had infiltrated my mind. My aunt was interested in how many gemstones the Sovereign House possessed, as well as a best guess to what the other Houses had. We relied on those stones to power the wards that kept the wraiths and other nasty beasts out of our Houses and outposts.

Why was she specifically interested in the numbers now though? Most of the Houses tried to keep best estimates of what the others had because it gave them an advantage during trade negotiations, but I didn't know what Carmilla was plotting.

It was too much. Everything was too fucking much. Vail's betrayal. Carmilla's coup. That bloody crown. My heart raced as I tried and failed to calm myself. I was imprisoned by my last surviving family member. Someone I cared about very much was also imprisoned, and any day now, they could decide he was no longer worth the risk of keeping around.

Carmilla could order the death of Draven, and I wouldn't know until it was too late. Cold, icy fear gripped my heart. I could lose him.

I tried to pick up my tea again, but my movements were so jerky that I knocked it over instead. It was a red tea blend, and it soaked into the creamy tablecloth like rusty blood. Before I knew what I was doing, I was on my feet and backing away from the table.

Apparently, this was the moment my mind decided to snap under the pressure of everything that had happened over the past two weeks. Ragged breaths tore from my throat. All I could think about was Draven chained up in the throne room the day we'd been captured.

Demetri stabbing him through the chest.

I could have lost him that day. I could still lose him. Magic so different from my Moroi nature rumbled to life, and—

Breath, young queen, the crown ordered. *All is not lost yet. And you will bring the roof down on our heads if you don't stop—not to mention on your lover in the basement.*

The magic died down instantly, but not before I felt it brush against that strange connection I had recently formed with Draven. For a few seconds, I could have sworn I felt his steady heartbeat down it. I had no idea what this was between us, but I grabbed on to it like a lifeline to calm down.

Kieran's parents glanced at me, eyebrows raised as they made their way to the table, but didn't comment. Carmilla's steady gaze fell on me from where she'd already reclaimed her seat, but before I could come up with some excuse for my outburst, Vail was suddenly there, a solid wall of muscle between me and everyone else.

Grey eyes looked down at me. He didn't say anything, just searched my face, looking for a clue as to what was wrong. I clawed back the maniacal laugh that threatened to spill out. What *wasn't* fucking wrong at this point?

Slowly, Vail raised a hand and placed it over my chest. His palm rested on the swell of my left breast, right where that tug I always felt towards him—and now Draven—always was. Nobody else could see us with his broad body blocking their view.

I raised my own hand and placed it against his chest in the exact same spot. A calm steadiness flowed between us. While I might treasure whatever this connection was between me and Draven, it seemed like such a bad idea with Vail. Our conversation from that night in the cave came floating back. When I'd asked why everything between us was so confusing.

"Because I should hate you, but I can't, and you shouldn't trust me, but you do."

How was it that everything and nothing had changed since then? I drew in a steady breath before tugging my hand away from Vail. His eyes flashed, and I sensed a wave of frustration and annoyance through our bond.

Well, that was new. Previously, I had just been able to feel his general whereabouts.

Great. Now I had direct access to the feelings of a man I couldn't—no, shouldn't—trust again, and he probably had the same to mine.

Gods, somehow things had managed to get more complicated between us.

I looked away from Vail's intense gaze and did what I'd done in the years after my parents' deaths when grief had threatened to overwhelm me. I gathered up all the intense emotions I was feeling, shoved them into a box, and buried it in the depths of my soul. Then I envisioned a stone wall between me and Vail. It felt a little clunky, but after a few seconds, the emotions I was feeling from him faded.

Without looking at Vail again, I reclaimed my seat at the table. After a frustrated growl, Vail returned to his post next to the door.

"Feeling alright, Samara?" Kieran's father asked in an attentive but gentle tone that I knew was a lie. I adored Kieran, but there was no one better than my sweet lover at trading one mask for another. Even I was envious of his ability to hide whatever he was feeling and have a completely different emotion on his face. I was good, but nowhere near his level.

And the man looking at me, brows furrowed and eyes shining with concern, was half the reason Kieran could lie so well. The woman next to him, wearing a similar expression, was the other half.

"I'm fine." I smiled at them both. It didn't reach my eyes, but I couldn't bring myself to care. I wasn't at my best at the moment. Even if I had been, I doubted I'd be able to fool these two with charming grins and fluttering eyelashes. It wasn't worth the effort to try. "It's been a long week."

"I'm sure," Narcisa said demurely and took a delicate bite of her food.

"How is Tamsen doing?" I asked politely. The Corvinus Heir was interesting. Her parents were even worse than Kieran's. Mora and Darius were the reason Nyx—Tamsen's younger sibling—had left Drudonia and become a ranger. It was rare for a member of a House bloodline to leave their birth House for anything other than a politically arranged marriage. To leave a House only to become a ranger for another was unheard of for someone like Nyx.

I wasn't close to Tamsen, but I'd interacted with her enough over the years to know she was the least trustworthy of all the House Heirs—except Demetri, obviously. Like her parents, Tamsen was skilled at hiding her emotions, and every exchange with her was like trying to find and avoid the carefully laid traps in her pretty words.

But Tamsen was also the reason Nyx had been able to get free of the toxic political bullshit of House Corvinus. She loved her younger sibling and had fought for them when it'd mattered—and had likely suffered the consequences.

It didn't mean I trusted her . . . but there was more of a question mark beside her name now, whereas before, I'd had her firmly in the box with the rest of her House.

"Our Heir is doing wonderfully." Narcisa beamed. "She's wrapped up in some negotiations with the *Velesians* right now; otherwise, she would have come herself. I fear that each round of trading we do with them becomes more tedious than the last, but Tamsen always does right by her parents. Mora and Darius are so fortunate to have one child who is loyal to the House and willing to put the work in."

I almost clapped at the performance. She'd managed to put down the Velesians and suggest that trading with them was failing as well as make a dig at both Nyx and Kieran. I had no doubt that she and her husband were well aware of my relationship with their son—the rumors of us finally getting together had been quick to spread, and they were the types of people who knew every rumor before the last word of it was even whispered. While Nyx had been with House Harker for years, their parents still probably considered the whole thing a black mark on their House.

"Strange, I very recently finished a trade with the Velesians and had no problems at all." I widened my eyes and gave first Narcisa then Davon a concerned look. "Is House Corvinus struggling with offering fair trading terms? I know how challenging it can be to run a House. We're fortunate in that House Harker is so well-established that sometimes I take our stability for granted." I let a hint of apology seep into my expression as I placed a hand on my chest. "Please let us know if we can be of assistance. Nobody wants to see House Corvinus fall on hard times."

Narcisa's eyes narrowed the barest fraction, but Davon just gave me a grateful nod. "You're too kind, Samara. I wish you good fortune in your *second* marriage—perhaps aiming lower than a fellow Heir will work out better for you? I do believe House Tepes has lots of second cousins available."

My smile sharpened, but before I could reply, Carmilla cut in. Probably for the best. I was too tired to come up with anything clever and probably would have just thrown the butter knife at Davon's head. It was blunt, but I was confident I could throw it hard enough to pierce his thick skull.

"It's actually very fortunate that you're here." Carmilla touched the crown on her head.

I stiffened. Kieran's parents might be horrible and represent the worst of the Moroi, but I wouldn't sit by and watch their free will be stripped away. "Don't—"

"You will not be the one to pay if you interfere," Carmilla cut me off, her dark gaze flicking downward for a second before meeting my eyes again. Draven. She would punish my prince.

My nails shifted to claws that bit straight through the tablecloth and into the wood, but I kept my mouth shut. If I were a better person, I probably would have fought regardless—even knowing it wouldn't matter. The only ally out of the dungeons I had was Vail, and he was questionable at best. Despite Draven's confidence in him, I didn't trust him not to betray me. Definitely not with Carmilla being here.

The last time Carmilla had ordered Vail to do something and I'd begged him not to, he'd sided with her. I had no doubt he would do so again.

Davon and Narcisa were watching Carmilla and me closely. Their expressions were polite with just a hint of curiosity. It was the mask Kieran wore when he was feeling uneasy about something.

"It seems you two have some things to discuss." Narcisa dabbed her mouth with a cloth napkin before folding it neatly on the table. "We wouldn't want to intrude on family affairs."

"Perhaps we can rest in our room and then catch up later this afternoon?" Davon offered as he began to rise from the table, Narcisa doing the same.

"*Sit and be quiet*," Carmilla ordered.

Both courtiers promptly dropped back to their chairs, and fear cracked through their calm facades as dread pooled in my gut.

"This isn't necessary," I tried again, hoping she wouldn't punish Draven for me merely pleading my case. "You said you would only use the crown when you had no other choice."

She gave me a placating smile. "My dear, you know how House Corvinus is. They are not to be trusted. Their loyalty is fleeting and always for sale. It's not a matter of if they will betray us, but when." Her gaze flicked to them. "Given the horrible ways they've treated Kieran over the years, I'm surprised you're defending them." Those green eyes met mine once more. "Or do you not love him the way you claim?"

"He wouldn't want this." I shook my head and glanced at

Kieran's parents. Narcisa's full lips were flattened into a hard line, and her eyes were wide with terror. Davon was trying to keep his expression neutral, but sweat was beading at his forehead. "Imprison them if you must, but please don't do this."

Carmilla tilted her head as she pondered me. "I thought I raised you to be more ruthless than this. This is the perfect opening to have high-level spies in House Corvinus. I will not pass up this opportunity. Unless you want to find out just how much blood your disgraced lover can lose, I suggest you watch what you say next."

A large hand fell on my shoulder. I didn't have to look up to know it was Vail. Whether he was doing it to keep me from doing anything rash or as a show of support, I had no idea.

Please. This time, it was the crown I begged. *You don't have to do this.*

This is why you cannot abandon me. I must obey the head I sit upon —even if I don't want to. She tried to use me on children the other day. Fighting back against that cost me. I do not have the strength to disobey as I am right now. There was a hint of despair in its tone. *I have broken so many. Do not let yourself be added to the list.*

"Davon and Narcisa Blake," Carmilla's voice rang out, filling the room. "From this day forward, you serve me—and only me."

The fear on Kieran's parents' faces was wiped away in an instant before relaxing into emotionless masks. They looked at Carmilla, their eyes hollow and blank. "Yes, my queen," they intoned.

CHAPTER EIGHT

—

Samara

I awoke with a start and rubbed my eyes as I looked around. Carmilla had kept me at her side all day, Kieran's parents trailing behind us like obedient pets as she'd checked in with the rangers and other staff of the household. Most had greeted her happily, while some had been a little more reserved but still polite. I'd tried to see if any of them were under the compulsion of the crown. There had been no obvious evidence, but that didn't mean she hadn't been more subtle about it than she had been with Davon and Narcisa.

Carmilla had ordered Vail away after breakfast, something he very much hadn't been happy about, but he hadn't disobeyed her. I'd been pissy about it at the time, even though I knew it wasn't like he'd actually had a choice. And even if he'd chosen that moment to stand up to her, it likely would have ended with him thrown into the dungeon next to me, which wouldn't have helped us in the long run.

Despite me logically knowing this, I'd still been fuming about it for an hour afterwards until the guard escorting me had been replaced by that prick Grigor. He kept finding reasons to touch me. Never in a super obvious way—even Carmilla wouldn't have allowed that—but his hand would momentarily slip from my lower back to my ass when escorting me through a door. Then there'd been the way his knuckles had accidentally brushed across the side of my breast when he'd been reaching for a cloak off the wall.

He'd only stopped because I'd snapped two of his fingers when Carmilla hadn't been looking, and he'd swallowed his scream of pain. Either because he hadn't wanted to risk me telling my aunt what he'd been doing, or because he hadn't wanted to admit that I'd gotten the better of him.

Asshole was lucky there hadn't been any sharp objects in my reach; otherwise, he would have lost those fingers entirely.

The crown hadn't spoken to me, even when I'd tried to coax it into talking. Occasionally, I'd swear I could feel it slipping into my mind. It didn't feel nefarious, rather I got the feeling that it was just seeking refuge somewhere. It didn't like the way it was being wielded. I couldn't explain exactly how I knew that . . . only that I did. Exactly what type of connection did my family have to the crown?

Lucian had joined us for dinner, but thankfully Demetri was nowhere to be seen. I'd thought about asking where he'd been but I hadn't wanted my aunt to construe that as interest in him. Even if she hadn't taken it that way, it wasn't like I trusted her to answer me honestly.

Lucian had been oddly friendly towards me. Apparently, Velika's ex-consort had decided he liked me. Good for him, but it wouldn't stop me from carving out his heart at the first opportunity. I hadn't forgotten his torturing of Draven over the years or the way he had shoved a sword through my prince's heart.

I had a list of people who needed to die—and Lucian was near the top of that list.

Fuck him and his charming smiles.

I looked around my cell. What had woken me up? Nothing looked out of place, and the Fae lanterns still flickered, casting the room in a warm glow. Vail wasn't anywhere to be seen. Not entirely unusual. He came and went as he pleased. Lately, he'd been sleeping on the floor just outside my cell though.

The hair rose on the back of my neck. Something was here. I was sure of it.

A soft chuckle came from the darkest corner of my cell, and then the shadows moved.

I was on my feet in an instant. On instinct, my hands dropped to my thighs—only, I didn't have any daggers strapped there as usual. I had nothing. Absolutely no weapons to defend myself, and it wasn't like anyone would hear me scream.

Damn it! Of all the fucking times for Vail to take a walk!

Shadows drifted through my cell, shifting around until they formed a vague outline of a person. A person with pointed ears.

I started to step back against the wall but stopped myself and moved forward instead. Being against the wall meant being trapped, I wanted to have room to move if needed. What I'd do with that space against a wraith, I had no idea.

"*Din tros.*" The title slithered between us as the shadowy figure gained more form until I could clearly make out the features of their face. Long hair trailed over their shoulder, whisps of shadow curling at the ends. When the wraith spoke again, his words had a distinct masculine tone, and he used the common tongue instead Seelie. "If I wanted you dead, I would have cut your throat while you slept." He raised a hand, and the slender fingertips morphed into beast-like claws.

Panic at the fact that he was right caused my already rapidly beating heart to go even faster. The wraiths were nothing but Seelie Fae trapped in shadows, but for a few seconds at a time, they could make those shadows solid.

A lot of damage could be done in that short window.

It's why they were the most dangerous of all the monsters in Lunaria. They could only be killed if they were solid, which meant you had to wait to strike until they were about to kill you. Fighting wraiths was not for the faint of heart.

"Alright." I willed my heart to slow down and straightened my shoulders. "If you're not here to kill me then I assume you're here to talk." Chin held high, I stepped forward until only a couple of feet separated us, putting me easily within their reach. "You clearly know who I am—the granddaughter of the *true* Seelie King—I believe it is only fair that I know who I am speaking with."

Shadows swirled as he cocked his head. It was hard to read his expression because so much was lost to the dark shadowy colors, but I thought he was surprised. Both at my fearless demeanor and how casually I talked about my ancestry and the Seelie monarchy.

Which was good because I was still scared out of my mind and had very little to go on when it came to Seelie politics. All I had were the claims from a freaking sentient crown and the fact that this Fae referred to me as the forgotten queen.

But if he thought I knew more than I did, perhaps he would be freer with what he spoke. Fake it 'til you make it. Kieran had taught me that strategy.

"I am Serill." His voice was even clearer now with an almost musical quality. Normally when the wraiths spoke, it sounded like multiple voices layered over each other. It made it challenging to understand them. I could still hear traces of that, but I had to almost strain to notice it. I didn't know what it meant that he was able to speak so clearly now. Probably nothing good.

"Pleased to meet you, Serill." I extended a hand out between us, concentrating hard on keeping it from shaking. "You may address me as Samara."

He looked at the hand for a moment before his lips curled into a grin. I forced myself to remain calm as he reached out to rest a hand beneath mine, shadowy fingers that I could sense but not feel wrapping around it. Then he bowed, and for a split second, his hand became solid as cool lips kissed the back of my hand.

A shudder threatened to race up my spine, but I squashed it and kept a pleasant smile fixed on my face as he rose.

"Even locked in the dungeons, still a queen of old. Despite everything, the blood ran true it seems." He gave me a sly smile. "More so than with the prince."

I assumed the *despite everything* was a reference to my mother's side of the family, and he got in a dig at Draven too. Nice.

"Perhaps it is the blood of my mother's people that strengthened me beyond what the Fae could ever dream of." I arched a dark brow. "And given the prince's heritage, I see it as a strength rather than a hindrance that he is his own person and not a *shadow* copy of his parents."

The Fae chuckled. "Truly, you are a delight. It has been some time since I've conversed with one as clever as you. It makes me remember the olden days."

It was a trap. He wanted me to ask what he spoke of. To reveal just how ignorant I was of Lunaria's past, and even knowing this, I desperately wanted to ask. Was he referring to the early days when the Fae had come to Lunaria? Or where they had been before? What in all the hells existed beyond the oceans surrounding our small continent?

"Perhaps I can have you over for tea sometime while you reminisce," I said breezily instead. "As you can see, my accommodations are not quite up to par for socializing at the moment."

"Indeed." He walked over to my cell and trailed his fingers across the bars. The shadows slipped through and around them easily. I was a little surprised that the iron in the bars seemed to have no impact on him. Maybe in their wraith forms, iron didn't bother them? I wondered if that meant that the enchanted silver weapons we used against the wraiths would be less effective on them if they fully reclaimed their Fae forms . . . I'd have to mention it to Vail so the rangers could be prepared. No matter how I felt about Carmilla and her plans, I didn't want our people to die fighting the wraiths or the Seelie Fae.

Serill turned to face me, his back to the bars and his hands clasped in front of him. "What if I told you we are not the villains you've painted us as? That we are merely trying to survive like you?"

"I'd ask if your survival required our death," I replied calmly. "Because from where I'm standing, the wraiths have been responsible for more Moroi deaths than all the other beasts of this land combined."

"Your concern is valid." He nodded. "But you must understand that our previous deal was with Queen Velika, and it was her idea to raid the outposts as we did. We needed those obsidian stones, and she wanted some population control. The food supplies of the Moroi are getting dangerously lower every year as your population swells."

Not a lie, but not entirely accurate either. We had to take riskier chances while growing crops, often planting in areas with no wards to protect the fields or the workers, but we were managing. Rangers protected the workers during the day, and they retreated to the outposts before the sun fell.

I didn't know if he was telling the truth about Velika. At the very least, she had known about their slaughter of the outposts while obtaining those stones and had done nothing about it. She was dead. It didn't really matter if it'd been her idea or not.

This felt like someone trying to cast the blame on another who couldn't defend themselves. I wanted to know why and what he'd come to offer me.

"That does sound like something Velika would do," I replied slowly like I wasn't entirely convinced but found it conceivable.

Serill pounced on my indecision. "There is so much we can share with you. Truly, we only want to survive in this land full of cruelty and lies. A false queen has risen to the Moroi throne. We would prefer you to sit on it."

My composure shattered for a moment, and I froze. I knew Carmilla had to be stopped, and while I hoped that would be imprisonment rather than death, I would do whatever I had to for our people. But never at the end of this had I seen myself sitting on a throne.

And absolutely not as the puppet queen of the Fae—because I had no doubt that would be all it was. I may not have known much about the Fae, but everything suggested they were not the type to share power.

"I will not allow our past to cloud my judgment of a potential alliance, but I trust you can understand my hesitancy here." I watched him closely, trying to glean any hint of how he was feeling from his movements and expressions, but the shadows made it so damn hard. "Putting aside the fraught history between our people, there is also the fact that I am the daughter of the Seelie King—and Erendriel is *not* the true king."

It was Serill's turn to go still for a moment; even the shadows rolling off his shoulders seemed to freeze. He recovered quickly and gave me a friendly but slightly condescending smile. "Young one, there is so much you don't know of our people. Of what the Fae have been since being exiled to these shores." His smile gained a shrewd edge. "Has the crown that rests on the false queen's head been whispering in your ear?"

"There are many things whispering in my ear these days," I answered vaguely.

"Such is the price of your lineage," he sympathized.

I didn't buy it. There was something about my bloodline that the Seelie Fae found useful—or feared. Perhaps it was the same reason Carmilla was suddenly interested in me marrying Demetri again. Once again, the urgency to get out of here hit me. I needed access to my mother's journals and to the secret room I'd found with Rynn beneath Lake Malov. One of those things had to have the answers I sought.

"What exactly are you proposing?" I fixed my features into a mixture of concern and wariness. "I would not have my people hurt, and not everyone in this House is responsible for my current predicament. If you mean to break me out by the same methods you used in the outposts, you will only make me your enemy."

"Queen Velika left many gaps in the wards here for us to come and go. I'm sure we can come up with a plan that would have minimal casualties while we retrieved you."

And delivered me straight into the hands of Erendriel.

"And what of Draven?"

"What of him?" Serill asked coldly. "His fate rotting in the dungeons below is better than what he would face outside of them. Forget about the *mikin.*"

Mikin. Traitor.

"I will need time to think on this." I waved a hand at my surroundings. "Something I have an abundance of, currently."

"Very well." Serill bowed his head. "I shall return in three days to discuss this further and offer options for getting you out." His form began to lose its sharpness before spreading into a more disembodied state.

"Serill."

The shadows snapped back into a Fae form, and he arched a brow at me in question.

"If I learn that Erendriel has ordered an attack on any outposts or any Moroi while I am thinking this over, any potential alliances will be dead."

"Of course, my young queen." Serill smiled. "Not a drop of blood shall be spilt . . . for now."

CHAPTER NINE

Kieran

"We're getting close," Desmond whispered quietly in that gravelly voice of his. I'd been a little surprised when both of Roth's brothers announced they'd be coming on this rescue mission. It was dangerous and a little insane. Plus, neither of them were close to Samara. Granted, we had explained the crown and our concern that it had fallen into the wrong hands, but still, part of me had expected them to lock Roth somewhere safe in their fortress and chuck the rest of us out.

When Roth's parents had announced that they'd also be going on this mission, I'd said as much. I *might* have phrased it in a poorly worded way that called into question their intentions. Actually, there was no might about it. While I didn't remember exactly what I'd said, Alaric and Roth had both winced at my choice of words, and if those two thought I'd been too blunt, then it must have been something really offensive.

The Devereux clan was an odd one though, and they'd just stared at me with a predatory focus. "You might claim Roth now, but they were ours first." Celestina, Roth's mother, smiled at me in a way that had all my instincts on alert. "Our youngest does not love easily. The fact that they have not only found it but that the person they love has chosen them with equal ferocity is something we will protect at all costs. You will not dissuade us from coming."

At the end of the day, despite my scheming and Alaric's near-constant research, it had been our antisocial and taciturn Roth who'd figured out a path forward to saving the woman we all loved. And hopefully Draven.

I was frustrated with myself over how quickly—and badly—I'd fallen apart. Samara and Draven were gone. Instead of keeping it together and doing everything I could to help them, I'd just . . . spiraled.

Sure, I'd done my best to gather gossip and call in favors, but at the end of the day, I'd had nothing to show for it. I'd promised Samara I'd always be there for her, but when it'd counted, I hadn't been. She'd never been bothered by the fact that I was just a courtier. Not when we'd been friends . . . nor when we'd become something more.

I heard the whispers though. People questioning her judgment or assuming I was just a passing fancy. When she was with me, it was easy to ignore them, but now all the doubts had crowded into my mind along with the frustration and terror that something really bad had happened to her.

And Draven. The prince I loved beyond reason. Who had used my lower status as a courtier to hurt and humiliate me. He'd done it to protect me from his mother's machinations, but that didn't make the wound any less raw. Nor did it help with all the insecurity I was feeling now.

I was so lost in my thoughts that I almost ran into Alaric when he suddenly stopped in front of me. Roth missed the message though.

"Oof!" They collided with me, causing me to bump into Alaric, who turned to glare at us both.

He peered around me. "Are you seriously reading a book right now, Roth?"

I turned, and sure enough, Roth had unwound the ropes on one of their forearms just enough to hold a small jar full of glowing stones. A little makeshift Fae lantern. How adorable. I filed it away to tease Roth about later. Ideally, when I wasn't trapped in an enclosed space with them.

"We don't know for sure how to open the door," they said defensively. "My brothers might be confident they can muscle their way through it, but I'd prefer to have an actual plan besides *smashy smashy*."

"It's a perfectly good plan, Rothie Bear," Desmond called from where he'd stopped at the front of the line. "And might, in fact, be necessary because there's supposed to be a door here according to the map . . . but there isn't."

"Let me see." Roth shoved past me and Alaric, grumbling something about being surrounded by idiots. They studied the wall, and we all did the same. The only sources of light were the few Fae lanterns we'd brought with us and Roth's jar of glowing stones, but our eyesight was more than good enough to see our surroundings, which consisted of compact dirt.

Ceiling, floor, walls . . . all dirt. It was a little unnerving because there weren't any support beams anywhere. Logic said that this tunnel should have caved in years ago—if not immediately—but we'd been walking underground for at least a mile, and there were no signs of any weakness anywhere.

It must have been made by the Seelie Fae and their earth magic. I was surprised that it had remained standing all this time though. Most of the Fae spells had burnt out and we'd had to replenish them with our own magic.

As spectacular as the construction of this tunnel was, our trip was pointless if we had no way of entering the Sovereign House from it.

"Are you sure we're in the area?" I squeezed past Alaric to

take the map from Taivan. "Or maybe it was marked incorrectly?"

I frowned at the fading lines and scribbles written in what I was guessing was Unseelie. If not for those hastily written words, I wouldn't even think this was the real thing. House Devereux had managed to successfully keep their treasure trove of Fae artifacts and writings hidden from the rest of the Moroi. While Roth might have been obsessed with Fae poetry, their family treasured something else—details about how all the Houses were constructed, including ways to break into and out of them.

I'd been impressed by it all, but Alaric had scowled so hard, I was surprised his face wasn't permanently stuck like that. He hadn't been pleased to learn that House Harker was included in their "information gathering" and that they knew all of our strengths and weaknesses.

It was thanks to their paranoia though that we had an undetected way into the Sovereign House, so he'd held his tongue. Mostly. Now we just needed to find the damn door.

Alaric reached for the map, but Roth was faster, snatching it from my hands.

"This is definitely the place," they murmured, casting their eyes from the map to the wall and back again. "Some type of illusion spell maybe?" Roth folded the map up and tucked it into the book before shoving both into a bag at their waist. "See if you can feel some type of release or glyph carved into the wall. Don't trust your eyes."

We each took a section of the wall and started searching. I ran my fingers across the cool earth, but nothing stood out. My frustration grew over the next few minutes, and I wasn't alone in that. It hadn't been easy to avoid all the patrols and find the entrance to this tunnel.

If it had all been for nothing—

I choked back the wounded sound that tried to escape, but

there was nothing I could do against the anguish rising in my gut, filling my thoughts and my soul with a hopeless despair I didn't know how to fight. Losing either Samara or Draven was unimaginable. Losing them both . . . I would never come back from that.

My search became more desperate. Nails shifted to claws as I tried to tear my way through the dirt. Blood scented the air, and then Alaric was cursing and pulling me away.

Just as I started to push past him and continue my frantic attempt at getting through, the wall trembled. Everyone froze. In an instant, all of Roth's family had their swords out. Taivan grabbed Roth and shoved his younger sibling behind their parents.

The wall exploded, the clumps of dirt hanging in the air for a few seconds before falling to the ground. I had my own sword free, as did Alaric, as we waited for the attack to come.

It never did.

"Forgive me, but this is a rescue mission, is it not? Shouldn't you all be moving a little quicker?" an amused voice asked. Dust still floated in the air, preventing me from seeing the person who spoke, but I recognized the voice.

In an instant, I was past the crumbled wall and in what appeared to be the dungeon—the map had been right after all, for the location at least. Whoever had said there'd been a door there had either been mistaken or had known some trick that we didn't.

None of that mattered though as my fingers closed around the bars that separated a cell from the rest of the room. Vibrant blue eyes threaded with red met mine.

"Hello, lover," Draven purred. "Out for a midnight stroll?"

"You know me," I replied, my voice catching. "A bit of a restless sleeper."

He chuckled and laid his hands over mine around the bars. "I promise to thoroughly tire you out after this."

"I don't need to hear this," Roth growled as they came to a stop beside me. "Iron bars," they mused.

"Can you feel it?" Draven asked, shooting Roth a curious look.

I wasn't sure what he meant by *feel it*, but when I glanced down at his hands over mine, I noticed he was being careful not to touch the bars.

"No." Roth's hazel eyes studied the cell, their brows coming together the longer they looked. "But I've seen this design before. Though the color is different from the metal composition the humans used." They frowned. "And anything the humans built had doors."

"Do we have you to thank for opening that wall?" Celestina jutted a thumb over her shoulder at the wreckage in the tunnel.

"Yes. I did my best to quiet the sound. Given that there aren't any guards flooding this room, I don't believe they heard anything." Draven eyed Celestina before looking around at all those gathered in the room, his gaze finally falling back on Roth, no doubt seeing the familial connection. He grinned when he noticed the new blood ropes around Roth's forearms. "Upgraded your ribbons, eh?"

He winked at them, and to my utter shock, Roth winked back. "The better to strangle you with."

"How'd you know we were there?" Celestina asked, her expression unreadable.

Some of the amusement drained from Draven's face, then he squeezed my fingers, being careful to avoid the bars. "I felt Kier's blood." His eyes didn't leave our fingers, and a tension rolled through him.

"No way you would be able to smell the blood through that wall." Desmond prodded some of the wreckage strewn about on the floor. "Too thick. Not even a Velesian would have been able to smell through it."

"Felt," Severen corrected his son. "He said *felt*, not smelled."

"I knew it!" Roth whispered loudly.

"Care to share with the rest of us?" Alaric said dryly. "Or was this just a gloating moment?"

Roth narrowed their eyes. "Don't be pissy because you've contributed nothing on this rescue. I'm sure Samara will still think you're pretty."

"What is going on?" I cut in, turning enough so I could glare at everyone in the room before looking at Draven again, who was avoiding my eyes. "How did you do that, Drav?"

Finally, he met my gaze, a half-hearted smile on his lips. "You know only you and Sam call me that, right?"

"Yeah," I told him softly. "I know."

Draven's eyes didn't leave mine as he gripped the bars with both hands for several seconds before pulling them away. His lightly tanned skin turned an angry red. It faded quickly, but I saw it.

I stared at his palms for a long moment. "Seelie Fae?" The question came out a little disconnected as my mind whirled. I didn't even know if that was possible because Draven was definitely Moroi . . . at least part Moroi anyway.

"Yes." Draven rubbed his hands against the sides of his pants like he wanted to wipe off the taint of the iron. "Half, courtesy of my asshole father." He opened his mouth to say more but then clamped it shut.

My sword suddenly felt very heavy in my hand. We'd told the Devereux clan the truth about the wraiths before coming here. That they were really the Seelie Fae. Roth hadn't wanted to hide that knowledge from their family, and we'd all agreed that they'd deserved to know the truth.

How would they react to knowing that some of the blood running through Draven's veins was the same as the shadow monsters' who had killed so many of their House? I wouldn't just let them hurt him, but I also knew I wouldn't win against them. And Alaric was foolish enough to stand by my side.

Had we come all this way to die?

"Well, your earth magic has already come in handy tonight," Severen said. "I'm sure it will again before this night is over."

Shock washed over me. "That's it?" I gaped at Roth's father and then at the rest of their family, who seemed to be rolling with this.

Celestina shrugged. "He's with Samara. Roth is with Samara. We're basically in-laws at this point."

"I'm kind of curious about how his earth magic can be used in a fight." Taivan gave Draven an appraising look. "If the wraiths manage to turn themselves back to their former Seelie Fae forms, then they'll have the same magic. Having someone to spar against will be really useful."

"Always thinking with your bloody sword," Roth grumbled.

"In more ways than one," Taivan agreed.

A tentative smile formed on Draven's lips. "I'll spar with you as much as you like if you get me and Samara out of here."

"Can you not use your magic to escape?" I studied the bars. They were a little thinner than my wrist, but when I tugged on them, there was zero give, and as Roth noted earlier, there was no door. How had they gotten him in there in the first place?

"No." Draven shook his head. "Interestingly, the bars don't block my magic—that's why I was able to tear that wall down when your blood leached into the dirt—but I cannot use my magic on the bars themselves, and there are more hidden in the walls of the cell."

"Must be because you're part Moroi too," Roth speculated. "Two forms of magic interfering with each other to create something new . . ." Their lips pursed together, and I could practically see their thoughts shifting. "Do you know where Samara is? Is she in a similar cell?"

"Three floors up," Draven confirmed. "It's only her presence here that keeps me from doing my best to tear down the entire building. I don't have enough control over my magic to ensure her protection."

"How do they open the cells?" I pushed, even as I looked around the room for a glyph or anything that would hint at how the magic worked.

"Blood." Draven sighed. "Certain blood is keyed to open the cells. I don't know everyone who has access, but Vail definitely does."

"Rumor is that Vail has been following Carmilla around like a loyal puppy," I said tightly. "Did he betray Samara?"

Draven cocked his head, causing his long, black-and-silver hair to shimmer in the dim lighting. "It's complicated."

"It's a yes or no question," Alaric growled, turquoise fractures forming in his seafoam green eyes.

"There is no black and white. There is no good and evil." Draven gave Alaric a patronizing close-lipped smile. "Don't be so boring."

Alaric looked like he was on the verge of leaving Draven here to rot.

"Samara can summon Vail," Draven added. His words only increased the tension in the room.

"Come again?" Severen frowned.

Draven opened his mouth—no doubt to say something lewd—but I cut him off. "How exactly can Samara do this?"

My princely lover gave me an annoyed look that clearly said *spoilsport.* "Just trust me on this. Samara can get Vail to come down here, and then we just have to convince him to let us out of these damn cells so we can all get the hells out of here."

"Three floors up, you said?" Celestina was already moving towards the door.

"Yes." Draven started to pace in his cell. "You shouldn't run into any guards—they're usually stationed at the very top entrance—but if you do, be quiet about how you deal with them."

"Not our first prison break, prince." Celestina jerked the door open. Her husband and sons followed after her as she walked into the hall.

I looked at Roth. "Your family is incredible, and I adore them."

"You're welcome to have them," they grumbled and started towards the door, but not before I caught the smirk on their face.

Alaric looked at me before narrowing his eyes coldly on Draven, and I was a little taken aback by his hostility. It felt personal, but I knew for a fact the two of them had rarely interacted before Draven had shown up at House Harker declaring he'd wanted to marry Samara.

Which . . . granted . . . could have been enough to piss off Alaric.

"Be right back," I promised Draven.

"Go get our girl." He cut a glance at Alaric before smirking at me. "If you have to sacrifice someone, I nominate him."

"Hilarious." Alaric started for the door. "It'll be such a shame if we have to leave you behind. Truly. I'll cry myself to sleep every night—after I make Samara scream my name for hours."

Draven chuckled. "Look at that. He *does* have a personality."

I smiled one last time at Draven before racing up the stairs to the third floor, where the others had already found Samara. Roth had slipped their slender arm through the bars to cup her face.

Dark purple eyes latched on to me. "Kier," she breathed out before taking in Alaric too. Then she frowned. "It was foolish of all of you to come and put yourselves at risk like this. You shouldn't have—oww!" she yelped and glared at Roth. "Did you seriously just pull my hair?"

"Don't say asinine things, and you won't get punished."

"It wasn't *asinine*," Samara muttered while rubbing a spot on her head.

"Draven said you could summon Vail," I said quickly. "We have a way out, but only if we get you both out of these cells."

"Quick would be good," Taivan added. "The prince said the guards are only stationed at the entrance, but I'm assuming they make regular rounds?"

"Yes," Samara answered, a crease forming between her brows as she concentrated. "Next one shouldn't be for almost an hour." She placed a hand over her chest, right over her heart. "I've never actually done this before, so I'm not sure if it will work."

I had no idea what *this* was, but I kept my mouth shut while Samara attempted to contact Vail. What had happened between them? I wasn't friends with Vail by any means, but I'd always respected him. His relationship with Samara was complicated, but recently, it'd seemed like it'd been getting better. Then she and Draven had been imprisoned—and he hadn't.

That reeked of betrayal, and yet Draven and Samara both seemed willing to call on him to help break them out of here. Clearly, we had a lot of catching up to do once we were somewhere safe.

Samara let out a sharp exhale.

"What?" I crowded closer to the bars. "Are you okay?"

"Pretty sure that asshole just gave me the middle finger through our connection." She frowned. "I wonder if there's a way I can slap him."

"Babe," Roth drawled. "Did you hit your head?"

Samara rolled her eyes. "Long story. Short version is that I have some type of empathic connection to Vail—and Draven. We can't hear each other's thoughts or anything, but we're . . . aware of the other."

I looked away from Samara and tried to ignore the spike of jealousy that hit. She'd been mine first. Why didn't *we* have a connection like that?

Warm fingers closed around mine where they were wrapped around the bars, and I raised my gaze to find Samara staring at me like I was the only person who existed.

"I hate that you're here, putting yourself in danger," she said softly. "But I'm so fucking happy to see you, Kier."

"Missed you, Sam." I rubbed my thumb across her fingers. "Sorry we didn't get here sooner."

"I never had any doubt that you'd come." Her bottom lip stuck out in a pout. "I was hoping to get myself out of here sooner. Kind of embarrassing that I needed to be rescued, honestly."

"It really is." I nodded, giving her a serious look.

Her pout turned into a wicked grin that had my heart skipping a beat. She opened her mouth to respond when we heard footsteps somewhere above us in the winding stairwell. There was nowhere for us to hide, so everyone except me moved to stand against the wall where the door was. I remained next to Samara so I could draw the attention of whoever entered, and Taivan nodded at me from where he stood closest to the door, his sword ready to skewer anyone who wasn't Vail.

A second later, the door swung open, but the Marshal of House Harker wisely did not charge blindly into the room. Instead, he waited in the hallway with a dagger in each hand. He didn't relax when he saw me; if anything, he looked more pissed off.

"You idiots chose the worst time to attempt a rescue." His

silver gaze slid to the right as if he could see through the wall. "Lower your fucking sword, Taivan, or I'll shove it up your ass."

The Devereux Heir snorted but lowered his sword, although he didn't sheath it. "Well, he's as cheerful as ever."

Vail stormed into the room then. "Carmilla recalled all the Sovereign House rangers, and most arrived this morning. There are five hundred rangers in the keep right now, and Lucian knows you're up to something."

CHAPTER TEN

—

Samara

"AND HOW DOES he know that exactly?" I narrowed my eyes at Vail.

"I didn't tell him," he growled as he stalked his way to my cell, not even acknowledging all the Devereux warriors eying him warily. Taivan and Desmond wore matching wolfish smiles that practically screamed trouble. One look from Roth, though, had those smiles dimming slightly, and they gave their younger sibling a chagrined look.

I had a lot to tell everyone once we were out of here, but I was dying to know what the deal was with Roth and their family and how exactly they had convinced not only their brothers but their freaking parents to come here.

But that would have to wait. We had more immediate problems, like the asshole slashing open the back of his hand and smearing the blood over his fingers.

"Then why does he suspect something?" I crossed my arms while Vail slammed his bloody fingers onto the center bar. Glyphs glowed red across a dozen of the bars before they vanished.

"You fucking yanked on our bond, and I damn near

collapsed." Vail didn't step back from the cell, which meant he was still blocking my exit as light silver bled through his dark grey eyes. "I was mid-sentence when it happened, and Lucian—obviously—thought it was strange. I might have cursed your name out loud. He put two and two together. I punched him in the face. Happy?"

My fist shot forward, and Vail stumbled back, blood pouring from his broken nose.

"Ecstatic." I bared my teeth at him before stepping out of my cell.

"Okay, I was skeptical before," Desmond rasped, "but I approve of your choice, little sib. She's a vicious thing."

"Do you really want to do this now?" Vail stepped towards me, but Alaric and Kieran blocked his way. He flashed his fangs at both of them before focusing on me once more. "How about you quit giving me shit so we can get out of here?"

I patted Kieran and Alaric on the shoulders, and they stepped aside to let me through. Alaric grumbled a little about it, but Kieran kissed me on the cheek. My sunshine and my grump. I'd missed them.

"I'm perfectly capable of doing two things at once." I dismissed Vail and started striding towards the door so we could free Draven when Vail grabbed my arm. Everyone tensed, and I heard Kieran and Alaric move, but they stopped at whatever they saw in his face.

Vail's lips curved into a tight smile before he leaned down to whisper in my ear, "Don't think I've forgotten how good you are at doing two things at once."

Heat rushed to my cheeks, and I felt my core tighten as I remembered what it felt like to have him and Draven both moving inside me. Draven's fingers gripping my thighs as I rode him hard while I swallowed Vail's cock, his fingers twisting in my hair, spurring me on.

The tension in the room increased as the scent of lust

permeated it. Fuck. I was at the tail end of the lust haze, but his damn words had it rising.

"I hate you." I shoved Vail away from me.

He released his grip on my arm and smiled. "It'd be easier if you did."

Was it possible to hate and love someone at the same time? Based on my complicated feelings towards Vail . . . the answer was yes. That didn't mean I trusted him though. Not when we were still standing in the aftermath of his betrayal, and not when the jagged pieces of my heart were still cutting through my soul.

Something flickered in Vail's silver eyes before they dropped to where my hand lingered on my chest. To where the bond between us was tight like a bowstring . . . feeling like the wrong move could make it snap.

"Come on." Kieran grabbed my hand and tugged me towards the door while Alaric appeared at my other side, and they guided me out of the room and down the stairs. Once Vail was out of my sight, it was like the world came crashing back in as I raced down the steps.

"Took you all long enough," Draven drawled as I burst through the door, the rest of the group right behind me. "Was starting to get worried the Marshal wouldn't come through."

"Drav." I crashed to a halt in front of his cell, and he raised his right hand, letting it hover an inch away from the bars. I did the same with my left, my palm tingling from the close proximity to the iron. "We're going to get you out of here."

"I don't think this is a good idea." Vail crossed his arms a few feet away. "We don't know for sure that we can trust him." I laughed and gave him an incredulous look, but he kept going. "Plus, his asshole father is likely going to come after him. The wraiths will be all over us."

"Who's his father?" Alaric peered at the prince as if he was searching for an answer in his features.

"Nobody," I answered at the same time Vail said, "The Seelie King."

We glared at each other.

"I take it back, Roth." Desmond's low voice rolled across the room. "Maybe you did choose poorly. I mean, she's hot and all, but this seems like a lot of dram—oow! Let go of my damn ear!"

I glanced over my shoulder to see Roth and Desmond swatting at each other like five year olds. The older Devereuxes, whom I'd met a few times over the years, just let out long sighs as they watched the squabble unfold.

Taivan rolled his eyes at his siblings before striding over to us. "What's the holdup? Spring the prince and let's go."

"Yeah, Vail." I crossed my arms and matched Vail's glower. "Open the fucking cell so we can get out of here. Unless you're just stalling so we can get caught. Will Carmilla give you a pat on the head then? Maybe a treat?"

His pissed-off gaze stayed locked on mine as he sliced open the back of his hand again, the cut from opening my cell already healed, and smeared some blood on his fingers before slapping them onto the iron bars. Out of the corner of my eye, I saw the same red glyphs glow before the bars disappeared.

In a heartbeat, Draven's lips were on Kieran's, who let out a surprised sound before kissing the prince back. That finally got me to look away from Vail to smile at them both.

"Roth, you're going to have to draw us a diagram or something later. Your relationship is complicated."

A rope shot through the air and wrapped around my waist, then I was yanked off my feet before being set down in front of Roth, who smirked at me. "The rest of them are still sorting themselves out. They're the complicated ones." Orange lines cracked through the haze like tiny lines of fire. "Me and her? We're golden."

Then their mouth crashed against mine.

I FROWNED at Alaric's back as we made our way through the tunnel. He'd pulled me away from Roth seconds after our kiss had begun—earning himself a lashing from their ropes. Then he'd almost gotten punched by Draven when he'd yanked him away from Kieran and shoved everyone towards the tunnel.

He was right of course. The middle of an escape was not the best time for make-out sessions, and I'd immediately wrestled my lust back under control, earning me a *"good girl"* from Roth that almost had me on my knees in front of them. The way their eyes had turned to pure fire told me they'd sensed just how turned on I'd been in that moment—and they'd be doing something about it later.

Apparently, this tunnel system was quite extensive, and there were some underground rooms towards the end that we could make use of to stay hidden a little longer. Draven had managed to put the wall back together after a few fumbled attempts. We couldn't be sure how it looked from the other side, so he'd carefully caved in parts of the tunnel behind us. Even if Carmilla and her rangers figured out how we'd escaped, they wouldn't be able to follow us this way.

In the past hour, as we'd walked towards our resting place for the night, Alaric had barely spoken to me. Nor had he touched me or even glanced in my direction. I didn't know what was going through that head of his, and it annoyed me.

"Got to hand it to Carmilla," Severen finally said. "I didn't see this coming."

I'd just finished recounting everything to them a few minutes ago. Kieran had to be physically restrained from going after Vail when he'd learned what he'd done. Alaric's jaw had tightened, but he hadn't said anything. While everyone was focused on keeping Kieran under control, Roth's ropes had wrapped around Vail and slammed him into the wall.

Repeatedly.

Kieran and Roth were now at the front of the group, followed by Roth's brothers. Draven and Alaric walked on either side of me with Vail—a little roughed up but mostly fine—behind us. Severen and Celestina brought up the rear.

It should've bothered me that Vail was at my back.

It didn't.

Which only made me pissed off at myself. Between that and my growing frustration with Alaric, I was in a bit of a foul mood.

"None of us saw this coming—obviously," I snapped. "She played us all for fools."

"Are she and Lucian really together?" Kieran asked from the front of the group. "He seemed so devoted to Velika."

"Seems they are." I thought about the little touches they'd given each other throughout dinners. "They're definitely sleeping together, and Carmilla trusts him enough to have him sitting in on most of her meetings. I'm not sure if they've always been a thing or if she seduced him away from Velika."

"Lucian is a treacherous bastard." Draven's hand brushed against mine, and I repeated the move back. "He might even be better than you, Kieran, at reading and manipulating people. I don't know for sure what his angle is with Carmilla, but I doubt it's love. The only person Lucian loves is himself. He'll serve her as long as he believes she's the strongest player in the game, but the second she slips, he'll stab her in the back. Likely for a price."

"Could we use him?" Alaric asked. "Offer him something to betray Carmilla?"

"Lucian dies," I half growled, causing Draven and most of the others to glance at me. My prince was the only one I focused on. "He hurt you. He fucking dies."

Draven's fingers wrapped around my hand before he raised

it so he could kiss my knuckles without ever breaking eye contact.

"Agreed," Kieran called out.

"I love it when you two get all murderous over me." Draven sighed.

Alaric let out an annoyed huff on my other side, which I ignored. I'd wait until we were alone to figure out what had made him even grouchier than normal.

"The Demetri bit is odd though," Kieran said. "Why is she so interested in the two of you getting back together? If she knew this was endgame, she could have just encouraged you to go back to him. We both know you would have done it if she'd asked, but instead, she let your divorce go through—supported it, even."

He was right. I had been loyal to Carmilla—up to a point; if she'd asked me to betray Rynn or Cali in some way, I wouldn't have done it. I hadn't been blindly loyal the way Vail had been, but if she'd asked me to sacrifice my happiness for the sake of the House? I would have done it in a heartbeat. I *had* done it when I'd agreed to marry Demetri.

"I don't know," I lied. "She must have her reasons though."

During my recap, I'd left out the part about my heritage. Draven and Vail knew I was part Fae, but they hadn't offered up that information, and I hadn't told anyone yet what the crown had told me. About who my father really was.

Everyone would have questions about it, and I had no answers—only more questions of my own.

I would tell the others about it. Just . . . later. When we were alone and had more time to discuss the implications. It wasn't that I didn't trust Roth's family; at this point, I trusted them more than my own House or any of the others. House Harker loyalties would likely be torn between me and Carmilla. The rest of the Houses . . . I only trusted them to do what was best for themselves.

But I wanted to tell my mates first.

My heart skipped a beat. Mates. The word had just flowed through my thoughts like water, but it felt right. The Fae hadn't used the term husband or wife—only mate. Growing up, I'd read so many poems of fated love. Of two Fae coming together despite all the odds against them.

I wondered if there were any Fae poems out there about multiple mates. My lips curled up in amusement. Maybe the crown would know.

The amusement died at that thought. *You cannot abandon me.*

For all its arrogance and sarcasm, there had been fear and loneliness in those words too.

I'm sorry, I pushed out even though I suspected I was too far away for it to hear me. *I will return for you. You are not forgotten.*

Even if I hadn't felt this odd responsibility towards the crown, we had to get it away from Carmilla. It was a weapon just waiting to be wielded against us. The crown might not have worked on me or anyone who had recently drank my blood, but it'd worked against Kieran's parents just fine. Not only were they powerful, but I suspected they regularly drank from the vein of the Corvinus family. They were close friends with the Heads of the House after all.

When Draven's mother had attempted to use the crown against House bloodlines, it hadn't worked well. At best, she'd been able to drive them insane until they'd become Strigoi, but she'd only had half the crown—Carmilla had united both halves. We didn't know what it was capable of now, and I didn't want to let her test its capabilities on the people I cared about.

There was also the fact that it could help us fill in the gaps of what we knew of Lunaria's history. Even with the crown's spotty memory, it might be able to tell us something new. Between that and the Harker journals I'd discover in the hidden cave, we might finally be able to piece together more of our history. Speaking of . . .

"Roth, where are the journals?" I didn't specify which ones because I knew they'd understand.

"Waiting for us at House Devereux," they tossed over their shoulder. "The ones you had anyway. The rest are where you left them."

In the secret room of the cavern by the sea. The Fae, it seemed, had been quite fond of secret rooms and passages. My brows pinched together as I cast glances around the tunnel. Come to think of it, all the secret rooms we'd discovered so far were underground, or at least covered by layers of rock like the cavern. Why had they been so obsessed with keeping things beneath the surface?

"Good." I let out a long breath, dismissing the eccentricities of the Fae for now. "Have you heard anything from Cali or Rynn?" My right thumb rubbed the spot on my finger where the ring Cali had crafted for me usually rested. I hated not knowing where they were, and I knew they likely weren't handling my sudden absence well.

Silence fell.

Kieran and Roth exchanged a look I couldn't decipher since I could only see their profiles. I glanced at Alaric and the muscle along his jaw flexed. "Reports indicate that Rynn is with the Alpha Pack in the north, but we haven't been able to confirm that with absolute certainty."

I nodded, having suspected as much. The last time I'd seen Rynn and the Alphas, they hadn't been getting along. In fact, Rynn had been adamant that she wouldn't be going with them despite the fact that she'd been promised to join their Pack for over a decade. She'd been delaying it for years, and I felt guilty that I hadn't read more into that. I'd been so preoccupied dealing with my failing marriage and trying to sort out my own life that I hadn't realized how desperate Rynn had been to avoid her fate.

Fuck, I was a shitty friend.

I'd make it up to her by busting her out of the Alpha Pack's stronghold—after we got the crown back and stopped Carmilla. For now, Rynn was in the safest place she could be.

"And Cali?" I asked quietly, dreading the answer.

"Nobody knows." Alaric sighed. "There have been no sightings of her anywhere."

He hesitated, and I could tell there was more.

"Spit it out, Alaric," I demanded, earning me a pissed-off look from him.

You can be pissy all you want, but you're going to fucking tell me. I held his gaze and raised my chin, and that muscle beneath his eye twitched.

"Two Furies stopped by House Harker before we left for Roth's House. They—"

"House Harker *is* Roth's House," I cut him off before giving Taivan a challenging look when he glanced over his shoulder at me. Severen and Celestina might be Roth's parents, but Taivan was their eldest sibling—and the House Devereux Heir. He was the one here who could lay claim to Roth. "*Mine*," I growled.

Eyes identical to Roth's sparked at the challenge, and he stopped. I and everyone else stopped with him.

"Taivan . . ." Roth warned and started towards me, only to be stopped by Desmond.

The Devereux Heir closed the distance between us. When Alaric and Draven moved to intercept, I slammed a hand against each of their chests and shoved them back. This was between me and Taivan. I didn't need them to fight this battle for me.

"Shouldn't you be a little more appreciative?" Taivan

raised a dark brow. "If not for us, your pretty ass would still be sitting in that cell."

"I would have gotten out eventually—you just moved up the timeline."

He gave me a patronizing smile. "Sure."

"You threw Roth away." I bared my teeth at him. "Finders keepers. You try to take them from me, and I'll carve out your fucking heart."

Several breaths passed between us, and the tension of those gathered shot up.

Then Taivan broke it when his smile widened and became something real. "Okay, I *definitely* approve of this." He patted me on the head before looking past me to his parents. "Looks like you finally get to plan that wedding, Pa!"

"Yes!" Desmond pumped a fist in the air. "That means we're off the hook for at least a decade."

Roth sighed, and I caught their eye. *What the fuck?* I mouthed. They just gave me a pitying look and turned to move down the tunnel in the direction we'd been headed.

We all started walking again, and Draven grumbled something under his breath when he had to step aside to make room next to me for Severen. A second later, Alaric did the same when Celestina took his spot.

"How do you feel about a summer wedding?" Severen asked.

Before I could answer, Celestina cut in. "You're good with a little pain, right? Our wedding vows are . . . intense."

"Don't worry," Severen said, again cutting me off from responding. "We have a little more time before we get to a safe place to rest. Plenty of time to hash out a plan to take care of this crown nonsense, kill your aunt, and coordinate a wedding."

"Maybe we should worry about the first two things before getting to the wedding bit," I suggested lightly.

Both of them slowed their pace.

"Are you trying to get out of marrying our youngest?" Celestina's voice was lethally quiet.

"No!" I cast helpless looks at both Draven and Alaric, who looked like they were trying to hold back their laughter.

"Excellent!" Severen slapped me on the back, causing me to stumble forward. "Which do you prefer, wildflowers or . . ."

CHAPTER ELEVEN

—

Samara

WE MADE it to our destination in just under an hour, and true to their word, Roth's parents had alternated between plans for how to retrieve the crown, murder Carmilla, and coordinate an epic wedding. Honestly, it was the wedding part that sounded the most complicated, as both the crown and Carmilla plan were basically "stabby stab."

Roth's family was insane. I now understood why they had fled to Drudonia.

I wasn't entirely on board with killing Carmilla. She absolutely had to be stopped—of that I agreed wholeheartedly—but my plan was to strip her of power and imprison her somewhere where she couldn't cause any harm. Nothing else was going to happen tonight though, so I decided to leave that argument for another time.

Because right now, I was tired. So damn tired. I just wanted to hopefully clean off and crawl into bed . . . with company of course. Suddenly, some of my weariness faded as lust slid into its place.

Yep. Still riding the tail end of the lust haze.

"We've found other places like this," Desmond explained as we all piled into a large, cavernous room. We were still underground—something I still found amazing—and the Fae had clearly planned on occasionally having to stay here because there were a dozen entryways off this main room. Several chairs and tables were organized around the room too, with shelves lining the walls. "All the rooms should have bathing chambers. This is our first time in this particular hideaway, but all the previous ones we found still had working water. No food though."

He pulled a few small containers from his pack and tossed them onto the table, and not a hint of dust rose. Despite not having been used in probably centuries and surrounded by dirt, the place was spotless.

Would I be able to do things like this once I understood my earth magic better? We didn't even understand how the Fae had done half the things they had. The glyphs to heat the water made sense because they were literally just a combination of the glyphs for fire and water. But how had they even gotten the water to run into the bathing chambers in the first place? And the bathing chambers' setup, much like the Fae lanterns, still worked all these centuries later, even though the Fae hadn't been here to maintain them.

Occasionally, we had to use our blood to activate glyphs or replace the gems and stones that stored magic, but the actual infrastructure was still working flawlessly.

"There's a room beneath House Harker that is similar to this." I looked around curiously. "How many of these places have you found?"

"We'll tell you"—Desmond grinned at me—"as a wedding present."

"Even take you on a tour of them," Taivan offered.

I rolled my eyes.

"Ignore them." Roth cut their brothers a scathing look

before grabbing my hand and pulling me into one of the rooms.

"Get some rest!" Celestina ordered. "We're going to find the exit from this tunnel system and do some scouting above."

I was still shaking my head at the ridiculousness of Roth's family when I came to a sudden halt just inside the room.

"Wow. Not what I was expecting . . ."

The room beneath House Harker had beds, but they were all single beds with one stacked on top of the other. Clearly, the point had been to jam as many Fae as possible into the space, but this room had only one bed—one huge bed—and a settee with several chairs arranged around it to the side.

Interesting. This was clearly a safe place to retreat, but they hadn't expected to house the masses here. I assumed the other rooms were laid out similarly. Which Fae got to stay here and which were sent to the cramped rooms beneath the Houses?

Kieran and Draven sauntered in, each giving the bed an appreciative smile before disappearing through a door on one side of the room. Probably the washroom Desmond had alluded to. A second later came the sound of running water, confirming my suspicions.

Gods, rinsing all the dirt and grime off would feel amazing right now. Even better if I had Kieran and Draven to help me with that. Heat started to build between my thighs, and Roth's gaze snapped towards me, the bright orange of their eyes flaring.

I took a step towards them until I realized not everyone had followed us into the room.

Alaric and Vail hovered in the doorway.

Dark grey eyes met mine, and for once, Vail held nothing back. Longing. Guilt. Confusion.

That'd always been Vail's story, not knowing how to handle his emotions, and somehow, I was always the one who bore the brunt of it.

I was fucking done.

Moving towards the door, I held out a hand to Alaric. Unlike Vail, his expression was unreadable. Something was bothering him, and I was going to get it out of him because Alaric's days of avoiding talking about things were over. He was mine.

And I'd fucking remind him of that.

A faint smirk played across his lips as if he'd just read my thoughts before he slipped his hand into mine. I tugged him into the room before giving Vail a flat stare . . . and then slammed the door in his face.

Roth let out a deep chuckle. "Good girl."

"What do you need?" Alaric asked in a light, casual tone.

I narrowed my eyes at him. That was all he had to say? Not *I missed you*. Or *I'm so glad you're okay*. Or even better, *I can't wait to be balls-deep inside you*.

Fine. The best way to deal with Alaric when he was in this emotionally distant state was to jar him out of it by being incredibly lewd and demanding—something I just so happened to excel at.

"What I need"—I moved towards him, rolling my hips, and a brief flicker of turquoise flashed across his eyes—"is to get cleaned off and then have all of you compete to see whose name I can scream the loudest." A smirk stretched across my lips. "Lately, I've got to say, Draven's been winning. Just a couple of days ago, he had me pinned against the wall with his cock stretching my puss—"

Alaric's mouth crashed against mine. Everything he'd been holding back came pouring out at once. Desperation. Terror. Rage.

Beneath it all was a demanding, possessive love that refused to bend.

There you are. I kissed him back with equal ferocity.

He broke our kiss and stared into my eyes like he was

convincing himself I was really here with him. "I missed you so fucking much."

"Same," I breathed out.

I felt a tremble run through him before his lips were on mine again. His hands slid under my shirt, going straight for my breasts. I moaned as he pinched both of my nipples, my own hands dropping to undo his pants as the lust I'd been fighting for the past few hours rose like a tidal wave.

Something rough moved around my waist, and I frowned against Alaric's lips. He pulled back, and we both looked down at the bloodred ropes wrapped around us.

"Wha—" I squealed as I was yanked away from Alaric, who let out his own bark of alarm.

"Shower first," Roth declared, marching towards the washroom and tugging us with them. Alaric and I stumbled forward towards the steam-filled room.

"Take your foreplay to the bed," Roth ordered. "We'll join you in a few."

I peered around Roth's lithe form and groaned as I took in the delicious sight before me. Draven was kneeling on the ground, Kieran's rock-hard cock pressed against his lips. Something told me Kieran's flush wasn't just from the hot water rushing down on them.

"You heard them." Draven licked a broad stroke up the underside of Kieran's rigid length, causing him to moan, before sucking him all the way into his mouth and then releasing him. "Time to change the scenery." He winked up at Kieran before rising to his feet.

"Are you sure we can't just stand here and watch a little more?" I asked breathily, my gaze locked on the two gorgeous Moroi males who were giving themselves one more rinse beneath the steaming water.

"Oh?" Kieran gave me a cheeky grin. "Didn't know you were a voyeur, Sam. Thought that was Alaric's kink."

"I didn't intentionally walk in on you both," Alaric said dryly.

"Of course not." I gave him a patronizing pat on the cheek that had him narrowing his eyes. I'd probably pay for it later . . . but I was very much looking forward to my punishment.

Draven and Kieran stepped out from underneath the water. I belatedly noted that they'd already rinsed their clothes and had them hanging off hooks on the wall.

Both of them sauntered past me, rippling muscles on display, and kissed me on the cheek.

"See you soon, love," Draven purred in my ear.

Kieran chuckled as they left the room, and I took a step after them without even realizing it. Only Roth's rope around my waist stopped me from following them into the bedroom.

"Dry yourselves off before getting into bed!" Roth commanded.

The only response was a groan that made me think one of them had just taken the other in his mouth. A pressing heat built between my thighs, and I pulled against Roth's rope— only to be yanked beneath the warm spray of water.

I sputtered as water doused my face, but the rope held me in place.

"Alaric," Roth said idly, "I do believe our girl needs some assistance getting out of her clothes—and with a few other things. Help her out, would you?"

The rope around my waist fell away as Alaric joined me under the hot water. Unlike Kieran, he wasn't sporting any scruff, and he'd clearly shaven his head recently. Alaric was always in control—even when he was losing his mind.

I traced my fingers along his sharp jawline, and he leaned into my touch and closed his eyes, savoring the moment. Roth cleared their throat, and Alaric's eyes flew open. We both grinned and started helping each other get our clothes off, holding them under the hot spray before tossing them onto the floor to hang up later.

Much later.

Once we were both naked, I turned to Roth and gave them a questioning look. I didn't exactly know how this was going to work. Alaric had already shared me with Kieran, and Draven and Kier were clearly a thing; those two had already hinted about being very excited about having me between them—something I was fully on board with. I suspected Alaric and Draven would just ignore each other. There was an animosity between them, at least on Alaric's side, that I didn't understand.

But to the best of my knowledge, Roth didn't like men. I didn't want them to be in a situation they were uncomfortable with . . .

Roth gave me a wry smile as they stepped beneath the spray and quickly stripped off their clothes.

"You're overthinking things, babe." They brushed my hair behind my ear as I leaned back against Alaric. "I have no interest in their cocks touching me, but I can't wait to see the way they make you scream." A devilish glint flared in their eyes. "Especially when I'm sitting on your face."

"Fuck," Alaric and I both swore at the same time.

Roth's grin widened, and they glanced at Alaric. "I think we should stall a bit—give Kier a little bit of alone time with his prince."

A deep groan came from the other room, proving Roth's point, and I chuckled. While I was very much looking forward to having them both at the same time, I was also happy they were enjoying each other now.

"It does sound like they need a little more time," Alaric agreed, his hands trailing up to cup my breasts as he kissed my neck. Something thick and hard pressed into my lower back, and I groaned as he ran a thumb over my pebbled nipple.

I started to reach back, suddenly desperate to feel his cock in my hand, when Roth dropped to their knees and shoved their face between my thighs.

"Oh, fuck!" I screamed, my head slamming back into Alaric's shoulder. If it weren't for him holding on to me, I probably would have slipped. He just chuckled against my neck and kicked my legs wider apart to give Roth better access as he alternated between squeezing my breasts and playing with my nipples.

Roth had two modes, I'd learned, when it came to eating me out. They'd either torment me for what felt like hours, edging around my pleasure until they drew an orgasm out of me that shut down my fucking mind. Or they'd devour me like they were starving and I was the feast they'd been promised.

Thank fuck Roth chose the latter this time.

A mewling sound bubbled up my throat as their tongue dove straight into my pussy. Then I felt them drag two fingers across the dripping mess they were creating and use the lubrication to roughly play with my clit. My hips bucked forward as Roth savagely licked and sucked me while their fingers practically demanded I climax for them right then and there.

"Be a good girl and come for us, Heir," Alaric crooned.

Oh. Fuck. Me.

Roth's fingers dug into my plump ass as I detonated, their nimble fingers playing my clit to perfection while they lapped up every bit of my desire.

I practically went limp in Alaric's arms, relying on him to hold me up while I rode out my orgasm. The water shut off a minute later, and Roth disappeared, only to return with a couple of towels. I reached for one, but they slapped my hand away and passed it to Alaric. Between the two of them, I was dried off quickly and my hair was wrung out.

My thoughts were still scattered, my lust haze riding me hard. Roth and Alaric grabbed a hand each and tugged me into the bedroom, where Kieran and Draven waited for us in bed. Kieran was on his back across the middle, his hands twisting the covers as Draven deepthroated him.

A whimper escaped my lips, and Draven paused, gripping Kieran's cock with one hand as he drew his mouth off to look at me. "Like what you see, love?"

All I could do was nod, my eyes glued to where Draven lazily stuck his tongue out and licked the slit, where a bead of precum formed. Kieran groaned, and I took a step towards the bed.

"Are you wet for us, Sam?" Kieran asked, and I finally drew my eyes away from Draven working his cock to find Kieran staring at me with a wicked glint in his eyes. I gave him another nod, and he grinned. "I think I should find out."

Alaric and Roth shoved me forward, and I took a few steps before looking back towards the two of them. "Are you coming?"

They both smiled wide.

"In a bit." Roth smirked. "We want to watch this first."

Lust flared, and my legs wobbled a bit at the thought of them watching me with Draven and Kieran. Alaric let out another dark chuckle. "I think our Heir likes that."

I really, really did. I didn't know when the two of them had become buddies, but I was here for it.

"*Sam.*" Kieran's voice, tinged with lust and amusement, drew my attention back to him. "Be a sweetheart and sit on my fucking face."

"Okay," I breathed out in a dazed tone. Between the lust haze, Alaric and Roth getting me off in the shower, and the show Kieran and Draven were putting on . . . it was difficult to string coherent thoughts together.

Draven chose that moment to wrap his lips around Kieran's cock and take him all the way down with zero hesitation. I stood there, mesmerized by Draven swallowing him whole and the way Kieran arched off the bed, making a sound that was pure sin.

Then a desperate ache building between my thighs had me scurrying to the bed and practically jumping onto it. Draven's head bobbed up and down as I threw a leg over Kieran's chest, straddling him. Through hooded eyes, he looked up at me, biting his lip, as if he was trying to hold back a scream.

"You ready to get *me* off while he gets *you* off, Kier?" I gave him a cocky smile. *Look at me using complete sentences.*

The gold that had been weaving its way through his brown eyes expanded as Kieran gripped my waist and hoisted me onto his face. I offered another silent thanks to the Fae who had decided these beds deserved a headboard as my fingers gripped the dark wood. My knees landed on either side of Kieran's head, and he shifted his grip to my ass.

Like Roth, Kieran didn't waste any time. His lips latched onto my clit and sucked hard.

Wood splintered beneath my grip as I climaxed instantly.

"Gods, the lust haze is a wonderful thing," someone—I was pretty sure it was Roth—said with a laugh.

"How many do you think we can get out of her before she passes out?" Alaric asked.

"At least six more," Draven answered in a deep, raspy voice before the sound of him slurping down Kieran's cock filled the room. My thighs clamped around Kieran's head, which only spurred him to start eating me out more.

I trembled as Kieran's grip remained firm, not giving me an opportunity to pull back as he continued to devour me. He alternated between diving his tongue deep inside my pussy to licking and sucking on my clit while I shamelessly rode his face, chasing another climax.

My only goal at the moment was to batter my brain with enough orgasms so I could pass out afterwards. I was pretty sure that was the only way I'd be able to sleep, and I desperately needed some rest.

So really, I was being responsible and taking care of myself.

"Fuck, Kier," I moaned as he dug his fingers harder into my flesh. Between that and the almost frantic way he was eating me out, I knew he was close to coming.

Then Kieran jerked underneath me and moaned directly into my cunt as he came. I joined him a second later when his tongue did something miraculous that I was pretty sure he could have only repeated by climaxing. We'd have to try this again.

For research.

My thighs were still trembling when Draven grabbed me and lifted me off Kieran's face. My sweet lover just gave me a lazy grin, his face glistening with the aftermath of making me come.

"Let's see how messy we can make this perfect pussy." Draven chuckled darkly as he settled me over Kieran's hips before pushing down on my back. My chest pressed against Kieran's, and his mouth crashed against mine just as Draven slowly slid his thick cock into me.

"Fuck, that's hot," Roth swore. Their voice was deep and husky, and I knew they were playing with themself. I wondered if Alaric was stroking his hard length, but just when I started to break my kiss with Kieran to look, Draven slapped my ass and slid his cock all the way in, filling me up.

I jolted up a little, a low groan slipping from me. Kieran groaned with me before licking my nipple and then closing his lips around it and sucking hard. I gasped, and he laughed against my flesh.

These two were going to be the death of me. And I was one hundred percent fine with that.

Draven slapped my ass again, hard enough to sting, then

groaned as my pussy tightened around his cock. "You like that, don't you?" He chuckled.

I was rapidly learning that I liked everything they did to me. Still, what I wanted most right now was for Draven to make good on his words. I glanced over my shoulder and almost came at the sight of him glistening with sweat, his long dark hair hanging around him and both hands gripping my ass hard enough to leave bruises.

"Show me how messy you can make me, prince. I want to feel you dripping down my legs." I turned to look at Alaric, who did indeed have his hand wrapped around his thick length as he watched me with a burning desire. "And then I want Alaric to fill me up too."

"You heard her, Draven." Alaric stroked himself harder.

"Make our girl scream," Roth added from where they were slumped on a chair that gave them a perfect side view of me getting fucked. The towel was across their lap, but I could see their hand moving beneath it.

As much as I wanted all of them to be touching me, I was discovering that I really liked to be watched. Especially with how much Alaric and Roth were clearly enjoying it.

Personally, I was really proud of myself for this self-reflection moment.

Draven apparently didn't need any more encouragement because his hands slid from my ass to grip my hips, and then he pounded roughly into me. Kieran gave me a devilish smile as his hands clamped down right above Draven's and he moved farther down the bed into the perfect position to lick and suck my tits.

All I could do was twist my fingers into the blanket and moan as Draven roughly fucked me. One of Kieran's hands drifted from my hip to play with my clit at the same moment he sank his fangs into the side of my breast.

The climax tore through me, and I screamed, but that

didn't slow either of them down. My own pleasure was dripping down my thighs, and the room was filled with the sounds of flesh on flesh and other obscene noises. Pain flashed in my hips as Draven's claws tore through flesh and his thrusts became more frantic.

"Gods, you are perfect," he grunted.

Then I felt him fill me with his seed, enough that some of it started leaking out. Gradually, Draven's thrusts became languid and slow. I suspected he was watching his dick sink into my wet and messy cunt and liking the view, but before I could turn around and look, Kieran pulled me down for a kiss. His tongue plundered my mouth, and I let out a lazy moan as his fingers rubbed my clit, which was still oversensitive from my last orgasm.

"Our turn," Roth announced.

My thoughts were so scrambled that it took me a moment to catch up when Draven pulled my back to his chest, his cock still buried inside me as Kieran slid out from underneath us. Then, in one smooth movement, Draven pulled out, and I found myself on my back, peering up at Alaric.

He grinned as he grabbed my legs and put them over his shoulders, lining up his cock with my entrance. There was something around his neck . . . I blinked. A dark red rope.

Roth's rope.

Alaric sank into me slowly, not the least bit bothered by Draven's cum.

"Oh fuck." I pushed my head back into the mattress, and suddenly Roth was stretched out in the bed next to me. One of their hands wrapped around my throat and squeezed gently before trailing down to play with my breasts.

"Alaric needs to blow off some steam, so he's going to unwind that tight hold he keeps over his bloodlust." Roth pinched one of my nipples and somehow timed it perfectly with Alaric pushing another inch into me. I gasped as my back arched off the bed, only to be yanked back down, courtesy of another one of Roth's ropes that had wrapped around my neck. A second later, two more ropes secured my wrists and tugged my arms above my head. "But he has control issues." Roth smiled broadly as I pulled on the ropes binding my wrists and found zero give. "I *excel* at control."

I whimpered. Alaric was holding my thighs against his chest with my knees over his shoulders. Between his unflinching hold and Roth's ropes, I could only move as much as either of them allowed.

Apparently, Roth liked playing with both of us because the thin, braided rope around Alaric's neck moved like a snake and tightened a little more. Turquoise lines bled into Alaric's eyes as he let more of his bloodlust rise.

I didn't actually believe Alaric lacked control of his bloodlust, but he thought so. We'd talked about it before, and I knew that letting his bloodlust rise for more than a few seconds frightened him. Seeing his cousin turn Strigoi when he'd been younger had left psychological damage that my grumpy lover refused to deal with. Instead, Alaric kept a stranglehold over his bloodlust, which meant it was always trying to break free. It was his denial of who and what he was that likely made it feel so chaotic.

But that was a truth I was more than willing to spend years getting him to see, and clearly Roth was on board with helping in the meantime.

"Still with us, babe?" Roth's hand traveled between my breasts at a frustratingly slow pace towards where I wanted their talented fingers. My clit was practically throbbing with need. Maybe it was greedy to want another orgasm after Draven and Kieran had made me come so many times, but I fucking deserved it.

Knowing Roth would only prolong my torment, I looked up at Alaric with wide eyes and slightly parted lips. The bastard laughed and moved his cock in the wrong fucking direction until his broad head was just barely inside me.

"Well, that's just mean," Kieran mused. "Excellent technique though."

I turned my head to glare at him. "Eat a dick, Kier."

"Oh, I plan to later." He winked at me, and Draven snickered. The two of them were cuddled up together on a small settee against the wall, holding hands as they enjoyed the show.

"You know what I'm in the mood for?" Roth asked slyly, drawing my attention back to them.

"If it's not giving me an orgasm while Alaric fucks me until my brain melts, I don't want to hear it," I deadpanned.

Alaric groaned, and more turquoise flared in his eyes, but he didn't slide his cock so much as an inch farther inside me.

"Poetry." Roth's fingers dipped straight into my dripping cunt, sliding past Alaric's cock and drawing out some slickness, which they smeared over my clit as they roughly played with it.

I let out a strangled scream and tried to pivot my hips up, only for Alaric to clamp down harder on my thighs and prevent the movement.

"Make me a fan of poetry, Sam," Alaric ordered, "and I'll give you what you want."

Roth's fingers pulled away from my clit, and they gave me a pointed look.

"*Pib' bomla fi ker,*" I started, only to scream when Alaric slammed all the way in with no warning. My pussy stretched around him as he pulled all the way out and paused with his cock notched at my entrance.

"You stop"—Roth's fingers lifted away from my trembling clit—"we stop."

"I hate you both," I breathed out.

The fuckers laughed.

"*Qu ib ofgi gef nalmo.*" Poetry spilt out of me. I was pretty sure I was mixing up some poems, but whatever. My pronunciation was perfect, so Roth could fucking bite me.

Only, it wasn't Roth who bit me—it was Alaric.

Sharp, delicious pain raced through me as Alaric's fangs pierced the inside of my thigh and Roth's rope tightened around my throat, cutting off my air as their fingers pinched my clit. Quite possibly the most intense orgasm of my life rolled through me, and every thought emptied from my mind.

Roth teased my clit as they loosened the rope before I could black out. I tried to shift away from them because it was too much. I just needed a second to recover, but neither of them were having it.

Alaric kept a death grip on my legs as he continued drinking from my thigh, all the while continuing to fuck my pussy hard and fast.

"Don't stop now, Sam." Roth's eyes were ablaze as they locked on mine before thrusting their fingers inside me in perfect time with Alaric's thrusts. Their thumb was playing with my clit and applying just the right amount of pressure.

"*B'ib qu ib mìr!*"

Alaric's fangs popped out of my thigh only for him to bite the other, drawing another groan out of me. My muscles trembled in anticipation as another climax started to build.

"*Goda sotlem qu fi mobof gef fi lìr,*" I panted as I writhed beneath the two of them. "*Kub qu ib*—fuck!" The scream tore from me as Roth bit my neck.

I came again, and this time, Alaric came with me, his hips slamming forward as he let out a deep groan, releasing my thigh so he could watch me fall apart with bright blue eyes that had only the faintest speck of green. I felt the gush of heat as he filled my already soaked pussy and it started seeping out.

"Messy," I mumbled with a delirious smile. "I go sleep now."

I didn't even wait for Alaric to pull out or for Roth to release their ropes before I passed the fuck out.

CHAPTER TWELVE

—

Roth

I was not a cuddler.

Which was why Samara was tucked between Draven and Alaric with Kieran resting his head on the prince's bare chest. Samara, the lazy shit, had slept through us carrying her to the washroom to clean her up. We'd all agreed to let her sleep a while since we didn't know when we'd have this opportunity again, but she'd woken up soon after we'd all climbed into bed, that sleepy, blissful smile still on her face.

I was sprawled across the bottom of the bed. These rooms had clearly been designed for the high-ranking Fae because this bed was enormous. It was even bigger than Samara's at House Harker. I was already plotting how we could come back here and steal it, because we'd definitely need a bigger bed so we all had room to sleep.

Maybe I could set up a chaise or something too? I'd liked sleeping in the same room as Samara before she'd been taken. Now I didn't think I'd be able to sleep without knowing she was there.

But I still didn't want to fucking cuddle.

I had to admit that this was nice though. All of us together —except Vail. But since he was my least favorite of the group, I didn't really care. The asshole had betrayed her. One word from me, and I knew my brothers would make him disappear. I wasn't sure if Samara would like that or not. She acted like she hated him, and every word they exchanged was caustic . . . but I saw the way Vail looked at her when he thought no one was watching.

And I saw the way Samara looked at him a second after he turned away.

It was the same look—full of hurt and longing.

I had no idea what the fuck to do about that. I'd have to ask Kieran or Draven about it later; Alaric was almost as useless as me when it came to navigating emotional clusterfucks.

But that could wait. My family wasn't back yet, so we could enjoy this peace and quiet a little longer before the world came crashing back in. Maybe I could nap . . .

"What is our priority going to be once we reach House Devereux?"

Of course, Alaric ruined the mellow vibe.

Everyone groaned, and I grinned. I decided Alaric did have his uses after all. He was worse than me at reading the room. It was nice not being the only socially awkward one.

I propped myself up, bending my elbow so I could rest my head on my hand and better see everyone. Alaric stared up at the ceiling, his mouth pressed into a hard line. "We have a lot of problems and no workable plans for any of them."

I mourned the nap that could have been.

"What? Killing everyone who opposes us isn't a workable plan?" Draven drawled. "Are your sword skills so lacking?"

"My sword skills are just fine," Alaric ground out.

Draven gave Samara a pitying look. "It's good that you

have me and Kieran. We're quite good with our swords—definitely better than *just fine.*"

"Stop antagonizing him," Samara chided Draven, her expression serious until her gaze collided with Kieran's, then her resolve crumpled in an instant. She made a sound that was somewhere between a snort and a laugh.

A hand flew to her face to cover it up, and we all stared at her. She did it again.

The irritated look on Alaric's face was quickly forgotten when he looked away from Draven to gaze down on Samara. A small, close-lipped smile graced his lips. Wow. I hadn't even known he was capable of smiling.

"It's not funny," she grumbled, even as her lips quirked up.

"False." The corners of Alaric's eyes crinkled slightly. "It's adorably funny."

I chuckled, as did Kieran and Draven.

"Mad at all of you." Samara sighed before scooting back on the bed until her back rested against the headboard. Then she crossed her legs underneath herself. "Alright, let's hash everything out." She chewed her bottom lip, a slight crease forming between her brows.

I knew that look. That was the *I have a lot of emotionally heavy shit to drop on everyone* look.

Oh, nap, how I miss you.

"Samara." Kieran raised his head off Draven's chest and sat up, mirroring her cross-legged pose. Draven took one look at Samara, released a long-suffering sigh, and maneuvered until he was sitting beside Kieran.

Clearly, they both recognized that expression too.

"What?" Alaric blinked at everyone, confusion etching his features.

"Wow." I stared at Alaric in wonder. "Someone more clueless than me at reading people."

Kieran started laughing so hard, tears streamed down his

cheeks. Alaric glared at him, then got distracted when Samara bent over and planted an upside-down kiss on his lips. My eyes flicked to Draven, and I found him admiring Kieran, like that laugh was the best thing he'd ever heard.

I knew Alaric still bore a grudge against the prince because of everything that had transpired between him and Kieran. Specifically how Draven humiliated Kieran at an event and then publicly ended their tryst. Alaric and Kieran had been best friends for a long time, and Alaric apparently wasn't as willing to forgive and forget what Draven had done.

I wasn't sure how he didn't see how much Draven loved Kieran though. It was nauseating, really. Kieran and Samara were the prince's *entire* world. If Alaric didn't figure that out soon, maybe I'd have to clue him in.

I chuckled under my breath. Who would have thought that *I* would ever be in a position to give someone emotional insight?

Gradually, Kieran got his laughter under control, and everyone seemed to settle down—although that crease between her dark brows was back on Samara's face. As if she sensed me studying her, those entrancing purple eyes fell on me, and she gave me a small smile. "How about you break things down for us, Roth? Then I'll add in my . . . information."

I was really curious about what Samara had learned, but she clearly needed to build up to telling us, so I did as she asked.

"We should group the problems together as much as we can to minimize how many plans we need." I held up one finger. "The crown and Carmilla are one. Getting the crown away from Carmilla will help neutralize her as a threat and make her easier to capture."

Everyone nodded in agreement as Samara bit her lip. This had to be tough on her. She was an incredibly rational person . . . but Carmilla was her family. I knew she would do what she had to, but I hoped we'd be able to simply imprison Carmilla and keep her from causing more trouble for Samara's sake.

I continued, a second finger joining the first. "Two. Tangentially related, but we need to determine how unstabilized the Moroi Houses have become. Right now, everyone is waiting for the dust to settle after Queen Velika's death and Carmilla rising to take her place. Nobody knows exactly what happened, and Carmilla is using that to her advantage, but when she is"—I glanced at Samara—"taken out of the running, there is going to be a power vacuum."

"House Tepes and House Devereux won't try to fill the void," Alaric said. "The Devereux are isolationists; they'll try to make it on their own." I made a noise of agreement. My birth House did not give a single shit about ruling the other Houses. "And Tepes already prefers to deal with the Velesians over the Moroi. This will only cause them to further separate themselves from the other Houses."

"House Salvatore is a bit of a wild card," Kieran added thoughtfully, "but my parents and House Corvinus will absolutely try to seize this opportunity to gain more power."

Samara went absolutely still, and her eyes widened in panic.

"Sam?" Kieran focused on her. "Why did you just tense up? Did something happen with my parents?"

Oh shit. Was that what she'd been keeping from us? No . . . She looked almost blindsided by the mention of Kieran's parents, like she'd forgotten something.

"They're still alive," Samara said quickly.

"More's the pity," Draven drawled, earning a smirk from Kieran, who then kissed his chest. Ugh. They were so grossly affectionate.

"I'm sorry, I should have told you sooner, Kier," Samara apologized. "But with the rescue and seeing you all again, it just slipped my mind and—"

"Sam," Kieran cut her off gently. "It's fine. I'm glad we were able to so thoroughly distract you." He winked at her, and she huffed a laugh, some of the worry fading from her face.

Okay. So sometimes his obnoxious, cutesy mannerisms had their uses. I'd put up with anything if it made Samara happy.

"They arrived at the Sovereign House a couple of days ago," Samara explained.

"Of course they did." Kieran sighed. "Let me guess, they were playing the roles of slightly bewildered but oh so supportive courtiers?"

"Yep," she said with a pop.

"Carmilla saw through their bullshit, used the crown on them, and sent them back to House Corvinus to act as spies?"

"Yep," Samara repeated.

"Something eventually is going to have to be done about House Corvinus," Alaric rubbed his forehead. "All the Houses are devious, but *their* plotting is on another level. They don't give a shit about all Moroi surviving, only their House."

"I know." Samara chewed on her bottom lip. "But that's a future problem. We have to stop Carmilla from brainwashing all the Houses one by one and then starting a potential war with the Velesians."

"That brings us to problem three." I wiggled three fingers in the air. "Moroi and Velesian relations have been growing more strained for years. Only House Tepes and House Harker had decent trade policies in place with them . . ."

"And now, thanks to Vail, House Harker can kiss its good relations goodbye." Samara chewed on her lip, debating if she should say something, then decided to just get it all out there. "And you should all know that I won't leave Rynn with the Alpha Pack if she doesn't want to be there."

"Another prison break." Kieran grinned. "Fun."

"Not fun." Alaric glared at him.

"Definitely fun," Draven agreed, earning himself a glare too.

While the three of them argued, I focused on Samara. She was trying to smile at their antics but kept failing. I knew why. The fourth problem.

Slowly, I held up my pinky finger to join the other three. I didn't say it because I wasn't sure if Samara was willing to broach this topic yet, and if she wanted me to drop it, I would. For now.

But my brave girl held my gaze and didn't shy away.

"Four," she said quietly. "Cali."

Everyone fell silent at the declaration. That Cali was indeed a problem. She was Samara's best friend, and we all knew that there was nothing Sam and Rynn wouldn't do for her, but we also knew the damage Cali could do if she truly lost herself. If that happened, then all our problem-solving wouldn't matter.

Because nothing in Lunaria would survive Cali's wrath.

She hadn't completely lost it yet, but something was definitely going on with her. I'd originally met Cali, Rynn, and Samara at Drudonia. The three of them were close and had tried to befriend me. Rynn had been the most successful since we were similar in nature. Samara had been determined to flirt with me—and had mostly fallen flat on her face because she'd been relying too much on her looks and not flaunting that magnificent mind of hers.

Cali had reminded me of my brothers. She was arrogant and brash. Most of our interactions had ended with one of us storming out of the room before violence could erupt.

Most Furies dedicated their lives to keeping their emotions level. They didn't allow themselves to feel anything. Anger. Happiness. Love. Hate. Of all the Moon Blessed, the Furies were the most volatile. Something about the original spell hadn't worked quite as well for them as it had for the Velesians and Moroi. The last couple of generations had stabilized by walling off all their emotions and largely isolating themselves from the rest of Lunaria.

Except Cali.

Few Furies had ever attended Drudonia—and never for years like Cali did—and Cali felt *everything*.

It had alarmed the shit out of me when I'd first met her, but I'd gradually gotten used to it. Even when her eyes had glowed with rage, Cali had still been in control of herself—of her magic.

But I'd witnessed a couple of interactions with Samara since I'd moved to House Harker. Something was different about Cali now. There was a chaotic edge to her rage that hadn't been there during our time at Drudonia, and I'd caught the way Samara looked at her friend now. It wasn't with exasperation or amusement like it had been years ago. Now, Samara looked at her friend with concern and fear.

Not *of* Cali—*for* her.

"The Furies that came looking for her wouldn't give us any specifics," Alaric said.

"One of them was worried." Kieran frowned. "Furies are so hard to read, but there was just something about him that made me think he was personally concerned about Cali."

"Big guy with dark, golden blond hair shaved on the sides?" Samara asked.

"Yeah." Kieran nodded. "You know him?"

Suddenly, Draven and Alaric were very interested in her answer. I rolled my eyes, not the least bit concerned with Samara's past lovers. She was mine now. Ours. That was all that mattered.

"Malachi." Samara pursed her lips. "He and Cali were involved a few years ago. The elders demanded that they break it off; they felt the two were growing too close. Cali refused . . . but Malachi did as he was ordered."

"Idiot," Kieran muttered.

Alaric gave his friend a stern look. "It may seem harsh, but the methods the elders have put in place are working. Only a handful of Furies have fallen in the last century."

"We can save the debate on the approach the Furie elders have dictated for another day." Samara rubbed her face. "I need to find Cali and see for myself how she's doing . . . and talk to her about Rynn—convince her that slaughtering the Alpha Pack to break Rynn out of their stronghold isn't a good idea."

I winced. I hadn't even thought about that. Here was hoping that wasn't where Cali had disappeared to. The only thing worse than the Velesians going to war against the Moroi was them doing it against the Furies. We'd be caught in the middle with no good option on who to support.

"Once we reach House Devereux, I'll ask Thessalia and Taivan to send rangers to search for her—discreetly," I offered. "Desmond is an excellent tracker; he'll probably choose to lead one of the groups."

"Thank you." Samara gave me a grateful smile.

"Of course." I hesitated slightly before asking, "And what information did you want to share with us? We might as well get everything out there."

Please don't be something really bad, I prayed to the gods, who I was pretty sure were long dead. We already had enough to deal with.

"The crown . . . is sentient." Samara let out a long breath while we all stared at her, wide-eyed. "It spoke to me."

"The crown," I said slowly. "It spoke to you? Like with actual words?"

"That's usually how speaking works," she said dryly.

I scowled at her. "Nothing I've ever read has implied that Fae artifacts could speak."

Samara smirked at me. I refused to acknowledge how

adorable she was and frowned harder, which only had her devilish eyes sparking with amusement. I was so going to punish her later.

"Did it ever converse with *you?*" Kieran glanced at Draven, who just shook his head.

"Yeah . . . about that." Samara's gaze fell on Draven. "I think the crown only speaks to the Seelie royal bloodline. Turns out your asshole father is a fake. He's not the true Seelie King—my paternal grandfather was."

"Your grandfather?" Alaric asked at the same time Kieran yelled, "*I'm fucking a princess?!*"

"*We're* fucking a princess," I corrected him and held up a hand, shushing him before he could ramble on. "Samara, please elaborate."

"Unfortunately, I don't have a whole lot more to share," she admitted. "Turns out, the crown is kind of sensitive, and I hurt its feelings. It refused to talk to me after that, and I never got a chance to make up for my rudeness."

"How exactly does one offend a crown?" Draven gave Samara a lopsided grin. "You're such an overachiever."

Samara gave him an obscene gesture that had his grin widening enough to show off his fangs.

"So you're half Fae—or at least close to it." I ignored their antics and studied Samara's face, trying to see how I'd missed that before. Then again, we really didn't know much about what the Fae looked like other than that they had tapered ears—something that neither Samara nor Draven had.

"Your father had to have known what he was . . ." Alaric trailed off before pointing at Draven. "Do you have magic like him?"

"I have a name, you know," Draven drawled.

"Nobody cares," Alaric replied in a bored tone.

"Pretty sure at least two people in this room do." Draven winked at me. "And I'm definitely growing on *Rothie Bear.*"

I narrowed my eyes at the prince. "I will carve you apart and have Alaric help me dispose of the remains if you ever call me that again."

"This bonding session is going fabulously, I've got to say." Kieran laughed.

A small grin tugged at the corners of Samara's mouth as her eyes scanned each of us. "So . . . none of you care that I'm at least part Fae?"

"I mean, obviously we all find you hideous now," I told her seriously before jerking my head towards Kieran. "Except him." My gaze slid pointedly to Draven before flicking back to Kieran. "He's clearly into the whole Fae thing."

"Maybe we can use him to suss out any other Fae amongst us," Alaric suggested.

"With his dick?" I tapped a nail against my bottom lip. "Kind of curious if it would work. Would we, like, lead him around on a leash like one of those hounds from the Fae murals?"

Draven and Samara glared at the both of us, but Kieran just chuckled.

"No, babe." I smirked at Samara. "We don't give a fuck about the Fae blood running through your veins. Any other surprises for us?"

"I spoke to a wraith while I was imprisoned." She sighed and leaned her head back against the headboard. "Apparently, with Velika dead, Erendriel is seeking a new alliance and would prefer me over my aunt."

"Which wraith?" Draven asked sharply. The charming prince was gone, and only a predator remained. One who sensed another encroaching on his territory.

"Serill," Samara supplied.

"Shit," Draven swore, concern bleeding into his stare as he looked at Samara. "He's basically my father's right hand. I suspected he would be the one leading the hunt after me . . . I don't like that he's so interested in you."

"What exactly did he say?" I asked, already thinking through the implications of facing a fight on two sides—Carmilla and Erendriel.

We listened as Samara recapped the short conversation, and Draven paled when Samara finished with Serill promising to return in three days . . . which, at this point, meant two more nights.

"How easily will he be able to track her?" I asked Draven.

"Unless we're behind a very strong ward in two days"—he rubbed his forehead—"we should expect a visit from Serill."

"Okay," I said slowly. "So we have two days to figure out how to either hide from the wraiths . . . or what to tell Serill to buy us more time when he comes calling."

"Erendriel isn't the patient sort," Draven warned. "And Serill hasn't risen to where he is by disappointing the Seelie King."

"Fake Seelie King," I pointed out.

Draven shrugged. "He's the one currently sitting on the throne, so he's the Seelie King now."

"Do we think there's a throne?" Kieran perked up. "And do we think we can steal it?"

"Dethrone the diabolical queen, rescue the lonely sentient crown, find out what the fuck is going on with my besties, and figure out how to outmaneuver beings known for being clever." Light sparked in Samara's deep purple eyes. "Sounds fun."

"The real question is, what will we do *next* week?" Kieran moved until he was lying down and tugged Samara to lie beside him. Draven followed suit, settling in next to Kieran and wrapping his body around him, one hand resting on Samara's collarbone.

"Fix the broken alliances between the Houses and

somehow make nice with the Velesians." Alaric rolled his eyes and then moved to Samara's other side.

"That sounds less fun." Kieran pouted.

Samara looked at me, clearly wondering what I was going to do. Oh fuck it. I crawled forward and shoved Alaric over. He rolled his eyes but let me settle between him and Samara as I rested my head on her chest and listened to her heartbeat.

"If any of you ever mention to my brothers that I willingly cuddled, I will skin you alive."

"Awww," Kieran cooed. "We love you too, Roth."

I grumbled more threats even as I tucked my face into Samara's body so none of them could see my smile.

"Where are you going?" I asked quietly as I propped myself up a little, being careful not to disturb Samara, who was still sleeping next to me.

Kieran paused halfway through getting up, his hand in Draven's, who was already standing next to the bed in a damp pair of pants and nothing else. We'd all done our best to rinse our clothes off earlier, but for all the niceties the Fae had given this place, it was still a damp, underground cave system. Our clothes would take forever to dry.

"We're going to search this place and see if we can find some clean clothes and maybe some weapons," Kieran whispered before standing.

"Good idea," I replied quietly. "We should be ready to go when my family gets back."

The two of them nodded and left. It was then I realized Alaric was already gone. Likely scouring the rooms for any information left behind by the Fae.

Usually, I would be all over the potential of finding new Fae books or scrolls.

Surprisingly . . . I didn't have any inclination to join him.

I looked at Samara's dark hair fanned around the bed and the warmth of her hand on my hip.

There was nowhere else I wanted to be right now.

Samara's brows furrowed slightly before smoothing out, and I narrowed my eyes at her.

"How long have you been awake?"

"Since Alaric elbowed me in the back when he got up." Dark eyelashes fluttered before dark purple eyes gazed at me full of humor. "The ass was just bitter about being on the outside of the bed. He should have been thankful I didn't shove him off it."

"We're going to have to get a bigger bed wherever we end up." I sighed. I'd have to get used to cuddling too.

It hadn't actually been that bad. It had been kind of nice to be cocooned in warmth.

"Yeah," she replied softly. That crease formed between her brows again and stayed there.

"What are you thinking about in that magnificent mind of yours?" I laid my head back down on the pillow so that our faces were only inches apart.

"Assuming we defeat Carmilla and find some way to do all the other things on our list . . . then what?" There was none of that brash bravado in her expression now. "House Laurent is a problem, obviously. Demetri's a piece of shit, and his mother would love nothing more than to see the demise of all Vele-sians. Corvinus has never been trustworthy. Your family's House is amazing, but they don't exactly play nicely with others. And while we're generally on good terms with House Tepes and Salvatore, I have no idea how they're going to react to all this. And then there is the Sovereign House . . ."

"What about it?" I frown. "You'll take it over. My House will back it up, and it's likely Tepes will too. The others will fall in line."

"I never planned on being queen, Roth," Samara argued. "My *plan* was to be Heir for at least another few decades until Carmilla stepped down and I rose—as the Head of House Harker, not the bloody queen of the Moroi!"

"You have to admit that The Blood Queen does have a nice ring to it though," I mused.

"Not. Helping." Samara huffed and rolled over until she stared up at the ceiling.

I pushed myself up so I was leaning on my arm and looking down at her. "Are you worried about this because you don't want to be queen . . . or because you do and you're concerned that you'll become as corrupt as the previous two?"

Her eyes darted to mine, and I knew I'd guessed right. I'd never be as astute as Kieran at reading people, but I did know how Samara's mind worked. She held herself to an almost impossible standard and was her own worst critic in many ways.

"First, I don't think for a second that you becoming an evil queen is even a possibility."

"You literally called me The Blood Queen a moment ago! That doesn't sound like a nice title, Roth!"

I snorted. "We're Moroi. There's nothing nice about us, and blood is intrinsic to who we are."

She pursed her lips, and I resisted the urge to lean down and kiss her because I didn't want to get distracted—and I absolutely would if my lips touched any part of her.

"But if you need further assurances," I told her softly, "you have us. Do you think Kieran would ever let you strip away the free will of others after growing up in that horribly manipulative House?"

She didn't even hesitate. "Of course not."

"Do you think Draven would let you lock up crying children in a dungeon after he holds himself responsible for the deaths of so many in the outposts?"

"None of that is his fault!" she snarled, her eyes flashing black. "That was fucking Erendriel's doing."

"It was," I agreed. "But there's the truth—and then there is the guilt he carries. He would never sit by while you harmed innocents."

"I know," she said softly.

"And Alaric cares deeply for the outposts because that is where his family is from," I reminded her, even though I knew I didn't have to.

"His parents are at an outpost now." She bunched her brows together again. "We should warn them in case Carmilla—"

"Already done." I reached up and brushed my thumb across her brow, smoothing out the wrinkles. "Alaric sent them a message before we left House Harker. He kept things vague, but they headed to one of the more remote outposts. They're as safe as they can be."

"Oh." She exhaled and closed her eyes as my thumb traced a path across her brow and then down her jawline. "And what about you?"

"What about me?" I tucked some of her dark locks behind her ear.

Those stunning eyes of hers slowly opened. "Will you keep me from becoming a tyrant?"

"Babe, I don't even let you be a tyrant in the bedroom. What makes you think I'll let you be one on the throne?"

A husky laugh tumbled from her lips, and I smiled. I loved hearing her laugh—especially when I was the one who caused it.

I didn't mention Vail, and neither did she. That just seemed like a way to derail this conversation. Besides, Draven seemed to have some vested interest in helping Vail succeed. I had no idea why, but I was more than willing to let him take the lead on that.

"The crown wants me to claim it," Samara said after her laughter died off.

"Do you want to?" I asked curiously. A sentient Fae artifact definitely fascinated me from an academic standpoint, even if the magic it was capable of horrified me.

She thought about it for a long moment, and I didn't push her, just continued playing with strands of her hair. It was so silky. I didn't think I'd ever grow tired of touching it.

"I do want to," she finally answered. "But not for its power —that, I find abhorrent. It's because I feel in my soul"—she placed a hand on her chest—"that it does belong with me. And it's so lonely."

It was my turn to laugh. "Of course you'd befriend an inanimate object."

"Honestly, it has a good sense of humor." She frowned. "We should come up with a name for it. Feels strange just referring to it as an 'it,' but I don't think it has any concept of gender. Maybe I'll just go with *they* for now and ask the crown if they have a preference . . ."

"We'll figure out something with the crown," I assured her. "Maybe there's a way to change its magic. Or we could just keep it—them—somewhere safe where you could regularly visit them."

She sighed and stared back up at the ceiling. "Another thing to add to the list."

"Hey." I tilted her face towards me, and those concerned eyes met mine. "I swear to you that I will help you figure this out. You are not alone in this." I swallowed. "I love you, Samara Harker."

Her eyes got a little misty. "I love you too, Astaroth Devereux."

I smiled at hearing my full name on her lips—the one I'd been running away from my whole life. I'd been running from the mantle of being part of the Devereux line but never really fitting in anywhere.

I was the lost scholar who'd finally found a home in her.

Samara scooted closer, laying her head on my shoulder and her hand over my heart, where heat suddenly flared—and a bond thrummed to life.

"You're mine, Roth," Samara breathed. "Always and forever."

"And you're mine too, my Blood Queen. Always and forever."

CHAPTER THIRTEEN

—

Samara

"We can't wait any longer." Taivan sighed. "Vail will have to find us."

"Are we sure he hasn't gone back to Carmilla?" Desmond looked to me for an answer.

I didn't have one, because while I didn't think he would have, I clearly couldn't trust myself when it came to Vail. I'd learned that lesson the hard way. There was another way I could tell though, one that made no sense but was real all the same. I concentrated on the thread between us, and it felt thinner now, strained.

Was that because of the physical distance? Or because of . . . everything else between us?

"South," I breathed out. "He's to the south of us."

Taivan mulled it over. "The Sovereign House is north, and most of their search parties haven't reached this far yet. If Vail is south of us, then it's unlikely he's met up with Carmilla or any of her rangers."

"What if he runs into them while making his way back to us?" Absently, I rubbed the spot on my chest where I felt the bond. As soon as I realized what I was doing, I dropped my hand. "Vail's a strong fighter, but he'd be outnumbered."

Not to mention the fact that Carmilla would likely make an example out of him if he were captured. He was a traitorous asshole, but if he was truly on our side, Vail would be useful. Just because I was still hurting over his betrayal didn't mean I'd waste such a valuable resource.

So pragmatic. I could practically hear Carmilla in my mind, and I shoved the thought away.

"Let's go then. We'll stick with the original plan and trust Vail to catch up." I nodded at Taivan. "We're following you."

"This way." He entered the tunnel outside the cavern we'd been resting in and went left. "My parents are waiting topside for us. We'll meet up with the Harker rangers—Adrienne, Emil, and Nyx—in a couple of miles. The storm is going to hit any minute, and we'll travel as far as we can. There are a few safe houses we can use, depending on where we end up."

The tunnel split into two directions, but Taivan sliced his finger open on his fang and tapped a glyph on the wall. The compact dirt shimmered, revealing a door, which Taivan pulled open and stepped through.

I started to move towards it when Kieran placed a hand on my forearm, halting me. Gold wove through his brown eyes, a little of his bloodlust peeking through. Everyone except Alaric was riding their bloodlust to some extent because we needed any advantage we could get.

Traveling on a night like this was insane. All kinds of wicked things prowled the Lunarian wilds after the sun set, and we were far from the top of the food chain, but we'd discussed it when Taivan and Desmond had returned and agreed it would be worth it. The storm would cover our tracks better than we could ever manage. With Carmilla and her rangers likely coming for us, I wanted to delay our reunion until I knew of some way to counteract the crown's magic.

"You good, Sam?" Kieran's lips quirked up into a lopsided grin as he tightened the cloak hanging around my neck. He and Draven had burst into the room after I'd formed the bond with Roth and Draven had felt the echoes of the new bond through his.

They'd both been happy for us, but I hadn't missed the uncertainty in Kieran's eyes. I'd tried to explain that I hadn't intentionally done it—not that I wasn't absolutely thrilled to be bonded with Roth—but I still didn't understand why this was happening. I didn't want Kieran to think I wasn't choosing him.

Kieran had seen right through my hasty explanations and assured me he was fine, but then he'd smiled at me in a way that I knew was false. Draven had frowned at him when he'd done it because he clearly recognized that fake smile too.

Unfortunately, that was when Roth's brothers had arrived, so I hadn't been able to discuss it with Kieran anymore.

We'd barely had time to get dressed in the clothing Kieran and Draven had found and adorn ourselves with weapons, which was why I was wearing a shirt that was a little baggy and pants that were way too tight.

On the plus side, two wicked daggers were now strapped to my thighs, and I'd been able to quickly recreate the blood magic I'd had on my previous ones, so now I could recall these to my hands after I threw them.

I reached up to double-check Kieran's cloak. "Absolutely. Who doesn't love a little midnight stroll?"

"The woods are great this time of year," Draven added, kneeling down to make sure the sheaths for my daggers were buckled to his satisfaction.

"Can't beat the weather either," Alaric said dryly as the crash of rainfall sounded from where Taivan had clearly opened another door.

"Definitely nothing else I'd rather be doing right now,"

Roth grumbled from beneath *three* cloaks. Apparently, their older brothers were very concerned about the cold. At one point, they'd been eying my cloak, clearly thinking about snagging it to give to their younger sibling, but Roth had snarled in their faces and they'd stomped away.

I might have offered *Rothie Bear* my cloak after that, and they might have threatened something along the lines of *you'll get the edging of your lifetime when this is over*.

Kieran booped me on the nose before darting up after Taivan and Desmond. Roth and Alaric both sighed before following, leaving me alone with Draven, who was still fiddling with the buckles on my thigh.

I chewed on my bottom lip. Vail was a good tracker, but the storm might make it more difficult for him to figure out where we'd gone. I could sense where he was through the bond we shared, but I wasn't sure if he could do it too. Draven and I had done some testing with our bond; he could sense where I was just as I could him, and he was also able to tug on it to summon me.

But Draven and I were both part Fae. What if that impacted whatever this connection was and Vail couldn't do the same? Not to mention the fact that the bond between us was stretched so thin . . .

My eyes dropped down to Draven. No. I couldn't ask that of him, and it was stupid to even think it. Vail had made his decision, and he wasn't my—

"Yes." Draven rose, his dark blue eyes twinkling with amusement. "I'll go find your Marshal."

"He's not my anything." I frowned and quickly scanned Draven. Like me, he'd loaded up on weapons. No whip, but he had two swords strapped to his back and half a dozen daggers hidden on his person. His black-and-silver hair was braided back, disappearing beneath his long black cloak. "And I didn't ask you a question."

"You thought it." He kissed my forehead. "It's okay to worry about him. Love's complicated."

"I'm only worried because Vail could be useful, and if he gets himself caught, we'll lose a valuable asset," I hissed.

Draven just gave me an infuriatingly patient look. "Of course."

I thought about stabbing him, but the way he was grinning at me now suggested he'd like it.

Stupid, hot prince.

KIERAN WAS . . . not pleased about Draven splitting off to retrieve Vail. I didn't blame him; I would have preferred for us all to stay together too. The fact that it was my fault Vail had gone off on his own only added to my guilt. I mean, I had every right to be angry with him, but he had helped us escape. It didn't mean I'd be inviting him back into my bed anytime soon. Still . . . I could have let him down easier instead of slamming the door in his face.

It'd been satisfying but not entirely mature of me.

Draven had promised that he was used to traveling in the woods at night and that he could use his magic to find Vail.

I'd asked if he could feel Vail through the bond, but he'd said no, that he could only sense me. He was confident he'd be able to track Vail down quickly though, and then he could use his connection to me to find wherever we currently were.

I looked around the dark forest, which felt extra ominous tonight. I hoped Draven found him and dragged his ass back soon. It could just be my general anxiety about being in the wilds at night, but I couldn't shake the feeling of dread that had been building since we'd left the tunnels.

We'd been traveling for almost an hour, and it was slow going. Severen and Celestina were in the front, Roth's brothers were guarding our backs, and Adrienne, Emil, and Nyx had met up with us not long ago and were guarding our flanks—Emil to our left, and the other two to my right. It felt good to see the rangers again and to have more backup in case some beastie tried to make a meal out of us.

Several times, one of the rangers or Roth's kin sensed something and held up a hand for us all to stop. The first time, we'd quietly climbed up into the trees as an enormous horned bear lumbered past us.

Even on all fours, it would have towered over us. The two horns that sprung from the top of its head before jutting forward brushed the leaves. It was the first time I'd ever seen one in person, as the bears preferred the mountains in the far north of Lunaria. The Velesians were used to dealing with them, since their realm bordered the mountain range, but the bears had only recently started coming into the Moroi realm.

Fortunately, they were usually easy to avoid and weren't as vicious as many of the other predators. As long as you didn't mess with them.

The second time, Emil had barely been able to give us enough warning as three kùsu had barreled through the trees. Luckily, they had been in hot pursuit of some swamp deer they'd managed to flush out of the brush. My heart had pounded rapidly as Kieran, Alaric, and I held ourselves flat against the trunk of a large tree while the twenty-foot-long insect-like beasts had scuttled past. The sounds of hundreds of legs moving across the forest floor while rain pounded around us would likely give me nightmares for weeks.

If Draven were here, he would have been able to use his earth magic to feel their approach far in advance. I'd tried to use my magic a few times, but I hadn't been able to consistently sense anything, and most of the time, it was a feeling that there was *something* there but nothing more. It still felt odd to even acknowledge that I had magic, considering I couldn't feel it most of the time.

So far, the only time I'd been able to use my earth magic was when I'd been desperate or angry—usually both. I'd just have to hope that I'd be able to rally it if we were in a near-death situation. No pressure.

In the meantime, I was using my senses like the others were doing to detect danger, which was difficult because of the storm doing its best to drown everything out. It was why we'd had so many close calls; we'd only detected the monsters seconds before they would have found us.

A blinding flash struck a tree fifty feet away from us, and the smell of burning wood filled the air while thunder roared across the sky. Summer thunderstorms were common, but this seemed more violent than normal. Or maybe it was because I normally enjoyed watching the storms from the safety of my room in a stone fortress and not traipsing through mud and undergrowth while dodging all the monsters that prowled the night.

Currently, the rain had slowed to a drizzle. Not that long ago, it had been a torrential downpour. We were damn lucky we weren't in an area prone to flash floods.

"Shit," I heard Severen say. His wife let out a torrent of swear words seconds later.

I closed the distance between us to stand next to them as I took in what had caused their reactions.

Oh. Apparently our luck had run out, because a river raged through the forest ahead of us. Given that Severen and Celestina had led us this way, I assumed it wasn't supposed to be here but was a creation of the storm. Maybe a watershed or a small creek that had been overrun by the rain.

"We could swim across it?" I suggested just as several large trees tore through the water, smashing into everything in their path. "Or maybe not."

"We'll have to double back," Celestina called out as the storm decided to kick it up a notch. "The ground gets higher to the east. We should be able to cross there."

I nodded and started to back up but froze when I felt it. The wrongness I'd been feeling all night intensified, like the forest itself was screaming at me to . . .

Run.

Without second-guessing, I lunged forward, darting to a tree with a thick trunk for cover and pulling Alaric and Kieran with me. Then I looked over my shoulder just in time to see Roth duck behind a large, rotting tree log, Taivan and Desmond ushering them to safety. Whether they were following my lead or had also sensed something, I didn't know.

When I peeked around the tree, I saw Severen and Celestina had vanished as well—only a few trembling tree branches gave a hint as to where they had gone. The Harker rangers were also nowhere to be seen.

Three howlers slithered through the trees and stopped to sniff the ground. Horror drenched me, and I had to bite down my tongue to keep from swearing out loud or screaming.

As if sensing my fear, one of howlers swung its head my way, and I quickly pivoted back behind the tree, a tremble racing through me.

It had no eyes because the howler was fucking dead. All it had were empty sockets surrounded by clumps of fur and rotting flesh.

I'd seen a lot of fucked-up shit in Lunaria, but something coming back from the dead? That was a new one.

Alaric and Kieran both looked around the tree only to pull back with shock-laced grimaces. Clearly, they weren't fans of this new type of monster either.

"Samaraaa," a voice rang out. Even through the rain, I recognized it. Demetri.

Everyone went still. Gold flooded Kieran's eyes as his

bloodlust rose while Alaric's eyes flashed turquoise but quickly returned to their normal light green as he pulled a long, curved dagger from the sheath at his thigh. Kieran's sword was in his hand a second later.

A smile curved at the corners of my lips, and I saw it reflected on Kieran's and Alaric's faces. Sure, we were deep in a Lunarian forest with three undead beasts hunting us down, but Demetri was here too. I didn't know how, but I assumed he was responsible for our walking-corpse friends. He also likely had some Moroi rangers with him.

None of that mattered though because Demetri was standing less than twenty feet from me. He wouldn't be walking out of this forest alive. I didn't care how many fucked-up nightmares I'd have to kill my way through—Demetri's death was mine to claim. My fingers closed around my daggers and silently pulled them free from the thigh sheaths. It was fitting that his blood would be the first to bless my new blades.

First, we needed to know exactly how many others he'd brought with him. I gave Kieran and Alaric a pointed look and mouthed, *Stay.* Both of them gave me murderous looks in return but didn't try to stop me when I stepped out from behind the tree.

Demetri loved the sound of his own voice. Might as well let him dig his own grave too.

I sauntered forward, twirling my daggers casually in my hands a few times before stopping a few feet from where Demetri stood behind the undead howlers that were just standing there, unmoving. Each one bore a leather collar with embedded sapphires. I'd missed that before on account of being shocked by their existence.

What type of magic could bring something back from the dead? And how had Demetri learned of it?

"Like my new pets?" he drawled from beneath his dark cloak. Most of his face was hidden, but his full mouth was curved into a smirk. "Turns out Velika had quite the treasure trove of Fae artifacts. We have no idea what most of them do, but these ones seemed pretty self-explanatory. The howlers make excellent tracking hounds, even if they smell a bit."

"I give you credit for attempting to find a creature more vile than yourself." I studied the beasts once more. Howlers were canine in shape, but they were taller and leaner than lycanthropes. They were built to run for miles on end. These ones were skeletally thin. In fact—I squinted—yep, I could see their bones in places.

A small amount of pity welled in me as I took in the creatures. Sure, howlers would rip me to shreds in a heartbeat if they could, but they were just predators trying to survive in a land of monsters, and they were pretty low on the hierarchy. It felt wrong for them to be used like this. Life in Lunaria was often cruel and heartless; they deserved to find peace.

My gaze lingered on the collars again. They were faint and hard to see in the dark, but two glyphs were carved into them between the sapphires.

Death. Awaken.

I held back my shudder and turned my attention back to Demetri. "They won't win any beauty contests, but if I had to choose between them and you, it's not even a question. Undead hounds all day. You remain the most vile of the Heirs."

Demetri's smirk blossomed into a smile. "Oh, I'm not an Heir anymore, my pet. You're looking at the new Head of House Laurent."

A dozen rangers stepped out of the dark forest, swords gleaming in the moonlight, to stand in a formation behind Demetri. All of them bore the Laurent crest on their tunics.

This time, I wasn't quite able to hide my disgust, so I just leaned into it and sneered at Demetri. "Killing your own mother might be a new low, even for you, Demetri."

Because there was no way Marvina Laurent had willingly handed over power to her son. That woman had ruled her House with an iron fist. It was all she'd cared about.

Demetri let out a cold laugh. "Come now, Samara. Are you really so upset about it? If you think she treated you badly to your face while we were married, I promise that what she said about you when you weren't in the room was far worse."

Not surprising. In many ways, Marvina represented everything that was wrong with the Moroi. She was arrogant and cruel and believed that the Moroi were inherently better than the Velesians and Furies. If I'd had to place a bet on which Moroi had been most likely to seize control of the Houses while wielding a mind-controlling crown, it would have been her.

I supposed the joke was on me that it was my own aunt who had proven to be the true villain.

I didn't mourn Marvina's death, but the fact that Demetri had murdered his own mother was still all kinds of fucked up.

A branch in the tree—the one I was fairly certain Roth's parents had climbed up—trembled slightly. It was behind Demetri and his rangers, so they didn't see it, and the rain swallowed up the sound of any movement. There were likely more Laurent rangers than just the ones I could see. I needed to buy the others time to take them out—hopefully quietly—so we could deal with these ones. As much as I wanted my revenge against Demetri, I wouldn't claim it at the risk of my friends.

"Your mother was no prize." I shrugged and tapped the flat blade of a dagger against my chin before pointing it at Demetri. "Still surprised you had the backbone to do it yourself. Or did you get one of your dogs to do it?" I glanced at the howlers that still hadn't moved. "And to be clear, I mean the rangers who swore an oath to their House and betrayed it."

"Fucking cunt," one of the rangers swore and took a step

forward, his sword hand raising, but halted when Demetri held his arms out to the side.

"Hey, Fletch." I winked at the ranger, who was still glaring at me. "Look at you using naughty words. Did your balls finally drop?" I twirled my daggers in an obnoxiously showy move before pointing one at him. "I can fix that for you."

"Careful, Samara," Demetri warned. "One way or another, you will be my wife again. You can live out the rest of your life in luxury . . . or in a dungeon."

Out of the corner of my eye, I caught more movement in the trees—someone timed their jump down right as thunder roared across the sky. Demetri's rangers shifted uncomfortably as they glanced around the forest. They were used to the forests along the coasts that, while still dangerous, were far less so than the ones farther inland like this one.

I was actually surprised Demetri had convinced them to come at all instead of waiting to track me down during the day. So much about this didn't make sense . . .

"Give me an honest answer, and I'll consider coming with you," I lied. "Why do you want to marry me again? Why go to all this trouble?"

He tilted his head, and his hood slipped a little, letting me see more of his aristocratic face that I'd once found very hand-some. When we'd been together, he almost always wore a lazy but charming expression. He'd spent all his time lazing about or entertaining courtiers—or fucking them, as I later learned—but there was a cunning glint to his eyes now that had been absent all those years.

Demetri had fooled everyone—myself included. It annoyed me that I'd missed it.

"My original deal with Carmilla was quite simple. She supports me as the new leader of House Laurent, and my House backs her as the new Sovereign." His mouth twisted like he'd just bitten something sour. "Then she changed it. Said that in addition to supporting her, I needed to father a child with you . . . for her to raise. She never did explain but made it quite clear it was nonnegotiable."

A chill ran through me that had nothing to do with the cold rain. She knew. At some point, Carmilla had figured out I was part Fae . . . and wanted a child of my bloodline.

"Why you?" I asked numbly.

My ex-husband watched me closely, likely looking for a hint about what made me so special.

Just wait a few minutes, and I'll show you.

"Like I said, she wasn't keen on going into the details." He gave me a sly grin. "If I had to guess, it seemed like she wanted to compensate for something in your bloodline. Wanted to make sure that a strong Moroi House bloodline was mixed in. Not all the Houses have male children—only Tepes and Devereux. Neither of those Houses were likely to agree to such a thing, but me?" His smile sharpened. "I've already had you before; I don't mind having you again."

"Pass," I said flatly.

"You don't have a choice, Samara." He snorted. "Technically, Carmilla only wants the child. The marriage was my condition."

"Funny. You didn't seem to care about the first one." My grip tightened around the daggers. The others better have taken out any other enemy rangers lurking around us because my patience was waning.

"Do you have any idea how much shit I had to listen to after you left?" he sneered. "At first, you were the butt of the jokes, considering how many courtiers I fucked right under your nose while you were too busy trying to be the perfect Heir, but then you had to go and start a *relationship* with Kieran. That got people's attention, and I had to listen to the rumors swirl about what was so wrong with me that you ran straight into the arms of a lesser Moroi. Let him stand beside you as if he were an equal."

I used to think, for all his flaws, that Demetri was different from his mother. That he hadn't inherited her bullshit beliefs about some Moroi being lesser than others simply because of the families they were born into, but the look of disgust and scorn on his face was an exact match to the one I'd seen on hers countless times.

Rage simmered inside me, knowing that Kieran had likely heard every word. I knew he worried that his station as a courtier made him not worthy of me. It was something I was more than happy to spend the rest of my life proving false to him.

In the meantime, I'd fucking kill anyone who made him doubt his self-worth.

"I'd offer to make you a list of all the ways you fail to measure up to Kieran, but it's too lengthy, and you're not going to live long enough to read it."

Demetri gave me a patronizing look. "I brought *forty* rangers with me." He gestured at the trees surrounding us. "Right now, the rest of them are killing whoever helped you break out—I'm guessing your pretty courtier and that surly advisor. I've only tolerated your pathetic attempt at stalling because I was hoping they would drag the broken bodies of your lovers out in front of you, but it seems they've abandoned you. No matter. My rangers still have orders to kill them."

Two bloodred ropes slowly slid from the trees above the heads of the rangers standing on either side of Demetri. Thanks to the thick foliage, nobody seemed to notice but me. A feral smile spilt across my lips.

"You want me?" I bared my teeth. "Come and get me."

Demetri narrowed his eyes, but like the coward he was, he didn't take a step forward. "Get her. Make sure she's tied up good for the journey back to House Laurent. I don't want to hear another fucking word out of that mouth."

Four rangers stepped forward with their weapons bared and a swirl of two different colors in their eyes as their blood-lust rose. These ones were clearly excited about the idea of hurting me, a cruelty that had been allowed to fester at House Laurent.

That would fucking end now.

The ropes that had been slithering their way through the branches shot forward and wrapped around the necks of two of the rangers moving to apprehend me before yanking them up into the trees. The other two rangers barely had a second to cry out in alarm before they dropped to their knees, screaming, courtesy of my daggers now protruding from their right eye sockets.

Demetri and the other rangers stood frozen in shock.

That was another difference between them and the House Harker rangers; Vail's people would have never hesitated.

I tugged on the magic connecting me to my daggers, and they ripped free of the rangers' eyes and flew back into my hands. Both rangers let out twin shrieks of pain before scrambling back as two bodies thudded to the ground, their throats slit and bodies disemboweled.

The two rangers with eye wounds were cut down by Alaric and Kieran as they leapt down from above us.

Roth's family melted out of the surrounding forest and cut through the remaining rangers like they were out on a morning stroll. A few Laurent rangers tried to flee once they saw that the Devereux clan was here, but their retreat was thwarted by Nyx, Adrienne, and Emil, who took care of them with ease.

Demetri stood frozen in the center of the chaos as his rangers were slaughtered. The undead hounds didn't react at all to the bloodbath around them either. They just stood perfectly still like statues. I got the sense that my earth magic didn't like their presence.

Things that were dead should stay dead.

I stalked towards Demetri, and whatever he saw in my face seemed to snap him out of it because he held up his hands and started backing up. "Samara, wait! We can negotiate a dea—"

Warm blood sprayed across my rain-soaked face as I slammed one dagger into his throat and the other into his groin. Demetri's hands weakly clawed at one of my wrists, but dark red ropes appeared and brutally pulled them away as he gurgled and I ripped my blades away.

The broken scream he released was music to my ears as he fell to the forest floor. Moroi were tough to kill—it was a blessing and a curse.

I watched as my former husband tried to crawl away from me, a cold satisfaction filling me. Kieran and Alaric appeared at my sides, the rain doing its best to wash the blood off their clothes. I sheathed my daggers and held a hand out, then Kieran placed his sword in my hand, and the two of them kissed me on the cheek before stepping back.

Around me, Roth's brothers were gleefully hacking off heads to ensure all the Laurent rangers wouldn't heal and come after us.

Demetri's fingers moved feebly as he drew a healing glyph on his neck, but he stopped when I closed the distance between us and slammed my foot into his ribs. He let out a strangled scream as he flipped onto his back. Blood soaked his shirt and pants, and his usually tan skin was pale.

"Deal," he rasped. "Make . . . deal."

"Oh Demetri," I purred. "The only thing I want from you is to bleed out at my feet." Then I swung the blade, and his scream abruptly ended as his head rolled off his shoulders. "And I can handle that just fine on my own, asshole."

CHAPTER FOURTEEN

—

Samara

"Thanks, love," I told Kieran when I tossed him back his sword.

"No problem, sweetheart." He flicked the blade to the side to get some of the blood off before resheathing it across his back.

"What should we do about that?" Alaric pointed at the three statue-like howlers as he sauntered over and crouched down to wipe his blade clean on the bottom corner of Demetri's pants.

The three of us slowly approached the howlers, who didn't react to our presence at all.

"That's creepy," Desmond said as he moved closer to Roth.

"Death. Awaken," Roth murmured as they tried to get closer to the hounds, only to be tugged back by their elder brother.

"I think whatever magic was used to bring them back from the dead didn't bring back the essence of what they are," I thought out loud. "Like their instincts, what made them predators, are missing. It feels like my earth magic is repulsed by their very presence. They're just empty vessels that can take commands, and it didn't occur to Demetri to order them to attack us."

"Your husband was an idiot," Taivan rumbled. "What'd you ever see in him anyway?"

"Ex-husband," Kieran and Alaric said at the same time.

"Dead ex-husband." Roth smiled.

I rolled my eyes. "Let's chalk up my failed marriage to the foolish and idealistic views of my younger self." I frowned at the hounds. "We should destroy the collars. If it's a spell that's reanimating them, that should allow their bodies to return to the earth."

We all looked at the creatures.

"So . . . uhh . . . who's going to do it?" Kieran scratched his head.

"Oh for fuck's sake," Roth growled, then the ropes that had returned to their forearms shot out and slipped underneath the collar of the nearest hound before ripping it free and tossing it to me. Within seconds, the howler fell apart into a pile of rotting flesh and bones.

I stepped back with a gag, and the others followed suit. Apparently, we didn't even have to destroy the collar, just remove it. With a grimace, Roth's brothers stepped forward and snapped the collars off the remaining howlers. The beasts didn't even move, just crumbled as soon as the leather broke contact with their bodies.

"Let's get the fuck out of here." I stared at the carnage around us before my gaze lingered on Demetri. His death had been too quick, but I was still glad it'd come at my hands.

I looked up to find Kieran also staring at Demetri's corpse, a troubled look on his face that I didn't like one bit. Demetri might have been dead, but the pain of his words was clearly still lingering in Kieran's mind.

Before I could say anything, the storm kicked up a notch,

and the rain became more like buckets of water being dumped on us.

"This way," Severen called from where he and Celestina waited in the forest. I shoved some loose strands of hair away from my face and reached out to grab Kieran's hand, pulling him with me.

Alaric glanced at his friend in concern and fell into step next to me. Roth was already bundled up between their brothers—and grumbling loudly about how they never wanted to be outdoors again.

I'd build them the library of their fucking dreams once this was all said and done.

We'd been walking for no more than five minutes when Severen and Celestina suddenly stopped. Everyone halted with them and looked around. Because of the damn rain, I could barely see twenty feet in front of me and definitely couldn't hear that far. All I could smell was the damn forest and the faint scent of ozone as lightning cracked across the sky.

"Run," Severen breathed out.

We all took off without second-guessing the order. Celestina yelled something harshly and Taivan immediately snapped Roth up and flung them over his shoulder, then peeled from the group, going left with Desmond hot on his heels.

Severen darted to my side. "Samara, take your group and go west. We'll keep going north. All three groups will meet—" He shoved me away, and I crashed into Kieran just as a bolt sank into Severen's shoulder.

Our group ground to a halt in the middle of a clearing, Kieran and Alaric on either side of me and the three rangers just to our right. Lightning flashed, and I inhaled sharply as I saw the dark forms taking shape in front of us, becoming easier to distinguish as they closed the distance.

Carmilla sat atop an enormous black steed, and behind her, in two neat lines, were a dozen rangers also on horseback.

Just like with Demetri, I had no doubt there were others in the trees surrounding us.

This wouldn't be like fighting Demetri and his rangers. For one, House Laurent wasn't known for creating strong warriors. Their rangers did the bare minimum to protect their lands.

A wordless whisper brushed against my mind.

Demetri also hadn't had a crown capable of warping minds. That was the true danger. Panic threatened to overwhelm me, but I shoved it down. Severen was letting out pained breaths behind me, and I could hear Celestina ripping fabric to tend to his wound. We already had one injured in our party, and two of our strongest fighters were hopefully getting Roth as far away as possible.

There would be no fighting our way out of this one. Unless . . .

I did my best to ignore Carmilla drawing her mount to a stop ten feet away in front of me, her rangers obediently stopping behind her. I followed the strange connection between me, Draven, and Vail. There. Less than three miles from us.

Still not great odds, but I was fairly confident that the crown's magic wouldn't work on me. In the past, it hadn't worked on anyone who had drunk a lot of my blood, which meant Kieran and Alaric should be protected. Maybe Nyx too, although it'd been well over a week since they'd had some, and they hadn't drank all that much to begin with.

Everyone else was vulnerable. I just needed to buy us time until Vail and Draven arrived. Carmilla had purposely driven us into this clearing because their horses wouldn't help them much in the thick of the forest. If we could cause a big enough distraction and get to the trees, we might be able to make a run for it.

During our standoff with Carmilla, the rain had decreased to a steady but less overwhelming amount.

"I thought I raised you to make better decisions than this,

niece." Carmilla's dark green eyes looked almost black, but I could still see the disdain in them.

Stall, I told myself. *Stay calm and keep her talking.*

"And I thought you were honorable and dedicated to your people, aunt," I said coolly. "It seems we're both disappointed."

Carmilla shook her head. "You're too weak to do what it takes for our people to survive. I tried to give you an opportunity, but you've spat on my reasonable requests." Her mount took a step forward. "Surrender. Return with me. You will marry Demetri and give me an Heir. One who will do right by me."

I felt Alaric and Kieran go still at my sides. It was an empty threat because she didn't know Demetri was dead. Still, it hurt to hear it from her lips.

Gods, we'd all been such fools. It still smarted that the woman we'd all respected as the Leader of our House had been the villain all along and not a single one of us had seen it.

That was something I'd have to come to terms with later. For now, we needed to survive—and I wanted more information.

It wasn't hard to let the pain of betrayal show on my face. "What did you just say?" I let my voice crack a little.

"Don't play coy, Samara." Carmilla narrowed her eyes. "You must have some idea of the importance of your bloodline by now."

I swallowed and looked at the ground like I was defeated before saying quietly, "I'm part Fae."

"Yes. Courtesy of your father. Knew there was a reason I never liked him." My aunt shook her head in disgust. "As soon as he came into the picture, my sister stopped listening to me. I should have killed him then. If I had, perhaps things would have played out differently."

She didn't look all that heartbroken about it.

"We both know that's bullshit," I snarled. "Was it even Velika's idea to kill them? Or was it an idea *you* whispered in her ear?" I took a step forward, only for someone to grab me and yank me back against a hard chest. Kieran's scent wrapped around me, but I just stared at my aunt. I thought about that scar running across Vail's face. "You tried to kill *us*." The words were barely more than a whisper.

For a second, something like regret flashed across Carmilla's face, but it was gone faster than the lightning dancing across the sky.

"I told your parents to leave you behind, but as usual, they didn't listen to me." A cold mask settled onto my aunt's face.

"Probably because they suspected you were a traitorous bitch!" I hissed, my hand slipping down to the dagger on my thigh, only to be stopped when Alaric clamped his fingers around my wrist.

Something dark and angry twisted inside my soul, and Carmilla's horse stamped its feet uneasily.

Magic. It was my magic I was feeling. Pity I had no idea how to use it. I took a deep breath. Now wasn't the time to dwell on that. I needed to be stalling, not picking a fight and probably getting someone I loved killed.

I did my best to ignore the earth magic churning inside me and instead sank further into my Moroi side, letting my blood-lust rise that much more. At least this magic I was familiar with. I let my nails shift into claws that bit into my flesh when I clenched my fists, the pain grounding me.

"You condemned Draven for being half Fae, yet you want a grandchild 'tainted' with the same blood?"

"The fallen prince was raised by two egotistical maniacs." Carmilla's mouth tightened. "I will teach the child to overcome their foul Fae blood and to wield their power for the greater good. Then I will pass the crown to them so that they might use it to its full potential."

Realization dawned on me. She knew the crown was

fighting her and must have thought it was because she wasn't of the right bloodline. It was partially true, but mostly, the crown thought she was a vindictive bitch and didn't want to obey her.

"We won't let you take her," Kieran said before I could come up with a response.

All three rangers stepped forward, placing themselves between us and Carmilla while Alaric and Kieran shoved me behind themselves, both of them drawing their own swords.

Damn it. This was escalating too quickly. I concentrated on the thread linking me to Draven and Vail. Still miles away. Had they run into trouble too?

Stop, I told myself. *Deal with the problem in front of you before you go asking for more.*

My aunt sighed. "Last chance to come willingly."

For a brief second, I thought about it. I'd escaped once, I could do it again, but I dismissed that idea. Kieran and Alaric wouldn't let me go without a fight, and they would likely not walk away from that. Our best option was to hit them hard and then run. Our chances would've been better if Vail and Draven were here, but it seemed our time was running out.

The river was less than half a mile from us. We just had to make it there and then hope we didn't get crushed by any trees while it swept us away. Once we lost Carmilla and her rangers, we'd have to backtrack to locate Vail and Draven. I had no doubt Roth's brothers could find us.

"Remember, this was your doing." Carmilla shook her head and reached into a bag hanging off the front of her saddle.

I inhaled sharply as she settled the crown of silver and gold onto her head. Lighting cracked in the sky above us, and several horses stamped their feet in alarm.

You shouldn't have left me behind, the crown whispered in my mind.

Please, I begged.

I'm sorry. Its voice was tinged with exhaustion and regret. *There is nothing I can do.*

My aunt's gaze fell on the rangers standing guard in front of us. "Nyx and Emil," she said in a clear, commanding voice. "Step forward and hold."

Both rangers moved forward, leaving Adrienne on her own.

"No!" I cried and lunged for them, but Kieran and Alaric grabbed me. I struggled in their hold as they pulled me back several feet.

"Keep her back," Adrienne ordered over her shoulder. Her eyes met mine for a brief moment, and I saw the sorrow and determination in them.

"Nyx, stay still. Emil . . ." Carmilla's dark gaze fell on the blonde ranger, who stared her down defiantly. "Kill Adrienne."

I fought to get free, but Kieran and Alaric just gripped me tighter and murmured apologies in my ear. In that moment, I hated them, even though I would have done the same in their positions.

Carmilla was using our friends to make a point. Even with everything she had done so far, part of me had still believed there would be a way to convince my aunt to step down or end this in a way that didn't require her death.

That belief was now shattered into a thousand pieces as I watched Emil and Nyx tremble like they were fighting the command with everything they were worth before going predatorily still.

"Strigoi," I whispered in horror as Nyx remained but Emil prowled forward.

All Moroi carried a bloodlust that had the potential to turn us into ruthless predators. For some, like myself, we could turn it on and off easily, and even when it was riding us high, we were still ourselves. For others, they became something else when bloodlust claimed them—but they retained the tiniest thread of control so that they could pull it back.

They were weapons you had to aim and then get out of the way.

But sometimes, Moroi lost themselves completely, all of their humanity drained and stripped away. Nothing but the predator remained, and there was no coming back. They became Strigoi.

Emil's eyes were usually a warm brown fractured by light green. Now, there was no brown to be seen. Only a green so pale, it appeared white every time lightning struck over our heads. And Nyx's sky-blue eyes were now the dark blue of midnight.

There was no hint of my friends to be seen. Not in their eyes nor in their expressions, and definitely not in the eerie way they moved towards Adrienne. Predators focused solely on their prey.

A low snarl tore from Emil towards Nyx, an alpha staking their claim. Nyx ducked their head and went still, their eyes still following Adrienne as she adjusted her stance to face Emil.

"I'm so sorry, my friend." Her words were a quiet echo across the clearing that shattered my heart.

"Carmilla!" I screamed. "Stop this!"

My aunt looked at me with cold resignation and shook her head once before focusing back on the brewing fight. I saw the instant her expression changed to intrigue. This show wasn't only to put me in my place. It was an opportunity for her to test the capabilities of the crown.

Growing up, I'd always respected Carmilla's pragmatism, but now I wished she'd demonstrate more humanity alongside it.

Several of Carmilla's rangers moved to stand closer to us. The message was clear—if we interfered, they'd put us down. I wouldn't be killed, but Kieran and Alaric likely would be. All we could do was watch as Emil slowly circled Adrienne with a cruel detachment.

"She's never beaten him." Heat burned behind my eyes, tears made of despair and fury. I'd seen the rangers spar more than once. Adrienne was good, but even she couldn't take down Emil. Any Moroi would struggle to take on a Strigo, no matter how well trained they were or how much they let their bloodlust rise. Holding on to even the smallest amount of our humanity came at a cost—we were slower and weaker.

Nothing held a Strigoi back.

"Adrienne could have bested Emil years ago," Kieran whispered quietly, his voice strained.

I jerked my gaze towards him. "What?"

"Emil started talking about how old he was getting and how he should retire. He's the last of his generation to still be an active ranger." Kieran swallowed and glanced at me. "He told her the day she could beat him would be the day he'd know it was time to hang up his ranger cloak."

We both turned back to the center of the clearing, where Emil had gone still as a statue while Adrienne watched him. Her preferred weapon—a broadsword—was gripped in her hands and held at shoulder level, its tip pointing towards the storm raging above us.

Emil ignored the sword strapped to his back and the daggers on his thighs. Normally, we could shift our nails into claws, but Strigoi took it one step further. Each of Emil's fingers now ended in black, three-inch-long talons, the inside curve of each was razor sharp. Perfect for ripping out throats.

Tension filled the clearing as neither ranger moved, both waiting for the other to attack first. Lightning flashed over our heads, and in the split second that Adrienne was blinded, Emil shot forward. As if she'd anticipated it, Adrienne stepped into his attack and started a diagonal strike, only to spin away at the last second.

It was like watching a dance that two performers had perfected over decades. Adrienne gracefully spun her sword until it was nothing but a silver blur. Emil's opening attack had been a feint, because he'd also twisted to the side, only now, he found his path blocked by steel. With no hesitation, he blurred to the right and tried to maim her thigh to slow her down enough to get in a killing blow.

Adrienne dodged the attack, her movements like flowing water. They danced around each other in the clearing, punctuated by lightning strikes, as if the storm were dancing with them.

Neither scored a hit. Neither slowed down.

My heart raced with every step they took. It felt wrong to root for Adrienne, but I didn't know what else to do as I watched two people I cared deeply about battle for their lives. Even if one of them was already lost.

Suddenly, Emil struck at Adrienne's neck, and when she stepped back to avoid it, his back was exposed. With only the slightest hesitation, Adrienne's sword cut vertically through the air towards Emil's neck. My heart clenched, but I couldn't make myself look away. Only, her blade found nothing but air as the Strigoi leaned backwards until his back was almost horizontal with the ground and the sword whistled over him.

He straightened and lunged for Adrienne's exposed side. She pulled her sword back to herself, trying to get it between her and those sharp talons.

Too slow.

A scream tore through the night sky, followed seconds later by the tangy scent of blood. Emil dove towards Adrienne again, and she raised her sword. I flinched as another burning flash of lightning forced me to close my eyes. When I opened them, I saw Adrienne staggering back, a pained grimace on her face as blood flowed through her torn leather vest. The thing that used to be Emil raised his hand and licked the blood from his talons.

Then, a low, hungry sound came from Nyx, who had stepped forward, only to be cut off by Emil's warning growl. The Strigoi took a step back, their hungry eyes still locked on a wounded Adrienne.

Adrienne resumed her stance, her feet shoulder-width apart, left foot slightly forward. Once again, she raised her sword so the point was to the sky. Blood ran down it. I frowned. When had she gotten him? The lightning strike? My eyes had only been shut for a second . . .

Emil stalked forward, spurred on by the scent of his prey's blood, but when he darted to the right, clearly intent on capitalizing on her already-wounded side, his steps faltered. Inside, I was screaming as Emil's body carried him forward, the momentum too much to stop even as his right leg buckled beneath him. Then he stumbled straight onto Adrienne's sword.

The blonde ranger choked back a sob as she released the hilt immediately and grabbed each of the Strigoi's wrists, preventing him from swiping those talons through her throat. She'd punctured his heart, but it would take him a few minutes to die.

"I'm so sorry. I'm so sorry," she sobbed over and over again as she lowered her friend to the ground. Emil only snarled in return, fighting to get free, even as his lifeblood poured into the ground beneath him. Slowly, she pulled her sword from his chest and rose to her full height.

I tore my gaze away from them and looked at my aunt as tears streaked down my rain-soaked face.

Her dark, stony gaze found mine, and without hesitation, she gave the next order. "Nyx, kill Adrienne."

"No!" I screamed and renewed my efforts to get free, only for Kieran and Alaric to hold me back.

"We can't, Sam," Kieran said through clenched teeth. "There's nothing we can fucking do."

I knew he was right even if I didn't want to accept it. The only reason I stopped fighting was because the rangers standing nearby took a threatening step forward.

Thunder and lightning cracked and sounded over us before the rainfall became more of a deluge as the sky opened up. I shoved my hair away from my face and looked to where Nyx had been waiting while Adrienne and Emil had fought.

The spot was empty.

Adrienne grunted as she brought up her sword just in time to keep Nyx from clawing out her eyes. She'd also angled her sword so that the flat side made contact with Nyx's forearm, a vicious snarl tearing from Nyx's throat as they darted back before hurling themself at Adrienne again.

There was no deadly elegance to their movements like there had been to Emil's and Adrienne's. Just a feral intensity to rend and claw through flesh. Again and again, they struck at Adrienne, and every time, she deflected Nyx's attacks without doing them harm.

But the defense-only tactic came with a cost, because Adrienne's blood now soaked the ground along with Emil's who, based on his slowly rising chest, was still alive but not long for this world.

"Nyx," I half whimpered, but there was no sign of my friend in those wild, dark eyes. My relationship with Nyx was complicated. I'd known them at Drudonia, then they'd disappeared and only reentered my life when I'd returned to House Harker, but in my time back, I'd picked up on how close they were with Vail and his rangers—especially Adrienne. I knew the older ranger viewed Nyx as a younger sibling.

And Carmilla had to know it too. For all the rage I felt towards her now, my aunt knew her people well. This was a test to see how far the crown could push people against their instincts. If it could turn them against those they loved. Her pitting Adrienne and Emil against each other had been bad enough, but Adrienne and Nyx?

Carmilla was responsible for so many deaths—including those of my parents—and while I hated her for it, those had been tactical and efficient. Carmilla could have just ordered her rangers to cut down anyone here with a crossbow bolt to the heart. This felt cruel for cruelty's sake. Something I hadn't thought her capable of until now.

Despite how much Adrienne was bleeding, it seemed obvious she could win this fight at any moment she chose. Emil had challenged her, forcing her to dig down deep and fight to the best of her abilities, but Nyx's fighting skills had devolved. Maybe because they were younger or because the crown's magic had hit them harder. They were only still standing because Adrienne couldn't bear to strike them down.

Alaric shifted his grip so that his arm was around my waist while Kieran's remained across my shoulders. Alaric had been quiet during all of this, but I could feel the tension and fear radiating off him. What we were watching was his greatest fear —losing himself to bloodlust and becoming Strigoi. He'd witnessed his cousin suffer a similar fate, and it still haunted him to this day.

Kieran had also grown silent. I knew he considered Adrienne a friend. All of us were silently suffering in our own hells as we watched Adrienne try to avoid hers—to kill a friend . . . or die by their hand.

The rangers close to us shifted on their feet as Nyx stumbled back from another of Adrienne's deflecting blows. Then Adrienne shoved the young ranger forward, even as they whirled and snarled at her.

"*Nyx*," my aunt's voice, infused with magic, rang out. "*Finish this.*"

Please, I begged the crown again. *Do something.*

I . . . cannot.

You must! I screamed through our connection and could practically feel it wince. *I will do anything. Just make this stop.*

Little queen, its voice whispered through my mind. *You have no idea the cruelties I've seen. This is one of many. If you do not wish to experience this again, you must reclaim what is yours.*

Whatever words I was about to hopelessly plead died as Nyx leapt towards Adrienne, talons outstretched. Adrienne backed up a few steps, but she was too close to the rangers who had moved to stand guard in front of Carmilla, and they shoved her forward. As if moving on instinct, Adrienne dropped one hand from the hilt of her sword to wrap it around Nyx's throat, catching them midair. Then, with one fluid movement, Adrienne had Nyx pinned to the ground by their throat . . . with her sword buried in their chest.

Her sword pierced Nyx at an angle, so if she pushed down on it, the blade would have shred their heart. The predator in Nyx sensed this and went still, their talon-tipped hands wrapped around Adrienne's hand on the hilt of the sword.

For a second, it felt like everything paused. I didn't hear the storm or feel the rain on my face. The only thing that existed was Adrienne and Nyx.

"I love you. Never forget that." Adrienne's voice didn't waver once, her golden hair draped around her face as she held the sword between herself and Nyx. "I know you will find your way back from this. Do not blame yourself."

With that promise and command voiced into the world, Adrienne pulled her hand away from Nyx's throat and loosened her grip on the sword.

Time unfroze, and I watched in horror as Nyx's talons shot up . . . and ripped out Adrienne's throat.

A fragmented scream of denial poured out of me, and Alaric's and Kieran's grasps didn't slip, but I felt their bodies go rigid next to mine.

Blood flowed from Adrienne's torn flesh directly into Nyx's mouth, and they lapped it up hungrily as I alternated between sobs and strangled screams.

"You could have avoided this, my dear, if you had just come with me when I asked," my aunt called out over the rain that pounded into the ground.

I raised my gaze from where Adrienne had collapsed on top of Nyx and pushed aside the hungry sounds of feeding to meet my aunt's eyes. "Someday, I might have forgiven you for what you did to me, maybe even what was done to Draven under your watch, but I will *never* forgive you for this. And if there are any rangers here tonight whose minds you haven't scrambled, let this be an example of how you repay loyalty."

A few of the rangers shifted uneasily and traded pointed looks with each other while others sneered at me, but most of those lined up directly behind Carmilla didn't react at all. They just continued to stare blankly ahead. Not even reacting to the Strigoi hungrily feasting on the blood of one of their own mere feet from where they sat astride their horses. Or to Emil—one of the most well-respected rangers in the Moroi realm—who had finally gone still.

A cold, hard bitterness settled in my gut. She had used the crown on them despite telling me many times that she would only use the crown's magic when absolutely necessary. Apparently she found it necessary to strip the free will of sixty rangers and force them to serve her.

As much as that disturbed me, there was a silver lining. The half of the crown that Vail had given her had the ability to see a soul. I took that to mean she could see a person's true intentions. If my aunt felt the need to compel loyalty from so many of these rangers . . . she must have seen that they didn't believe in her plan.

I had to figure out a way to break them free of the crown's

magic and to get it away from her so she couldn't cause any more harm to our people.

"Do I need to continue the demonstration, or will you—" Carmilla's words were cut off when an agonized howl cut through the night.

My gaze fell back to Nyx, and I inhaled sharply. Kieran and Alaric did the same beside me.

The only occurrences of Strigoi becoming Moroi again had been the first generation of Moroi—the humans who had used magic to become something else. The Moroi, Velesians, and Furies. That first generation was special for each of our groups. For the Moroi, they were the only ones we knew of who had lost their humanity . . . and reclaimed it.

Outside of that generation though, it was a known fact that once a Moroi became a Strigoi, there was no coming back.

Nyx was no longer feeding on Adrienne. Instead, they were cradling her close and rocking her back and forth. I saw their lips moving, but I couldn't hear their words over the rainfall. Nobody moved as Nyx grieved the ranger they had loved like a sister.

"'I'm sorry. Please wake up,'" Kieran murmured, somehow figuring out what Nyx kept repeating.

Oh gods.

"Nyx." My voice broke as I called to them. Slowly, they raised their head to look at me. "Not possible," I breathed out, because Nyx's eyes were no longer the solid deep blue of night. Now, bright blue threads weaved their way through the darkness.

When Moroi let their bloodlust rise, it was like racing along the edge of a cliff. Most made sure to keep a decent amount of space between them and that edge—some, like Alaric, preferred to never go near it. The rangers liked to live danger-ously, trusted themselves not to slip while getting as close as possible.

Nyx had gone over that edge. I was sure of it. Now, they were clawing themself back up.

But when another ranger stepped forward, the brightness in their eyes faded, and Nyx released a sharp snarl in warning. Not all the way back . . . but not completely lost to us either.

"Interesting," Carmilla murmured. I tore my gaze from Nyx and glared at my aunt, who was staring at the young ranger in quiet contemplation. "It would be handy to be able to turn humanity on and off like a switch."

Nyx swiveled their head towards my aunt. I couldn't see their expression, but whatever was in it had Carmilla blanching. Carefully, Nyx settled Adrienne onto the ground and rose, black talons once again extending from their fingers.

"Stop," Carmilla ordered, her horse shifting its hooves nervously beneath her. Nyx stopped and held still for a heartbeat . . . then they took another step. "Do not move."

I held my breath as Nyx once again stopped, then took another step after a few seconds passed.

Well, isn't that fascinating? the crown's voice swept through my mind.

"How?" I choked as the word slipped from my lips. I felt Kieran's and Alaric's gazes on me but couldn't look away from where Nyx was fighting to get to Carmilla.

I don't know, the crown finally admitted after hesitating.

Several of the horses snorted in distress and pulled against their reins as the rangers tried to keep them under control. Carmilla glanced at them with a frown before looking around the woods. I did the same, scanning the darkness, looking for any sign of a threat.

For quite possibly the first time in my life, I wished for a monster attack. We needed a diversion, and I had faith in us to use the chaos to our advantage and slip away—with Nyx, because there was no chance I was leaving them behind.

Carmilla's mount reared up, and the unease of the rest of

the horses increased. Something had them seriously spooked, I just had no idea what. My aunt looked past me, the corners of her eyes and mouth pinched. "I have no quarrel with House Devereux, but I'll be taking the members of my House. If you choose to fight me, know that we'll hunt down your children."

"You can try, bitch," Celestina snarled.

I glanced quickly over my shoulder and saw her standing in front of her husband, a long, curved sword in her hands and eyes glowing with menace.

She would fight. And she would die.

My eyes went to Emil and Adrienne. No more deaths tonight. I'd escaped Carmilla's grasp once. I could do it again.

I moved my hand behind me, where it would be visible to Roth's parents, and made the signal for *stand down*. All rangers, regardless of which House they owed allegiance, used a system of gestures for communicating when speaking aloud was ill-advised. Technically, none of Roth's family were rangers, but House Devereux was a warrior clan, so I had no doubt they knew the gestures.

"Nyx goes with them." I jerked my head over my shoulder towards Roth. "You've caused them enough pain."

"No. Nyx comes too. I want to—" Carmilla cursed as her horse reared again. As soon as its hooves hit the ground, it shied into the ranger's horse next to it. "Grab Nyx and Samara and let's go," she said through gritted teeth as her mount tried to bolt and she barely kept it in check. All the horses looked on the verge of running. I could hear ours stamping their feet behind us as well.

Something was coming.

Half a dozen rangers stepped towards Nyx and another half a dozen towards us.

"Anyone have any bright ideas on how to get out of this?" Kieran asked tightly as he angled himself slightly in front of me.

"Nothing's coming to mind," Alaric replied in an equally strained voice. Both of them were looking at the rangers approaching us. Something, a vague feeling, had me looking to the sky, which meant I saw what no one else did—the dark streak flying through the air on silent wings made of night and shadow.

The rangers were halfway to us when she slammed into the earth between us, cutting off their approach. Leathery black wings spread out from the Furie's back as shadows spun around her, like the night was thrilled by her presence.

Then, glowing golden eyes met mine as the Furie looked over her shoulder.

"Cali," I breathed out.

CHAPTER FIFTEEN

—

Alaric

FOR A FRACTION OF A SECOND, relief hit me when Cali landed in front of us. The Furies were few in number compared to the Moroi and the Velesians, but they were ruthless in battle, and there was nobody as skilled—and terrifying—as Calypso Rayne.

But then those mesmerizing golden eyes slid from Samara's tear-streaked face to the chaos erupting around us, and I realized we weren't saved—we were fucked. Because something had driven Cali over the edge, and now she was nothing but wrath made flesh.

"Shit!" Kieran swore from the other side of Samara, clearly coming to the same realization as Cali's predatory gaze zeroed in on the rangers tasked with apprehending us.

Carmilla seized the opportunity to turn tail and run, not that her horse needed much encouragement. Over half the rangers lost their battle with their mounts as the horses took off running after the new Moroi Queen. A few tripped over upraised roots, dumping their riders.

"Stall her!" Carmilla commanded over her shoulder, not

showing any concern for the rangers she was leaving behind for what would likely be a gruesome death.

I tried to pull Samara back to shove her behind myself, but the leash Cali held over her own magic finally broke. Shadows exploded across the clearing as an alien presence speared my mind, and time seemed to stop only to jump forward and then freeze again.

It felt like someone had placed a vice around my head and was slowly cranking it tighter, all while a rage that was not mine burned hotter than any fire. At some point, I fell to my knees, and I was faintly aware of ripping my nails as I tore at the ground.

Cali vanished into shadow only to reappear behind the rangers, who were clutching their heads and screaming. Her sword flashed. Heads rolled.

More rangers poured into the clearing, only to fall as Cali's magic ripped their minds to shreds, leaving them as easy pickings for her blade.

I didn't know how House Devereux were fairing, but I hoped they didn't do something foolish like try to attack Cali. Taking down Furies when they lost themselves like this required far greater numbers than anything we had at our disposal. It also required careful planning, the element of surprise . . . and the knowledge that you would have to sacrifice some of your own to land a killing blow.

Kieran was kneeling next to me, his face locked in a pained grimace as blood leaked from his nose and ears. There were only three people still standing in the clearing. Cali. Samara. Nyx.

The Furie's molten gaze fell on Nyx, who still seemed to be wavering between Moroi and Strigoi—their eyes mostly midnight blue, but a few light strands remained. I didn't know what it meant, if they could truly come back from turning Strigoi, if they'd want to after what they'd been forced to do—

but none of that mattered if we didn't survive the next few minutes.

"Samara!" I half whispered the warning before groaning as another wave of Cali's magic hit me and that vice squeezed a little tighter. Warm blood dripped from my nose. "Not. Your. Friend."

I loved Samara Harker with every bit of my pragmatic heart, and I understood her well. Her greatest strength—and weakness—was that she was loyal to a fault. She did not give that loyalty lightly, but once she did, there was no taking it back.

Even if the person who held it turned into a monster.

When Furies lost themselves, they didn't become mindless beasts. They remained what they'd always been —apex predators who took out the biggest threats first. And right now, Cali had decided that Nyx was the threat that needed neutralizing.

She took a step towards the broken ranger while Nyx held their ground, a silent snarl on their face, even as the flicker of something else danced in their eyes. Cali's golden stare held nothing but cold detachment. I tried to get up—to do what, I had no idea—but a sharp pain cut through my mind, immediately driving me back to my hands and knees.

In a desperate attempt, I tried to let my bloodlust rise to combat Cali's magic, but I'd kept it too ruthlessly locked down . . . so it did not answer when I called

All I could do was watch helplessly as Samara smoothly moved to stand in front of Cali, putting Nyx at her back. Internally, I screamed at the risk she was putting herself in. Cali was not her friend anymore, and only a fool would let a Strigoi be at their back.

Nyx's muscles tensed for a second, and I knew they were about to launch themself at Samara's exposed neck and back, but then they squeezed their eyes shut and jerked their head, stumbling backwards. When their eyelids fluttered open a second later, more light blue was threaded through the dark. Slowly, Nyx took another step back, as if they were trying to remove themselves as a threat.

"Cali," Samara barked. The pressure on my mind eased slightly. "Enough."

"What are you doing?" I asked tightly. Reasoning with Furies in this state was useless. We needed to figure out how to retreat. Maybe get Cali to chase after Carmilla . . .

Samara ignored me. Of course she did. Gods, I was going to strangle her when this was done.

"All these years," Samara sneered, "everyone has been saying you would fall. *'Calypso Rayne is already half mad and too powerful. Better to put her down now,'*" she mocked as she stepped closer to Cali, who had gone stock-still. "I was the harlot, Rynn the screwup, and you the mad bitch."

The magic bearing down on my mind came back, and I growled as I tried to push against it. Kieran crawled closer to me, and we both grimaced as we looked at each other before focusing once again on the reckless woman who held both our hearts.

Samara's hand shot out to grip the front of Cali's blood-soaked vest. "We do not yield!" she snarled into her friend's face. "Pull yourself together! Everything is fucked right now, and I can't do this without you."

I hated the way her voice broke on that last word. *So fucking do something about it, asshole,* I chided myself.

Cali's clawed hands gripped Samara's, piercing her flesh, but she didn't attack her friend. To my amazement, Samara was actually getting through to Cali, even though everything I knew about Furies said that should be impossible when they were in this state.

We just needed to give Cali another push.

Shoving aside the pain that still had a grip on my mind, I rose to my feet. Cali's head snapped towards me. "I think I know where Rynn might be," I said quickly but clearly before rushing to get the rest out. "There is much we need to catch you up on, Cali, and Samara is right, we will need your help because you will be able to retrieve Rynn faster than any of us."

I was embellishing a little. Okay, a lot. I suspected I knew where Rynn was because it was the only place that made sense. Assuming I was right about her being in the far northern reaches of the Velesian realm, Cali was our only hope of reaching her because we definitely wouldn't make it there on foot.

Kieran got to his feet next to me but didn't make a move towards Cali. We'd both experienced a Furie's wrath before, but that time had been only the barest splash of it, and that Furie had never been given the chance to come back. She'd been hunted down and exterminated.

Samara would never allow that to happen to Cali though, and against all odds, it did feel like Cali was drawing her rage back. I could still feel it on the outskirts of my mind, but the blood was no longer pouring from my nose, and I was capable of thinking for more than a few seconds at a time.

Which was why I was able to contemplate the way Cali had moved. In addition to the strange mental attacks Furies could invoke, they all had a little bit of shadow magic. That was the true reason they'd always felt apart from the Moroi and Velesians. Their shadow magic was just a little too similar to the wraiths that haunted these lands.

Over the generations, the Furies had learned to lock down their magic. They only wielded their mental attacks as a last result, and most refused to touch their shadow magic altogether.

Except Cali.

She'd always been the exception. Much like Samara was somewhat of an exception amongst the Moroi, as she frequently flaunted her bloodlust. And Rynn had her own eccentricities that set her apart from the rest of the Velesians.

It was almost like fate had drawn the three of them together. Bonded them on some deep level that no one else could touch.

I normally didn't believe in such things, but it was hard to deny it as the most powerful Furie in existence clawed back her magic, looked at her friend, and wept.

I didn't know what to do, so I looked at Kieran.

He looked at me wide-eyed. "This is outside my area of expertise."

Great.

I rubbed the back of my head and turned away from Samara and Cali. Something told me the Furie wouldn't want anyone to see her cry, and I really liked my head being attached to my body.

Kieran moved to huddle next to me. "Go check on Roth," he said quietly. "I'll make sure Nyx is . . . alright."

Nyx was definitely not alright.

I jerked my head in a nod and strode towards the Devereux clan. Other than a few patches of dark red hair, I couldn't even see Roth past all the muscled bodies guarding them.

"Samara has it under control," I told Taivan and Desmond as I approached. They'd put themselves in front of their sibling with Severen and Celestina guarding their children from the sides.

"Does she?" Desmond rasped.

"She does," I said flatly.

The brothers traded a look that said they didn't quite believe that, but then they both let out twin shrieks as Roth grabbed them by the ears and yanked.

"I'm officially out of patience." Roth shoved past their brothers and crashed to a halt in front of me, their eyes a burning orange. "Move, or I'll move you."

"I was actually coming to get you." I gave them a wry smile.

"Oh." Some of the fire banked in their eyes. "Let's go then."

Roth started to walk past me before turning back around to face their family. "Uhh . . . thank you for keeping me alive."

Severen rubbed his face, clearly at a loss for patience when dealing with his youngest child, but a faint smile of amusement teased Celestina's lips. Meanwhile, Roth's brothers both smiled like they'd just been paid the highest of compliments.

That was clearly too much emotion for Roth because they practically fled past me, and I quickly followed after them, not wanting to be left behind to deal with the strange family dynamic that was House Devereux.

We walked across the clearing to where Samara was wiping some of the blood off Cali's face while offering soothing words. I cut a glance to Kieran and found him standing a few feet away from Nyx, who was rooted to the same spot, tension rolling off them, but at least they weren't actively hunting anyone nor had they bolted into the woods, so I'd take that as a win.

Samara's dark gaze cut to us as Roth and I approached, then she dropped her hand to her side and moved her fingers in a way that had to be some type of signal. A ranger signal maybe? Kieran spent a lot of time sparring with the rangers, so he probably would have known what it meant, but I had no idea. I opened my mouth to ask when Roth's fingers briefly closed around my forearm, drawing me to a stop.

Wait and hold, they mouthed.

Surprise flickered through me. It was well-known that every member of House Devereux went through ranger training, but I'd assumed Roth had been exempt from it because they were . . . well . . . they were Roth. If it wasn't a book—or Samara— they didn't give a shit.

Any musings I'd had about Roth and their upbringing evaporated as Samara tucked a strand of hair behind Cali's ear and started asking her questions—ones I was really curious about the answers to.

"How did you know where to find us?" Samara asked her friend gently.

"Whispers." Cali's eyes were wide. "Don't you hear them?"

Roth and I shared a look. Furies were prone to madness. Nobody knew why. The Moroi lost themselves to bloodlust, but the Furies . . . they lost themselves to rage. If our hunger for blood was its own entity, then so was that fury that burned within them.

Only the Velesians had no such hardships.

It was one of the many mysteries I and so many others had pondered over the years.

"I don't hear anything." Samara shook her head, keeping her voice calm and soothing. "These voices . . . they told you to come here?"

Cali's head snapped towards the north. The sudden movement had me reaching for the dagger on my thigh, but I stilled my hand.

"He told me. I've never heard his voice so clearly before." She turned back to face us—Sam, really. I didn't think she was entirely registering our presence at the moment. Her mouth hardened into a flat line as her brows furrowed together. "The lake."

"Lake Malov?" Samara prodded, reaching out to grip her friend's hands.

The Furie looked down at where their bloody fingers were intertwined, then her eyes cleared a little more, the glow dimming. "You were missing," she said slowly. "So was Rynn. The last place I knew you were was Lake Malov."

I cursed under my breath, drawing Samara's attention for a moment and letting me see the fear in her eyes. Fear for her friend, who had said that all Furies avoided the area around Lake Malov because it made them uneasy . . . but that it had always called to her.

Something had been trying to get Cali to go to Lake Malov for a long time—and it just got its wish.

"Can't we just go one fucking day without more fucked-up bullshit raining down on us?" I half growled.

Someone grunted next to me, and I almost jumped out of my skin. Taivan's eyes never strayed from Cali, but the corners of his mouth quirked up into a grin, clearly amused at having scared the shit out of me. I glowered at him. How did someone that large move so quietly?

"This is Lunaria." Taivan gave me a sly look before returning their vigilant gaze to the Furie. "There's never a time when it's not fucked."

I snorted. True enough.

"Do you still hear it—him?" Samara corrected herself, once again focused on her best friend.

Cali tilted her head as if she was listening for something, and we all waited for a few tension-filled seconds until her shoulders sagged in relief. She smiled weakly at Sam. "No. I think I burned myself out. The whispers will be back—he'll be back—but for now, it's quiet."

Lightning flashed across the sky, and thunder rumbled in the distance a few seconds later. The downpour had lightened up, but the rain showed no sign of stopping anytime soon.

As if reading my thoughts, Samara looked up to the sky and then surveyed all of us, her eyes lingering for a moment on the fallen forms of Adrienne and Emil. A hint of grief broke through her calm and determined mask before she hid it.

For years, I thought Samara was self-serving because she'd always seemed so above everyone. Always breezing into a room with a confident swagger that had immediately put me into a foul mood, but now I realized what that had cost her. Samara never allowed anyone—in our House or any other—to see her as anything but unbreakable.

So many times, I'd said something cruel to her just to try to get a reaction. I almost never got one. Instead, she'd say something back that would have me seeing red and usually storming out of the room, but I suspected my words had always cut far deeper than I'd imagined. She was just better at hiding her wounds than I.

Fuck. I'd been such an asshole. To make it worse, Kieran had always seen the truth of Samara, and he had hinted at it over the years. I'd just chosen to not believe him because of the often conflicting feelings I'd had towards the House Heir.

That was all in the past though. I could make up for it now—starting with not making Samara bear all of this alone.

"We need to regroup. Preferably somewhere indoors and behind wards. We can't be that far from House Salvatore." Cautiously, I closed the distance between myself and Samara, keeping part of my attention on Cali. She seemed calmer now, more like her usual self, but I didn't want to risk upsetting her.

The Furie just gave me a tired, wan smile and extended her wings up, curving them forward slightly to provide a little bit of shelter from the rain.

"We don't know where House Salvatore stands with Carmilla's rise to power." Samara chewed on her bottom lip, her eyes distant as she thought it through. "Draven and Vail are south of us. We could rendezvous with them and then continue to Salvatore. Hopefully Carmilla hasn't sunk her claws into them."

Or used the crown's magic. Although we still didn't know if the crown could be wielded against a House bloodline as it could any other Moroi. Nyx might be one of our rangers, but they were technically of the House Corvinus bloodline.

I didn't know if Carmilla had intentionally turned them into a Strigoi or if, even with both halves united, that was still the only way it could work on a House bloodline. She'd definitely been able to control them. I thought about the way Nyx had been fighting towards the end. One rebellious step at a time.

Something about the crown's magic hadn't entirely worked on Nyx.

A howl rose in the night, sounding a few miles away from us. "No matter what, I think we want to head south." I reached out and brushed back the hair that was plastered to Samara's face. "We're lucky we haven't drawn the attention of wraiths or any other nasty creatures." I glanced around before looking back at Samara and suggesting a plan of action. "Find Draven and Vail. Evaluate House Salvatore when we get there. If anything appears suspicious, we don't set foot inside their walls and we continue on to House Devereux."

"Okay." Samara nodded and then glanced at Taivan, who hadn't tried to crowd in under Cali's wings and was just standing in the rain, not looking the least bit bothered by it. "Does that plan work for you?"

"Yes." The Heir of House Devereux nodded. "We've had scouts keeping an extra close eye on House Salvatore since Roth arrived home. Best we can tell, they've had no communication with Carmilla."

"Good enough for me." Samara looked around at the corpses littering the clearing—Cali's work. Again, I saw that hint of sadness in her eyes before she tucked it away. Some of them might have willingly served Carmilla, but not all. "We can't take them with us," Samara said softly.

There were far too many for us to carry, and we needed to move swiftly. It was a miracle that the Lunarian beasts hadn't already come to investigate the tang of blood in the air. The storm might be making us all miserable and cold, but at least it was keeping scents down.

"I'll send my people to come and collect the dead as soon as I can," Taivan offered.

It was nice of him, but we all knew there wouldn't be much left. The beasts that prowled the forests were not ones to waste such a meal.

Suddenly, Nyx snapped out of their almost comatose stance, causing everyone to stiffen. Taivan had a blade in his hand in an instant, but Nyx ignored him along with the rest of us as they walked over to where Adrienne lay and carefully lifted her, cradling the ranger to their chest, as if they could protect her in death.

Not a flicker of emotion appeared on Nyx's face as they looked to where Emil rested. Wordlessly, Cali tucked her wings back and strode over to the other ranger, easily picking him up. Together, Nyx and Cali began walking south.

The rest of us followed, leaving the dead behind.

CHAPTER SIXTEEN

—

Draven

"These howler nests look like they were abandoned weeks ago." I toed a pile of branches, leaves, and other debris collected from the forest.

Vail just grunted. That seemed to be his main form of communication since I'd tracked him down half an hour ago.

I sighed. It hadn't taken me long to find him, but Vail kept coming up with reasons to slow our journey back to the others. "We should keep going. The rest of the group is only a few miles away, and I'd prefer to be at Samara's side."

Usually, I loved being out at night. Thanks to my magic, I could sense the nastier of the monsters and avoid them. There was something thrilling about sharing the forest with them, of being just another monster trying to survive, but that thrill was dimmed tonight because Samara was out here too, and she didn't have a good enough grasp on her earth magic to wield it like I did—something we'd absolutely be working on once we had time.

"Carmilla is no doubt hunting her down." I hesitated before adding, "And my father is going to seek retribution for

Velika's death. He might decide to take out his frustration on Samara."

Moonlit silver eyes finally met mine. "Will he not come after you?"

"Eventually." I shrugged. "But he'll want revenge for Velika's death first. There was no love lost between the two of them, but Velika helped him get access to those obsidian stones by figuring out which outposts were built over the human towns. She also shared information with him about the other Moroi Houses."

Thunder rumbled in the clouds above us.

"You really don't care that she's dead, do you?" Vail tilted his head as he studied me.

"Actually, I'm quite upset about it. I was really looking forward to killing her myself."

A slight tug pulled on the bond, there and gone in an instant. Based on the way Vail stiffened, I suspected he felt it too.

"Let's go. Samara wants us all together."

"*She* slammed the door in *my* face. So, clearly, she doesn't want us *all* together." He pushed off the tree he'd been leaning against. "I'll keep scouting ahead. You go running back to *her*," he tossed over his shoulder as he stalked farther into the woods.

My temper snapped.

Between one blink and the next, I had Vail pinned against a tree while roots shot out of the ground, winding around his waist and legs. My claw-tipped fingers dug into his throat, and his dagger pressed against mine.

I missed my whip. That would be priority number one once we reached House Devereux. No doubt they had a large weapons stash for me to raid and I could find something that would work.

"Get your hands off me, pretty boy," Vail snarled, "before I cut off your fingers and shove them down your throat."

"You're already on Samara's bad side." I snorted. "My fingers are her second favorite part of my body." My brows bunched together. "Maybe her third, I'm not sure where my tongue lies exactly. I'm good, but I have Kier to compete with, and his tongue skills are—"

Vail shoved me away, his blade drawing a bit of blood in the process, and started slashing at the roots holding his lower body. I sighed. This wasn't my problem to fix, and he *had* betrayed Samara, which was something he hadn't really accepted yet. In his mind, he was trying to be loyal to two people at once, but that wasn't possible when they were so opposed to each other.

I didn't particularly like Vail, but I understood what it was like to give your loyalty to the wrong person and suffer the cost. Vail was starting to understand, but I needed to give him a nudge to ensure he didn't betray Samara again.

Try to anyway. I'd kill him before he ever got another chance, which would break Samara's heart—which was the other reason I was trying to help the stubborn asshole out. I had no doubt that Samara still loved Vail, it was just hidden beneath a mound of hurt and fury.

Half a thought from me had the roots slipping back into the earth. Vail stalked away—in the opposite direction of Samara—so I ripped open the wound in my soul that I'd tried so hard not to think about.

"My father killed my older brother."

Rain started spattering against the thick forest canopy. I focused on that sound, doing my best to block out the resounding crack that always came to mind when I thought about Kalias.

Vail stopped mid-step, not turning around but clearly listening.

"Kalias was my half brother. I think it was hard for the Fae to procreate, and the Seelie turning themselves into shadow monsters probably didn't help," I said evenly, as if I were discussing someone else's family history. The branches above me moved closer together to provide me a little bit of shelter from the rain. They did that sometimes, helped without me having to ask. I patted the rough bark of the tree in thanks. "Erendriel was the first of the wraiths to figure out how to get his Fae form back."

"Who was the mother?" Vail asked, still facing away from me.

"A Velesian." I swallowed. "She died shortly after Kalias was born. We . . . were never able to find out anything about her. Not even her name." *Or if she'd been willing*, I thought darkly.

A twig snapped when Vail finally turned to face me. My magic lashed out, silencing the rest beneath his feet. His gaze dropped to the forest floor and back to me. "That's how you're able to move about so quietly—you use your magic to quiet your footsteps."

I nodded shallowly. "Stumbled across that ability by accident." The sound of bone snapping echoed across my mind, and I flinched. "Kalias was five years older than me. I'd met him a few times growing up, but it wasn't until I was twelve and Erendriel took me to live with him that I really got to spend more time with my brother."

"Did he have magic?"

"No." I closed my eyes briefly. "Pure-blooded Fae come into their magic in their early twenties, but they typically start showing signs of it earlier. Kalias was seventeen when I arrived, and it was becoming clearer with every passing year that he wouldn't have magic."

Something our father derided him about every day.

"But you do," Vail pointed out.

I gave him a smile that didn't reach my eyes. "Yes."

"Does your father know?"

The rain started to fall harder, and Vail took a few steps closer so he could hear me. It took me a moment to decide how to answer him. I was already telling him a story I hadn't told anyone else, so I might as well speak the truth.

"Yes," I finally answered. "But he doesn't know how much."

Something that I couldn't read flickered in Vail's eyes, but he didn't say anything. He was a patient bastard when he wanted to be.

"I started showing signs of having earth magic when I was eleven. Minor things like making flowers bloom early, being able to sense nearby animals. As my powers grew, Velika became more . . . perturbed by me." I blocked out the painful memories full of blood and screaming. "But it was the first time Erendriel ever showed an interest."

Few people truly knew me. I was the charming Moroi Prince to most. To some, I was a villain—but those were mostly people I'd killed or those who had been slaughtered in front of me while I'd been forced to stand by. Only Samara and Kieran truly knew me, and even still, they'd probably be surprised to know just how gullible I'd been all those years ago.

That I'd seen the hand Erendriel had stretched out to me as salvation when it had really just been damnation wrapped up in pretty words.

Nobody lied better than the Fae. I'd learned that lesson too late.

"I'd spent the first twelve years of my life under the thumb of someone who despised me. Erendriel treated me like a person, asked my opinions on things, praised me when I did something right. I'd never experienced such a thing, so I naturally gravitated towards it." A bitter smile stretched across my lips. "I was too young to understand the way he was manipulating me."

A small crease formed between Vail's brows, but he didn't say anything, so I continued.

"Erendriel had no interest in Kalias—he'd already written him off—but I liked having an older brother, and Kalias took me under his wing." The bitterness in my smile faded slightly as I thought about Kalias. *Crack.* The smile vanished. "He knew our father was disappointed in him for not having magic, so he tried to make himself useful in other ways."

"Did he betray the Velesians the way you did the Moroi?"

"I was a child manipulated by a centuries-old Fae and then had the pleasure of having my mind shredded by my psychopath of a mother." I gave him a cold look. "What's your excuse?"

Vail looked away.

"To answer your question, Kalias had no interaction with the Velesians—bad or good." I tried not to think about how many times I'd caught him staring at paw prints in the mud belonging to Lycanthropes or other Velesians. My brother had been caught between two worlds, unable to shift into an animal form but unable to do magic like a Fae.

Erendriel had thought he'd been a failure, but to me he'd just been my brother. We'd both been too caught up in trying to win the praise of our father to realize we hadn't needed it. We'd been enough.

"What is the point of this story?" Vail asked when I fell silent. He still wasn't looking at me, but he was idly rubbing his chest in the spot where I guessed he felt the same tug I did.

"During my time living with the wraiths, I was mostly kept away from everything. Erendriel would occasionally ask me to perform small acts of magic, but he dodged any questions I had about him and the Fae. How they'd become wraiths. What they were trying to do. I never truly learned anything about what was driving Erendriel."

Lightning tore across the sky. *Crack.*

"One day, Erendriel brought me and Kalias to a remote Moroi outpost with a handful of his wraiths." Vail's silver eyes suddenly focused on me again. "He passed me a knife, told me several Seelie words, and then pointed to the blood ward protecting the outpost. I hesitated. Despite my naivety, I knew wraiths had killed Moroi before. I'd convinced myself that it hadn't been on the orders of Erendriel . . . but it was the dead of night and the Moroi were sleeping peacefully in their homes."

"The attacks on the outposts didn't start until recently. You're talking about almost a decade ago," Vail commented.

"It was a test," I said tightly. "One that I failed."

The branches above us creaked, and I felt the forest reach out to me, trying to heal the old wound. I flinched when one of the branches cracked.

"There is so much I don't understand about the Fae, even after being around Erendriel and his followers for so long, but one thing I do know—they plan everything ten steps ahead." I moved towards a tree and laid my palm against it. The branches settled, but the hollowness inside my chest remained. "He needed to know that when the time came, he could get across the wards, and he didn't want to rely on Velika. She was a tool to be used—not trusted."

"What did you do?" The accusing expression on Vail's face told me what he suspected my answer would be. That I'd betrayed our people. A dark part of me wished I could tell him that's what I'd done, because maybe if I'd made a different decision that night, I would have saved my brother. I sure as shit hadn't saved those outposts—only delayed the inevitable. Because those were the outposts Erendriel had slaughtered years later.

Crack.

"I refused," I rasped. "I loved Erendriel. He has this . . . presence about him, and he was my father. I thought he must have valid reasons for anything he did, even if I found some of them suspicious. He had my loyalty—beyond a shadow of a doubt." The muscles along my jawline tensed. "But I did not have his."

"He threatened Kalias if you didn't do it?" Vail guessed.

A humorless laugh escaped me. "That's the other thing about the Fae. They prefer punishment over ultimatums. He snapped Kalias' neck in front of me and then threw his body to the ground. The wraiths he'd brought with him ripped Kalias to shreds. There was nothing left of my brother to bury. It was like he never existed."

A hollow ache settled in the pit of my stomach. I so rarely let myself dwell on Kalias and his fate. But while the others were pissed off at Vail for betraying Samara—and rightfully so —I understood why he'd done it.

Sometimes it's hard to see the monster beneath the mask of someone you love.

Vail looked at me for a long moment with an unreadable expression. "What happened next?"

"Erendriel and his wraiths left me there. The Moroi who lived in the outpost found me crying in the morning. I was returned to my mother and became a tool for her and Erendriel to use when they needed. Erendriel didn't need me to cast the spell to get past the wards. He only needed to slice me open and hold my bleeding body over them while reciting the spell. The night he brought me and Kalias to that outpost had been a test. Not to see if the spell worked, but to see if I would do as commanded."

"Why tell me this?" Vail's brows furrowed. "I don't understand you, prince."

"Few do. Samara is one of them, and she loves you despite herself." I shrugged. "If you attempt to betray her again, I will carve you apart and scatter your body across the earth." Roots rose from the ground and snapped at Vail's feet, causing him to leap back. "It will be like *you* never existed. This is a warning to better choose who you give your loyalty to."

He glared at me. "Carmilla isn't the same as Erendriel. She thinks she's doing what she has to for all of us. I just need to get her to see reaso—"

"Believe me when I say that Carmilla knows exactly what she is doing. Or have you forgotten about the families—with children—still locked in the dungeons of the Sovereign House?" I cut him off. "Samara has already come to harm once because of your inability to see who Carmilla truly is. I know you love her. Do not fuck up again."

His mulish expression morphed into one of uncertainty. "She'll never forgive me," he murmured. "I've tried to explain, but she—"

"Have you tried saying the words, 'I'm sorry?' That's usually a good starting point."

The tug on my chest became more insistent, and I frowned before looking in the direction it was pulling me. Then I exhaled sharply when the tug became a panicked yank and heard Vail do the same.

We looked at each other, then took off at a dead run.

Vail kept pace with me as we raced through the woods towards Samara. The frantic pulling had dimmed, and emotions slid through me that weren't my own. One of them was so strong, it almost took me to my knees.

Grief.

It was still hard to decipher things from the bond, but I was fairly certain Samara was at least physically alright. It wasn't bodily pain I was feeling from her—only emotional.

Something very bad had happened while I'd been fetching Vail. I had no gods to pray to. Instead, I begged the moon that

Kieran wasn't the reason Samara was feeling such despair. If my love had suffered because Vail was too fucking stubborn to face what he'd done . . . the Marshal wouldn't have to worry about his conflicting loyalties or emotions anymore. Despite how much I saw myself reflected in Vail's struggles, I'd fucking kill him if anything had happened to Kieran.

The storm was getting worse, and the rain was coming down in sheets now as thunder roared overhead. The thick forest underbrush was getting soggy, and it made running tiring, but on the plus side, most of the beasts that prowled the night had clearly decided to hunker down at this point and wait it out.

Vail's eyes were almost a solid silver—he'd allowed his bloodlust to rise to give him that extra boost of speed. I'd done the same. We were closing in on Samara and the group now, but they'd changed direction slightly. Still heading south but angling west towards House Salvatore.

It was risky to go there to seek shelter—if that's what Samara and the others intended. Dominique was a bit of a wild card. If I were Carmilla, she would have been one of the first Houses I'd use the crown on and force their subservience. Samara was clever, and she knew her aunt better than I did; this must have occurred to her as well, which meant something bad enough had happened to make it worth the risk.

I ran faster.

Almost there. Just a little farther.

The tree line broke, and a flash of lighting revealed a small group of people on the main road to House Salvatore.

"Samara! Kieran!" I called out as I sprinted towards them, only to halt when a half-mad Furie with glowing golden eyes landed in front of me.

"Cali! No!" I heard Samara scream.

The fact that neither I nor Vail drew our weapons was probably the only reason Cali didn't follow through on her attack. Her bright eyes dimmed as she took us in and realized we weren't a threat. There was something still off about her though. I'd met Cali a few times, and she'd always had this swaggering arrogance about her. There was none of that to be seen right now, and it made my panic increase until I saw Kieran shove his way past the Furie, as if that wasn't courting death.

"You're okay," I breathed out as Kieran wrapped his arms around me.

"'Okay' probably isn't the right word, but I'm not seriously injured."

I didn't like the *not seriously* part of that statement, so I pulled back and quickly started scouring him for wounds, tugging at his clothing where it was ripped so I could see the bare skin beneath it.

"Drav," he said softly, pulling my attention away from my manic inspection to his beautiful brown eyes threaded with gold. "I'm fine. I promise."

I let out a shuddered breath and nodded. "I'm not leaving your or Samara's sides until this is over. Not for any reason."

Kieran kissed me and then breathed across my lips, "Good."

"What happene—"

My question was cut off by a rumbling growl and someone crashing into Vail. Two figures rolled across the rain-soaked ground, and I tugged Kieran out of their path as they traded blows.

"Nyx!" Vail grunted. "What the fuck are you doing?"

Nyx? The young ranger who was part of Vail's ranger unit and was friends with Samara? Why were they attacking Vail?

Samara rushed forward but was cut off by Cali, who dove towards the two brawling Moroi and broke them apart. She grabbed Nyx by the throat and held them back when they tried to lunge for Vail again.

I started when I saw Nyx's eyes—they were a solid midnight blue.

Even when I let my bloodlust rise, I still had faint traces of blue in my eyes. Vail's silver eyes had small dark spots of grey, hinting at his tenuous hold on humanity. Samara was the only Moroi I'd ever encountered whose eyes turned the solid color of their bloodlust while remaining herself.

Nyx was clearly not themself; otherwise, they wouldn't have been attacking Vail this way. Between that and their eye color . . . Nyx had turned Strigoi.

"Calm yourself!" Cali commanded and shook Nyx as if they weighed nothing.

I pushed Kieran behind me as I prepared to defend him, but he just threaded his fingers through mine and moved to stand by my side.

"It's not what you think," Samara said as she appeared at my other side, her expression forlorn.

Roth and their family appeared, quietly creating a half circle around Vail and Cali, who were still struggling to keep Nyx under control. They all wore matching expressions of sadness. Alaric stood on the edges of everyone gathered, frowning as if he didn't know what to do. It took me a moment to realize there were two people missing.

"Where are Adrienne and Emil?" It was hard to see more than ten feet in front of me with the rain, but my magic didn't sense any other Moroi in the immediate vicinity.

For a few seconds, it felt like even the storm paused at my question.

Then Nyx let out an anguished scream and renewed their attack on Vail.

"Get him the fuck out of here," Cali grunted as she tried to hold Nyx back. Even with the rain, the scent of Furie blood filled the air as Nyx's claws tore through her skin.

Samara surged forward and grabbed Vail, pulling him

away as Cali finally gave up and shot up into the sky with Nyx clamped against her, flying off into the raging storm.

"What's going on?" I asked Kieran.

Mournful eyes looked at me, but before he could answer, Vail released a pained sound.

I looked over my shoulder just in time to see the Marshal of House Harker fall to his knees in front of two bloodied bodies. My magic only sensed the living, and I got nothing from the two broken forms in front of Vail.

Any hopes I'd had that Adrienne and Emil had gone scouting ahead were dashed. I hadn't known them well, but they'd seemed like good people, and they'd come through for Samara when she'd needed them most. For that alone, I would have been loyal to them for the rest of their days.

But it seemed that their days were no more.

"Carmilla found us," Kieran said quietly. "She used the crown on Emil and Nyx. Ordered them to kill Adrienne. She killed Emil . . . but she couldn't bring herself to do the same to Nyx."

My mind flashed back to Selia—the woman who had raised me when my own mother couldn't be bothered. Velika had ordered her to kill me one day, and in less than a second, the person who I knew for a fact had loved me had attempted to rip out my throat. I knew the power of that fucking crown better than anyone.

But if Nyx had turned Strigoi . . . why hadn't the others put them down?

I had my answer a moment later when Cali and Nyx joined us again. The latter still had dark blue eyes, but now there were the faintest lines of bright blue running through them.

They'd come back. Shock rolled through me. I'd never heard of a Strigoi regaining their humanity. There was still something not right about Nyx though. Their movements had a predatory quality to them that was unique to Strigoi. Something about it just set my instincts on edge.

But they made no move to attack anyone and seemed to be in control of themself. I still not so subtly maneuvered myself to stand between them and Kieran. Samara was far enough away that I was confident I could stop Nyx if they tried to attack her.

The young ranger only had eyes for Vail though, who finally seemed to sense their attention. He raised his head in a daze to look at the not-quite Strigoi.

"She did this," Nyx hissed in a low, otherworldly voice. "The woman you so loyally serve. She ordered their deaths." For a split second, the bright blue vanished from their eyes before appearing again. "I still taste Adrienne's blood in my mouth. I don't think I'll ever stop remembering it."

Kieran's fingers tightened around mine, and we all watched as the strong and resilient Marshal of House Harker looked at his two fallen rangers . . . and broke.

CHAPTER SEVENTEEN

—

Samara

"How are we going to handle this?" Alaric's sharp green eyes looked down at the castle from the ridge we'd stopped to rest on. The storm had finally broken, and the rays of the early morning sun were starting to peek through the clouds.

I studied House Salvatore from where I stood next to Alaric. It was a risk to stop here; they were the closest geographically to the Sovereign House. To my knowledge, Carmilla hadn't come here since acquiring the crown, and I hadn't heard of Dominique, the Head of the House, nor her Heir, Aniela, visiting Carmilla. Vail hadn't either.

It seemed odd that Carmilla wouldn't have immediately used the crown to secure her control of House Salvatore, given how close they were.

She didn't need to do anything about House Harker since everyone there would be loyal to her—at least until they learned the truth of what was going on. Some might still follow Carmilla, but I knew many wouldn't be keen on someone manipulating the minds of other Moroi.

For now, House Harker would be low on her list. She already had plans in place for House Laurent and House Corvinus, and I didn't think she'd bother trying to use the crown against House Devereux. If I were her, I'd gain control of the other Houses and then wipe out Devereux—they were too powerful to be left standing.

That left House Salvatore and House Tepes as the wild cards.

Movement to my left drew my attention. Nyx strode towards the ledge, and my heart thudded, as it seemed like they were just going to keep walking. Before I could move, Cali was there. She didn't touch Nyx, but they slowed at her presence, and both came to a stop an inch from the edge.

Nyx hadn't spoken for hours. Not since their outburst at Vail, who had also been quiet after that. I fought the urge to turn and look at the two freshly dug graves behind us. There wasn't time to bring Adrienne and Emil back to House Harker, so we'd chosen this spot for their final resting place. Draven had used his magic to dig deep into the earth, to ensure no beasts would disturb them, and then coaxed some roots to stretch over the tops of their graves for good measure.

Absently, I rubbed my chest, just over my heart. I grieved the loss of the rangers, but it was nothing to what Vail was feeling right now. His grief was like a poker that had been thrust into flames. I could feel the rage beginning to burn, growing hotter by the hour.

We needed to determine if House Salvatore was compromised and warn them of Carmilla if they weren't, but Nyx couldn't set foot inside that castle. We knew they weren't Strigoi —not completely anyway—but they'd slipped more than once on the way here and tried to attack Vail. If the Salvatore rangers saw Nyx lose it like that, they'd kill the ranger.

Strigoi were always put down.

I didn't know what was going on with Nyx, but I wasn't going to give up on them.

"Celestina," I addressed Roth's mother, who was standing

not far behind Nyx and Cali. "Would you and your family be willing to escort Nyx back to your House? And keep them . . . comfortable?" *Don't kill them or allow them to harm others.*

"Of course." She hesitated before looking at Roth as they moved to stand next to me.

"I'm staying with Samara," Roth declared.

"Maybe it would be better if you—" I started, only to have my words cut off as one of Roth's ropes wound around my lower face, covering my mouth.

"Babe, it's in your best interest that you don't finish that sentence." Roth glared at me. "I'm staying."

I nodded in reluctant acceptance. Part of me was happy they were staying, but another part wished Roth were going back to House Devereux, where they'd be surrounded by thick walls and quite possibly the most homicidal bloodline of all the Moroi.

"Take care of our favorite sib," Desmond rumbled as he gave me and then Kieran, Alaric, and Draven a pointed look.

"There will be consequences if you don't," Taivan added. Then the two enormous Moroi swept Roth up into a hug, which resulted in some very creative curses being thrown about before they moved off to wait by the tree line.

Roth shuffled on their feet as Celestina and Severen approached.

"I know we messed up when you were younger," Celestina said softly. "We never meant to make you feel unwanted or like you were less than because you're not interested in the warrior path."

"We thought giving you space was what you wanted." Severen reached out slowly, giving Roth time to pull back, but when they didn't, he laid a hand on their shoulder. "Then we let ourselves get caught up in training your brothers and the rest of the rangers. You seemed happy enough to spend time with Thessalia that we just . . . left you alone."

"But we have always loved you, child." Celestina rested her hand on Roth's other shoulder. "And we're so fucking proud of who you grew up to be."

Roth's eyes got a little glossy. "I love you." Then they glanced at their brothers. "And those big idiots too."

Celestina and Severen smiled at their youngest child, and despite everything that had happened last night and the grief I was feeling, my heart felt a little lighter at seeing Roth and their family repairing what had been broken.

I stepped around Roth to give them another minute with their parents and walked over to Nyx. They were looking over the ridge and didn't acknowledge my presence. Cali and I traded a look.

"Nyx," I said carefully. "You're going to go with the Devereuxes, okay?"

The ranger turned their head to look at me. There was something unnerving about the way they moved now. The Nyx I'd always known had moved with this lightness, like despite all the fucked-up shit in the world, they'd never let it truly get to them. Nyx had been quick to smile and easy to befriend.

Now, the easygoing ranger was nowhere in sight. Even in control of their bloodlust, Nyx moved like a Strigoi. Cold and predatory.

"I'm one of the monsters now." A chilling, dark laugh spilt from their lips. "Shouldn't you just kill me?"

Something deep inside me cracked at the hollowness of their words.

Fuck. This.

My hand snapped out, and I wrapped it around Nyx's neck, letting my nails shift to claws that tore into their skin. They didn't even try to stop me. Just looked at me with dark eyes that *welcomed* death.

I let my own bloodlust rise until I knew my eyes were just as dark as theirs.

"We all have monsters crawling beneath our skin—yours is just no longer hidden." My fingers tightened, and more blood dripped down their neck. "You are my *friend*, Nyx, and I won't let you go."

A small amount of light blue bled back into their eyes like glowing rivers in the dark. "Promise me you'll make her pay."

"I promise," I swore and released my hold on their neck. "Stay alive, Nyx."

They held my gaze for a long moment before giving me a deep nod. Then those new strange eyes of theirs flicked to Cali, who just arched a brow at them.

"A little insanity is good for the soul, my pretty fanged friend."

Nyx's eyes darkened in a way that I didn't think was remotely connected to their new not-quite-Strigoi status, and a familiar, lazy smile stretched across their lips. For a second, it was almost like I was looking at my old friend before Carmilla had broken them. "See you around, my beautiful winged friend."

Cali blinked as Nyx moved like a shadow, sliding between us and striding towards where Roth's family was waiting for them. Nyx nodded in farewell towards Alaric, Kieran, and Draven but didn't spare Vail a single glance.

I rejoined the others, Vail moving a little closer, and Cali followed me. "Alright, let's go see what we're dealing with. Carmilla might be licking her wounds after Cali's dramatic appearance"—the Furie snorted at my words—"but I have no doubt she's already plotting. We shouldn't plan on staying here too long one way or another."

If House Salvatore was compromised, we might have to fight our way out, and even if they weren't, I didn't want to stay so close to the Sovereign House.

"Long enough to get cleaned up though, right?" Kieran frowned down at his tunic, which had once been a light cream but was now stained with blood, mud, and gods knew what else. "And maybe something to eat?"

"I'd also like to snag a whip from their armory," Draven chimed in. "I'm feeling a little inadequate without it, especially since Roth has those fancy ropes and you have your clever knives." He looked jealously at the daggers strapped to my thighs that I'd imbued with blood magic.

"Sure," I drawled. "Anyone else have any requests?"

"I want to check out their library." Roth's eyes lit up. "Might need help stealing some shit."

We all chuckled. It felt weird to be joking around, given . . . everything, but I thought we all recognized that we needed some sort of lightness right now. Only Vail didn't join in.

"I'll wait outside the walls. My presence will set them on edge. If I don't receive an all-clear signal from you within one hour, then I'm walking through that front gate. They're welcome to try to stop me." Cali wrapped her dark wings around her shoulders like a cloak, pulled the hood of her cowl up, hiding her distinctive red hair, and started down the path that led to House Salvatore.

Unease rippled through me. Cali had a massive overprotective streak when it came to me and Rynn. She wasn't wrong that her being with us would draw attention, but I was an *Heir*. Only Aniela or Dominique could deny our entry, and they would have to come out and do it in person.

I watched my friend disappear down the trail. Something told me Cali didn't want to go in there because she didn't trust her control. It felt like someone had wrapped a cold hand around my heart and squeezed. For as long as I could remember, people had been terrified of Cali.

I had never been scared of Calypso Rayne—the most powerful Furie to ever exist—but I was sure as shit scared *for* her.

Kill Carmilla. Stabilize the Moroi Houses. Do . . . something about the wraiths. Try to mend things between the Moroi and Velesians. Figure out what the fuck was going on with Cali.

Gods, I would give Vail's right hand right now just to have an easy-to-fix problem so I could get that little thrill at actually solving something.

I thought about our night in the cave that felt like ages ago but had only been a couple of weeks. Maybe his left hand. If I ever decided to forgive him one day, that right hand was *talented*.

A laugh bubbled up my throat and got stuck. Was this what it was like to lose your mind? Because I was drained in every sense of the word. Emotionally. Mentally. Physically.

The world could get fucked.

Suddenly, I felt the weight of several gazes on me, and I briefly wondered if my manic laugh had actually made it past my lips. Then I realized that everyone except Vail had started to follow Cali but stopped when they realized I wasn't moving.

Because I was having a minor mental breakdown. No big deal.

I caught Draven's attention, knowing Kieran and Alaric would be stubborn about this, and briefly slid my gaze to Vail before giving Draven a heavy look. He pursed his lips but jerked his head in a nod, then proceeded to pull Alaric and Kieran away, but not before they both leveled a death glare at Vail.

The Marshal failed to notice. He just stared down at House Salvatore with a distant look in his eyes.

I stood next to him in weighted silence. I was far from forgiving Vail for what he'd done, but I no longer had any doubts about his loyalty. Carmilla had severely miscalculated by targeting the rangers. Maybe she hadn't realized that, despite Vail helping us escape, he hadn't completely turned against her. He would never side with her now. The rangers— especially those rangers—were Vail's family.

"She dies." He finally turned away from the horizon to look at me with eyes of silver fire. "There will be no deal. No life of imprisonment when this is all done. Carmilla fucking dies."

The fury that had been slowly building in Vail ignited into a bonfire that swallowed his grief and forged it into something new.

I let him see the rage I was feeling before I allowed myself to look at the graves of our fallen friends. Carmilla was someone I'd looked up to for most of my life. In many ways, she was the reason I was who I was. Not to mention that she was my last living blood relative . . . which was her doing, since she'd done nothing when my parents had been murdered. It didn't matter that she hadn't been the one to order their deaths. She could have stopped them.

Nobody had forced Carmilla on this path. She'd chosen to be the villain and played us all for fools.

I turned away from the graves to look at Vail. "Painfully. She dies painfully."

<hr>

THE MOOD inside House Salvatore was tense. I suspected if I were anyone other than an Heir, the guards at the front gate would have turned us away. As it was, they had granted us entry, and we'd been quickly ushered into a guest wing.

Half a dozen rangers stood outside our door, and the message was very clear that we were to wait. I assumed for Dominique or Aniela, but the rangers weren't exactly forthcoming with information.

It didn't feel like a trap though, because the air reeked of fear and uncertainty.

The room we were in did have a bathing chamber, so we all took turns cleaning ourselves up as best we could; although, without fresh clothes to change into, there wasn't much we could do.

"We'll give it another ten minutes," I said quietly. The rangers would no doubt hear anything we said, so we were all being careful with our words. "Then I'll insist on seeing Aniela or Dominique."

Everyone nodded while Roth went back to frowning at the small collection of books in the room, as if they were personally offended at the meager offerings. Kieran was cuddled up on the small settee with Draven, his head resting on the prince's shoulder. I hadn't gotten a chance to speak with him alone since our encounters with Demetri and Carmilla. Demetri's words about him being a courtier had no doubt struck at an old wound. I scowled, wishing I could kill my ex-husband all over again.

I caught Draven's eye, and something passed between us, then he gave me a tight smile before kissing the top of Kieran's head. A soothing sensation passed down the bond, and I assumed it was from him because Vail was currently pacing the room like a trapped animal.

Definitely not soothing.

Alaric walked out of the washroom, and for a solid ten seconds, I stopped thinking about all the ways we were fucked.

He carried a damp shirt, leaving his carved chest and abs on display. Like Kieran, Alaric was built on the leaner side. Unlike his best friend though, Alaric spent a lot of time running and rock climbing—something I'd only recently learned about him.

"You're drooling," he said dryly as he closed the distance between us, the corners of his lips curling up into the smallest of smiles. "And you missed a spot."

He used his thumb to brush at my jawline. I closed my eyes and enjoyed his touch. It still didn't feel real that Alaric Lockwood was being affectionate with me.

"I could really go for some hot springs right now," I mused.

Alaric's thumb went still, and I cracked my eyes open to find him looking at me with such wanton desire that my heart started beating faster.

A soft laugh came from the couch as Kieran stirred in Draven's arms. "I think Alaric would go for the dessert this time."

Roth snorted, which made me suspect Kieran had told them about the time Alaric had walked in on the two of us getting hot and heavy and Kieran had asked Alaric if he was there for "dessert."

"I do love how sweet you taste," Alaric said, never taking his eyes off me as his thumb started stroking my jawline again.

A spear of jealousy slammed into me, and I inhaled sharply before glancing at Vail, who was still pacing the room—now with clenched fists.

Despite how frayed our bond was, his emotions were practically screaming down it.

I opened my mouth to say something to hopefully calm him down a bit just so I could think without getting bombarded by his feelings, when I heard the faint sounds of footsteps from the hall outside our room. Kieran and Draven detangled and smoothly got to their feet. I pushed feelings of gratitude down the bond as Draven nudged Kieran behind himself. It seemed unlikely that we'd be attacked now, given that they'd shown us to a guest room and not a dungeon, but after the past week, I wasn't sure anything would surprise me anymore.

Vail stalked over to stand by my side, something that earned him a warning look from Draven that I also felt echoed down the bond. Argh. It was really confusing to feel emotions that weren't mine. Hopefully I'd get used to it over time.

I glanced at Alaric—who'd thankfully put his shirt back on, because if anyone else drooled over him I'd carve their eyes out

—and jerked my head towards Roth. He pursed his lips but did as I requested and went to join them.

If Salvatore did decide to attack us, we were spread out across the room and would force them to divide their attention.

The door slammed open, and a beautiful, very pissed-off redhead stormed into the room. Usually the Salvatore Heir exuded a sultry energy while she glided through life. It was often easy to forget that Aniela was a ruthless predator while she batted her long, dark eyelashes.

That was not the case now.

"What the fuck is going on, Samara?" She crashed to a halt in front of me, green eyes flashing in warning. Only two rangers followed her into the room, but given the reputation of the twin sisters, that was all the backup Aniela needed.

Petra and Brennan bared their teeth while burnt umber eyes shone brightly against their rich brown skin. The dual Marshals of House Salvatore.

"You tell me, Aniela," I responded coolly while I arched an eyebrow. "Things seem a little tense around here, and shoving the Heir of another House into a room like this and locking the door isn't exactly good manners."

Cunning eyes searched mine, and I responded in kind. If Aniela had been mind-fucked by Carmilla, I would think she would act like her normal self-assured self and try to keep us placated while she informed my aunt that we were here.

Granted, she could have sent a striker with a message while we'd been sequestered and was now putting on a show to see how we would react, but I didn't think that was the case. Behind the anger brimming in her eyes was something else. Fear.

Something had happened that had put the usually unshakeable Heir on alert.

"Answer the fucking question," Aniela growled. Thin lines

of a green so light, it was practically white wove their way through her green eyes. *Interesting.* I could count on one hand the number of times I'd seen Aniela let her bloodlust rise.

Aniela liked to be underestimated, relying on that pretty face to distract the foolish while she angled a dagger at their backs.

The question was . . . was this just another act? Was there a knife at my back?

"I'll tell you," I said slowly, "but first . . . where is Dominique?"

I had a split second to see Aniela's eyes turn almost a solid white before she threw herself at me. My back crashed against the low table in front of the settee, and I let out a harsh grunt as something sharp jammed its way between my ribs.

The sounds of fighting filled the room, but I was a bit preoccupied with keeping Aniela from stabbing me again. I wrapped one hand around her throat, and the other clung to her wrist when she tried to pull the dagger free.

"You did this!" She let out a strangled hiss as she tried to get my hand off her neck. The blade in my side wasn't great, but we both knew I'd recover from that. She wouldn't recover if I tore her throat out, which was why her claws were digging into my wrist.

"Not. Your. Enemy," I ground out.

"Liar!" she growled and twisted the knife.

I gasped as pain laced up my side. Fuck this. I shoved my hips up to unbalance her, earning myself another flash of pain just as I yanked her down by the throat.

Aniela didn't let go of my wrist, so her entire body dipped forward as I leaned up to slam my forehead into her nose.

Blood erupted as Aniela shrieked and her grip on my wrist slipped before I shoved her off me. A fresh wave of pain tore through me as she pulled the knife with her, but I didn't let it slow me down as I lunged forward and hammered another punch to her face.

"Aniela!" one of the Marshals screamed. I rarely heard them speak, so I couldn't tell them apart by voice.

Everyone in the room seemed to freeze, the sounds of fighting abruptly stopping, but I kept my attention on Aniela, trusting Alaric to keep Roth safe and Kieran, Draven . . . and Vail to keep the others off my back.

The Salvatore Heir panted beneath me, her nearly white eyes feral with rage. I held one of my blood daggers at her throat while my other hand caught her wrist before she could raise her own dagger in defense.

"Do it," she spat. "I don't know what you did to my cousin, but I sure as fuck won't be your lapdog. So fucking kill me already."

I narrowed my eyes. "Dominique is with Carmilla, isn't she?"

Aniela went still, and I knew I had guessed right. That alone wouldn't have set her off like this though. I quickly thought through several possibilities, not letting go of Aniela's wrist or decreasing the pressure of my blade against her skin.

"Let me guess." I held Aniela's gaze. "Dominique did something completely out of character. Maybe issued an order that you know she would never give and one that you don't want to follow?"

"Won't," Aniela whispered. "*Won't* follow."

Slowly, I pulled the dagger away from Aniela's throat. I didn't release my hold on her wrist until I rolled back onto the balls of my feet, then I smoothly rose and took a couple of steps back. A quick glance around the room showed everyone a little bloody, but there didn't appear to be any major injuries.

Petra and Brennan sported bloody lips. They looked damn near identical, but Petra's eyes were a touch darker, which was how I knew it was her giving Vail a look that promised death.

He smiled at her in return.

More rangers had poured into the room while I'd been fighting Aniela. To my annoyance, Alaric and Roth were standing next to Kieran and Draven; the four of them had held off the flood of newcomers. I sent Alaric a cool look for failing to keep Roth out of the fighting, only to yelp when one of Roth's ropes snapped against my ass.

Hard.

Roth arched an eyebrow at me while I rubbed my soft flesh, trying to ease the sting. They smirked at me as the thin ropes slipped through the air to wind back around their forearms.

I slid the dagger back into the sheath on my thigh and gave a pointed look at the others. Kieran and Draven immediately put their weapons away, but Alaric hesitated for a second before doing the same. Silver eyes glared at me for a long moment before Vail resheathed his sword and threw a dagger back to Petra . . . a little harder than necessary.

Oh, no wonder she was so pissed. Vail had managed to at least partially disarm her.

"So," I drawled as Aniela rose to her feet, "how about we try this again? Maybe start with talking? We can always stab each other later."

CHAPTER EIGHTEEN

—

Samara

THE RANGERS who had burst into the room filed out at some silent command from Aniela. I settled onto the largest of the settees that almost resembled a crescent moon. Kieran sat to my left with Draven on his other side. Alaric narrowly beat Roth to sit next to me and earned himself a sour look that he didn't seem the least bit concerned about.

That left Vail standing awkwardly by himself, since Aniela and her two Marshals had claimed the other settee.

"Vail, would you mind letting *our friend* know that we're alright for now." I gave him a pointed look. Cali might have been acting strange, but I had no doubt that she would keep her word and absolutely slaughter her way through House Salvatore if we didn't let her know we were okay, and it was getting really close to her one-hour mark.

"Brennan, go with him," Aniela ordered. "Just let Cali in."

I arched an eyebrow at the Salvatore Heir, and she rolled her eyes. "You wouldn't be worried about a single Moroi breaking into our keep, and it is well-known that you, Cali, and Rynn are a bit of a package deal."

Something bothered me about that statement, even as I

made a noise of agreement. How was she so sure it wasn't Rynn? Sure, Cali was scarier, but as Aniela had said, Rynn was also a known friend of mine, and Velesians were tricky.

Vail started to stiffly walk towards the door behind where I was seated, and I reached up to grab his arm. He halted as my fingers closed around his forearm, dark grey eyes meeting mine as I felt his fingers graze my arm almost tentatively.

I didn't know exactly where I stood with Aniela. I was fairly certain she wasn't under Carmilla's control, but that didn't mean we were on the same side, which meant I had to be careful about the information I offered up.

"Go." I held Vail's unflinching stare. "Come back quickly."

Strong, thick fingers tightened around my forearm as he bent down to whisper in my ear, "I'll set whatever pace I damn well feel like, Heir."

It was like a dozen emotions collided inside me. Lust. Amusement. Rage. Somehow, I managed to keep all of that off my face as I gave him a brief nod and released my grip.

Vail's fingers lingered for another second before they dropped away and he strode towards the door. He didn't look back as he left.

Once again, I found myself confused as fuck about Vail Ferenc.

Argh.

"Tell us where your cousin is, Aniela, and why you reacted to our presence the way you did." I returned my attention to the Salvatore Heir and shoved my confused feelings about Vail aside. "And I'll tell you what we know."

Aniela looked at me for a long moment, and I got the impression she was searching for something in my expression. She didn't find it.

"Two days ago, Dominique was summoned to the Sovereign House by Carmilla." Her mouth tightened before she threw the towel she'd been using to clean the blood off herself onto the floor. If she wanted me to feel bad about that, she'd have to try harder. My side had mostly healed, but it still smarted from where she'd freaking stabbed me. "It's a short flight for our strikers from here to there. Before the sun set that day, we received a message from my cousin."

Petra held a folded letter out to us, and I reached for it, but Alaric grabbed it first. Roth read it over his shoulder, and both of their expressions grew grimmer by the second.

"Dominique has ordered the majority of the Salvatore rangers to set up a perimeter around the edges of House Devereux territory." Alaric raised a brow. "We've also all been declared traitors, and House Salvatore is under orders to capture most of us alive if they see us."

"*Most?*" I eyed Aniela while my hand slid towards the dagger on my right thigh.

Petra started to go for her weapon but stopped when Aniela held up a hand. "How did she sign the letter, Alaric?" she asked, not taking her eyes off me.

"She just put her name," Alaric said. "Dominique."

A smile that didn't reach her eyes touched Aniela's heart-shaped mouth. "My cousin might be Dominique to everyone else, but to family, she's always been Mika."

"She's fighting it," Draven mused.

I leaned forward and twisted slightly to look around Kieran so I could see Draven better, letting my hand drop away from the dagger on my thigh. "Even with the power boost of the crown being united, it's still not enough to fully control those of House bloodlines." My brows furrowed together. "It's not happy about how it's being used, so maybe it's also leaving loopholes in the minds of those it's wielded against—and Dominique seized it."

"So it's true then." Aniela traded a weighted look with Petra. "Velika had a way to control our minds, and now Carmilla has it."

"You knew about the crown?" I went still as surprise flickered through me. Up until recently, I'd never suspected such a thing existed, let alone that Velika had been wielding it.

"Why do you think we stayed to ourselves so much?" Aniela said dryly. "It was impossible to know who we could trust. Everyone thought it was because Dominique was young and inexperienced—we leaned into that, even if it did make our House appear weaker."

"How?" Roth narrowed their eyes at Aniela. "How did you find out about the crown?"

"We didn't actually know it was a crown," Aniela admitted. "There were little things that alerted Dominique's parents to something not quite right. Sometimes, their minds would feel . . . tired after visiting with Queen Velika. And there were other things—advisors and courtiers visiting the Sovereign House and coming back slightly different. Not like major personality changes, but saying things that were out of character."

"The soul crown is a Fae artifact," I explained. "Velika only had half of it. She was able to bind souls to obey her, but the effects were temporary. My aunt has both pieces. It's considerably more powerful now. House bloodlines still have some protection against it—but clearly, they're not immune, given that Dominique has been compromised."

"You said *they*." Aniela narrowed her eyes. "Are you not including yourself in the House bloodlines?"

I pursed my lips as I thought about what to say. We needed allies to defeat Carmilla, and the more information they had, the better prepared they would be. But I was still coming to terms with the fact that I was half Fae . . . and that the crown was my birthright.

Everything was far more broken between the Houses than I had thought. They wouldn't be happy to learn that the crown that could steal their will and control their minds wanted to be united with me. I had no intention of ruling over everyone, but they would never believe that—I certainly wouldn't trust any of them with that kind of power.

"Your father had Fae blood, didn't he?" Petra's sharp eyes studied my face.

I barely managed to stifle the startled motion at the question. It felt like my heartbeat plunged for a few seconds before beating rapidly.

Petra and her twin sister were the same generation as me but older by several decades. They'd served Dominique's parents before they'd been killed.

Oh, shit. Did Dominique know her father hadn't been killed in that attack? That he'd actually been taken prisoner and Velika had experimented on him with the crown? That she'd been trying to figure out how to use it on House bloodlines?

According to Draven, she'd never truly been successful, but she had broken him down enough that he'd turned Strigoi and had been well and truly mad by that point.

Draven had killed him as a mercy.

I decided to not volunteer that information for now. Nothing could change the past, and it was irrelevant to our current situation. Still, I'd have to monitor for any signs that they knew and make sure Draven hadn't been responsible for the former Salvatore Head's imprisonment and torture.

It would be unfortunate to have to kill Dominique and Aniela—and probably their Marshals—over a pointless attempt at vengeance, but I'd do it. Nobody fucked with what was mine.

And Draven was absolutely *mine*.

I tucked away that thought as something to deal with later —or maybe I'd just take the truth of what happened to the grave—and pondered how to answer the question of my lineage. Maybe it was time for the truth, even if that was an odd sentiment in our culture. If the Moroi Houses were going to survive long-term, we'd need to start trusting each other a little more. With some things anyway.

"My father was half Fae." I left out the royalty part because I wasn't ready to share that just yet; plus, I wanted to have more information. All I had was the claim of a sentient crown. "I only learned this recently." I narrowed my gaze at Petra. "What made you suspect he had Fae blood?"

The corners of her lips tilted up ever so slightly. It was the closest I'd ever seen her come to a true smile and not just a baring of teeth.

"He saved me once. I was traveling alone and had been injured thanks to a run-in with a large howler pack. My blood drew the attention of some kusu, and I thought I was done for." She grimaced. "Damn near lost my leg when one of them got me with their pincers. Before they could finish me off, roots shot out of the ground and tore the kusu apart."

Note to self, definitely prioritize learning magic. I loved my blood daggers, but being able to summon roots out of the ground to, at the very least, hold monsters at bay would come in handy.

"You never told me that." Aniela looked at her Marshal. There wasn't anger or reprisal in her eyes—she looked more curious than anything.

Petra's shoulders rose in what I was pretty sure was the smallest shrug I'd ever seen. "When I asked him about it, he said I was delirious and seeing things." A faint smile stretched across her lips for a second. "I was bleeding heavily from head trauma, and my right leg had been holding on by a few shredded tendons, so I wasn't in any shape to argue, and I never mentioned it because I had no proof. Plus, he saved my life that day, and it seemed in poor form to go spreading rumors about him."

"Fair." Aniela nodded and turned her attention back to me.

"So you also have Fae blood, and you think this protects you from the effects of the crown?"

"It is my father's bloodline that protects me, yes," I answered. It was the truth—in a sleight of hand kind of way. It wasn't just that my father was Fae; it was that he belonged to the Seelie royal bloodline that was responsible for the creation of the crown in the first place.

At least according to the smart-ass Fae artifact. The wraith I'd spoken with seemed to back that up. Still . . . it'd be nice to get my hands on some unbiased information to shed light on all of this.

Aniela glanced at the door before her eyes flicked back to me. "How do we break the control Carmilla has over Dominique?"

"It's hard to say," Draven answered. "My mother only had one half of the crown. Typically, she had to renew her hold on someone at least once a month, sometimes sooner if they were particularly strong of will. With both halves of the crown united, I imagine it will last longer."

"We could ask it . . . the crown, I mean," I said in an even tone, like it wasn't crazy to suggest talking to an inanimate object.

"Come again?" Aniela arched an eyebrow.

"Phrasing," Kieran muttered under his breath, earning himself a glare from Alaric.

"The crown is sentient," I explained. "It spoke in my mind while I was being held captive at the Sovereign House."

"You're saying the Fae created a crown capable of stealing someone's will . . . and gave it a mind of its own?" Aniela stared at me wide-eyed. "Are you fucking shitting me right now? How is that even possible?"

"Like with most things that involve the Fae"—I rubbed my forehead—"I have no idea, but it definitely talked to me, and it has quite the personality."

Again, Aniela looked towards the door. This time, I noticed the tension in her shoulders. Was she expecting someone else? Or was she worried about Cali getting here? If it was the latter . . . why?

"Something on your mind, Aniela?" I watched her carefully as she swallowed and met my gaze again.

"I don't know who to trust, Samara," she admitted. "I've always liked you, even when Dominique threw you in with Carmilla—who she was always suspicious of because of your aunt's friendship with Queen Velika—but Ary trusts you."

A hint of softness entered her eyes. There was something between Aniela and Ary—the Heir of House Tepes. He was definitely carrying a torch for her, and up until this moment, I hadn't been sure she'd felt the same.

I didn't say anything, and the others followed my lead. Aniela was hiding something, and whatever it was, she feared Cali learning about it.

The moment of vulnerability in Aniela's expression left and was replaced by grim determination. Then she squared her shoulders as she sat straighter and raised her chin while holding my gaze.

"Rynn is locked up in our dungeon."

Well, fuck.

"We haven't harmed her," Aniela rushed on before wincing. "But she was quite injured when the rangers found her two days ago. She kept attacking us when we tried to see to her wounds, so we put her in a cell as much for our safety as hers. Hostilities seem to be rising against the Velesians. I thought it best to keep her out of sight."

"Two days ago," I murmured and then asked sharply, "Does Dominique know she's here?"

If she did, it seemed likely that Carmilla knew as well, and my aunt would absolutely try to capture Rynn as a way to control me. There was nothing I wouldn't do for Rynn and Cali.

"No," Aniela said softly. "The rangers found her in the badlands. She didn't arrive here until after I got that message from Mika. I haven't sent a response back yet."

"Okay." I nodded and rose to my feet. "Aniela, come with me to fetch Rynn. Everyone else, stay here and keep Cali distracted when she arrives."

"Absolutely not," Petra and Alaric said at the same time before glowering at each other.

"Perhaps one of us should go with you," Kieran suggested.

I shook my head. "Cali is . . . testy right now. It'll make me feel better knowing you're all here to help keep her calm. Besides, Aniela picked a fight with me once and lost—badly."

"You kicked me right in the cunt." Aniela glared at me before rising from the settee.

I rolled my eyes. "You punched my tit. Twice."

"What type of fight was this exactly?" Both of Kieran's brows rose.

"A drunk one," Aniela and I said at once.

"Why don't I go get Rynn," Alaric volunteered.

"No." I made a halting motion when Alaric started to stand. "I haven't spoken to Rynn since we separated at Lake Malov. I need to make sure she doesn't lose her shit when she sees Vail—and more importantly, that she doesn't tell Cali."

"What exactly did Vail do?" Aniela arched a dark red brow at me.

"It doesn't matter," I said tightly, not wanting to go into detail about Vail's betrayal and then have to explain why the fuck he wasn't dead in a ditch somewhere, or at least locked up in a cell. I realized I was absently rubbing my chest just over my heart and dropped my hand.

"Funny," Aniela drawled. "It *sounds* like it matters."

I gave her an obscene gesture that had her barking out a laugh.

"I'll be fine," I promised, making eye contact with Kieran, Draven, and Roth before lingering on Alaric, who was clenching his jaw so hard, I was worried he'd crack a tooth. I bent down and kissed him with the intention of it being a quick, reassuring type of thing, but when he wrapped his hand in my hair and pulled me close, I lost myself until someone cleared their throat.

"Cali's gonna be here any minute." Roth gave me an amused grin. "You can make out with grumpy-pants later." Then they shoved Alaric's face away so they could lean forward and kiss me. This time, it was a quick one because they pulled back and pointedly looked at the door.

"So you've got the wicked prince, the heartthrob courtier, the gorgeous advisor, and the cunning scholar . . ." Aniela asked as we walked to the door. "Bit greedy, aren't you?"

I snorted. "Jealous?"

"Little bit, yeah."

"Uh, how exactly are we supposed to keep Cali occupied, Sam?" Kieran asked just as Aniela and I started to leave.

"I'm sure you'll think of something, Kier," I said confidently. If anyone excelled at small talk, it was Kieran. "But feel free to tell her about Dominique. We won't be long." I glanced at Aniela. "Right?"

I didn't know exactly where the dungeon was in House Salvatore, but if it was like House Harker and the Sovereign House, the entrance would be towards the center of the first floor, which we were on.

"Fifteen minutes at most."

"When we're back, we'll plan our next move—with Rynn."

On that final note, Aniela and I started at a quick pace down the hallway. I still couldn't believe Rynn was *here*. She must have had some reason for leaving the Velesian realm. I sighed. Or not.

Most of the time, Rynn was the most levelheaded of the three of us. Cali and I both had tempers that sometimes got the better of us, but Rynn did have a habit of being reckless when she got frustrated—of not taking into account the bigger picture.

So would she have decided to run away from the Alpha Pack on a whim because of some comment they made that she took great offense to? Yes. Was Rynn capable of avoiding a realm's worth of Velesians and sneaking into Moroi territory? Also yes.

My friend was a sneaky bitch, and usually I adored that about her, but it felt like we were on a collision course with all-out war between the Moroi and Velesians. So Rynn choosing this moment to hold up her middle finger to the Alpha Pack and seek sanctuary with us wasn't ideal.

That said, if Rynn didn't want to go back to the Alpha Pricks, then they could kiss my luscious ass. She'd been mine first.

The Alpha Pack was a secondary problem though, because if Cali learned that Aniela had locked an injured Rynn in the basement . . . things would get bloody real fast. Cali was over-protective of both of us, but normally, she just glowered threat-eningly, and that was enough. Something was clearly going on with her though. I had little doubt that she would respond with violence at seeing Rynn imprisoned, and we couldn't afford to have our potential allies killed.

Plus, I liked Aniela and looked forward to teasing her mercilessly about Ary when we weren't dealing with a mad, egomaniac queen, conniving and murderous wraiths, and an impending war with the Velesians.

"I need to go on a holiday," I muttered.

"What's that?" Aniela gave me a side-eyed look as we

turned a corner and headed down another hallway towards a door guarded by four guards.

"A holiday," I repeated. "It's something I came across in some Fae writings. Basically, it's like a trip you take, but for fun."

"Where in all the hells did they go in Lunaria for fun?" Aniela scoffed. "The beautiful beaches with tentacled monsters hiding just beneath the surface? Or maybe the badlands with its oppressive heat and enormous spiders that hide beneath the ground to jump out and grab you? Oh! I know!" She waved a hand at the guards, and they obediently opened the door at our approach, giving me a curious look but nothing more as we walked past them. "The lovely northern forests! Where moon devils fuck with your head and send you running into huge carnivorous flowers that will spend days sucking you dry before spitting out your dried corpse."

"Actually, I think they went somewhere else."

Aniela stopped on the narrow stairwell, and I did the same. We both stared at each other for a long moment before we burst out laughing.

"Everything is so fucked!" she sputtered between laughs. "Lunaria is the absolute worst!"

"It truly is." I wiped the tears away from my eyes. "Maybe someday, we'll find out what the Fae did to find themselves here."

"Come on." Aniela started down the stairs again. "She's just one level down."

I followed after her, still laughing under my breath. This place truly was fucked, and it only seemed to get worse as the years dragged on. Clearly, something in the spell our human ancestors had cast to turn themselves into monsters had also ingrained a dark sense of humor in all of us.

Good call on their part. We all would have gone insane

ages ago if we couldn't look at the dark, cruel world around us and laugh in its face.

Two more guards waited outside the door on the next floor. Aniela had put way more security on Rynn than Carmilla had on me, which made me wonder if my aunt had underestimated my ability to escape . . . or if she'd needed those rangers somewhere else.

"Aniela." The tall, blond guard on the right nodded deeply towards the Heir he served before giving me a shallow nod. "Harker."

Grief slammed into me hard and fast. His hair was the same golden blonde shade as Adrienne's. They weren't related—Adrienne hadn't had any surviving family—and he looked nothing like her in any other aspect, but my grief for her and Emil was still an open wound. One that I'd hastily slapped a bandage on in the name of survival, but it'd just slipped, leaving my wound bloody and raw.

"Samara?" Aniela gave me a puzzled look, her hand braced on the door she'd just started to open.

I slammed the wrapping back on the wound made of grief and rage and gave her a tight smile. "Let's grab Rynn and get back before Cali loses her shit."

"Calypso Rayne is here?" The ginger-haired guard traded glances with the blond one. "Inside our walls?"

"You Moroi are such pussies," a gravelly voice called out from behind the door. "Now let my friend through before she punches you both in the dick. It's her favorite move."

Both guards looked at me.

"She's not wrong." I shrugged.

To their credit, neither backed away, although they weren't really blocking me anyway. More or less, they were crowding my space and forcing me to walk between them, which I did—before I tapped them both on the dick faster than they could block me.

Both flinched and cursed under their breath as I sauntered into the room where my lycanthrope bestie was confined.

"Well," I drawled, "this is considerably better than where Carmilla had me locked up." Half of the room was walled off with thick bars, but that portion had a rather soft-looking bed, a comfy chair, a bookcase, and I was guessing there was a small washroom behind the curtain.

I could smell Rynn's blood, mostly old and dry, in the air. She must have been seriously wounded if she'd still been bleeding when she'd arrived here.

"About fucking time." Rynn smoothly leapt to her feet from where she'd been lying on the bed. Her usually tanned skin was pale, and there were dark circles under her mismatched eyes, but otherwise, she appeared okay.

She strode out the cell door that Aniela had opened with a languid grace and stopped in front of me, hands braced on her hips. One eye was a bright golden brown and the other a deep vivid blue.

Earth and sky. That's what they always reminded me of.

"You look like shit." She arched a brow at me.

"Not all of us have been living that pampered life . . ." I remembered the nickname the Alpha Pack had given her that drove her insane. "*Princess.*"

Her nostrils flared. "Sure you want to play that game?" A sly grin spilt across her lips. "Your *Majesty*?"

CHAPTER NINETEEN

—

Kieran

"WHY DON'T you get freshened up while we wait for Samara to return?" I gestured towards the small washroom and gave Cali a bright, charming smile. It was the one I used when high-ranking Moroi started arguments during House events and I needed to de-escalate the situation. Not flirty exactly, but confident with just a hint of mischievousness.

I'd practiced the smile a lot, and it had never let me down. Samara, Alaric, and even Roth might be great at keeping track of facts and the specifics of a trade negotiation, but nobody was better at reading people and manipulating their emotions than I.

"I'm not some simpering fool courting House favor, Kieran," Cali sneered. "So you can wipe that stupid smile off your ugly face."

Apparently, Cali was immune to my charm.

"Rude." I glared at her. "My face is *stunning*."

"Yes, it is," Draven agreed from where he was sprawled on the settee, watching me and Cali square off. Alaric and Roth were also still seated, and I got the impression that they wished they had wine to sip or food to munch on while they watched me try to handle Cali.

Meanwhile, Vail and the Salvatore Marshals were taking turns glaring at each other and watching Cali like she was a predator someone had thrown into the room and locked the door behind.

Which . . . was kind of accurate. Cali had stalked in with a pissed-off expression a few minutes ago, which had turned murderous when she hadn't seen Samara. A quick reassurance from me that Samara would be back soon and that she'd asked us all to wait for her was the only thing that kept the Furie from rampaging past Vail and Brennan, who had followed after her—hands on their weapons.

Cali had glanced around the room and relaxed slightly at seeing Alaric, Roth, and Draven all seated and looking unworried. She must have come to the conclusion that nothing was wrong—at least that nothing in the last forty minutes had gone wrong—and that Samara would be returning.

That didn't mean she was happy about the situation though, and I was trying to make sure no blood was shed while Samara fetched Rynn—something that was growing more difficult by the minute.

"Whose face do you find prettier, Draven?" Cali's head snapped towards the prince. "Kieran's or Samara's?"

Someone—I was pretty sure it was Roth—let out an exaggerated whistle. I was starting to suspect that they were every bit as much of a shit-stirrer as their older brothers and had just hidden it well all this time.

"That's an impossible question, Furie," Draven drawled. "How fortunate for me that I don't have to choose. Instead, I get to enjoy both of their exquisite faces."

"I'm so going to swallow you whole until I choke later." I gave him a smoldering look and was rewarded by his eyes darkening before I returned my attention to Cali.

"What?" she snapped when I just stared at her and didn't say anything. Given how tightly wound she was, I should probably continue trying to calm her, but technically, Samara had just ordered that I keep her distracted, so . . .

I cocked my head. "So, you and Malachi fucking again?"

Her eyes widened to an almost comical degree. "Excuse me?"

Bullseye. I'd known something had been off when that Furie had come looking for her at House Harker. It hadn't been one particular thing, but a bunch of little tells. The way he'd said Cali's name with a hint of dark possession, how the muscles along his jawline had flexed when we'd said we hadn't seen or heard from her in weeks, and how he'd been somewhat reluctant to leave when the other Furie with him had announced they'd tried their best but needed to return home.

"You know, big bastard, about yay high." I held my hand up way above my head. I wasn't short by any means, a solid six feet, unlike Draven and Vail, who both had several inches on me. My hand was above where even their heads would be. "Dark eyes, messy, shoulder-length black hair, leathery wings. Not ringing any bells?"

"That's the Furie who stopped by House Harker looking for Cali," Alaric said out loud—I assumed for Draven's benefit because Alaric and Roth had been there that day, and I didn't think Alaric gave a single fuck about keeping Vail in the loop.

Draven hummed in response. "Interesting."

"It's not!" Cali scowled at him before crossing her arms and glaring daggers at me. "You're mistaken. Clearly, you're losing your touch for reading situations, Kieran."

"Actually, I wasn't *entirely* sure the two of you were at it again." I grinned. "But I am now."

The Furies didn't do relationships or emotional commitments of any kind. It was a strategy to keep their emotions under control and limit the chances of them losing themselves to that all-consuming rage that always burned within them. Cali wasn't one to follow rules, and she'd been involved with Malachi before, but when the Furie elders had ordered them to cease their relationship, Malachi had obeyed.

I was surprised he'd decided to disobey now, and even more surprised that Cali had taken him back and not slit his throat.

Cali's golden eyes glowed, and I saw Vail stiffen out of the corner of my eye, but I just let my grin widen at the pissed-off Furie. "If he disrespects you again, let us know. We'll make sure his body is never discovered and find you a nice Moroi to fuck."

She snorted, and the glow faded from her eyes. "Thanks for the offer, but I'm pretty sure I'd break a Moroi."

Before I could start naming potential fuck buddies for Cali—ones who probably wouldn't mind being broken by the beautiful Furie—the sound of footsteps came from the hall, and we all looked towards the closed door. A few moments later, it opened, and Samara strode inside with Rynn and Aniela behind her.

"Rynn?" Cali started. "What are you doing here?"

"Enjoying Moroi hospitality," she said dryly, flicking her long brown hair that was in desperate need of a good brush over her shoulder.

Samara coughed politely as Cali's piercing stare bounced back and forth between the three of them. I decided that I didn't want to be standing between Cali and Rynn, so I practically dove for the settee and reclaimed my seat next to Draven.

"Smooth," Alaric muttered on my other side.

"Blow me."

Alaric snorted. "Pretty sure that's pretty boy's job."

"You think I'm pretty?" Draven arched a brow at Alaric.

My best friend scowled, sinking further into the cushions.

Ignoring us, Cali marched across the room. Her path took

her directly where I'd been standing, and I had no doubt that, had I still been there, she would have flung me out of her way.

"You're okay?" She crashed to a halt in front of Rynn, her hands quickly and efficiently checking her for injuries.

"I'm fine. Quite fussing!" Rynn slapped Cali's hands away, only for the Furie to key in on a spot of dried blood on her tunic and yank the clothing up, exposing Rynn's ribs. Several claw marks were still healing, and she had dark bruises, but nothing life-threatening. Still, it must have been bad if she hadn't healed completely already.

"What the fuck is this?" Cali demanded.

"I'll get to that!" Rynn snapped and again smacked Cali's hands away. She gave Samara a pleading look. "Will you please tell her I'm okay?!"

Samara tapped a finger against her bottom lip. "Mmmm . . . no. We were both worried about you, so you'll just have to deal with some light fussing."

I laughed under my breath, but not quietly enough because Rynn's wolfish eyes narrowed on me. I killed any hint of amusement on my face and gave her a small, supportive smile instead. She wasn't buying it, but when Cali tugged her tunic up again, she broke our stare off and went back to pulling her clothes out of Cali's grip.

Pissing off Cali meant you had to watch your back for a while. She'd never kill anyone Samara cared about, but she wasn't above stabbing you a few times. Nonlethally, of course.

Personally, I preferred that over Rynn's method of revenge. The lycanthrope had a very creative mind when it came to pranks, as I'd learned years ago when I'd been flirting with a courtier from another House in front of Samara. In my defense, Samara had been talking about Demetri all week after visiting him. He hadn't revealed his assholeness back then, and she'd actually liked him.

So I'd flirted with the pretty courtier, whose name I didn't even remember. Samara had cried, and Rynn had put some type of dye into my hair products that could only be described as puke green.

My options had been letting it grow out or shaving my head. I'd chosen the latter and learned that, while Alaric could pull off a closely shorn haircut quite well, I could not.

I'd been very careful to not piss off Rynn again after that.

"Those are wraith wounds." Cali finally gave up on trying to get a better look at Rynn's side but didn't step back. "What. Happened." She somehow made it more of an order than a question.

Clearly sensing how on edge her friend was, Rynn's shoulders sagged and some of the defiance fled from her face. "It's a long story, so I'm going to give you all the short version because we need to get back as soon as possible."

"Get back where, exactly?" Alaric gave Rynn a questioning look.

Rynn opened her mouth but closed it, glancing at Aniela and then to Samara.

It was a gamble, but we needed more help, and my gut told me to trust Aniela. Apparently, Samara felt the same because she gave her best friend a curt nod.

"Ruined temple," Rynn answered. "In the badlands."

"I know that place . . ." Aniela trailed off with a frown. "What does that have to do with anything?"

"It's where we got our asses kicked by some wraiths and barely survived." My brows furrowed together. "Why exactly would we go back there?"

"Because I couldn't remove the scrolls and books I found, and they have answers we need. Plus, Samara can read Unseelie faster than I can, and I'm pretty sure one of the books talks about the Seelie royal line." She frowned. "Although why the Unseelie were writing about that, I'm not sure . . ."

Everyone stared at the lycan. I sighed and glanced at Samara, who was now sitting on the arm of the settee, leaning against Roth, the two of them smirking. They were used to Rynn's roundabout way of explaining things.

I caught Samara's eye and arched an eyebrow. She arched one back but took my hint to steer her friend back onto the trail. "Rynn," she said evenly, "why don't you start at the beginning? Like how you got from the far northern part of the Velesian realm to the badlands?"

"Oh . . . right." Rynn nodded. "I found another one of those hidden rooms, like the one under Lake Malov, but underneath the Alpha House. I . . . uhh . . . might have locked the Alphas out and then stepped through a mirror that took me to another room, which turned out to be underneath that shitty, abandoned temple."

"Feels like there's a lot to unpack there," Draven said in a completely even tone.

I chuckled while Alaric rubbed his forehead and Vail redirected his glare from Cali to Rynn.

Aniela pondered all of us from where she was settled between Petra and Brennan, her lips quirked up in a barely there smirk.

"Fae mirrors," Roth said slowly and then looked up at Samara. "We've read about them, but it seemed like they were for communication—not travel."

"Maybe the Fae here adapted them?" Samara mused. "I mean, it makes sense, right? Before they turned themselves into wraiths, they would have had to travel through this fucked-up land of monsters too. That'd be a lot easier if they could just step through a mirror in one location and end up on the other side of the continent."

"I'm sorry," Brennan cut in, leaning forward slightly. "Did you just say that the wraiths used to be Fae?"

Samara nodded.

Brennan looked around Aniela and pointed aggressively at Petra. "I fucking *told you* they were Fae! The Unseelie fucked up their shadow magic somehow."

"Actually, it was the Seelie," Samara corrected. "We don't exactly know what happened to the Unseelie, but the Seelie did something to steal their shadows. I'm guessing the Unseelie are dead."

"Can we focus please?" Vail growled.

For the first time since entering the room, Rynn looked at Vail, and a golden sheen rolled over her eyes before she went predatorily still. Samara cleared her throat, and after a second, Rynn relaxed. Slightly.

Something told me it wouldn't be a humiliating but ultimately harmless prank she played on him in the future. Vail had knocked her out and stolen the crown off her unconscious form before absconding with it. Sure, he might have stashed her body behind a magical ward to keep her safe until she'd woken up, but that didn't change the fact that he'd fucking attacked her.

For a second, there was regret in Vail's dark grey eyes before he hid it. "You found another hidden room beneath the Alpha Pack stronghold. Somehow—and I don't give a fuck about the specifics or the historical implications"—he gave Samara and Roth a hard look before focusing on Rynn again —"you used the mirror to travel across Lunaria and ended up in a different hidden room, this time beneath the abandoned temple, yes?"

"Correct." Rynn started pacing, stepping around Cali. "It's, like, triple the size of the one beneath the lake. I think maybe it was some kind of archive—"

"Stop," Vail cut her off again, earning himself a warning growl from Cali, which he ignored. Brave man. Stupid too. Pissing off Cali seemed like a good way to get your dick cut off.

"Why did you leave the room, Rynn? What sent you into the badlands instead of back through that mirror and to the safety of the Alpha Pack?"

"Cade can fucking bite me," Rynn snarled. "And Bastian can get fucked! Ryker too!"

Guess that answered the question about if things were getting better between her and the Alpha Pack. I bit back my sigh but didn't miss the look between Cali and Samara. Our priority might be dealing with Carmilla and figuring out what Erendriel and the wraiths were up to, but I had no doubt those two were also plotting how to get Rynn out of her messy situation.

I didn't know the Alpha Pack that well. Most of my inter-actions had been with Bastian. The panther shifter served as an ambassador of sorts and used to make regular trips to the Moroi realm. He was difficult to read because, like me, he was exceptional at slipping into different masks based on the situa-tion. Sometimes, he was self-deprecating and charming. Other times, he had an edge like he was just itching to spill some blood.

Then there was Cade, the de facto leader of the Alpha Pack. He was calm and steady . . . until he wasn't. I'd once seen him tear the head off a rabid howler like it had been nothing.

Ryker was the youngest and a bit of a hothead.

Technically, there was a fourth member of the Pack, but I'd never met them.

Rynn paused her pacing and chewed on her bottom lip. I supposed there were five members of the Alpha Pack now. Even if the fifth one might never go back if her friends had anything to say about it.

"What did you find, Rynn?" I prodded gently. Something had sent her running through the badlands on her own. Rynn could be rash, but even she wouldn't have done that unless she were desperate.

Rynn went back to chewing her lip and looked at Samara. My dark-haired beauty held her gaze for a long moment before giving a deep nod, like she was giving Rynn permission.

"I'm guessing some of you already know this, but Samara's grandfather was the Seelie King—the *true* Seelie King. Erendriel is just a pretender." Aniela and her Marshals gave Samara appraising looks but didn't say anything. "I didn't get through all the documents, but I saw enough to know that I needed to warn you." Rynn smiled at her friend. "You've always acted like a queen. I should have known you actually were one."

"Wasn't acting like a queen when she pulled my hair and kicked me in the crotch," Aniela muttered.

"Anything I do is queenly," Samara replied with a sniff.

I. Adore. Her.

"The wraiths can't get into those hidden rooms," Rynn continued. "Trust me when I say they tried once they realized I was in there, but however they managed to break through the blood wards around our outposts clearly doesn't work for these rooms. More importantly, there are things in the room that I couldn't open either—I think only the Seelie royal line can."

"That's why Erendriel is suddenly interested in you." Draven gave Samara a worried look. "Somehow, he learned the truth of your lineage, and now he's trying to sway you to his side. He'll start with pretty words, and when that doesn't work, he'll use other methods. Find your weaknesses and exploit them until you have no choice but to bend to his will. He can use his magic to—" He flinched and abruptly stopped talking.

Apparently, he'd been about to say something that was still protected by whatever spell Erendriel had put on him. His face contorted in frustration and fury at not being able to share whatever knowledge was locked away in his mind.

I turned and cupped his face in my hands. "You know we're going to kill him, right? For everything he's done to you?"

Draven's deep blue eyes warmed. "You say the sweetest things, love."

"Can we please get back to the room full of secret treasures and away from this gross display of affection?" Roth complained.

Samara snickered and leaned down to kiss their cheek, causing the taciturn librarian to blush slightly.

I opened my mouth to tease them, but Alaric gave me a stern look to knock it off, so I pouted and settled back against Draven instead.

"So you left to find Samara," Vail guessed, "but the wraiths found you first?"

"I bolted as soon as the sun rose, causing the wraiths to scatter." Color stained Rynn's cheeks, and she muttered something.

"What was that?" Cali crossed her arms and stared at her best friend.

"I fell into a spider's trap!" A sheen rolled over Rynn's eyes again. "It was an old one, and some debris had fallen over it, so I missed the signs."

Cali threw her hands up. "This is exactly why I've told the two of you to stay out of the badlands if I'm not there! You should have gone back to the Alpha Pack and sent us a message. You could have gotten yourself killed, Rynn!"

I groaned as Rynn closed the distance between them.

"I'm not some helpless pup!" Rynn growled and stopped a hair's breadth from Cali so they were practically touching, aggression rolling off both of them. Samara was the short one of the trio, while Rynn and Cali were almost the same height, but Cali had at least thirty pounds of muscle on her leaner friend. Not that Rynn cared. If she were in her wolf form, her hackles would have been raised. As it was, her words had more of a gravelly tone to them than usual. "Samara needed to be warned, and I didn't know where you were."

She tried to shove the Furie, but Cali didn't move an inch, which only pissed Rynn off more.

"We protect each other, Cali. It's what we do." Rynn pointed a finger in Cali's face. "So don't you fucking *dare* tell me to retreat with my tail between my legs while you two fight!"

"I'm sure that's not what she meant—" Samara started.

"Oh, shut it!" Rynn and Cali both snarled at her.

Roth and Alaric snickered as Samara sulked and crossed her arms. It was really strange how well the two of them were getting on, but I guess it made sense, since they were both grumpy assholes most of the time. I was glad Alaric's friend circle was expanding. He'd always be my best friend; I wasn't the least bit threatened there. Mostly because I knew Roth's ability to socialize had limits, and they were more than happy to disappear for days at a time in the library.

"Are they always like this?" Petra asked Vail.

"Unfortunately." He sighed.

Suddenly, his hand snapped up, and he caught a dagger an inch before it sunk into his face.

"Seriously?" He glared at Samara, who just turned the hand that had thrown the dagger palm up.

"I'll take that back now."

Vail slid the dagger into an empty sheath on his belt and fastened a leather strap over it so Samara couldn't summon it back. "Finders keepers. You're welcome to try to take it."

I didn't miss the flash of desire cross Samara's face before it was replaced with a rage that rivaled a Furie's. Yeah . . . I wasn't going to touch that mess of a situation. The four of us —Draven, Roth, Alaric, and I—had already agreed to let Samara figure out what to do with Vail, but if he gave even the slightest sign of betraying or hurting her again, we'd kill him.

Or tell Cali, and she'd kill him for us. Dead was dead after all, and my face *was* too pretty to get smashed in by Vail's meaty fists.

Draven seemed confident that Vail wouldn't betray Samara again. I'd been doubtful . . . until his rangers had been killed. Now, there was no chance of him going back to Carmilla. That didn't mean he couldn't still hurt Samara though. She was in love with him—had been for a long time—but I knew her. She was a spiteful thing.

I just didn't want her to hurt herself more in an attempt to punish Vail.

"Why do you think we should go back to the room, Rynn?" Samara asked, dragging her gaze away from Vail. "It's not that I don't want to see it, but maybe it shouldn't be a priority? Unless you think there is something in there that can nullify the crown's magic?"

"I'm not sure," Rynn said slowly, her argument with Cali already forgotten. "But I think there is a better chance of finding it there than anywhere else—except maybe the room under Lake Malov. I don't know how to or even if we can change where the mirrors lead, and some of us definitely don't want to cross into Velesian territory right now." She cut a glance towards Vail.

He winced before killing the motion. Vail had always been on friendly terms with the Velesians, but I suspected that had come to an end. Even if Rynn hadn't told them what Vail had done, they had likely been the ones to find her, and they would have smelled Vail on her. Between that and the missing crown, it would have been obvious what had happened.

Vail's days of running with any of the Velesian Packs were over.

"Three days," Draven murmured before looking at Rynn. "You're positive the wraiths couldn't get into the room?"

She nodded. "Absolutely. It sounded like they tore down

half the bloody temple in a fit of rage over not being able to get to me."

I caught on to what Draven was driving at and locked stares with Samara. "It doesn't matter if that room has the answers we need for the crown or not. Serill told you he'd be back in three days—that's tonight. We need to get you behind a ward that even the wraiths can't break through."

Because I sure as hell wasn't going to lose her again.

CHAPTER TWENTY

Samara

IT WASN'T that I'd forgotten about Serril's promise to return, but on my list of problems to solve, I'd been placing the wraiths below Carmilla. The wraiths had always plagued our lands. Sure, now we knew more about them, but they were still an old threat in my mind—one that was escalating but seemed less urgent than my aunt.

The longer we let Carmilla go unchecked, the more she would use the crown on the Moroi Houses. She was clearly targeting House Salvatore, Corvinus, and Laurent. All she had to do was get the key players, and those Houses would be under her thumb. Then she could concentrate on wiping House Devereux out and likely Tepes as well.

As much as I wanted to go back and secure House Harker, there were plenty of people there who loved Carmilla. It was unlikely that they'd believe me if I told them she was now our enemy. Even if they did accept that she had a crown capable of subverting someone's will, they'd probably still defend Carmilla. Claim she wouldn't abuse her power. I wasn't so naive to think there weren't people within House Harker who wouldn't mind if our House became synonymous with the Sovereign House—as the true rulers of the Moroi realm.

There was a very real possibility that Carmilla would have complete control over all the Moroi Houses within months. After that, she'd likely turn her attention to the Velesians. The Packs were in a worse state than the Moroi Houses; it was doubtful they'd be able to mount a unified defense. Plus, Carmilla could use the crown on key players to further sow dissension in the ranks.

The Furies were the wild card, as they'd pulled back so much over the last few decades. Cali was the first and last Furie to ever attend Drudonia for more than a year, and she'd done that in defiance of the elders. Most of the Furies rarely left the badlands.

On the plus side, that hopefully meant they wouldn't help Carmilla with her quest to rule over the Moroi and the Velesians. If it came to it, I'd beg the Furie Elders for support, but I knew it was unlikely they'd agree to get involved. It didn't help that the Fury Elders didn't like me because of my close friendship with Cali. I knew they'd ordered Cali to stay away from me and Rynn after we'd left Drudonia, but she'd refused.

For all their power, the Elders couldn't completely control Cali—and they held me at least partially to blame for that. I couldn't depend on any other Furies coming to our aid, and as powerful as my friend was, she was still only one person.

Carmilla was no doubt plotting a way to deal with her. In the back of my mind, I was trying to think of a way to convince Cali to take Rynn somewhere safe—out of reach of the Alpha Pack. If it worked, they would both be out of harm's reach. I just needed to frame it in a way that didn't sound like I was trying to keep Cali out of the fight for her own safety.

I was kidding myself of course. Both of them would tell me to go fuck myself if I suggested they hole up somewhere and hide.

All of this was exactly why I'd been shoving the wraith problem to the side. I'd already survived one chat with Serril. Surely I could do it again and buy us a little more time.

Draven felt otherwise, and to my annoyance, Kieran had backed him up without hesitation. So had Vail.

I'd suggested that we track down Ary and warn House Tepes instead, then retreat to House Devereux. Only Roth and Alaric had agreed with me on that plan, but when Vail had just shrugged and said he was happy to tie me up and throw me onto the back of a horse to get me to the temple in the badlands, neither of them had argued.

I'd decided I'd be withholding sex from all of them. A minute later, I'd changed my mind because I wasn't going to punish myself for their treachery. They'd just have to get down on their knees and get creative with their begging.

"Still mad?" Kieran tucked some of my hair behind my ear, and I glared up at him. All of us were standing around in one of the side courtyards, waiting for the stablehands to fetch horses for us. Fast ones. We had less than eight hours to make it to the temple before the sun set. It was doable, but we'd have to push the horses hard.

I missed Zosa. My fiery mare would have raced across the badlands like she had wings, but she was safe at House Harker, where I would hopefully be reunited with her when this was over.

"What do you think? You're supposed to always have my back, Kier." I pursed my lips together and tried to ignore how gorgeous he looked because of the late morning sun hitting his golden blond hair just right.

Strong arms wrapped around my waist and pulled me back against a hard chest. A second later, Draven kissed the side of my neck, and I barely managed to swallow down the moan that tried to escape. "Don't be mad, love." He hadn't shaved in a couple of days, and the stubble scraped deliciously against my skin as he nuzzled my neck. "I know Serril. He's a tricky bastard. We need to make sure you're out of his reach so we can plan accordingly."

"But House Devereux—"

"Can't keep you safe. Not from wraiths." Kieran stepped closer until his chest was against mine and I was sandwiched between them. Then he claimed my mouth while Draven alternated between kissing and nipping my neck. Both of them had their hands on my hips and were gripping me hard.

Mad. You're mad at them, I reminded myself. *Furious. Don't let them—*

"Oh!" I exhaled sharply when Draven slipped his hand between me and Kieran to rub the seam of my pants.

"Get a room," Alaric muttered.

Kieran broke our kiss to grin at his best friend. "Why? So you can walk in on us again?"

"Wait, is that your kink, Alaric?" I asked a little breathlessly. "Is *that* why you never knock?"

Alaric gave me an unamused look, even as his lips twitched like he was fighting a laugh.

Fuck. It was impossible to stay mad at them. Even if I still didn't love the idea of going to the temple. It was so isolated there. I felt like I was running away when I should be staying and fighting.

Still, I'd be lying if I said I wasn't curious about what treasures the room might hold, especially in the spaces that were locked. I mean, someone—it had to have been the Fae—had gone to a lot of trouble to set up these hidden locations. What had they found so important that they'd decided it needed an extra layer of protection?

And assuming the Fae were responsible for these hidden treasure troves, why couldn't Erendriel get in? He seemed to have at least mostly reverted back to his original Fae form. He was no longer trapped in shadows like most of the Fae.

I loved me a good mystery. I'd love it even more if Lunaria weren't on the brink of collapse.

"Sam," Kieran said in a singsong voice.

"What?" I blinked and found him smirking at me.

Draven chuckled, his hand that had been rubbing my overeager clit through my pants sliding up to wrap around my waist.

"I forgot that's the trick to making you forget you're mad at us—not kisses—uncovering Fae mysteries." Kier kissed me on the nose and walked to the rangers, who were leading out horses, then Draven kissed me on the cheek before following him.

I wrinkled my nose and opened my mouth to argue.

"Samara, you're with me," Vail announced.

"What?" My head whipped to Vail as he strode over to a large black horse and took the reins from the stablehand, who gave him a respectful nod.

Vail didn't even turn to look at me as he secured several bags to the front of the saddle. "Salvatore can only spare three horses. They already don't have enough to relocate most of their people to House Devereux." He quickly and efficiently started lifting the horse's hooves and inspecting them. "I'm not riding with anyone else. So either you ride with me, or someone stays behind. Horses can only carry two."

The fucking *audacity* of this man.

"Fine," I said evenly. "Then you can go with Aniela and her rangers to warn Ary."

The majority of House Salvatore was going to seek refuge at House Devereux. Roth had written a note to their family explaining the situation. Just like Draven and I had discovered at House Harker, there was a large underground level beneath Roth's birth House. It would be a little cramped, but they'd be able to fit everyone inside.

Aniela's Marshals hadn't been happy about the Heir's insistence on going to find Ary, but she refused to back down. I understood where she was coming from because I would have done the same in her place. I also knew that Ary could be a stubborn ass at times and it would take Aniela to convince him to relocate—albeit temporarily—to House Devereux.

Technically, Ary was an Heir, but he acted more like a ranger. Similar to House Devereux, House Tepes had never had much patience for Moroi politics. They preferred to be in the wilds. Because of how close they were to the border of the Velesian realm, Ary and his rangers spent a lot of time there as well.

Or at least they had. I wasn't sure how much longer even they would be welcome with the rising tensions across Lunaria.

"Not a chance." He finished checking the horse's hooves and patted the mare's neck before looking at me. "I'm not leaving your side."

I recognized the stubborn look quite well. Even if we did have time to spare—which we didn't—there would be no dissuading him.

"Fine," I ground out. "But I get the reins."

He grunted in reply before turning towards the enormous white wolf that trotted into the courtyard. Rynn gave Vail a silent snarl before butting her head against my thigh and damn near toppling me over.

"You sure you're up for running the whole way?" I guided my hand down her side, fingers slipping through her thick coat, searching for any signs of injury. Shifting helped the Velesians heal faster, and I didn't feel so much as a scab. Even if all her injuries were resolved, the amount of healing she'd had to do in the last two days had been taxing on her system. "Cali could carry you."

I barely managed to pull my hand away when Rynn snapped and let out a warning growl.

Touchy, touchy.

"Quit fussing, Sam," Cali said as she landed silently next to me, a mocking smile on her face.

I squinted at her. "Worried I'm going to take your spot as the resident fussian?"

"That's not a word." She rolled her eyes.

"You're not a word." Was I the perfect representation of maturity at twenty-three?

Yes. Yes, I was.

"I don't even know how to respond to that." Cali rolled her shoulders before glancing at the sun. "Follow my lead once we get to the badlands. I'll do my best to guide you all around the worst of it." She grimaced. "But it's leading up to the trapper's breeding season."

"Wonderful," Alaric muttered. "More fucking arachnids. As if those starfish things a couple of months ago weren't bad enough."

"You good?" I tried and failed to keep from laughing as he awkwardly tried to figure out where to hold on to Kieran on the back of their bay gelding. Kieran gave me a mischievous smirk before nudging the horse to the side, and Alaric immediately wrapped his arms around his friend's waist with a panicked expression.

He really was the worst rider.

Roth didn't look happy, but I suspected that had more to do with them having to hold on to Draven and not so much being on horseback. They didn't really like physical contact with people—except me, which made me feel warm and fuzzy inside.

"We're heading out," Aniela announced from astride a white horse, Brennan mounted behind her. She pulled their horse to a stop a few feet from me, and the mare pranced and snorted in Rynn's direction, clearly not thrilled about being so close to a wolf. "Most of my rangers are escorting the elderly and children on horseback. The rest will help those who are traveling on foot."

I tried not to think about all the ways that could go wrong. On horseback, it was a two-day ride to House Devereux. Less if they rode fast, but that was unlikely considering the people riding. Walking would take a solid week.

There were some outposts they could stay at along the way, but that meant collecting more travelers since they'd have to explain things to the locals. All the outposts between here and House Devereux were under Salvatore's control, and Aniela was confident the residents wouldn't question the order to evacuate.

The sentiment that there was something deeply wrong with the Sovereign House had been brewing for a long time amongst the Salvatore Moroi. The abrupt change of leadership would only further their suspicions.

I hoped we all survived this so that we could work on repairing that distrust. For too long, we've had an every-House-for-themself mentality, and that wasn't great for longtime Moroi survival. It was something Carmilla and I apparently agreed on—we just differed on how to achieve unification.

"My brothers should receive my message by this evening," Roth told Aniela. "If all goes according to plan, they'll meet your people with additional rangers on the road."

"You have my thanks." Aniela nodded deeply. "We'll be unreachable while we travel to House Tepes, but I'll send word once we're there."

"Travel safe, friend," I said sincerely. Their trip was just as dangerous as ours. House Tepes was in the north of the Moroi realm. The safe route was to travel to the Sovereign House, then cut west, but obviously that wasn't an option. So Aniela and her small group of rangers would be cutting straight through the forests in the center of our realm. All sorts of nasty things prowled there.

"You as well." Aniela glanced to where Vail waited for me by the horse, an increasingly impatient look on his face. "And good luck with that."

She waved goodbye and turned her horse to leave. Brennan hadn't acknowledged us once. Super friendly, that one.

It was time for us to get moving, yet I couldn't convince my feet to budge. Everything between Vail and me was so fucked. I was excellent at compartmentalizing, but even I had my limits. Keeping physical contact with Vail to a minimum had helped keep him in the category of *useful tool to be wielded as necessary.*

An eight-hour ride was going to smash that to pieces.

Something Vail damn well knew because the bastard *knew* me.

"Sure you don't want us to kill him?" Cali said casually, not even trying to be quiet. Rynn let out a low growl, her gaze locked on Vail.

He apparently wasn't the least bit concerned about my two best friends plotting his death because the asshole just smiled.

"If anyone kills him, it's going to be me," I muttered. "Let's get on with it." I glanced down at Rynn. "Don't fall into anything this time."

Her head snapped away from Vail, and her growl deepened as a golden sheen rolled over her mismatched eyes, which seemed brighter in this form.

If she thought we would ever let her live that down, she had another thing coming.

Holding on to that amusement, I stalked towards Vail and easily swung up onto the beast of a horse. A second later, he landed behind me, one large arm looping around my waist while the other rested on my thigh.

A shiver ran through me before I could stop it. Something told me this ride was going to feel a lot longer than eight hours.

I'D TRAINED myself to be a very patient person. It didn't come naturally to me, which was why sometimes my temper won out, but in general, I didn't mind the quiet. Most people couldn't handle silence in a conversation or negotiation, so they seeked to fill the void. My willingness to embrace the quiet had won me many a trade deal.

Vail hadn't spoken in five hours.

Five. Fucking. Hours.

His arm remained looped around my abdomen, and his hand had only strayed from my thigh to retrieve the water bottle—of which he'd made sure I'd also taken a drink. Not by asking. Just by holding it up for me.

I'd expected him to use this time to once again explain to me why he'd done what he had. That he'd been being loyal to Carmilla and hadn't realized she was seriously fucked in the head. Or that he'd assumed I'd be able to work things out with her and everything would be fine.

None of this would have been news to me. He'd said it all before when I'd been imprisoned and I'd had no choice but to listen to him explain in great detail why he'd chosen to attack my best friend, steal the crown, and do nothing as Draven was tortured and both he and I were thrown in the dungeons.

Sure, he'd done what he could to help me get through my menstrual cycle, but he was the reason I'd been locked up in the first place.

And he hadn't apologized. The moon fucking forbid that the words, *I fucked up and I'm sorry*, passed through Vail Ferenc's lips.

Argh. Maybe I could shove him off the horse?

Subtly, I shifted in the saddle, trying to determine how solid of a grip he had on me.

"Don't even think about it," he grunted.

"Think about what?" I asked casually, as if we hadn't been riding in tense silence for hours.

"Trying to shove me off the horse. That will only result in both of us going down." His breath tickled my left ear as the hand on my thigh dug in a little harder. "And if you're that eager to have a tussle with me, I'm sure we can figure something out at the temple."

Before Vail, I hadn't thought it had been possible to be confused, enraged, and horny all at once. Honestly? Could have gone my whole life without ever experiencing that.

"You're insufferable," I seethed and gripped the reins with one hand so I could reach back and grab my dagger—the one he'd refused to give back after I'd thrown it at him—off his belt. He didn't try to stop me, but I could feel his amusement as I fumbled a bit before getting it free. I considered stabbing him —not lethally, just a flesh wound—but the bastard would have probably just taken that as encouragement, so I slid it back into the sheath on my thigh and left it there.

Right next to his hand.

"I'm a lot of things these days," he said evenly. His grip on my thigh loosened, and he started lazily tracing loops on it. I liked it. The slow, methodical pace was relaxing. Between that and his broad chest against my back, I felt safe.

Which was ridiculous. The man behind me was anything but safe. He'd proven that over and over again. Sure, he might not go back to Carmilla after what she'd done to his rangers, but I had no doubt Vail would find some other way to fuck me over.

I hated that I still liked his touch. *Craved* it.

It had to be this stupid magic tying us together. Maybe I'd find some answers in the temple as to what this was and how to get rid of it. Then I'd be able to think straight when it came to him.

"Why exactly did you insist on riding with me?" I did my best to ignore his damn fingers and narrowed my eyes at the others, who rode ahead of us, giving Vail and me time to clear the air, apparently. I had no doubt that had been Draven and Kieran's doing because Alaric and Roth occasionally turned around to glare at Vail.

Well, mostly Roth. Alaric tried to a couple of times and almost fell off the saddle. He'd gotten considerably better with a crossbow, but riding was clearly never going to be his thing.

Rynn was scouting ahead—I could just barely make out her furry white ass—and Cali was soaring above us. One advantage of the badlands was that they were flat in every direction. Once in a while, a mesa would rise out of the ground, but it was impossible for anyone to sneak up on us.

Above ground, anyway.

Vail didn't answer my question right away, and just as I was about to push him for a response, I felt the echoes of grief and trepidation inside my chest. Not mine . . . I'd tucked my grief for Adrienne and Emil into a box and shoved it onto its metaphorical shelf with all the others. Close to it was the angst and stress for Nyx.

No. What I was feeling now belonged to Vail.

Whatever this emotional feedback was, it seemed to only happen when we were in close contact, and it wasn't all the time. With Draven and Roth, it was more consistent, but between Vail and me, it felt more strained, like flashes of emotions here and there.

"Carmilla . . ." Vail trailed off, then another feeling shot through our connection, so intense, it made me inhale sharply.

White-hot rage.

"What about her?" I rasped, my hand tightening on the reins, causing the mare to toss her head in annoyance.

"Did she have anything to do with our parents' deaths?" He spoke the words so quietly, I knew the others hadn't heard. Not that it mattered. Most of them had been there when Carmilla had stated what she'd done, and I'd told Roth later.

I'd been planning on telling Vail but had figured it could

wait. There was nothing to be done for it now, and he was still grieving his rangers. No purpose in opening up an old wound when there was a fresh new one still seeping blood.

"Yes." I forced myself to relax my grip on the reins as a numbness took hold. It wasn't coming from Vail. This was all me. The problem, I was learning, with compartmentalizing things was that, sooner or later, you had to deal with them.

I'd never dealt with losing my parents. I'd just let my grief fester in that damn box.

Something told me Vail had done something similar. He'd thrown himself into becoming the perfect ranger and then taking up the mantle of Marshal—just like his parents. I'd dedicated myself to being the unfathomable Heir and then to solidifying our alliance with House Laurent by marrying Demetri.

Both of us had looked to Carmilla as that stand-in parental figure. She'd shaped us into weapons she could wield—and had made sure to destroy our childhood friendship so that we'd relied only on her in those early years. Before I went to Drudonia and became close with Cali and Rynn. Before Vail bonded with rangers like Adrienne, Emil, and later Nyx.

Looking back, I realized that she had tried to sabotage my relationship with Cali and Rynn, making little comments here and there, but I'd lived at Drudonia, and that distance between me and Carmilla was probably what had saved me. If I hadn't had my friends and if I hadn't carved out a piece of myself outside of that constant pressure to impress Carmilla, would I have left Demetri?

Or would I have remained at House Laurent in a loveless marriage? Carmilla probably had plans to take out Marvina at some point, and then Demetri and I would have risen to the Heads of House role. Carmilla would have had two Heads under her thumb without even needing a Fae crown.

That was what my parents had died for.

Something wet and hot streaked down my face. I raised my right hand from where it had been resting on the handle of the dagger to brush the tears away, but a large hand caught mine and tucked it against my chest—right over where that connection thrummed.

Vail's other hand rose, and he gently brushed my cheeks, wiping away the tears before wrapping that arm around me too.

He rested the side of his head against mine as I silently sobbed in his arms, finally grieving the loss of my parents after denying it for so long. Vail didn't say anything, just held me as I felt his own grief wind through mine. We'd both lost so much because of Carmilla's obsession with power.

Slowly, something else wrapped around my grief. Something enduring and resilient.

It was love. The unbreakable kind.

At first, it was just coming from Draven, but then Roth's bond intertwined with his. I'd been learning over the last couple of days the subtle distances between how their emotions felt through the bond. Another choked sob broke from my lips when Vail's bond joined. Tentatively, like it wasn't sure it was allowed to be there.

I might have lost my parents—and my aunt to her own greed—but I still had family, and they wouldn't ever let me go.

So I let myself fall apart and finally weep for the parents I'd loved and lost . . . in the arms of a man who had broken my heart.

CHAPTER TWENTY-ONE

Vail

"Stop!" Cali ordered a second after the white wolf loping ahead of us skidded to a less than graceful stop.

"What is it?" Samara called out even as she tugged on the reins, drawing our mount to a halt. Draven and Kieran did the same.

I leaned to the side a little more so I could scan the ground but didn't release my hold on Samara. She'd stopped crying half an hour ago, and we'd both been content to ride in silence. Not the tense kind of these past couple of weeks, but a strangely comforting one. I didn't think everything between us was resolved, but for the first time, I had hope that I could actually fix them.

I just needed more time to do that, which meant we needed to make it to that damn temple alive. Cali and Rynn had both sensed something—even if I couldn't see it. I grimaced. If it wasn't on the surface, then it was below.

Trapper spiders.

Most of Lunaria was covered in forests, ranging from tropical to snow-covered; it was impressive how quickly the climate changed between the northern and southern ends of the continent. Then there were the badlands, a unique ecosystem that contrasted sharply with everything else. They were flat and arid—so much so that the ground cracked and faint lines scattered out in every direction, as if the earth itself was begging for rain, which it rarely got, as the storms seemed to always bypass it.

Cali landed in front of us, wisps of red hair plastered to her face where they'd slipped free from her braid. We were lucky it was overcast, but even without the sun beating down on us, the heat was stifling. The horses were sweating but so far seemed okay with our steady jog.

"Spotted a trapper." Cali's mouth twisted in distaste. "Where there's one . . ."

"There's more." I grunted and tightened my grip around Samara's waist. "If it's a colony, their tunnels could extend for miles."

"Or it could be just a few that split off from the group," Draven said, but he sounded doubtful.

It seemed unlikely we'd get that lucky.

"I fucking hate spiders," Alaric muttered.

"Same," Samara echoed. "I had nightmares for a solid week after the cave." A chill seemed to run through her, and she leaned further into my embrace—something I greedily accepted as I inhaled her delicious scent.

I'd never admit it, but even I'd had a nightmare or two after we'd encountered those arachnid-like starfish in the cave outside House Harker. The creatures themselves had been nightmare-inducing, but what really terrified me was remembering Samara dangling off the ledge with a tentacle wrapped around her leg while a monstrous starfish waited beneath to devour her.

Those things had been unexpected. At least trappers I'd unfortunately dealt with before.

There weren't as many predators in the badlands because

of the harsh terrain and climate, but the ones that dwelled here were crafty. Trappers were spiders as large as Rynn in her wolf form that lived in tunnels beneath the ground. They'd earned their name because they built pits hidden beneath trapdoors in their tunnels. When they felt the vibrations of something walking by, they leapt out and dragged the unsuspecting prey underneath, where the walls were lined with their sticky webs.

Thanks to all the cracks in the ground, it was difficult to tell where the trapdoors were. To make matters worse, their breeding season was coming up, and they were stocking up on food to feed their young, which meant there were probably twice as many traps as usual and the spiders would be extra aggressive.

Because Lunaria was the gift that kept on giving.

Reluctantly, I let go of Samara and slid off the horse. Cali was clearly stressed, because she didn't even bother giving me one of her death stares when I moved to stand beside her.

"You've been in the badlands more than any of us." I kept my gaze locked on the ground in front of us. "What do you think we should do?"

"Throw your body out there, wait for the trappers to jump out, run real fast," she replied without missing a beat.

I laughed darkly, drawing Rynn's attention from where she was also seeking out the trapdoors. Fangs that were several inches long flashed at me as she snarled before going back to trying to find a path.

Remorse hit me hard. I'd always respected Rynn. She was smart and clever, and while she could be blunt at times—she lacked Samara's ability to speak honeyed words—she'd always spoken the truth. I liked her no-bullshit approach to things.

It wasn't just Samara I'd lost when I'd taken that crown and handed it over to Carmilla. It was Rynn . . . and the Velesians too.

Samara, I hoped to win back, but I wasn't sure if Rynn

would ever trust me again—and the Alpha Pack would be out for blood.

"As delicious a snack as Vail is," Samara said as she swaggered to Cali's other side, "I don't think he'll be enough to distract all of them. Not if they have a large colony."

My dick instantly hardened at Samara referring to me as delicious, and I had to subtly adjust my pants.

"Won't know until he tries." Alaric shrugged before half falling, half leaping off the horse he'd been riding with Kieran.

I didn't bother hiding my smirk at his ungraceful dismount.

"Knock it off." Samara gave me and then Alaric a warning look. "Both of you."

"Could you fly us across, Cali?" Kieran asked from behind us, where he and Roth were holding on to the three horses. I looked around, trying to spot where Draven had gone, and tried not to be envious of how quietly he could move. It didn't take long to find him, crouching down with his hand flat against the earth a short distance away from us.

"Possibly," Cali answered Kieran. "It'd be easier if we backtracked and climbed up one of the mesas so I could glide and not waste energy just trying to get off the ground. Even then, I'm not sure if I could carry Draven or the asshole."

I assumed I was the asshole.

Fair.

Samara chewed on her bottom lip. I wanted to reach out and brush my thumb across it to get her to stop, but I wasn't sure if my touch would be welcomed. Despite what had transpired when we'd been riding together, I didn't think we were there yet—and I didn't want to fuck up what progress I'd made. So instead, I had to watch as Alaric brushed *his* thumb across her lip and Samara gave *him* a small smile in return.

Cold, green eyes cut to me as soon as Samara turned her attention to where Rynn was nimbly trotting back to us, then Alaric arched a dark brow at me. Out of all of Samara's lovers, he seemed to be the one who had the biggest problem with me, which I found interesting because he was also the one who had been the cruelest towards her.

Sure, I'd tried to kill Samara a few times, but Alaric had spent his teenage years delivering perfectly crafted insults that cut right through her armor. He'd picked that habit back up as soon as she'd returned to House Harker. One day, they were at each other's throats—the next, he was in her bed.

I didn't get it, which was probably how he felt about me and Samara.

Figuring out how this would all work long-term would be challenging, and I suspected there might be a little bloodshed. Samara clearly wasn't going to choose between us. I just needed to make sure she chose me at all.

Which meant I couldn't punch that arrogant expression off Alaric's face.

Rynn finished making her way to us and shifted back to her human form. I almost rolled my eyes at how Alaric suddenly found the ground so interesting. Clearly, he hadn't spent much time around Velesians because nudity was nothing to them.

Unless mates were involved and someone was being disrespectful, but while the Alpha Pack had claimed Rynn, there was no mate bond between them—and likely wouldn't be, given the way things were going.

"Thoughts?" I kept my gaze on Rynn's eyes. Velesians were comfortable wearing nothing, but leering was still considered rude—or an invitation. Neither was of interest to me. I only had eyes for my dark-haired, curvy beauty, but I hoped to mend some bridges with Rynn, so I waited respectfully for her to answer.

Rynn glanced at me, a cool distance in her gaze, before she sighed. "I suspect this colony goes on for a ways. There are a lot of trapdoors, and from what I could see, they don't decrease in any direction. So we could walk for miles and still be in it."

"We don't have that kind of time." I frowned. It was past midday. We'd traveled a good distance, but we still had a ways to go before reaching the temple. Dealing with trappers was difficult but doable—we just had to avoid those damn doors. If darkness fell and the wraiths came for us though . . . we wouldn't be able to fight them *and* avoid the trappers.

"Can you sense anything?" Kieran called out to Draven.

The former prince shook his head and rose, dusting off his hands as he walked back towards us. "Yes, but it's not all that useful. I'm pretty sure I can feel the tunnel system, but I can't differentiate between what are tunnels and what are traps. My magic only senses the spiders when they move; otherwise, I just kind of have an awareness of them but not an exact location."

He ran a hand through his long hair, causing the silver strands to shimmer as they caught the few rays of sun that peeked through the clouds. I tried not to roll my eyes as both Kieran and Samara practically drooled.

"Well, you're doing better than me." Samara wrinkled her nose. "I can't sense anything."

Draven gave her a small smile. "You only found out you had magic a few weeks ago. It takes practice to draw it out and then manipulate it to your will. Even I struggle with it, and I've been practicing a lot longer than you."

Samara nodded, but I could tell it still bothered her. Samara liked to be the best at everything. She was one of the most competitive people I'd ever met. It was probably driving her insane that she had a well of magic inside her that she had no idea how to wield.

I frowned at the ground, imagining the tunnels running beneath them, before glancing at Draven. "Could you collapse the tunnels?"

"I thought about it," he admitted. "But I doubt I could do it all at once. I'd probably have to pick a spot and then expand. It would give them time to escape to the surface."

"Yeah, let's not do that." Kieran kissed Draven's cheek. "I'd prefer to not be suddenly surrounded by dozens of giant spiders."

"More like hundreds," Rynn commented idly, her mind clearly trying to work through other options.

"In the words of Samara responding to that asshole Demetri's marriage proposal . . ." Kieran grinned at Samara. "Pass."

She snorted. "He really was the worst."

My frown deepened. I was happy he was dead—and that she'd killed him—but I'd kind of been looking forward to twisting his head clean off his shoulders, and I hadn't even gotten to see Samara cut the fucker's head off.

Didn't seem fair after I'd had to listen to him run his mouth for weeks.

"So we leave the horses behind and walk through," Samara said, interrupting my internal griping. "Rynn, Cali, and I all have experience spotting the doors because we visited the badlands often when we were at Drudonia. We can forge a path."

I almost pointed out that Rynn had fallen into a trap on her way to us, but I bit my tongue. In some ways, the active trapdoors were easier to spot because the trappers kept the areas clear, whereas the abandoned ones were covered by dried up plants and other random debris.

Cali glanced up at the sun and grimaced before giving Roth an appraising look. "Without the horses, we'll have to run to make it to the temple before nightfall."

"Your point?" Roth asked flatly. I glanced over my shoulder to find them scowling at Cali and rubbed my hand over my mouth to hide my grin. Cali was only voicing what we were all thinking—Roth's idea of physical activity was getting a book down from the highest shelf in the library.

And they'd created magical freaking ropes to help them

with that . . . amongst other things, I suspected, based on how I'd caught Samara blushing sometimes when Roth's ropes shifted on their forearms.

"I can carry them if need be," I offered.

Samara's jaw practically dropped as she stared at me.

"What?" I asked, shuffling a little on my feet.

"Aww, he wants to feel useful," Kieran joked. "Let him put all those muscles to use, Rothie Bear."

Roth and I both glared at the blond courtier, but he just smiled wider. Then one of Roth's ropes started to unwind from their forearms—likely to choke Kieran—but Samara smoothly cut in.

"Thank you for the offer, Vail." She walked over to Roth and took their hand, gently wrapping the rope back around their forearm while Roth continued staring daggers at Kieran. "Roth, will you be okay running?"

Bright orange lines bled through Roth's hazel eyes as their bloodlust rose. "Don't worry about my stamina, Samara. I can sure as fuck outlast Kieran."

"That sounds like a fun game," Kieran murmured.

"I do like games that are a win-win for me." Samara grinned smugly. "Let's make it to the temple, and then we can play."

My mind ever so helpfully conjured up the memory of Samara tied up in that cabin while Draven and I tried to make her scream.

Fuck.

"You okay there, Marshal?" Cali drawled. Her tone was casual, but she still looked at me like prey she was determined to take down.

I'd have to be careful as we made our way through trapper territory. Something told me that if Cali saw an opportunity to *accidentally* knock me into a trapdoor, she'd take it.

"If we're going to do this, we should get moving," I said

gruffly, trying to ignore how uncomfortably tight my pants felt right now and willing my hard-on to go away. "Rynn has the best senses out of all of us. She shifts and takes the lead. Cali can scout from overhead. I'll take the rear guard."

It was so easy to fall back into ranger mode, I hadn't even realized I'd done it until I'd given the orders . . . ones I would have given to Adrienne, Emil, and Nyx in different times.

I wouldn't be doing that again. Two of my rangers were dead, and Nyx . . . I didn't know what Nyx was.

For a second, the grief and rage I felt were almost crippling. Until I ruthlessly shoved them into the depths of my soul, slammed the door shut, and threw away the key. Dwelling on what had happened wouldn't help us now. Carmilla would pay. I'd make sure of it.

"It's a good plan," Draven said, cutting off Cali, who looked pissed off at being told what to do. I hadn't meant to give her orders like that, they'd just slipped out. "I'll do my best to sense the spiders if they go on the move, but I likely won't be able to give much warning if it's them springing a trap."

"Understood." I nodded at him thankfully—something I never thought I would be doing. "Let's see to the horses and then get going."

I strode back to the black mare Samara and I had ridden, took the reins that Kieran wordlessly passed to me, and started untying my bags. Suddenly, Samara was there, holding out her hand.

"I can carry it a—"

"Or you can stop being difficult and let me carry one of them." She curled her fingers quickly several times in a very clear hand-it-over gesture. "Crossbow too. I'm a better shot, and you know it."

I grunted because it was true. Samara was shit with a sword, but she was the best shot I'd ever seen with a bow—or a throwing dagger.

"Aim for dead center between their eyes and fangs. It won't kill them, but it will mess up their sense of direction." I passed her the bag, waited for her to secure it to her back, and then unlatched the crossbow. She greedily took it from my hands and checked it over quickly before accepting the quiver of bolts from me as well.

Once she was satisfied, she swung the crossbow over her shoulder. "We should take their bridles off so they don't get caught on anything."

I nodded and slipped the bridle off the mare, who had stood here patiently this whole time. House Salvatore was known for breeding and training some of the best horses—I suspected it was where Zosa had originally come from. How Samara had managed to get her hands on such an incredible horse, I had no idea. These ones might not be as stunning as Zosa, but I had no doubt they were trained to return home. With no riders slowing them down, they could make it before the sun set.

Roth passed the reins of the chestnut horse they'd ridden with Draven to Samara, who patted the horse's head before slipping off its bridle. A minute later, all three horses were cantering away in the direction of home. A few rangers had volunteered to stay behind at House Salvatore to keep watch, so they'd be able to let the horses in—if they made it.

There were no guarantees in Lunaria. Although I suspected the horses were going to have a better trip than us.

I pulled my sword free and jerked my head towards where Rynn waited for us in her wolf form. "Let's get on with it."

Alaric and Kieran both pulled swords similar to mine free and started walking. They both trained regularly with my rangers and were pretty good. Roth's ropes unwound a little from their forearms and dangled at their sides as they followed after the other two.

A low, husky laugh spilt from Samara's lips as Draven whispered something in her ear before pulling the whip coiled at his side free. I still thought a whip was a stupid weapon, even if the prince did wield it well.

By the time we reached Rynn, Cali had taken to the sky above us, and we fell into a single file line. Draven had sped up to be at the front behind Rynn, with me at the end. Nobody spoke as Rynn found us a path through the traps. First one mile. Then another.

An hour ticked by, and I was still spotting trapdoors. How fucking big was this colony?

I spotted some hoof tracks here and there from the deer who cut through the badlands to avoid all the predators that roamed the forests. The trappers were converging where the prey was.

Lucky us.

More than once, Rynn made us backtrack to find an alternate route. I trusted her judgment, but the fourth time she did it, I couldn't stop myself from glancing up at the sun that was rapidly moving across the sky. We still had at least two hours until sunset, but we were also a solid five miles from the temple, if not more. If we didn't get out of trapper territory soon, we would be in serious trouble.

"Wait," Draven said harshly. Everyone froze. "Something's coming. A lot of somethings."

Cali shot higher into the sky.

"It's a deer herd," she called out. "And unless they alter their course . . . they're going to run straight into us."

"Fuck," I growled. "Can you scare them in a different direction?"

"Doubtful." Cali darted down to hover above the ground a few feet away from us. "There are too many of them. I'd be lucky to get half to switch direction."

"So let's use it to our advantage," Samara said quickly.

"The trappers will converge on the deer. We wait until they do, then we run like hell."

"The deer are going to trample anything in their path," I argued. "Or impale it."

A crazy light flared in Samara's eyes, and she grinned at Cali. "Remember that time we got drunk on your twentieth birthday?"

The Furie laughed darkly. "Hard to forget waking up naked in a tree covered in sticky berry juice and wearing your panties as a hat."

"Did you three *ever* study at Drudonia?" Alaric gave Samara an incredulous look.

"Cali definitely didn't," Roth muttered.

"Before the tree, we made a bet over who could hold out the longest against stampeding deer," Samara said smugly. "You lost, Cali, but you split the herd."

"We need to discuss fun ways to celebrate a birthday." Kieran shook his head. "I'll give you a hint . . . it should involve too much wine and sweet treats. Not rampaging, horned monsters."

"Don't tell me how to celebrate my birthdays, pretty boy." Cali shrugged.

Faint vibrations started to rumble through the ground, and we all looked towards where a dust cloud was rising into the sky. The deer were still far enough away that I couldn't make out individuals, but Cali wasn't wrong; the herd was massive.

One-on-one, Lunarian deer weren't dangerous. True, they were large—about the size of an average horse—and the twisted horns that rose from their skulls were as sharp as any dagger, but generally, they avoided conflict. It made them hard to hunt because at the first hint of danger, the entire herd took off. Exactly like they were doing now, with their heads lowered so they could spear or trample anything in their way.

We had the unfortunate luck of being in their path. We'd

never outrun them, and if we tried, the trapper spiders would be on us immediately.

I knew what Samara was suggesting. It was absolutely crazy . . . but it could work. Maybe. Like a fifty-fifty chance. Honestly, we had no other options because that fucking herd would be on us in minutes.

"We need to group together and make ourselves as small as possible if we're going to pull this off," I ordered.

Roth grabbed Samara and tugged her close while Draven, Kieran, and Alaric closed ranks around them and I stepped to Samara's back.

"Rynn!" Samara yelled.

The large white wolf shoved her way between all of us, and I flinched when she nipped my leg but shuffled a little to make room for her. Cali moved to stand in front of us, her black, leathery wings tucked in tight, and her deep red hair spilling down her back like liquid fire as the afternoon sun finally broke free of the clouds.

"Might want to prepare yourselves," she warned in a low, dangerous tone. "There's bound to be some spillover with me being so close to you all."

All we could do was wait for the herd to reach us. If this was going to work, the timing needed to be absolutely perfect. Out of the corner of my eye, I saw a few long legs prod out from the earth before quickly sliding back beneath the trap-doors. The vibrations were making the trappers antsy.

"Get ready!" Cali ordered as the deer thundered towards us, blood already staining some of their stark-white horns. I threw my arms around Samara and ducked my head, nestling into her hair, then I breathed in her scent deeply to ground myself as I heard Cali snap her wings open and release a bloodcurdling scream.

Chaotic magic full of unyielding rage brushed against my mind, and the thread connecting me to Samara thrummed between us as if it was anchoring me to her. I held on to it as the deer raced past us—not into us.

Fuck me. It actually worked.

The ground shook as the deer thundered across the badlands. Then the spiders attacked, and terrified shrieks filled the air.

Cali cut her scream off, her magic abruptly vanishing, and I instantly straightened. The bulk of the herd had passed us, but there were still stragglers trying to catch up to the rest.

That wasn't the problem though. Random deer, we could dodge. No, the problem was that the spiders were launching themselves out of their trapdoors. If they caught a deer, they did their best to drag it back into their tunnel. Sometimes they won . . . sometimes they found themselves speared and stomped to death.

The hard white surface of the badlands was quickly being stained with red blood and a dark green ichor.

Amongst all the chaos were the trappers who hadn't caught anything but also hadn't been trampled—they were hunting now.

It was hard to believe something so large could be lurking beneath the surface. Their bulbous abdomens were a deep red, and it was the only part of their bodies that had coarse hairs covering it. The rest of their bodies were a shiny black, including the three-inch curved fangs, which delivered a toxin that would start breaking down tissue almost immediately.

A thick carapace protected the top half of their bodies, and the exoskeleton on their legs was equally strong. The abdomen was the most vulnerable spot, as it was the only soft bit of their bodies. I'd learned from experience though that they could shoot those fucking hairs to burrow under your skin or puncture your eyes.

There was also the small problem that the spiders were

taller than my waist, and if they reared up onto their hind legs, they would tower over me.

I loved me a good fight, but I also wasn't an idiot.

"*Run!*" I shoved Samara and the others forward.

Nobody needed any further encouragement as we took off at a dead sprint. Deer snorted as they galloped past us, but an enormous one with horns stained completely red, bits of torn flesh still hanging off them, altered its direction to charge straight for us. Kieran was in front, and he started to veer left, only to jerk back when a spider leapt from a trap.

Draven's whip wrapped around one of the trapper's outstretched legs, bright red spikes shooting out from the whip a second before he yanked the whip down. The spider let out a high-pitched shriek as it crashed to the ground and its injured leg snapped in half.

"Take out the fucking deer!" I yelled.

Another spider leapt from a trap, only for Cali to dive from the skies and shove her blade into the space between its abdomen and upper body. The thing let out an ungodly sound, and Cali screamed as its hairs shot out and pierced her wings.

Alaric and Kieran raised their swords as the enraged deer got closer, only for a white blur to leap from the side. Rynn's jaws closed around the deer's throat as her body continued its forward momentum and swung to the other side, jerking the deer with it. The two men were too close to change course, so they jumped over the deer while the rest of us went around it.

To her credit, Samara didn't slow down, not even as Rynn and Cali continued their respective battles. I felt her worry through our link, but she had absolute faith in her friends to come out on top. More spiders poured from the earth, some finding prey to occupy themselves with, others still looking.

If we stopped, we died.

"Six trappers up ahead!" Draven warned, then glanced

over his shoulder to make sure I was with Samara. Unlike the others, he trusted me to keep her safe.

A trapdoor opened to our right, and Alaric shoved Roth left before rolling underneath the spider as it launched itself out. Silver flashed, and dark ichor poured onto the earth as Alaric sliced open the underside of the trapper's abdomen. Without missing a beat, he sprung back to his feet and was running again.

I didn't have much time to be impressed though because the spiders Draven had warned us about darted forward. Rynn and Cali hadn't caught up to us yet, which meant it was the six of us against the six of them. Not the odds I would have preferred.

"Make room!" Samara shouted.

Alaric grabbed Roth's hand and pulled them to the right while Draven and Kieran went left, giving Samara a clear shot at the spiders. Samara slammed to a halt and snapped the crossbow up. In the span of a single breath, two bolts soared through the air. Two spiders jerked and crashed into each other as a bolt sunk into the exact two-inch spot on their heads I'd told Samara about earlier.

She reloaded the crossbow and fired again. Two more spiders went down.

The others raced ahead, even as the two remaining trappers keyed in on them. Samara took out the one on the right, and Draven's whip cracked, taking out two legs of the one on the left.

Samara swung the crossbow onto her back again, but I grabbed her before she could dart after the others.

"Wha—"

Her words were cut off when my mouth crashed against hers in a quick but brutal kiss.

I pulled back and grinned wildly at her. "Nice shooting, my queen. Now it's time to run."

CHAPTER TWENTY-TWO

—

Samara

THE MEMORY of Vail's scorching-hot kiss was all I thought about as we raced across the badlands, chasing the dying light.

"My queen." Vail had called me his queen.

After we'd broken apart, he'd pulled me into a run, and we hadn't spoken since. There hadn't been time because those fucking spiders had cost us. We were lucky that most of us had come out unscathed. Rynn's white coat was now a mix of deep red and dark green ichor, but she only had a few minor wounds. Cali was the worst off. Her wings were still fucked from the hairs the trapper had launched at her. Each one would have to be removed before she could fly again, but we didn't have time to do that now, so she was running with the rest of us.

Everyone had let their bloodlust rise to give them an extra boost of speed and stamina—except Alaric. He was stubbornly keeping his locked down. The fact that he was still keeping pace with us was impressive, but then he did run for fun almost every day because he was a psychopath.

Who ran for fun? Someone who didn't have to deal with thigh chafing, that's who.

I slid Alaric, who was on my right, a dirty look, and he glanced at me with a small grin. If we weren't in such a hurry, I would have tripped the bastard for enjoying this.

Kieran was on my left, and his hand briefly brushed mine for the dozenth time. He'd been doing these light touches frequently since we'd been reunited, like he was reassuring himself I was still there. Roth was sandwiched between Kier and Draven, their eyes burning like two suns as they rode their bloodlust hard.

Behind us, I could feel Vail's attention on me, as it had been since he'd dropped behind us to guard our backs.

The faint outline of the temple appeared on the horizon, and I could have wept. I tried to calculate how much farther we had to go but gave up with a huff.

"How far?" I wiped at the sweat dripping down my forehead before it got in my eyes.

"Five miles," Draven replied roughly.

My lungs burned at the answer. The sun was dipping into the horizon ahead of us. Even if we picked up the pace—which I was doubtful we were capable of—we wouldn't make it before nightfall.

Luck, you spiteful bitch, please be on our side for once and do not let the wraiths show up, I begged—to whom or what, I had no idea. We were so damn close to safety.

Shadows started to sneak across the ground as the sun fell beneath the horizon, slowly taking with it the last of its rays. Even if I couldn't see it, I could *feel* day giving way to night. My senses became a little keener. Speed a little faster. We were Moon Blessed. We were made for the night.

Unfortunately, so were the wraiths.

"Almost there," I panted, more for my sake than anything else. The temple loomed before us, and I could make out its towering columns and large open entrance.

Rynn and Cali ran faster, and the rest of us did the same.

Straight through the entrance, past the first room, make a right, down the stairs. I reminded myself where Rynn said the door to the secret room was.

The last of the light leached from the skies, and the badlands fell into darkness. At some point in our mad dash to the temple, the clouds had rolled back in and blocked the stars. Moonrise was still hours away.

Between one blink and the next, my vision adapted for the night. No sign of wraiths anywhere.

Relief coursed through me. Within minutes, we'd be at the safety of the temple. We only had to make it a little farthe—

Shrieks echoed through the dark, and as one, we all slammed to a halt.

The terror that gripped me was instant, but I breathed through it and let it settle in my bones. I'd long since learned that it was impossible to shove fear entirely aside, but you could use it to make your instincts sharper.

Rynn and Cali sprinted back towards us until we all stood in a circle with our backs to each other. Draven stood to my right and Vail to my left. I didn't bother with the crossbow; instead, I pulled out my blood daggers. Vail pulled a dagger from his thigh and passed it to Roth, who grimaced but accepted it because their ropes would be useless against wraiths.

Shadows emerged from the earth like water from a spring, then slid across the ground and circled us.

"Serril?" I called out. Maybe I could talk our way out of this. Erendriel clearly wanted me for something, and Serril served him. I had no problem lying and agreeing to work with them if it meant we got out of this alive.

One of the shadows crept along the ground and twisted before snapping into the shape of a kùsu. Shadows rolled off the long insect as it skittered forward. One by one, the wraiths chose different beasts to imitate. Some I recognized, some I didn't. All of them had fangs and claws though that could tear us to shreds.

"Not Serril, I'm guessing." If he were here, I suspected he would have taken on that Fae form again and tried to speak with me. I'd only met him the one time, but Serril had come across as someone who would use words to terrify you—not rely on monstrous forms.

My fingers tightened around the handles of my daggers. There was no point in throwing them—only blades with a specific enchantment could hurt the wraiths in their shadow forms, and my daggers didn't have it. Crafting the enchantment was time-consuming and required resources that were hard to come by, which was why only the rangers carried enchanted blades—like Vail's sword.

The rest of us would only be able to harm the wraiths for the split second their shadow forms turned solid—and hope we killed them before they killed us.

The wraiths continued circling around us, forming a perimeter.

"I want to be clear that I'm not complaining," Kieran started, "but why aren't they attacking us?"

"Are you seriously whining about the fact that we're not all monster food right now?" Cali growled.

"I said I *wasn't* complaining, Cali!"

"You were definitely complaining, love," Draven said lightly before sighing. "As to why they're not attacking, it's because these are the lost ones—wraiths that don't even remember being Fae. They're what Strigoi are to Moroi. Mindless monsters that only care about killing."

I pondered the wraiths that were making no move against us. "Like Kieran said when he was complaining—"

"I *wasn't* complaini—"

"They're not trying to kill us," I pointed out.

"Left to their own devices, they're nothing but killing

machines, but they can be controlled. Serril uses them like hounds to track and sometimes attack prey." Draven glanced down at me. "He likely ordered them to wait in areas where he thought you might make an appearance and delay you until he arrives. I'm sure some of them fled the moment they detected you to alert their master."

"If that's the case," I said slowly, "then I'm technically the safest one in the group. They won't harm me, but they will follow me."

"No," Vail growled.

I turned away from Draven to look up at Vail and arched an eyebrow. "I'm sorry, did you just tell *your queen* no? You sure did a quick turnabout on that one."

"Feels like we missed something," Alaric muttered.

"Vail probably did something dramatic and asinine," Roth agreed.

"You're not using yourself as bait." Vail glared at me, ignoring the commentary.

"It could work," Cali said from where she stood behind me. "Some of us stay with Samara, the rest get to the safe room and make sure the path is clear."

"As much as I despise agreeing with Vail," Kieran cut in, "I don't like the idea of us splitting up."

"It'll only be for a few minutes," I argued, eying a wraith that had molded its shadows into an enormous feline monster with spikes running down its back. What in the actual fuck was that thing? I had never seen a beast like it in Lunaria. "The temple is right fucking there." I pointed towards the structure. "We'll be right behind you."

What I didn't say was that we were going with my plan one way or another. These wraiths—the lost ones, as Draven had called them—might be under orders to not harm me, but I doubted that extended to everyone else. The way they would occasionally drift a little closer before almost reluctantly going back to circling us didn't escape my notice. We had no idea when Serril would get here; he could be hours away.

And there was every chance he would kill everyone but me when he arrived.

Icy fear crept through my veins at the thought of losing even one of the people with me. My true family. I'd do whatever it took to keep them alive. Even if that meant drawing a bunch of bloodthirsty wraiths after me. The question was, who was I going to involve in this crazy plan?

As much as I would have preferred to do it on my own, even I knew that wasn't a good idea because I very much wanted to make it to the safe room. This wasn't me sacrificing my life—it was me giving those I loved time to get to safety so that I could then join them.

Then we could have *Holy Fuck We're Still Alive* victory sex. I might even let Vail watch.

"I can take two of them out temporarily—maybe three." Draven uncoiled his whip.

I nodded. "Okay, Draven and Vail, with me." If Draven could even temporarily put some of the wraiths down, then I wanted him with me—and I knew it wasn't worth arguing with Vail. "Everyone else, get to the room. Rynn, once everyone is there, come back out and wait by the main entrance so we can follow you, since we'll likely be coming in hot."

"Bullshit!" Cali snapped. "I'm coming with you. Vail can go with the others."

"Like hells—" Vail started, but I cut him off.

"You've been limping for the last two miles and trying to hide it, Cali. It's more than your wings that are injured. Your magic won't work on the wraiths anyway. Draven and Vail are the best suited for fighting them, and you know it."

Vail was the only one who had a weapon that could hurt the wraiths in their shadow state, and Draven had experience fighting them.

Cali's lips pressed into a flat line while her eyes glowed with rage, but she didn't argue any further. She knew I was right.

"We'll make this quick." I leaned forward slightly on the balls of my feet. "The three of us will run away from the temple, just enough for you lot to get inside the entrance, then we'll turn around and sprint back. I'll take point since the wraiths won't kill me."

Hopefully. I was counting on them fearing Erendriel enough to obey his orders and deny the drive every predator had to chase down prey and slaughter it.

The kùsu-shaped wraith got too close to one that looked like a seriously fucked-up bear, and the two shrieked at each other.

"Go!" I spun around and shoved Kieran and Alaric hard. "Now!"

Without waiting to see if they obeyed, I took off in the opposite direction. Curses sounded behind me, but when I chanced a look over my shoulder, I saw everyone racing towards the temple. Two of the wraiths started to chase after them, only to stop and shake their heads violently, causing shadows to swirl through the air before twisting back in my direction. Both released pissed-off screams, then charged after me.

Well, my plan worked. Yay?

Draven's whip cracked, and something snarled to my right. In front of us, shadows writhed on the ground before bursting upward and snapping into the form of an enormous beast with wings.

"Oh, fuck me!" I skidded to a stop, Vail and Draven doing the same next to me. "Is that a dragon? Why is it so big?"

"What the fuck is a dragon?" Vail cursed as we all tilted our heads to look at the towering monster.

"I don't know!" I took a step away. "There was a picture of one in a book!"

The shadow dragon snaked its long neck forward until its head, adorned with spikes, was only a few feet from us. A mix of fear and adrenaline slammed into me as the other wraiths closed in behind us, leaving us nowhere to go.

Then it spoke one word in Unseelie, its voice so broken that it took me a second to understand.

"*Birreb*." Kneel.

"*Mur keb!*" I screamed. Fuck you.

The dragon roared, and the other wraiths let out their own shrieks.

"Pissing them off further probably isn't a wise move, Sam," Draven chided even as amusement coated his words and a crazy smile lit up his face. He flipped his whip so that the length stretched across the ground before gripping the handle with both hands and then pulling them apart.

I blinked as a *second* whip peeled away from the first—made entirely of blood.

"I knew I saw you with two whips before!" The bloodred whip looked almost exactly like the first, aside from the color. I pointed one of my daggers at him. "You're teaching me how you did that."

Because having an endless supply of blood daggers I could throw at people who pissed me off sounded *amazing*.

"Maybe. If you ask me nicely." Draven winked at me. "Get ready to run again, love."

The wraith dragon growled and opened its maw to roar at us again, but Draven's bloodred whip snapped forward, growing impossibly long before cutting directly through the dragon's head. Instead of passing harmlessly through the shadows, as most weapons would, a deep red mist burst out from the whip, and the wraith reared back with a pained scream. Then the dragon shape fell apart, as if the wraith had lost control of its shadows, which were now writhing across the ground like a puddle of darkness.

Draven's whip snapped around to the wraiths behind us, but I didn't wait to see what would happen. I just took off running back towards the temple with Vail and Draven hot on my heels. Several wraiths were convulsing on the ground like puddles of liquid night, just like the dragon shadow had.

Unfortunately, not all of them, because the one that was shaped like a kùsu and the feline sporting spikes down its spine cut off our retreat to the temple.

Once again, I slammed to a halt. Damn it. Less than fifty feet separated us from the temple, where I could see Rynn's white wolf form pacing.

"Can you do the whip thing again?" I looked to my left, where Draven panted, then dropped my gaze to the single whip he was holding and felt my hope extinguish.

"No," he ground out. "I can only get in a few hits with the blood whip before it disintegrates. It doesn't kill the wraiths either, just fucks with their ability to control their shadows."

"For how long?" Vail moved to stand between me and the two wraiths

"Another five minutes at most," Draven answered tightly.

I eyed the two wraiths. "They won't hurt me. What if I—"

"Don't even think about suggesting that you run one way and we go the other," Vail growled. "I went along with your plan the first time. The others are safe. I'm not leaving your fucking side."

I opened my mouth to argue, but Draven cut me off.

"I agree with the Marshal." Any trace of amusement was gone from Draven's tone. "Besides, even if they won't kill you, they'll absolutely hurt you."

"Fine." I gripped my daggers tighter. "Then we stick close together and just edge our way towards the temple."

"Quickly though." Draven glanced over his shoulder at the shrieking wraiths. "Those ones are going to be extra pissed once they're capable of moving again. We need to be behind that ward before then."

They could still follow us inside the temple, but Rynn was there to help, and it wouldn't be far to the safe room. We'd made it all this way. I refused to falter now.

Slowly, we started walking towards the temple entrance. I took the lead, Draven and Vail walking at an angle so their backs were towards mine. The two remaining wraiths paced aggressively around us, clearly wanting to attack but bound by the order to not kill me.

A minute passed, and we were halfway to the entrance. Hope started to flutter inside my chest that we might actually make it.

I should have known better.

The feline wraith pounced forward, its clawed paw swiping out for my legs. I leapt straight up into the air, its paw passing underneath me. Then Rynn barked in warning, but it was too late. The kùsu wraith plowed straight into my side with the top of its head. The cool shadows momentarily turned solid, which sent me hurtling away from the temple—and from Vail and Draven.

"Samara!" Draven screamed. I heard his whip crack before one of the wraiths hissed in pain, but it wasn't the agonizing scream his blood whip had gotten.

Then I hit the ground and rolled, barely avoiding stabbing myself with my dagger before springing upright. Twenty feet now separated me from the others.

Rynn had charged into the fight. She and Draven were squaring off against the feline wraith. Every time it turned solid to attack one of them, the other would counter.

Based on the fresh blood on Rynn's coat and the way Draven's arm was hanging limply at his side, it wasn't going well. We only had a small window to inflict any type of injury on wraiths, and as soon as they turned back to shadows, they healed. Rynn's teeth couldn't do any lasting damage, and Draven's enchanted whip could barely do any better.

The kùsu circled me, its long, dark body cutting off my view. I had no idea where Vail had gone, but he hadn't been with Draven and Rynn.

I gripped my dagger, even though it was basically useless. Then an eerie sound filled the night, and I realized it was the kùsu wraith laughing.

It weaved its long body around me. Without the light of the moon or the stars, it was hard to distinguish it from the dark of night.

"*Din tros,*" it mocked. Forgotten queen.

Fuck this. I darted forward, intending to run straight through its shadows, but it snapped its massive form towards me. The hard body knocked me backwards before vanishing into cool shadows once more. Out of the corner of my eye, I could see the other wraiths starting to gain control of their shadows.

We were running out of time.

I shoved myself up, ignoring the bite of pain in my leg. Something had crunched when I'd landed, but I could still put weight on it, which was all that mattered. The wraith could only turn solid for two or three seconds, tops. I just needed to time it better.

Before I could attempt to race through it again, its shadowy form rippled, and it jerked its head up with a shriek as Vail's sword sliced through its midsection, momentarily parting the shadows, before he rolled through it.

"Vail!" I raced towards him but then had to leap back when the wraith scuttled between us. It lunged forward, its pinchers snapping towards Vail, but unlike mine, Vail's timing was perfect. He sidestepped the attack and plunged his sword into the wraith's eye for the split second it was corporeal.

It screamed and reared back, creating a clear path for me. I raced forward but halted when Vail held up a hand.

"I'm sorry, Sam." There was a note of finality to Vail's tone that sent a chill down my spine. Shimmering eyes of silver bored into my soul. "I've always loved you. Even when I hated you." He laughed darkly. "There is no force in this world that could have ever stopped me from loving you. I'm so sorry I fucked it all up."

"Don't," I growled and took a step towards him only for him to move back. "Whatever it is you're thinking of doing, don't you fucking dare."

He smiled at me, and in that moment, I didn't think there was anything I hated more. "I was wrong about the prince too. I'm happy you have him and the others. They'll keep you safe. Now *run*."

"Vail!" I shot forward, then jerked myself back as the kùsu-shaped wraith recovered and dove at Vail. Just as the wraith solidified and snapped its pinchers, Vail dove underneath it and shoved his sword through the beast's skull.

For a second, I felt relief at knowing Vail had survived his stupid fucking attack—but then the second wraith pounced. The shadow form of the feline wraith lunged towards Vail with his taloned paws extended. It felt like time froze as the outstretched claws swept towards Vail and turned solid for an instant. That was all it took for blood to spray as three jagged wounds opened across Vail's stomach.

"No!" I screamed.

Vail clamped one hand over his abdomen but stayed on his feet. The two wraiths momentarily forgot about me as they found something to vent their rage on.

Just as I was about to dash after Vail—because there was no way I was obeying his order to run and leave him to die—Draven grabbed me and hauled me back.

"Let me go!" I struggled to break out of his iron grip.

"Close your eyes!" Draven ordered.

"Wha—"

Before I could get the word out, a flash of white bounded past us. Rynn. She had a glowing orb in her mouth as she sprinted towards Vail and the wraiths. She tossed her head back, and the orb flew, arcing upward, impossibly bright. The last thing I saw before one of Draven's hands left my waist to cover my eyes was Rynn shifting to her human form, grabbing the orb out of the air, and throwing it down—directly beneath the wraiths.

Through the cracks of Draven's fingers, I caught the blinding light. If I thought the wraiths had screamed before, it had been nothing compared to now. They were still shrieking when Draven's hand fell from my face, grabbed my hand, and yanked me forward.

"Wait!" I tried to pull free. "Vail—"

"I got him!" Rynn yelled as she half dragged Vail. He was conscious but barely, based on the way he struggled to put one foot in front of the other, a trail of blood leaking behind him.

"We'll fix him inside!" Draven scooped me up in his arms. "We're out of both luck and time!"

The four of us raced towards the temple as the last of the light from the orb faded. Cali and Kieran darted out, helping Rynn carry the now-unconscious Vail the rest of the way. Dark shapes rippled across the ground and walls as the wraiths gave chase through the temple, only to slam into an invisible wall as we darted down the secret stairs and across the ward.

We'd survived.

I sucked in a shaky breath as Draven carefully set me onto my feet.

Rynn glanced at me. "Did that wraith turn into a fucking dragon?"

"What's a dragon?" Cali perked up. "And can I kill it?"

I sighed.

An hour later, Vail limped into the room we'd all set up in after leaving him passed out but mostly healed on a bed. This space under the temple was massive. It was far larger than the secret room I'd discovered near House Harker or the one under Lake Malov. It reminded me a little of the tunnel system the Devereux clan had found. There were multiple levels beneath this one with living quarters, and beneath that was another level that had some rooms for storage and—much to Kieran's delight—a cavern full of hot springs.

We'd only explored enough to get our bearings and make sure everything was secure. The wraiths were still prowling the temple above us, but Rynn had been right—they couldn't get in here, which was something they were extremely enraged about, based on the way they had screamed and trashed some of the marble structures. I was a little worried they were going to bring the whole temple down in their temper tantrum, but it was still standing for now.

I'd gone back to the entrance a couple of times, but there was no sign of Serril yet. He'd get here eventually, I had no doubt.

Alaric, Roth, and Rynn were pouring through some texts that had been locked away in a chest. Rynn had also been right about me being able to unlock the more secured items. It was a simple locking glyph, but it'd been keyed to my blood. I'd opened everything I could find, and we were sorting through the items now. Most of them were books and scrolls, but there were also some weapons and other artifacts.

Normally, I would have been positively giddy about finding lost Fae treasures and my nose would have been in those books immediately, but I was too fucking pissed to concentrate.

The source of my ire was currently slumped in a chair at one of the tables where we'd piled up the weapons and artifacts, which Draven and Kieran were going through. Cali was passed out and snoring in one of the rooms downstairs. We were under orders to wake her up when "it was time to kill something."

"Find anything good?" Vail asked in a gravelly tone as he idly scanned the weapons laid out before him. He still looked like shit. His normally tan skin was pale, and he'd had none of his lethal grace when he'd walked across the room.

Draven grunted in response, but Kieran just shook his head with an *oh, you poor idiot* look on his face. Kieran had been watching me stew in my rage for the past hour. He knew exactly how explosive my temper could be because he'd witnessed it more than once. Back then, it had been Alaric pissing me off. Now, Vail decided to take that spot.

"How are you feeling?" I fixed my features into one of concern as I walked towards the table. Draven and Kieran scooted aside so I could stand directly opposite from Vail and lean forward, placing my hands on the smooth wood surface.

Right next to so many wonderfully sharp, pointy items.

"Fine," Vail said slowly. His instincts were likely warning him about danger, but he didn't know what to make of my worried demeanor. "Thank you for saving me, but you shouldn't have. I don't want you to ever risk your life for me, Sam."

My smile gained a sharp edge.

"Did you mean what you said?" I leaned forward a little more. The table wasn't that wide. Vail could easily close the distance and kiss me. Based on the way his gaze dropped to my lips, I knew he was thinking about it. "That you're sorry . . . and that you love me?"

His eyes snapped back to mine. "Every word."

"That's what I thought." I nodded. My fingers closed around the two daggers my hands had been drifting towards. Normally, Vail's reaction time was better than mine, but he was tired and still hurting—and I was really fucking motivated. Faster than he could react, I slammed them through the backs of his hands—pinning them to the table.

"Fuck!" he swore. "What in the fuck, Sam?"

I hammered a punch to his jaw, and pain ricocheted up my arm. Why did he have to have such a strong jawline? That fucking hurt. Worth it though. My arm shot back to punch him again, but then Kieran had his arms around my waist, laughing as he pulled me back.

"How fucking *dare* you apologize, tell me you love me, and then sacrifice yourself!" I screamed and flailed in Kieran's hold, who just laughed harder at my antics. "If you fucking die before I forgive you, I will drag you back from whatever hells exist just so I can kill you myself, Vail Ferenc!"

"I was trying to save your damn life!" Vail bellowed as he jerked his hands upward. They hit the flat handle of the daggers, and the blades pulled free from the table, drawing another pained grunt from him. "You should be thanking me!" Blood poured from his hands as he rose and glared at me from the other side of the table. Good. I hoped it fucking hurt.

"Gods, he's dumb," Roth muttered.

"Impressively so," Alaric agreed.

"Can this lover's spat be taken somewhere else?" Rynn growled. "Some of us are trying to read and find solutions to our many problems."

I stopped fighting Kieran, but he didn't release me—because again, he knew better. Instead, he kept his arms wrapped around my waist and started kissing my neck, which did admittedly feel nice, but I excelled at multitasking, so I was perfectly capable of being turned on by Kieran and enraged at Vail.

"Samara, love," Draven purred as he sauntered over to stand in front of me and Kieran. He gently gripped my chin and forced me to look at him and end my stare off with Vail.

Amusement danced in his eyes as he brushed a thumb across my bottom lip. "I spotted some clothes in one of the bedrooms downstairs. Why don't you get cleaned up and rest a bit?"

Beneath the desire that Kieran and Draven were drumming up—and the anger towards Vail—exhaustion was tugging at me. Even if I wanted to help with the research, I suspected I'd have to read everything three times before it sank in. We were safe enough here for now. I could afford an hour or two of sleep to better get my wits about me.

"You all should take breaks too," I said begrudgingly.

"We will," Draven assured me.

I managed to turn my head enough to glance at the others, who were all buried in books. "Make sure Roth and Rynn eat something."

"We're not children," Roth said wryly as they flicked their eyes away from the text they were reading long enough to scowl at me before immediately dropping them again. Rynn didn't even bother looking at me, just made a rude gesture with her fingers as she kept reading.

"We will," Kieran echoed Draven's response, and I could feel him grin against my skin. "You going to behave if I let you go?"

"Yes," I promised.

Kieran chuckled and pulled me tighter against his body while Draven leaned forward to whisper in my ear, "Be a good girl, and we'll reward you later."

"I mean, you could reward me now?" I fluttered my eyelashes at him when he pulled back, but he grinned at me before giving me an all-too-quick kiss.

"Go get some sleep, Sam." Kieran released me and gently pushed me forward.

I made it halfway to the door before my anger cut through the dirty thoughts Kieran and Draven had planted in my mind, and I spun back around to face Vail. "Our discussion isn't over, and I'm still mad at you."

"You being mad at me is nothing new, Sam." Dark grey eyes looked at me in challenge. "How about you do what you're told and go get some sleep . . . my queen." He bared his teeth at me.

"Fuck you!" I spat before stomping towards the door—only because I knew Kieran and Draven wouldn't let me beat the shit out of Vail again.

"Fuck you too!" Vail growled.

I was halfway down the hall when I heard Draven say, "Maybe I need to explain how apologies are supposed to work . . ."

CHAPTER TWENTY-THREE

—

Samara

Hours later, I had to admit that I did feel a lot better. The rage towards Vail and the stupid fucking stunt he'd pulled was still simmering, but I was capable of putting that aside to help search this place for something useful. Roth had pointed out the chest where they'd found that orb of light. There'd only been one, but that didn't mean there weren't more somewhere else. Or maybe one of the texts would mention how it had been made.

If we could figure out how to create more, we'd have an actual weapon we could wield against the wraiths. It was a hell of a lot more effective than the enchantments on the rangers' weapons.

Draven's blood whip worked well against the wraiths, and while we'd been exploring this secret level of the temple, I'd asked him more about it. The good news was that I was fairly confident I could recreate the spell on my daggers, making them even more useful. The bad news was that while the spell itself was simple, it required a lot of blood—Fae blood.

Or at least half-Fae blood. Which meant we were limited

based on how much blood Draven or I could spill on any given day. Not ideal.

My eyes slid over the murals painted on the walls. Most of the other places we'd found were utilitarian. The living spaces underneath House Harker were clearly meant to house a large number of people—they had the basics and nothing more. The tunnel system we'd stayed at had been a bit more extravagant, with actual bedrooms instead of just a large space with rows of identical beds.

This space felt like someone had lived here though. Something about the rooms just felt more homey than the other places. The clothes hanging in the closets had that distinct look of having been worn before. I tugged at the thin fabric of the deep purple gown I'd found after washing my clothes and hanging them to dry. Whoever had been here before had had good taste, but they'd clearly been taller and thinner than me. Luckily, the material was stretchy, so it still fit.

The dress even had *pockets*.

And these murals . . . I traced the vibrant petals of the wildflowers painted on the bottom half of the wall.

It was a meadow . . . but not like one I'd ever seen around here. The flowers were too dainty and delicate, and it had a peaceful vibe to it that we simply didn't get here. In Lunaria, even the fucking flowers wanted to eat you.

"Where did you all go?" I murmured aloud, because woven into the beautiful painting was poetry—Unseelie poetry.

The Seelie had turned into the wraiths, but there was no hint of where the Unseelie had gone. It couldn't have been a coincidence that the Unseelie had been known for their shadow magic and the Seelie were now trapped in shadows. Somebody had protected this place to keep the wraiths out . . . or maybe some Unseelie had designed it to keep out their own kind?

The hallway ended in a stairwell, and I started to climb up.

Between this place, the Harker journals, and the room beneath Lake Malov, we had to start finding some answers. Although, given that the Alpha Pack was probably tearing the Velesian realm apart looking for Rynn and that we were almost certainly not welcome there, I wasn't sure how we'd get back into that room.

Only my footsteps sounded as I made my way up—the wraiths had gone quiet. I worried my bottom lip and hesitated when I reached the level where everyone was likely still convened. Hopefully some of them were resting.

My gaze flicked up more stairs to a small landing that led to an archway. On the other side were a few more stairs and then the rest of the temple, but that archway was where the ward started. If I went up there, I could at least peek out and see if I could spot any of the wraiths—or maybe even Serril— waiting.

Decision made, I tiptoed up the rest of the stairs and peered out into the darkness. The last time I'd been in this temple had been to investigate wraith activity. That night had ended with us thinking Draven was the enemy and wraiths attacking us. Vail had almost lost himself to bloodlust and attacked me—then saved me. During the process, he'd ripped open a hole in the ceiling.

The moon had risen while I'd been asleep. I looked longingly at the moonbeams rippling across the temple floor, beckoning me to come and lie on the cool surface and gaze up into the night sky.

"Does it call to you?" a deep voice asked from the shadows.

I'd noticed that I wasn't alone only a split second before he'd spoken, but even then, I'd barely managed to stop myself from jumping. Or taking a step back from the archway as the figure stepped into the moonlight and strolled down the stairs to stand on the opposite side.

Not Serril.

Dark golden-blond hair framed a handsome, masculine face. I saw echoes of Draven in it. The strong jawline, chiseled cheekbones, and those eyes—lapis lazuli blue—were the exact same shade as Draven's. Only, these had no red fractures interrupting the blue.

"Hello, Erendriel." I leaned against my side of the archway like I wasn't the least bit surprised that the Seelie King was standing a foot away from me. Here was hoping that the Fae didn't have sensitive hearing; otherwise, he'd hear my heart pounding so hard, it was a miracle my ribs weren't rattling.

The last time I'd seen him, there had been shadows trailing in his wake, but there were none now. He looked every bit as flesh and blood as I.

Suddenly, my heart, which had been beating rapidly a second ago, felt like it froze.

Did that mean he could walk through the ward? Had he figured out how to turn himself completely back to Fae? I smothered the alarm that threatened to choke me. No. He'd clearly been waiting for me. If he could have gotten past the ward, he would have by now.

Either the ward was also designed to keep out Seelie Fae, or Erendriel had enough wraith left in him that he was still forbidden from passing.

Not all traps were the physical kind. He was here because he wanted something from me, and something told me a centuries-old Fae was just as capable of ensnaring me with words as he was with actions.

I should have been frightened by this—and I was a little unnerved—but I couldn't deny the thrill that ran up my spine. I was about to try to outwit the Seelie King. Sure, he was a throne-stealing bastard, but he'd been clever enough to depose the previous one and hold on to power all this time.

Let's fucking play.

He leaned his broad frame against the stone archway,

mirroring my pose. "Are we on a first-name basis now, Samara?" The grin he gave me was almost playful. "Usually I demand more respect from my subjects, but I suppose you are basically my daughter-in-law, so allowances can be made." He winked.

"Am I?" I gave him a lazy smile, even though I didn't buy his casual and harmless act for a second.

Those cunning eyes studied me. Erendriel had this ageless quality about him. He appeared to be in his early thirties and could have passed for Draven's older brother, but those eyes . . . there was something ancient about them.

"I didn't know my bastard son had it in him," he mused. "Hiding his magic from me all this time." His gaze dropped to my chest, not in a leering way, but like he could see the connection to Draven. "And one or both of you have enough magic to form a mating bond." A crease formed between his brows. "You have . . . three bonds. With who, I wonder?"

Mating bond. The words bounced around in my mind even as I kept a bemused expression on my face, as if Erendriel hadn't just casually solved a major mystery for me.

The strange connections I had with Draven, Roth, and Vail were mating bonds. Holy shit. In my head, I'd occasionally thought of them as my mates, but in name only. I hadn't thought it was possible that we had a true mating bond like the Fae talked about in their stories.

Draven and I might have been half Fae, but Roth and Vail weren't. Did my Fae nature make up for that? What else could these bonds do? Moon bless us, please let the books downstairs have at least some explanations.

Erendriel laughed softly. "You're good. Many in my court would be jealous of your ability to mask your emotions so well."

"I'd be happy to give them lessons." My smile widened. "For a price, of course."

"I see why Serril was so captivated by you. It's hard to impress him, but he was quite intrigued when he returned. It's why I just had to come tonight to see what all the fuss was about."

The Seelie King tilted his head, causing some of his hair to slide over his shoulder, the silky strands falling to his chest. His dark blue shirt was unbuttoned enough to give me a good view of his extremely well-muscled chest, and the fabric clung to his biceps as he crossed his arms.

It all felt very . . . posed.

"Oh!" I snorted and then covered my mouth as giggles escaped. "Was your plan tonight to seduce me? After acknowledging I had a *mating bond* with your son? Maybe you should let Draven show you how it's done. He does the 'effortlessly gorgeous' thing a lot better."

Erendriel straightened, and the charming facade fell like a mask he'd pulled off.

"It seemed worth a try." He shrugged. "Velika was easy enough to manipulate."

"What do you want, Erendriel?" I deliberately didn't use the word *king* to see if it would annoy him. If it did, he hid it well.

"You by my side. As my queen."

I waited for him to laugh. He did not.

"First, no. As you noted, I already have a few mating bonds—and I'm quite happy with all of them." Okay, maybe not the Vail part of it, but whatever. "And before you ask again, you should know I cut the head off the last man who tried to force me to marry him." I narrowed my eyes. "Secondly, why?"

It had to be my bloodline. He must have only recently learned that my father had been the son of the previous Seelie King. The question was, how? And what precisely did he want me for? To get into places like this?

"Mating bonds can be broken."

Dread hit me, and I knew I'd failed to keep it off my face. I had no intention of breaking my mating bond with Draven and Roth, and as soon as I could figure out how to share it with Kieran and Alaric, I would be doing so.

Vail . . . I had no idea what I was going to do about Vail. I was still feeling kind of stabby towards him.

Luckily, Erendriel was looking over my shoulder to the stairs below, so he missed all the misgivings in my expression. "Whatever you find in here will not give you the answers you seek. This place was built by the Unseelie Princes—and they are liars."

Are. Not were. The Unseelie Fae were still alive. At least Erendriel believed them to be.

"And you'll tell me nothing but the truth, right?" I huffed, slipping back into a mask of haughty indifference to not even hint at what information Erendriel had just given away.

His gaze snapped back to me.

"Join me, and I'll take care of your aunt for you. The crown has no control over my mind, but it will tell you if I'm lying or not." He placed his hands on either side of the archway, leaning forward until only a few inches and the thin boundary of the ward separated us. "Right now, you're a queen in name only. Let me make you one legitimately. Right now, the Moroi and the other Moon Blessed are just children stumbling around in the dark and hoping to not get eaten by the monsters."

I snapped my fangs at him. "We hold our own."

"Barely."

"So light it up for me. Convince me to at least *entertain* the idea of trusting you. Why did you kill my grandfather?" I adjusted my position so that I stood directly in front of him. He was easily a foot and a half taller than me, so I had to tilt my head back. "You were his faithful general, no? If you betrayed him, it wouldn't seem that out of character for you to do the same to me once you get what you want—whatever that is."

He pondered me for a long moment. "I want to go home."

"Home," I repeated and thought about the murals here and in all the Fae fortresses left behind.

"Yes." He flashed his teeth at me. "The one your grandfather cost us because he refused to listen to me and allied himself with those traitorous Unseelie Princes. He's the reason we ended up here in this fucking prison."

Prison. That's why this place was like one of the hells the Fae poetry sometimes alluded to. It was a punishment—for the Fae.

"Why were the humans brought here? Were they part of the rebellion?"

It was Erendriel's turn to scoff. "We were hardly going to grow our own crops or scrub our own floors."

"Of course not." I gave him a flat look.

His gaze hardened. "Don't think your grandfather was some hero to the humans. His father had been a good and strong king; he was the only reason I served Lachlan for as long as I did, but Eirac would have been disgusted to learn his only son made a bargain with the Unseelie and lost everything because of it. I did your family a favor by removing Lachlan from the throne."

"Sure," I said smoothly. "Absolutely nothing about it was self-serving at all, *King* Erendriel."

His mouth tightened. "You have no idea what it was like where we came from. How the Fae were treated. We were fighting for a better world—I still am fighting for a better world."

I really wanted to know more about the world outside Lunaria, but I was sitting on a treasure trove of information. Sure, it might be biased, but so was Erendriel, and he'd already given me quite a bit of information in the last ten minutes.

Amateur.

"And whose neck will you step on for your better world?" I drawled. "Or were you planning on taking all of the Moon Blessed with you?"

A faint sneer that he tried and failed to hide trembled across his lips.

I shook my head with a laugh. *"Chil muréd."* Get fucked.

The last of Erendriel's control snapped as he slammed his palms against the stone, and even through the ward, I felt the power of his magic ripple forth as the ground shifted slightly beneath my feet.

"You've only survived this long because my attention has been elsewhere." He snarled. "When I leave this place—and I will leave Lunaria—I will take you with me as my queen." His fingers danced across the invisible boundary. "If you ask me nicely, I might even let you bring my ungrateful son and whatever other lovers you want to slum it with. I'm only interested in your bloodline, not your cunt."

I rolled my eyes. Did he think crude insults were going to get a rise out of me? Vail and Alaric had already had that covered for the last *decade*. Maybe I should suggest he take lessons from them too?

"As fun as this chat has been"—I tapped my claws against the stone—"I'm starting to feel a bit bored. What specifically are you proposing? I'm not any more interested in your cock than you are in my cunt. My lovers have been keeping me *very* satisfied, and I'll definitely be adding a few more mate bonds in the future."

"You should be begging to be my queen." Erendriel's mouth twisted in distaste.

"The only thing I beg for is Kieran's co—"

"There are more hidden spaces like this throughout Lunaria," he cut me off, clearly annoyed that I did dirty talk way better than he. "If we form a mating bond, I'm confident it will give me access to them."

"To do what exactly?" I arched a brow. "The knowledge within these walls is useful to me, but you likely know all of it already."

He went still for a moment. "Agree to work with me, and I'll tell you."

"I'll think about it." I blew him a kiss and turned to walk back down the stairs.

"My patience only goes so far, Samara," he warned. "You don't want to find out what happens if I set my sights on you as an enemy."

"Likewise, usurper." I glanced over my shoulder, pulling on my bloodlust hard enough to let my eyes bleed black. "You asked me if the moon calls to me? She does. *We* are her beloved monsters. Lunaria might be the prison you were forced into, but it's the fire that forged us."

"*Qìnol, din tros. Leb are fi fel keb' fapnik.*" Careful, forgotten queen. We are the monsters you fear.

I snapped my fangs at him. "*Keb' are fi kuspa fel. Leb are fi men ones.*" You're the old monsters. We're the new ones.

AN ENDLESS STREAM of thoughts swirled through my mind as I made my way down the stairs. I needed to inform everyone that I'd just had a conversation with the fucking Seelie King so we could dissect every word that had been spoken. There was so much to glean from my encounter—both about the history of Lunaria and what he needed us for.

What he needed *me* for.

I stepped out of the stairwell into the hallway of the first under level, only for Alaric to grab me by the waist and pivot my back to the wall.

"Alaric!" I squeaked. "What are you do—"

His mouth crashed against mine, demanding and possessive. I parted my lips, and his tongue slipped inside to taste me, then his hands slid from my waist to my ass, cupping me and hoisting me up. Thanks to the high slits on either side of the dress, I was able to wrap my legs around him easily as my arms wound around his neck.

Alaric ground against me, eliciting a moan. One hand gripped my ass harder, while the other roughly tugged the dress off my shoulders, causing my breasts to spill out because I hadn't found a chest band to wear while mine was drying.

"Seelie King," I panted when Alaric tore his mouth away from mine. "He was here. We spoke."

"I know." His head ducked down, and he sucked on my breast before palming it. "I heard every word that asshole said."

"Need to tell the others." I didn't know what had gotten Alaric so worked up, but he was making it increasingly difficult to stay focused on anything other than getting his pants off. "Alaric—oh, fuck!"

The hand that had been cupping my breast ran down my body until it slid between my thighs. There was no hesitation as he yanked my panties to the side and thrust three fingers into me. My hips bucked forward as Alaric pumped his fingers while his tongue teased my nipple.

All I could do was hold on and ride Alaric's hand as he fucked me. I could feel my climax building when he brushed his thumb over my clit before pushing down on it, making me scream his name as I came apart.

He laughed huskily against my skin, his breath tickling my hard nipple before raising his head to meet my gaze again. A satisfied smile stretched across his full mouth as he slowly played with the hot slickness dripping out of my pussy and down my thighs.

"I'll never get tired of feeling you come." A small amount of turquoise bled into his green eyes. "On my cock. My tongue. My hand." He thrust his fingers back inside my needy cunt, drawing another moan out of me.

"We need to tell—" My half-hearted protest was cut off when Alaric snapped his hips forward and I felt every inch of him through his pants. Suddenly, I desperately wanted something other than his fingers inside me.

"They can wait." Alaric grinned at me, desire and need lighting up his handsome face. The knowledge that nobody but me made him smile like that sent a thrill running down my spine. Mine. That smile was mine—just like he was. "Rynn and Roth are passed out. They literally fell asleep on top of the books, and they didn't didn't stir once as Kieran and I carried them downstairs to the room where Cali is still passed out. Kieran and Draven went off to *talk*." He rolled his eyes.

I let out a breathy laugh. No doubt their conversation was similar to the one Alaric and I were having. "And Vail?"

Alaric let out a wicked chuckle. "Knocked out cold on the floor."

"What happened?" I started, only to moan when he slid his fingers over my clit.

"Rynn happened." His gaze fell to where his fingers pumped in and out of me. "Knocked his ass out less than a minute after you left. It was a good hit. Asshole hasn't stirred once."

Any concerns I had for Vail vanished when Alaric shoved his fingers into me and fucked me roughly. I arched my hips into him, spurring him on, only to whimper when he withdrew them.

"I was on my way to find you when I heard you speaking with Erendriel." Fabric rustled, and then something hard and thick pushed into my core.

We both groaned as Alaric bottomed out and my pussy clenched around him.

"Did you mean what you said?" His eyes searched mine as more flecks of turquoise pierced through the green. I didn't even think he was aware of his bloodlust rising. I wasn't the least bit worried, but I was pleased to see him releasing some of that iron grip he kept on himself.

"About what?" I braced my hands on his shoulders, enough that I was able to rise up a bit before sinking back down onto his cock.

"Fuck," he ground out as he gripped my ass with both of his hands and pulled me harder onto him. I tilted my head back against the wall and enjoyed the thrill of him pounding into me. Alaric was always so in control—I loved being the one to make him lose it.

One of his hands left my ass to twist into my hair and force me to look at him again, the blue in his eyes snaking through the green like rivers.

"You have a mate bond with Draven, Roth, and Vail." Not a question—a statement. His pace changed from hard and fast to slow and torturous just as I was on the verge of climaxing again. I hissed in frustration and tried to lift myself up again, only for Alaric to grab my wrists and hold them above my head, his hips and body pinning me against the wall. "Did you mean what you said about forming a bond with all of us?"

"Yes, but if you don't have me coming in the next ten seconds, I might seriously rethink it," I growled.

Alaric stared at me. "I've been going out of my mind with jealousy over that fucking connection you have with those three assholes."

"Draven's not an asshol—"

"I know what he said to Kieran, so yes, Draven *is* an asshole." Alaric glared. "But I'm willing to make allowances since you two seem to like him."

"How gracious of you."

"And Vail is your problem, but just say the word, and we'll happily kill him for you." He maneuvered his hold until he secured both of my wrists in one hand so his other could go back gripping my ass. "I know I should say something clever and charming to assure you that you're making the right decision in forming the mate bond with me."

A flicker of uncertainty flashed in those beautifully mesmerizing eyes of his. After everything we'd been through, some part of him still thought I wouldn't choose him in the end.

"I don't need you to be charming, Alaric," I said honestly. "I just need you to be mine."

He leaned in until our foreheads touched. "Yours," he breathed across my lips. "Always."

"I love you, Alaric." I brushed my lips against his.

"I love you too, Sam." He kissed me again, this one tender and sweet, and yet it still left us breathless when we broke apart a moment later.

When he looked at me, his eyes were almost solid turquoise. I saw the moment he felt it, the panic that bled into his features as he tried to claw his bloodlust back. His hand dropped from my wrist, and he started to pull out of me to set me down but froze when I cupped his face in my hands.

"You're fine, my love." I kissed the corners of his mouth. "Your bloodlust has been rising this whole time, but nothing bad has happened. You won't turn Strigoi, I promise."

He swallowed. "We can't know for sure. I could hurt you or—"

I cut him off with a kiss before nipping his bottom lip. "You won't. Trust me." I leaned back enough so that I could slide my hand through the opening of his shirt and lay my palm flat over his heart. "Trust us."

A new bond burned and sizzled to life. I couldn't explain

how I knew it would happen—only that I did with absolute certainty.

Alaric's eyes widened. "I can *feel* you."

"Show me." I shifted my hips slightly where we were still joined. "Fuck me, Alaric. Make your mate scream."

"As my queen demands." He grinned and stepped back from the wall, taking me with him, his cock still buried inside me. "But we're going down to the hot springs."

CHAPTER TWENTY-FOUR

—

Draven

KIERAN FOLLOWED me down the hallway, away from the room we'd left Rynn and Roth sleeping in. Cali had cracked open one golden eye at us but then drifted back into her healing slumber. Rynn and Samara had been the ones to remove the hairs the trapper spider had shot into her wings, and it hadn't been pretty. The hairs were covered in hundreds of little barbs that did just as much damage coming out as they did going in.

Blood magic didn't work on Furies, just as their shadow magic didn't work directly on us, so we couldn't aid her healing. She'd heal fast though, all Furies did, and sleeping it off would help.

Alaric had murmured something about checking on Samara, who was also still sleeping, but based on the pointed look he gave me, I knew he was giving me and Kieran some alone time.

Out of all of Samara's friends and lovers, he was the one I had the most difficulty reading. He and Roth were both equally standoffish, but Roth would just let things go for the most part. If it wasn't a book or Samara, they didn't seem to have the energy to care about it for long. Except for their family. For all their blustering, it was clear how much Roth loved their unhinged brothers and parents.

But at best, Alaric gave me cool looks. Most of the time though, he just acted like he was on the verge of tearing my throat out. I deliberately ignored his antics because I didn't really give a shit; all I needed was Samara and Kieran, and I had them both—and I'd never let them go again. Also, I was fairly certain I knew why Alaric treated me the way he did.

The grumpy asshole might be shit at choosing his words, but he loved Samara and Kieran was his best friend. He was protective of them both, and I'd hurt Kieran. Badly.

Kier might have already forgiven me for the things I'd said to break things off with him a year ago, but Alaric hadn't. It honestly made me respect him more, and I was thankful Kier had someone like that in his life.

Fortunately for me, I wasn't Vail. I knew how to apologize and right previous wrongs, which is something I'd be proving to Kier—and by extension, Alaric—for the rest of my life.

And that's exactly why I was leading Kier to the room at the very back of this floor, away from everyone else. I wanted to make sure we had privacy for this conversation, and for all the niceties of the living quarters here, I hadn't noticed any silencing glyphs.

Over the past few days, I'd been able to draw enough information out of Roth to get an idea of how things had been while Samara and I had been imprisoned. How Kieran had exhausted every single one of his contacts and grown more distant and snappish as they'd failed to provide anything useful. I knew how Kieran thought. He must have believed he was letting us down because my beloved courtier always felt he had something to prove, like he wasn't worthy of being loved.

For all of his confident swagger, Kieran eyed that gulf

between our stations. I was a prince, twice over. Sure, mommy dearest was dead and Erendriel was a usurper, but even a fallen prince was still a prince.

Samara was the Harker Heir and likely soon to be Head of House Harker—maybe more, depending on what happened with the Sovereign House after Carmilla's inevitable demise. Plus the whole minor detail of her being the granddaughter of the former Seelie King.

In Kieran's eyes, he was less than us. Something that prick Demetri had only made worse. Samara had shared some of the hateful things Demetri had said during their final encounter, such as the reason he'd been so obsessed with forcing Samara to marry him again. How—in his words—he'd had no choice.

Samara had practically trembled with fury when she'd repeated what he'd said about Kieran. Demetri had wanted to save face because of the stupid gossip in his court about her falling in love with a courtier. His ego had been bruised, and he'd wanted to punish Samara for it.

It was a shame that Samara had killed him because I would have loved to cut out Demetri's hateful tongue and make him choke on it.

"I know the others are excited about the treasures upstairs, but honestly, these clothes are amazing," Kieran drawled as he explored the armoire against the wall of the room we'd ducked into. He held up a deep blue tunic embroidered with gold stitching. "Whatever Fae built this place had amazing taste. Hopefully they don't ever return to look for their stuff because I'm absolutely stealing all this and taking it back to House Harker."

"No doubt it will look better on you than any Fae." I grinned at him.

Kieran smiled back, but it faltered as he carefully folded the tunic and put it back onto the shelf. "I suppose maybe you and Samara won't be returning to House Harker though." He turned away from me and closed the doors to the armoire. "Everything is so fucked in Lunaria right now. You two might have to stay at the Sovereign House while it all gets fixed. Alaric will be useful in negotiating with the Houses, and Roth has a good mind for determining strategies for harvests and trades. Probably not much use for a courtier though." He snorted. "I don't think lavish balls and lazy mornings trading gossip are going to be in our future any time soon."

"Most likely not," I agreed and closed the distance between us. Kieran went still as I wrapped my arms around him, tugging his back to my chest. "But you know what is in my future?"

"What?" he asked tightly.

"You." I kissed his neck. "Always you, Kier."

Some of the tension eased from him, but not enough, so I spun him around until his back was against the armoire and I leaned my body against his. Kieran was only an inch shorter than me, but he was built a lot leaner.

"So this is why you chose a room so far from the others . . ." His brown eyes lit up, and a playful grin stretched across his mouth while he toyed with the ends of my hair.

It was a lie.

Kieran had as many masks as he did clothes—and he changed them far easier. Before everything had fallen apart between us, I'd adored watching him flit about the stupid parties Velika had been obsessed with throwing to boost her ego.

Between one breath and the next, Kieran would change from a sultry lover to an empathetic shoulder to cry on to a charming and self-deprecating friend.

I loved watching him work a crowd, seeing how he could

get so many people to eat out of his hand and spill their secrets without even realizing what they were doing.

I did *not* love when he used one of those masks on me.

"Kier," I purred and ran a hand through his tousled blond hair before letting it trail down the side of his face. "What did I tell you about wearing those false smiles around me?"

Those beautiful brown eyes blinked, and then Kieran gasped when my hand dropped to his throat and tightened. "Drav," he rasped.

My mouth crashed against his, hungry and possessive, then I broke off the kiss almost as quickly as I'd started it, leaving Kieran breathless.

"Let me make this perfectly clear." I loosened my hold on his throat but didn't remove my hand. "I have done terrible things in my life. Things that will haunt my dreams until I take my last breath."

"You didn't have a choi—"

"Sometimes I did," I cut him off. "Most of the time, it's true that either Erendriel or Velika forced me to do things." A lump formed in my throat as I thought of the outposts Erendriel had been able to break into because of me. I hadn't been willing, but it'd been my blood all the same that had allowed all those Moroi to be slaughtered while they slept. Their screams still echoed in my mind. I swallowed as I pushed out the other truth. "But, sometimes, I just wanted to avoid more pain . . . and I did as I was commanded."

"What happened?" Kieran asked softly, no judgment in his eyes.

Fuck. I didn't deserve him.

"Erendriel spends most of his time in the mountains above the Velesian realm, but the wraiths have different strongholds throughout Lunaria, including this temple for a while. More than one ranger has stumbled across them and seen too much." I dropped my gaze to Kieran's throat, where I had absently started running my thumb over his pulse. That constant reminder that he was alive. I focused on that while I continued, "When Erendriel was gone—which was often—he left Serril in charge. That prick reveled in making me choose between being subjected to whatever fun torture he had recently thought up . . . or ending the life of the ranger."

My spine itched where Serril had broken it in multiple places. For all his pretty words and calm demeanor, there was something seriously fucked up about Serril. I didn't know if he'd always been that way or if centuries of living as a wraith had twisted him. My father was a cruel bastard, but at least he didn't take pleasure in it the way Serril did.

Although he had to have known what his right-hand was like and still left him in charge. I shook my head to clear the dark memories.

Then I lifted my eyes to meet Kier's once more, expecting to see at least a hint of disgust, but there was none.

The corners of his lips curled into a lopsided smile that I knew was his real one. "This is Lunaria, Drav. We endure and survive, but that doesn't mean we come out unscathed. Those rangers were dead the moment they were captured. You can't regret granting them what I'm sure was a kinder death than the wraiths would have given them."

"I don't," I said truthfully. "Am I proud that I chose my life over theirs? No. Would I do it again? Absolutely."

He didn't say anything as I dropped both of my hands to his waist and tilted my head to touch my forehead to his. A second later, his hands rested over mine.

"The only thing in my wretched life that I regret is how much I hurt you that night," I whispered, because in my worst nightmares, I relived the scene of Kieran coming to one of my mother's parties and me breaking his heart in front of everyone. That beautiful smile falling from his face as I loudly announced that I was bored with him. That he should watch how he spoke to me since he was just a courtier.

Fuck. I was just one of many who had thrown Kieran's station in his face.

The nightmares never ended there though. No, the grand finale was always me finding Kieran's broken body somewhere. It was me waking up in panic with a pit in my soul, thinking Kieran was dead—and that I'd never have the chance to make things right between us.

That ended now.

"You are everything to me, Kier. I'm the one who's not worthy of you." I pulled back enough to look him in the eyes, which were glistening with tears. "But I will spend the rest of my life proving how much I fucking love you, if you'll let me."

"You have nothing to prove to me," Kieran said forcefully. When I opened my mouth, he clamped a hand over it. A few tears raced down his cheeks, but he was smiling at me. "And I'm more than happy to spend the rest of my life convincing you that you are worthy of being loved, because I absolutely love you beyond reason."

Then he dropped his hand from my mouth and kissed me.

The taste of him flooded my mouth, and when he bit my bottom lip hard enough to draw blood, I moaned. That sound was apparently his undoing because Kieran shoved me back a few steps and tore my tunic off before roughly yanking my pants down.

Before I knew what was happening, he was on his knees and swallowing my cock.

"Fuck, Kier." I grunted as my hand fell to the back of his head, fingers twisting in his hair. "I was planning on doing this to you."

He looked up at me as his lips slid back up my hard length. His tongue circled my broad head before releasing me completely. "Sorry, love." He gripped my base with his right hand and squeezed, giving me a cheeky grin that had me almost coming all over his damn perfect face. "But I was already intending on doing this, and I'm absolutely not stopping now. So how about you be the charming prince you are and fuck my mouth hard enough that I gag?"

"As you demand." I used my hand to push his head onto my cock at the same moment I thrust my hips forward.

Without breaking eye contact, he took me all the way in, his hand moving to cup my balls while his head bobbed up and down. I hadn't been lying, I'd been intending to throw him onto the bed and lavish him with praise and pleasure.

But if this was what my love wanted, who was I to deny him?

My thrusts became harder and more punishing, and Kieran let out a muffled moan as my cock hit the back of his throat over and over again. I felt myself start to coil and tighten. Gods, he was already going to make me come, like I was some inexperienced youth getting off for the first time.

"Kier," I ground out and yanked him off me. "I'm not ready yet, and your mouth is too fucking perfect."

He rose to his feet, that same playful grin on his face as he forced me to walk backwards until I hit the bed. I sat down, and Kieran shoved me onto my back. I was bigger than him and could have held my own, but I was kind of liking this bossy side of him, so I stretched across the bed, propping myself up on my elbows so I could watch him strip.

I gripped myself and lazily moved my hand up and down my cock while I admired Kieran's lean and hard body. Kieran watched me hungrily as he pulled a small glass vial from his pocket before ditching the rest of his clothes.

"Remember the game we used to play at parties?" Kieran moved to the edge of the bed and gripped my legs, pulling me closer to himself before angling them over his shoulders. Then he tipped the vial, letting some of the clear fluid seep out onto his fingers until they glistened.

"Oh, fuck me," I moaned when his hand slid under my ass and those slick fingers started teasing me.

"That was definitely part of the game." He chuckled darkly. "What was the other part?"

One finger slid in, stretching me out, and I bit back the second groan that tried to slip free. "To be quiet," I breathed. "You used to love fucking me near that damned veranda."

"And your favorite spot was in that alcove right behind where the musicians played." He pushed another finger inside me, and this time, I couldn't stop myself from moaning. "The others are only a few doors down. Trust me when I say that you don't want to be around Cali when her sleep gets disturbed."

"You're kind of wicked, Kier." I stroked myself harder.

"You love it." He grinned down at me and added a third finger.

"I do," I panted. "I really fucking do, but if you don't get your cock inside me in the next ten seconds, I'm going to bend you over this bed and—*fuck*!"

I thrust hard into my own hand as Kieran did exactly what I demanded. His thick length glided into me as he spread my legs a little wider over his shoulders.

"That's not staying quiet, my love." He hammered into me again before stopping, buried balls-deep inside. "Now put that hand of yours to work around that gorgeous cock."

His grip on my thighs tightened as he started fucking me hard and fast. I did as he ordered, sliding my hand up and down my length in rhythm with him. His gaze drank in every ounce of my pleasure, darting from where I bit my lip to try to choke back the moans, to where my hand was fisting my cock, and finally to where he was taking me over and over again.

It was getting harder and harder to stay quiet.

Kieran saw how close I was to losing it because gold bled into his brown eyes as he pushed my legs wider so he could lean down between them. I released my cock and pulled him to me, kissing him hard and then moaning when one of his hands found my rigid length.

He broke our kiss and turned his head, bearing his neck for me. I struck just as a scream threatened to escape my throat. My fangs slid into his soft flesh, and he let out a low moan as his sweet blood filled my mouth. His thrusts became rougher as he fucked me while I drank him down.

Then he groaned his release as my own orgasm tore through me. I slid my fangs free from his neck, and he collapsed next to me. Blood trailed down his neck and my cum coated my stomach and chest, but Kieran didn't give a single shit as he cuddled into my side.

Suddenly, a familiar heat flared inside my chest.

"Is that . . ." Kieran trailed off as he stared at the same spot on his own chest before his brown eyes flecked with gold looked up at me.

"Yes," I breathed out.

Whatever bond I had with Samara, I now had with him too.

An hour later, we were both clean and in fresh clothes, thanks to the Fae who had left their clothing behind. Kieran straightened the tunic he'd been eying earlier as we started up the stairs. Cali and the others must have really needed their sleep because, somehow, we hadn't woken them when we'd started round two . . . or three.

Samara, however, was no longer in bed. There were no signs of Alaric either.

"So, what do you think?" Kieran glanced at me over his

shoulder, his golden blond hair still dark from rinsing off. "Are they actually working upstairs . . . or fucking on one of the tables?"

I started to answer when a faint moan echoed up the stairwell.

We both stopped midstep.

"Neither." I laughed.

Kieran's eyes lit up. "I wonder if Alaric locked the door . . ."

I grinned mischievously. "Let me grab something real quick, and then we'll go find out."

A moment later, we were standing outside the large door that led to the underground hot springs. I'd actually been planning on convincing Samara to come down here later with me and Kieran, but it seemed Alaric had beat us there. Now we'd find out how much the grumpy asshole was up for sharing.

I suspected he'd be swayed when I presented the peace offering I held in my hand.

"Oh, fuck!" Samara screamed from the other side of the door. "Harder!"

Kieran reached out and slowly twisted the doorknob, which turned easily. He chuckled. "All his bitching, and he didn't lock the door either."

He flung the door open and we strode in without any hesitation.

The room—really more of a cavern—was completely open, with various pools of steaming water spilling into the others, courtesy of the mini-waterfalls that connected them all, and Fae lanterns cast the entire space in a soft, warm light.

It was one of the most beautiful sights I'd ever seen in Lunaria, but it paled in comparison to what was currently captivating all my attention—Samara leaning over the edge of one of the pools, her long, black hair hugging her body, and giving us a glorious view of her breasts as they bounced while Alaric fucked her hard from behind.

Her eyes widened when she saw us, and a second later, Alaric spotted us too. He slammed into her one more time and held still, his eyes a mix of turquoise and light green.

Interesting. I'd rarely seen him let his bloodlust out, and even then, it'd only been for brief flashes here and there.

"So that's what it feels like," Alaric said dryly, although his tone had a deep rasp to it now.

Kieran and I both let out dark chuckles. He'd told me about Alaric's proclivity of walking in on Samara getting fucked and the tantrums he'd thrown over it.

Samara moaned when Alaric thrust into her again while wrapping his hand around her dark hair and pulling back, forcing her to push those absolutely perfect tits out farther.

My concerns over Alaric not being keen on company vanished, which was good because my cock was getting uncomfortably tight in my pants.

"Need I remind you both that we are in a life-or-death situation here?" Kieran said sternly, even as he stripped and strode towards the pool.

"All the more reason to get some last-minute orgasms in while we can," Samara snarked before yelping when Alaric smacked her ass.

"She does have a good point, love," I said idly, tossing my own clothes aside.

Samara's bloodlust was out to play, and her eyes were like solid black gemstones as she hungrily looked at Kieran's cock and then mine. She was insatiable—I really loved that about her.

"I always have good point—wait." She went still, and Alaric loosened his hold on her hair but didn't pull out of her. Samara's hand fell to her chest as she looked at Kieran, then me. "I can feel Kier . . . through you."

Kieran blushed. Like honest to the moon *blushed*.

"We have . . ." I smiled softly at Kier. "We have what you and I have." My gaze went to Alaric, and I sensed what I hadn't noticed at first—that I could feel him too. "And apparently what you and him have now."

"Holy fuck!" Kieran beamed at his friend. "You two are . . . whatever this is?"

"Mates," Samara said softly. "It's a Fae mating bond."

The magic that coiled in my soul shuffled almost happily at the declaration.

"How . . ." I swallowed. "How do you know?"

For a second, the stupid happy grin slipped from Samara's face. "I'll tell you later—it can wait—let's celebrate." Alaric's hand trailed down her spine to grip her other hip, and she groaned as he shoved his hips forward. "Get your gorgeous asses in this pool."

"So demanding, Sam," Kieran chided before practically leaping into the water.

"Actually," I drawled as I leisurely closed the distance between me and Samara. "I have an idea."

"Oh?" she breathed out as Alaric slowly pumped in and out of her.

"Mm-hmm." I fell to my knees in front of Samara, just far enough away that her mouth couldn't reach my cock the way I knew she wanted to based on how she licked her lips while she stared at it. "It'll require a little rearranging though."

"Not a fan of that idea," Alaric grunted.

"Oh, you will be." Kieran chuckled as he grabbed a handful of Samara's hair and twisted her head enough so his mouth could claim hers.

"What my *mate* means to say"—happiness bloomed inside my chest at calling Kieran that, and I felt it echoed down our bond—"is that we brought you a present."

Alaric looked towards me as I held out the small vial. For a second, he just stared, but then his lips stretched into a smile that could only be described as sinful.

After one more hard thrust that had Samara moaning into Kieran's mouth, he pulled out.

"What?" Samara growled and started to look over her shoulder, only to exhale sharply as Kieran picked her up and slammed her down onto his cock in one smooth motion. "Oh, fuck," she moaned and wrapped her legs and arms around him.

Kieran kissed her as she continued lifting herself up slightly before slamming down on him while he walked them over to a shallower ledge and perched on the edge. Samara straddled him, continuing to ride his cock as the water splashed around them. The back of the pool slanted slightly, allowing Kieran to lean back and pull Samara forward with him.

"I still think you're an asshole." Alaric took the bottle from me.

"Honestly, same." I shrugged.

"You ever break Kieran's or Samara's hearts again, I'll carve out yours and stick it in a jar to decorate my office," he said casually.

"If I ever do that again, I'll let you." It wasn't a lie. I'd sooner break my chest open and rip out my own heart than hurt them again.

Kieran did something to make Samara let out a half-strangled moan, and both of us looked over at them.

"Alright." Alaric glanced down at the vial in his hand. "Let's go fuck our mate until her voice gives out."

I got to my feet as Alaric strode through the water to where Kieran had sat up enough to suck on one of Samara's breasts while his fingers teased the nipple of the other. Her head was tilted back in pure ecstasy as she continued to bounce up and down on his cock.

Sensing our approach, she glanced over her shoulder to

where Alaric now stood behind her before looking up at me. "You look like you have a plan, prince." She smirked.

"I do, my queen." I concentrated until the rocks to the left of where Kieran sat moved to form another ledge that jutted out into the water a couple of feet. Kieran raised his head from Samara's chest, and they both watched me take my place on my newly formed seat next to them.

My fingers closed around my cock as I slid my hand up and down before reaching out and stroking Samara's face. "You're going to take all of me and also both of them. Can you do that for us, love?"

"Yes," she breathed out before groaning as Alaric slid a finger into the tight ring of her ass.

"Such a good girl," Kieran crooned. "You're going to be dripping with all our cum soon."

"Fuck, Kier," Alaric ground out. "Maybe tone it down until I'm inside this perfect ass. I'm so hard, it fucking hurts."

"What are you waiting for?" Samara teased. "You were very adamant about claiming my ass, Alaric, so do it already."

She moaned when Alaric slapped her ass hard, but it was cut off when I gripped her by the chin and forced her head back. "That's enough sass out of you." I ran my thumb roughly over her bottom lip before forcing it into her mouth. "He's making sure you're ready to take his cock, because we're going to fuck you hard until you're a trembling mess . . . and then we're going to do it again. We don't want to break you too early."

Her tongue licked my thumb while she sucked on it, a glazed look in her eyes. "Yes, *my prince*."

I groaned. How did she make that sound so hot?

Fuck it. I pulled my thumb from her mouth and pushed my cock against her lips, smearing the bead of precum over them.

Kieran leaned forward and licked the side of my shaft

while Samara's tongue darted out to swirl around my thick head.

"You two are going to be the death of me," I ground out as Kieran and Samara continued worshipping my cock with their tongues. Part of me was desperate to come right now and cover their faces with my seed. If it'd just been the three of us, I probably would have.

But there was no chance I was letting Alaric outlast me. Luckily, I suspected as soon as he was inside Samara's tight ass, he'd be having control issues too.

I let my head fall back and rested my hand on Samara's head as she and Kieran took turns sucking me off. Only when Samara gasped did I look down at them again. Kieran was watching her face with rapt attention, and he'd momentarily stopped thrusting into her.

"Fuck, Sam," Alaric said in a strained tone as he gripped her hips. "You feel amazing."

Samara panted as Alaric pulled back before pushing in again. My hand slipped up and down my cock, still wet from Sam and Kier playing with it, and it grew even harder as Kieran started moving in time with his best friend.

Strangled sounds slipped from Samara's lips as she writhed between the two of them. Kieran's hands moved to her ass and he spread her wide for Alaric. I was tempted to adjust my position so I could watch Samara take both of them, but then Alaric reached up and wrapped his hand around Samara's long hair, tugging her head back.

"Put that pretty mouth of yours to use." He directed her face towards my lap. "Swallow the prince's cock."

Obediently, Samara opened her mouth, and I didn't hesitate. She let out a choked moan as I slammed my cock all the way in, tears streaming down her cheeks as she gagged but kept going.

"You take all of us so beautifully." Kieran licked some of

the tears off Samara's cheeks before tilting his head back. Seeing that blissed out look on his face while Samara took us both was becoming one of my favorite things.

The water started to splash more as Alaric's thrusts became harder, and Kieran groaned as Samara was pushed further onto his cock. Fuck, we were doing round two after this. I wanted Kieran to claim her ass while I sank into her pussy.

I hoped Samara knew she wasn't getting any sleep for at least a couple more hours.

Alaric released his hold on Samara's hair so that he could grip her hip with one hand and reach around to play with her clit with the other. She screamed around my cock, and I grabbed her by the hair, pulling her off.

Words poured from her lips in the common tongue, Seelie, and Unseelie, as Kieran and Alaric continued to fuck her hard. I watched as she climaxed, her black-as-night eyes rolling to the back of her head as neither man paused. If anything, they started thrusting into her harder.

It wasn't long until she was coming again, but this time, Alaric came with her with a loud groan, and Kieran followed a few seconds later. I forced her to look at me again. "Don't swallow, my queen," I ordered.

Samara whimpered but nodded and parted her lips as I slid my cock back into her mouth. I set a punishing pace, and she gagged several times but kept trying to take me further.

"Good girl," Kieran praised. "Relax your throat and take him deeper."

I felt myself tighten when she did as Kieran bade. Just before I came, I pulled my cock almost all of the way out of her mouth, and she parted her lips enough that I could watch my seed spill all over her pink tongue. Only when I'd completely filled her mouth did I fully remove myself and push her towards Kieran.

Neither of them hesitated as they kissed each other. When

a small amount of my cum dripped out of Samara's mouth, Kieran broke their kiss so he could lick it off her.

Inside my chest, my two mate bonds thrummed happily as Samara collapsed onto Kieran's chest, letting out a low groan as Alaric pulled out of her.

The moody asshole looked decidedly less grumpy as he settled on the other side of Kieran and Samara. I met his gaze over them, and he gave me the smallest of smiles. "Perhaps you're not the worst after all."

CHAPTER TWENTY-FIVE

—

Samara

"Erendriel was here?" Rynn squeaked. "And you didn't wake us up to tell us that immediately!?"

"Cali was sleeping like the dead!" I pointed at my friend, who was leaning her hip against one of the workshop tables. "And then I got . . . distracted . . ."

"With dick?" Cali arched a brow.

I shrugged. "It happens."

"Tragically, I wouldn't know," she lamented. "My pussy is drier than the badlands these days."

Roth and Alaric laughed from where they stood opposite Cali. It was early afternoon, and we were all gathered in the same room as yesterday. It was the only room on this floor that had places to sit and tables for laying things out. The rest of the rooms contained more books, scrolls, weapons, and other odds and ends.

It would take us years to go through everything and thoroughly catalog, which was something I hoped we'd have time to do. The scholars at Drudonia might literally lose their minds over the knowledge contained here.

Kieran gave Cali an exaggerated look of concern. "I didn't

356

realize things were that dire, Cal. As I said previously, I can find some sturdy, non-drama-causing Moroi to help you with that." He cocked his head while twirling a hand through the air. "Do you have any preferences—"

"Can we please stop talking about dicks and pussies for a second?" A golden sheen rolled over Rynn's eyes, and a snarl undermined her words.

"Speaking of not getting any . . ." Kieran said lightly.

Rynn turned her wolfish glare on him and growled, causing him to grab Roth and thrust them in front of him.

"Seriously?" Roth sighed and elbowed Kieran in the gut.

"Sam, control your—" Rynn turned to me and frowned. "What are we calling them? Paramours? Consorts?"

"Mates." I smiled. "I did indeed have a conversation with the Seelie King last night, and during it, he sensed the connections. They're Fae mate bonds."

Cali arched her eyebrows. "What does that mean, exactly?"

"Oh, I have no idea." I shrugged. "I only read the romantic shit about them growing up, but none of the poems had any actual useful information.

"Of course not." She snorted.

"Mate bonds," Roth murmured as they rubbed the spot on their chest over their heart. "That feels . . . right."

I smiled softly. "It does." My gaze went to the shelves of books lining the walls. "If we come across any books that mention them, let's pull them aside to review later. As much as I want to know more about the bonds, it's not as urgent as everything else."

"Fair." Roth nodded. "I'm definitely curious about what they can do and how they are formed." They glanced at me and then Alaric. "You two have one now, right? I can't feel his emotions, but I think I can feel the new bond between you both."

"Gods, Sam." Cali smirked at me. "Here I am living the celibate life, and you have five freaking mates."

"Four, technically," Kieran said. "Sam and I don't have one yet."

The smirk fell off Cali's face, and she rubbed the back of her neck awkwardly as silence fell. *Sorry*, she mouthed at me.

A pit of guilt settled in my stomach. I would have tried to bond with Kieran last night, but he had just done so with Draven, and I hadn't wanted to take anything away from that. What they had was just as valid and special as what I had with Kier, and I loved that they were happy.

But given that Kieran had hang-ups about thinking he wasn't enough, had I messed up? What if he thought I didn't *want* to form a mate bond with him? If I had hurt him—even unintentionally—I'd never forgive mysel—

"Sam." Kieran stepped forward and cupped my face in his hands before kissing the corners of my mouth. "Stop panicking. My feelings aren't hurt. You had just bonded with Alaric, and I had just done the same with Draven. We don't have to rush this."

"Are you sure?" I closed my eyes and leaned into his touch. "Because in my heart, you're already my mate, Kier. I just wanted to give you and Drav some time to settle into your mating bond before we threw ours on top of it."

"I figured." He smiled, and there was so much joy and love in it that my worries instantly evaporated. "Because I very much want to be your mate—in both the name and magic bond kind of way—but I want us to be able to celebrate it."

Alaric sighed. "You want a party, don't you?"

"Of course I want a party." Kieran sniffed and stepped away from me so he could shove his friend's shoulder. "Samara is obviously saving the best for last. That deserves a celebration." He looked at Roth. "Think your parents will be up for throwing a double wedding or something?"

Roth rubbed their forehead. "They would no doubt be thrilled."

I opened my mouth to tease them when Rynn stalked off to the table of books and started flipping through them.

Shit. I exchanged a look with Cali before we both looked at Rynn in concern.

I hadn't thought about how all this talk of mates would affect her.

Normally, Moroi didn't refer to their spouses or lovers as mates, but the Velesians did. They'd been the only ones to pick up that habit from the Fae. It was a big deal for them, although I didn't know the specifics of what it entailed. They kept it all very hush-hush, and it was one of the few things Rynn never talked about.

I did know that mates were *never* forced in the Velesian realm. Rynn might not have had a choice in joining the Alpha Pack, but she didn't have to choose them as mates. Nor did they have to choose her.

But the chances of her finding a mate outside of her pack was complicated. Technically, she could, but how would she know if they truly wanted her or just wanted a way to join the Alpha Pack, who rarely accepted anyone into their inner circle?

Rynn had been a political pawn her entire life. The only people who had ever chosen her just for being who she was were me and Cali. We might be her best friends for life . . . but we weren't her mates.

A good fuckfest might make Cali happy—at least for a while—but I doubted that would work for Rynn. She wanted something more than that.

My heart ached for my friend. I couldn't fix her problems now—or possibly ever—but I could at least distract her.

"Mate bonds aside, there were a lot of other interesting things I learned from the Seelie King." I walked over to one of the tables and perched my butt on it. The others settled into chairs or leaned against tables while I recounted everything Erendriel had said.

"What is with people wanting to marry you?" Vail muttered.

"Jealous?" I arched a brow at him and already started thinking of a pithy response for when he no doubt lost his temper.

"Marriage is too simple a word for what I want from you," he said in a low, deep tone that had me clenching my thighs together. "If Erendriel tries to take you from me, I will tear him apart limb from limb and offer you his still-beating heart as a gift."

The snarky response I'd had ready to go died on my tongue. For once, I had no idea what to say. The sincerity and intense need I saw on Vail's face was echoed in the bond. He really did mean it.

"Wow, Rynn." Kieran clapped slowly. "You should knock Vail out more often. He finally figured out how to use his words."

Instead of getting angry, the corners of Vail's mouth twitched.

May the moons damn it all. Did he almost *laugh*?

"I definitely plan on punching Vail again," Rynn said absently as she stared unseeingly at a spot on the floor while she processed everything I'd recounted before her gaze snapped to me. "He said the Unseelie Princes *are* liars? Not *were*?"

"Definitely present tense," I confirmed. "No idea where the rest of the Unseelie are or if they're still alive, but their princes are still kicking around somewhere."

"There's something in the mountains," Draven mused. "Erendriel spends most of his time there."

"Maybe the princes are there." I looked at the floor-to-ceiling bookshelves that lined the room. "Or maybe there are more places like this in the mountains that don't have wards in place preventing him entry. I don't think he liked that we were able to get into this room. Either because he wants what's in here for himself, or he thinks there is something here that we'll be able to use against him."

"Probably both." Draven snorted and reached behind himself to swipe a dagger off the table. Then he tossed it to me, and I snatched it out of the air.

"These glyphs . . ." I ran a finger down the silver handle. "They're like the ones the rangers use on their weapons but way more complicated."

Erendriel hadn't been wrong when he'd said we were like children bumping around in the dark. We'd only figured out that we could use the magic in our blood to reactivate the Fae glyphs a century or so ago. From there, we'd been able to derive spells of our own, usually by combining glyphs. It'd taken us a while to figure out that we had to pour our intention into the spells as well as our blood.

It took a lot of trial and error, and we still didn't really understand *how* any of this worked, only that it did. I glanced at the mirror that resided in the corner of the room. Rynn had walked through a blood mirror and traveled almost a thousand miles.

That was a little beyond using glyphs to make water hot.

Alaric rose from where he'd been sitting and walked over to me, then held out his hand, and I passed him the dagger.

"These are Unseelie glyphs," he noted, likely spotting the same small flourishes that distinguished their glyphs from the Seelie's. He pointed at the glyph carved into the actual blade of the dagger. "*Gùlma âmâm.*" Light green eyes flicked up from the blade to me. "Shadow killer. Why would the Unseelie make weapons to use against their own kind?"

"Maybe that's not what it does?" I took the dagger back

from him and studied the glyphs more. Several of them on the handle I didn't recognize.

Cali sighed and pushed off the bookshelf she'd been leaning against. She stopped a few feet from me, but a shadow version of herself stepped out of her body and kept going.

Everyone except me, Rynn, and Roth stiffened.

We were used to Cali's abilities. The others had seen her shadow form before—she usually used it to communicate long distances and had even given Rynn a ring that allowed her to do the same—but there was still something about seeing the endless pit of darkness peel itself away from Cali that was unnerving.

It was so wraith-like that I often wondered if our human ancestors' spell had been similar to the one used by the Seelie that resulted in them becoming wraiths.

The shadow version of Cali strode forward while the flesh-and-blood version stood there with an impassive expression. We all watched as a shadowy hand stretched out to touch the tip of the blade.

"Maybe this isn't a good ide—" Alaric started, only to be cut off when Cali's shadows exploded, covering sections of the room in darkness.

I fell from the table I'd been sitting on, my knees slamming to the floor and the dagger clattering a second later. My hands clamped around my ears as if that would help as Cali screamed.

Vaguely, I was aware of everyone else hitting the ground too. Pressure built in my head, and it felt like my mind was being shredded as Cali's magic slammed into it.

"Cal," I panted. "*Stop.*"

My back arched in pain as every single nerve lit up.

A large white wolf leapt over a table and barreled into Cali —the real one. She hit the ground hard, and the screaming abruptly cut off, then the shadows that had been convulsing suddenly vanished.

The wolf very ungracefully flopped to her side next to Cali, and a second later, a trembling Rynn was there with a sheen of sweat over her skin.

In their animal form, Velesians weren't as impacted by a Furie's magic, but they weren't entirely immune either. I dropped my hands from my head and groaned as I got to my feet. We were lucky Cali wasn't at full strength and some part of her hadn't wanted to hurt us. Her magical assault had been painful, but at least she hadn't driven us mad.

"Fuck," I ground out and leaned against the table. "What the hells happened, Cali?"

Around me, everyone else was getting up. Draven helped Kieran over to a chair while Roth and Alaric leaned on each other. I glanced at Vail, half expecting him to have a weapon in his hand and looking at Cali like he was figuring out the best way to take her down; instead, I found him looking at me, his hands hanging by his sides—empty.

There was tension in his posture—he still viewed Cali as a threat—but he trusted me to handle my best friend. Silver eyes bored into mine, and I could almost see the question in them. *You okay?*

I gave him a small but genuine smile and pushed a wave of gratitude down our bond. I knew it worked when the tension running through him relaxed slightly and he nodded once.

A very naked Rynn sat up and glared at Cali, who was still lying on the ground, then she smacked the back of her hand against the Furie's ribs. "I second Sam's question. What in the actual fuck, Cal?"

"Give me a second," Cali groaned as she flinched in response. "That was really unpleasant."

"You don't say," Roth deadpanned.

Kieran snort-laughed and then quickly winced and rubbed his temples.

I pushed off the table and took a few wobbly steps before swiping the dagger up off the ground. "Are there more weapons with these glyphs?"

"Yes." Draven gestured towards a neat pile of daggers on the table. "All of these."

"There might be more in the other rooms," Kieran added from where he was seated next to Draven. "We haven't looked at them all that closely."

"Okay, so we potentially have a weapon that can be wielded against the wraiths." I looked at Cali, who had managed to sit up, but her skin, which usually had a healthy tan to it, looked pale and almost sickly. Part of me was troubled by the fact that someone could use these daggers against her. She'd only pricked her finger with the end of it; what would happen if she were stabbed with one? And would the daggers work on her flesh as well as her shadows?

"Don't worry about me." Cali gave me a knowing look. "Now that I know what those daggers do, I'll make sure I don't ever get stabbed with one. And let's be real, nobody in Lunaria is a match for me." A cocky grin stretched across her lips. It would have been more believable if she didn't look like a butterfly could knock her over.

"Can you summon your shadows now?" Alaric's piercing gaze was locked on Cali. "Did it have any lingering effects on your magic?"

Cali concentrated, and then her eyes widened. "I can't feel them." Panic drenched her words. "My shadows . . ." She held up her hands and stared at them with golden eyes that started to glow.

A pressure started to build at the base of my spine. "Cali," I warned.

The feeling disappeared, and she gave me an apologetic

look. "Sorry." She dropped her hands. "I felt a flicker of them for a second. My shadow magic is still there; it's just currently out of reach." She paused for a second, and the glow of her eyes brightened before fading. "It doesn't seem to have impacted my mental magic at all."

"We can't be sure how well they'll work against Erendriel." I walked over to the table with the rest of the weapons and placed the dagger onto it. "I didn't see a trace of shadows on him last night, so he might be fully back to his Seelie form now."

"It's possible," Draven admitted reluctantly. "Although, if anyone could figure out how to retain a bit of shadow magic and also get back his original form, it would be that asshole."

"He'll be back to speak with me," I said confidently. "I'll try to suss out a little more of his magic then. In the meantime, Carmilla is just as much of a threat as Erendriel—maybe more so."

Roth nodded. "War will break out in the Moroi realm. My House will never follow her, and it's unlikely that Tepes or Salvatore will either. She'd likely been counting on quietly taking control, going House by House and using the crown to manipulate key players."

I thought about Kieran's parents and how she'd sent them back to House Corvinus to be her puppets. "Most likely," I agreed. "We're ruining that plan because we know the truth and can gather allies. The crown might be a powerful weapon, but it's not making it easy for her."

Because it wanted to sit on my head. It was odd, but some part of me wanted that too. Not for the crown's abilities, but just because it felt . . . right. Some part of me was drawn to the crown—and wanted it back.

"Sooner or later, Carmilla is going to figure out where we are," Vail spoke up. "There could be a traitor amongst Salvatore, or one of the rangers loyal to her could have seen us on the way here. Even if they didn't track us the whole way, there aren't a lot of places in the badlands to seek refuge."

"True. I wouldn't be surprised if she already knows where we are." My gaze fell on Cali. "She'll figure out a way to get you off the board if she can."

"Let the bitch try." Cali bared her teeth.

I shook my head. "We can't afford to doubt Carmilla. She'll come at the problem from an angle we're not seeing. I don't think we need to worry about her attacking while you're here, but we can't count on that. This place might be secure against Erendriel and the wraiths, but we'll be cornered if Carmilla sends a bunch of rangers in here."

"Rynn," Kieran said slowly. "You said you blocked the Alpha Pack from following you into the secret room underneath their castle . . . how did you do that?"

"A glyph . . ." Rynn chewed her bottom lip as her brows furrowed in concentration. "It all happened so fast, but there were some markings on the wall beside the door. A barrier spell—one I'd never seen before."

There definitely wasn't one by the doorway here because I would have noticed last night during my chat with Erendriel. Odd that the room Rynn had found had one and not this place.

"A spell of that kind could be useful," Draven mused.

An idea bloomed in my head. It was kind of crazy, and I'd need to figure out several key elements for it to work, but it could solve two of our biggest problems in one go.

"Rynn and I will go take a look at that glyph to see if we can replicate it here," I said evenly. "Alaric and Roth, you can continue scouring the books to see if you find anything useful. Draven and Vail, go through the weapons and pull out any that can be used against the wraiths."

"Is splitting up wise?" Alaric hedged.

"We're literally just going to step through that mirror."

Rynn pointed to where the Fae artifact stood in the corner. "You all can peep your heads through if you want. The room is a lot smaller on the other side, so there's not enough space for all of us. You'd all just be standing around while Samara and I figure out how that glyph works. Trust me." She wrinkled her nose. "Nobody wants to avoid being caught by the Alpha Pack more than I."

Cali grumbled something under her breath.

"You're not killing them," Rynn huffed at her. "Just because I hate their smug, arrogant faces doesn't mean they're not good for the Velesians in general. Two things can be true at once."

"Whatever." Cali flopped back onto the floor, stretching out her wings and whacking Rynn in the face with one. The Velesian growled down at her, but Cali just pouted up at the ceiling. "You lot never let me kill anything, and it's getting tiresome."

Draven chuckled and started going through a stack of daggers on the table. Alaric and Roth came over and kissed me on the cheek before pulling some books from shelves and settling into chairs.

"And what about me?" Kieran arched a brow.

I grinned at him. "You're coming with us. On the off chance one of the Alpha Pack members is waiting on the other side of the barrier, it's your job to sweet-talk them while we steal their shit."

"Sounds fun." His eyes lit up. "I hope it's Bastian. He's fun to play with."

My grin slid from my face, and I narrowed my eyes at him—and across the room, I heard the sound of weapons clattering against each other. I glanced at Draven to find him glaring at Kieran too.

"Linguistically." Kieran rolled his eyes. "The overgrown pussycat is fun to play with *linguistically*."

"You'll be my favorite Moroi forever if you call Bastian that to his face," Rynn said seriously before springing to her feet and trotting over to the mirror.

Kieran chuffed. "I'm already your favorite Moroi. You just let Samara pretend she is to protect her delicate sensibilities— oww!" He rubbed the back of his head where I'd smacked him. "Rude."

"Come on." I grabbed his arm and started tugging him towards where Rynn was waiting for us, only pausing to grab a few sheets of paper and sharpened pieces of charcoal so I could sketch out the glyph for reference.

I thrust them into the pockets of my dress before coming up short when Vail stomped over, shoving between me and Kieran. "If there is even a *hint* of the barrier being down when you get into that room, you get that nice ass back here immediately. The Alpha Pack isn't going to react reasonably if they see you with Rynn."

"You need to work on your compliments as much as your apologies." I poked him in the chest. "And I don't have a nice ass—I have an *amazing* ass."

"Sam," Vail growled.

"Vail," I mockingly growled back.

My heart quickened when he smiled at me before leaning down to whisper in my ear, "If you don't bring that *amazing* ass back in one piece, I'm going to think of all kinds of ways to punish it." Before I could get out a clever retort, Vail's hand gripped the back of my head, and his lips crashed against mine in a searing kiss. Heat coursed through me as I molded my body into his.

Yes. I was still mad at him.

Yes. I was enjoying the hells out of this kiss.

As Rynn had said before, two things could be true at once.

"Stop getting distracted by dick!" Rynn barked sharply.

Vail and I broke apart, both of us breathing a little heavily.

"Also"—his eyes slid to where Kieran was now waiting with

Rynn, a stupid grin on his face—"I want credit for allowing you to go with just the wolf and peacock."

"You don't *allow* me to do anything," I sputtered, but Vail was already stalking back towards the weapons table.

Draven shook his head at him. "You almost had it but fumbled the landing."

"Shut up," Vail growled.

"Let's go." Rynn grabbed me. "Deal with your obnoxiously possessive and bossy mates later. Cade and the others are usually patrolling at this hour, and I'd like to get in and out without them noticing," she snapped before shoving me face-first into the mirror.

<hr>

"Oh fuck, that was weird." I hopped from one foot to the other as I stared wide-eyed at the mirror. The reflective surface looked solid, but as soon as I made contact, it felt like a cold, viscous liquid slipping over my skin. My mind told me I should be dripping wet right now, but my skin was dry and unblemished.

Aside from the weird sensation, it'd been fine. Nothing like when Draven had tripped the glyph at the bottom of House Harker and my stomach had tried to relocate to my throat as we fell.

"Rynn wasn't kidding." Kieran glanced around the space we had landed in. "I'm not even sure Vail would have fit in here, and Draven's ego definitely wouldn't have."

"I'm going to tell Draven you said that." I peered at the completely packed shelves that I could only see parts of, thanks to the wooden crates full of more books and scrolls stacked precariously in front of them.

"Go for it." Kieran grinned at me. "I like his punishments."

I thought of when Draven had used his whip to tie me up in the cabin.

"Good point. Tell him I talked shit about him too."

Kieran snorted. "This place actually makes Roth's room look neat and tidy." He reached out to the nearest stack of books just as Rynn stepped through the mirror.

"Don't"—the books tumbled over with a loud crash—"touch anything," Rynn finished tensely and looked towards the open doorway that led into another small room.

The three of us held still, waiting to see if the Alpha Pack would barge in. We were close enough to the mirror that we could make it back through and smash the one on the other side . . . probably.

Velesians were fast fuckers.

A little tension bled out of Rynn's shoulders when nothing happened. Either they weren't here or the barrier was still holding.

"Come on." She slipped past me and Kieran—somehow managing not to knock over more books—and headed towards the small room that must have been the entryway. "Let's do what we came here to do and get the fuck out before one of those assholes comes . . ."

She trailed off and came to a slow halt a foot past the arched doorway like prey that suddenly realized it was no longer alone.

Immediately, I dashed towards her with Kieran hot on my heels, books crashing behind us in our haste. I'd been right—this room was just a small entryway that led to the stairwell. Another archway was directly to our right, which hadn't been visible from the other room. Clearly, it used to have a door because the black hinges were still attached to the stone—mostly anyway—but now, they were twisted and half torn out, like someone had wrenched the door free with their bare hands.

My bet was on Cade. The ursanthrope spoke with even words and calming smiles most of the time, but when he lost it, you got to see what a three-thousand-pound, pissed-off bear looked like up close.

It wasn't the leader of the Alphas who was waiting for us though. Nor was it Bastian or Ryker—the latter of whom I was happy not to see because Rynn didn't act rationally around the other lycanthrope. Plus, I didn't want to be around two snappish wolves any more than I wanted to deal with the bear.

Leaning against the wall on the other side of the doorway was a man with deep brown skin so dark, it was as if it had been kissed by midnight. His black hair was cut short, and the neatly trimmed beard somehow called even more attention to his handsome features.

I had five extremely gorgeous lovers, and I was not the least bit interested in another, but even I had to acknowledge that this man was hot.

Like, impossibly so.

I also had no fucking idea who he was.

Though I was pretty sure Rynn did, based on the intensity she was staring him down with. She still hadn't moved from her spot, but I recognized the almost cautious aggression sending trembles up her lithe frame. If she were in wolf form, her hackles would've been raised right now.

The handsome stranger's golden yellow eyes barely glanced at me and Kieran before falling back to her. He said nothing, but I saw the hatred burning in his eyes.

"I was wondering when you were going to bother showing up." Rynn finally spoke in a low, raspy voice. "You smell even worse in person."

Kieran and I traded a weighted look. Velesians were kind of particular about scents—especially their own. Telling one of them they stank was a sure way to get your throat ripped out.

"Rynn, who—"

"Just copy the glyph, Samara," Rynn cut me off. "The barrier is up. He can't get through."

Right. I pulled the papers and charcoal from my pocket and strode towards the doorway. The golden-eyed Velesian didn't move, but his eyes did flick towards me for a second before returning to Rynn.

No vertical slits. So he wasn't a panther shifter. All the ursanthropes I'd met had a much larger build. He could be a lycanthrope, but something about that didn't feel right. If I was correct, then that meant he was an aetanthrope—an eagle shifter.

Kieran followed me as I quickly laid the paper over the glyph and then scratched the charcoal over it until the pattern appeared on the sheet. I handed it to Kieran, and he carefully folded it so it wouldn't smudge before tucking it into his pocket. On another sheet, I made some notes about how the glyph was positioned on the wall and some other finer details that might not have come through in my charcoal imprint.

After handing that paper to him and tucking the charcoal back into my pocket, I studied the glyph for a few minutes. My memory was pretty good, so between that and the papers, I was confident I could recreate this glyph.

The man hadn't broken his silence once. It was kind of unnerving. I was burning to ask Rynn who the fuck he was, but she hadn't offered up that information, and the situation felt volatile enough that I didn't want to push her about it.

When I stepped back from the wall to stand beside Rynn, the man finally deigned to speak. "I'm going to enjoy stripping the flesh from your bones, traitor," he said in a deep melodic voice.

"Try me, Warrick," Rynn sneered.

Warrick. Holy. Shit. The missing member of the Alpha Pack. Or at least, a member who nobody in the Moroi realm had seen in decades. We'd all assumed he was dead and that his death was the reason the Alpha Pack had been less inclined to talk to us recently.

Kieran had clearly been thinking similar thoughts because he gave the Velesian a leering look and drawled, "You're looking pretty good for a dead man."

Warrick's cold, predatory gaze flicked to him. "I don't speak to Moroi whores."

"Technically, you just did," Kieran pointed out and leaned an elbow on my shoulder. "Given your whole vibe, I think you really need to get laid. I know I'm absolutely stunning, but unfortunately for you, I'm off the market, so you'll have to look elsewhere."

Rynn choked on a laugh, finally snapping out of her stare off with Warrick, and slid a glance to Kieran. "You are definitely my favorite."

"I know." Kieran nodded sagely.

Warrick's eyes burned with fury, but before he could say anything else, footsteps echoed down the stairwell, and a moment later, Bastian appeared.

In the dim lighting, his usually vertical pupils had rounded out, and he gave Warrick a brief warning look before turning his attention to us. While Warrick exuded a quiet deadliness, Bastian was all sleek underhandedness.

"Rynn," he said smoothly, "I'm delighted that you've returned to us."

"Oh go fuck yoursel—" Her words were cut off as Kieran clamped a hand over her mouth and pulled her snug against his chest. Both Velesians' eyes narrowed at him holding her.

Shit. *Diplomacy*, I reminded myself. *Don't make things worse.*

"Apologies, Bastian." I stepped in front of Rynn. "She's helping us with a minor issue in the Moroi realm."

Sharp green eyes cut to me. "The minor issue being your aunt overthrowing the Sovereign House, seizing power, and according to a few rumors, being in possession of a Fae crown capable of controlling minds."

"You have to admit, he has a way with words," Kieran chimed in. "It's kind of hot."

I gave Kieran a scathing look over my shoulder before returning my focus to Bastian. "I have things under control." Or, really, I had a vague outline of an absolutely insane plan that had a small chance of working.

The daemon is in the details, as the Fae used to say. I had no idea what a daemon was, but it sounded neat.

"Do you?" Bastian cocked his head at me.

"Yes." I took a step back and heard Kieran drag Rynn towards the other room, where the mirror waited for us. "We have no interest in a war with the Velesians. I *will* handle things in the Moroi realm."

"The traitor stays," Warrick said in a calm tone that I didn't believe for a second.

"No." I gave him a cool look. "Rynn's with me."

Aggression rolled off Warrick, but Bastian stepped in front of him in a move very similar to what I'd done to Rynn.

"What my friend means to say is that Rynn belongs with us," Bastian said in that polite tone of his that I always found a little annoying. "She is a member of the Alpha Pack after all."

"Is she?" I gave him a friendly smile. "Because your *friend* seems to feel otherwise."

A muscle in Bastian's face ticked before he could hide it. I stepped forward until I was less than a foot away from the barrier.

"It will solve a lot of problems if you release Rynn from your Pack," I said quietly. "The Alpha Pack clearly doesn't want her." My eyes flicked briefly to where Warrick stood behind the panther shifter. "Just let her go."

Bastian studied me, and for a second, I thought he was

going to go for it before he dashed that hope. "That's not possible, I'm afraid."

"Why?" I ground out. "She doesn't want to be here—you all don't want her. This is an easy solution to a delicate situation, and you know it."

"Do you need assistance with Carmilla?" Bastian asked. The change in topic threw me for a loop for a second.

"We're not helping her," Warrick growled.

A brief flicker of irritation rolled over Bastian's eyes. It seemed the Alpha Pack wasn't quite the cohesive unit I'd thought it was. If I wanted to destabilize the Velesian realm, I would have rejoiced in that observation, but despite my desire to free Rynn from them, I did want the Alpha Pack to succeed in holding power. If the Velesian realm fell to chaos, it would spill over into the Moroi realm.

Just as they needed me to hold my people together, I needed them to do the same.

"Like I said," I told Bastian, ignoring Warrick, "I have it handled."

He held my gaze for a long moment before dipping his head in acknowledgment. "Then I look forward to discussing future relations between the Velesians and the Moroi—with the new queen."

It wasn't a cold dread that settled in my gut at the inference of me becoming the Moroi Queen. Only acceptance. Perhaps a little reluctance, but acceptance all the same.

My people would survive. All of the Moon Blessed would. I didn't give a single fuck about the Fae and whoever had banished them here. We would not be casualties of their bullshit.

"And I look forward to discussing our future alliance as well." I nodded at him before turning and walking to the other room, where I heard Kieran and Rynn fiercely whispering to each other.

"Samara," Bastian said just as I was about to pass into the other room. I halted and looked back towards him. "We won't let her go. She is *ours*."

Somewhere in front of me, Rynn let out a deep, rolling growl.

"Rynn belongs to no one but herself," I told him simply. "I will not force her to return."

"Even if it means war?" Bastian asked, and for the first time in our conversation, a hint of defiant rage crept into his tone.

"She is my best friend," I told him simply. "Fucking try to take her from me. I'll burn down your world."

CHAPTER TWENTY-SIX

—

Samara

"Okay . . . that could have gone better," Kieran drawled once we stepped back through the mirror.

"Understatement," Rynn growled.

Cali instantly perked up from where she'd been picking through the weapons table. "Do I get to kill the Alpha Pack?"

The leader part of me wanted to say no because the Alpha Pack was all that was keeping the Velesian realm somewhat stable and Cade *could* be reasoned with. But then I thought about the hate brimming in Warrick's eyes when he'd looked at Rynn, and the monster side of me rejoiced at the idea of Cali melting his fucking mind while carving him apart with her sword.

I didn't understand why he'd been so hostile to my friend, especially since it seemed like that had been the first time they'd met in person. Now, I was even less excited about the idea of Rynn going back there. Before, she hadn't been happy but was at least safe. I wasn't sure if that was true anymore.

Rynn stared at the mirror with a defeated expression. "I love you both, but we all know I have to go back."

"No," I said firmly. "You don't."

She turned away from the mirror and gave me a sad smile. "I heard what you said to Bastian, and I have no doubt that you would burn down their realm, but I won't be responsible for the Moroi and Velesian realms going to war. Both realms are already too precarious as it is. We need to figure out how to stabilize them, which means I have to go back—after I help you here."

I deflated a little. As much as I hated to admit it, she was right.

"Fine, but I want a contract."

"Of course you do." Rynn rolled her eyes.

"Will they even be open to that?" Draven asked. "All my interactions with the Alpha Pack have been pretty hostile."

"They never liked Queen Velika," Vail said, not bothering to look away from the sword he was inspecting. "Bastian thought your mother smelled like—and these are his exact words—sour jealousy and rotting deceit with a hint of rancid insanity."

Draven blinked. "Wow. That's actually quite accurate."

"Guess that explains why he spent more time with the other Houses," Kieran mused. "But if we go back through the mirror and catch Bastian before he leaves, I think he'll be willing to work with us. Rynn technically *is* supposed to be with them." He gave my friend an apologetic look. "But we heard Warrick's threat, so we have valid reasons to be concerned about Rynn's welfare."

"What threat?" Cali asked sharply, her golden eyes glowing slightly.

"We'll handle it," I said quickly before looking at Alaric, who was leaning back in a chair behind a table with five open books scattered in front of him. "Are you up for negotiating with Bastian?"

"Sure." He raised his brows. "You don't want to do it yourself?"

"I don't think I'd be able to keep a cool head," I admitted. "I trust you to do it."

Something in his green eyes softened. I believed in him to keep my best friend safe, which was a bigger deal than me trusting him with my own life in a lot of ways.

"I'll go with you," Kieran said. "Bastian and I have always had good rapport."

"Thank you." Alaric nodded and rose to his feet, going to stand next to Kieran.

"Should I go too?" Rynn asked uncertainly. "It feels weird to make the two of you deal with my fucked-up situation."

"Given how hot some tempers are running, I think it's best if you remain here." Kieran gave her a small, reassuring smile. "We got this, Rynn."

"Roth absconded with an armful of books shortly after you all left—they said Cali was breathing too loud," Alaric said in a dry tone, even as amusement danced in his eyes. Cali snorted as she plucked a dagger from the table and slid it into a holster on her thigh. Alaric continued, "I'm not sure what they've found, but I've been reading your notes about this transformation spell, and I think you're onto something. I found a few more books that go into detail about it and might be useful."

Rynn was hurrying over to the table before he'd even finished his last word.

I walked over to Alaric and Kieran. "Thank you both for doing this."

"Of course, love." Kieran shrugged. "Rynn's family."

Both of them kissed me on the cheek and strode back through the mirror—which was still strange to watch. I walked over to it and studied the glyphs etched into the dark wood frame. Some of them I recognized, but most I didn't.

My eyes drifted to the right, where something tall was covered with a black cloak. I stepped closer and tugged the cloak off. Another mirror. Interesting.

"There is a second mirror in the room beneath the Alpha House too," Rynn said from across the room. "Different glyphs than the travel mirrors. I messed around with it a bit but couldn't figure out what it did."

"Hmm." I looked the markings over, similar to the other mirror, but I only knew what a handful of them meant. "Mystery for another day, I guess."

"I need to stretch my wings for a bit," Cali announced.

"Are you sure that's a good idea?" I turned away from the mirror. "There could be wraiths lurking in the dark spots of the temple."

She shrugged. "Then I'll get to kill something."

Vail and Draven both chuckled, and I rolled my eyes. "Fine, but be careful, and don't go far."

"Yes, Mom." She gave me a finger salute before sauntering out of the room. Rynn laughed at that one.

"It wasn't that funny," I grumbled as I joined her at the table and grabbed one of the books Alaric had left out.

"Yes, it was." Rynn glanced up with a smirk on her face. "Only you would fuss over quite possibly the most lethal warrior in Lunaria going out for a flight in the middle of the day."

"She's not invulnerable," I pointed out. "Plus, I know Carmilla—she's working on a way to get Cali off the board."

The amusement bled from Rynn's face. "You think she's going to send stealth units?"

Over the last few decades, the Furies had gotten better about controlling their magic. It was rare for one to completely lose it, but it did happen. Sometimes they would deal with the problems themselves, but sometimes they would ask for assistance. That was where the stealth units came in. Some Moroi and Velesians were specifically trained to take down rogue Furies. They used a mix of long-range weapons and other tactics to get close enough to do lethal damage fast before the Furie could shred their minds.

It was easily the most dangerous task in Lunaria, but unfortunately a necessary one. Vail had been trained to take down Furies . . . so had Adrienne and Emil. I doubted Nyx had because usually it was only rangers with a couple of decades of experience who went through the training.

Nyx. Sadness washed over me. They'd been so happy being a ranger and belonging to a unit. Technically, they should have served as an advisor or some other high-ranking role in House Corvinus because they were the youngest child of the Heads of that House. If Nyx had remained in their birth House, they'd probably be safe right now. Not trying to piece together a shredded soul.

But they also likely would have been forced into a political marriage they didn't want.

Not a lot of happily-ever-after stories in Lunaria like there were in some of the Fae stories I'd read. I looked across the room to where Draven and Vail quietly bickered over weapons.

We'd get our fucking happy ending. I'd make sure of it.

"She'll leave that as a last resort." I turned my attention back to Rynn's question. "Carmilla would probably like to permanently take Cali out, but without the Furie Elders officially declaring Cali a danger, Carmilla's hands are a bit tied. I don't particularly like them, but the Furie Elders will retaliate harshly if Carmilla kills one of their own without cause. She can't afford that."

"So she'll come at the problem sideways." Rynn pursed her lips, her eyes going distant in that way that meant she was thinking through the possibilities.

"Yep," I agreed. "Hard to say how she'll do it, but if whatever she thinks up is successful and we're separated from Cali, we'll have to be ready for an attack afterwards."

Rynn hummed her agreement. "She'll punch a hole through our defense and then take advantage."

I had no idea how Carmilla would get Cali to willingly leave us, but I wasn't going to underestimate my aunt. She'd think of something, and as soon as she did, the countdown would start for her finding us—if she didn't already know where we were—and attacking.

A plan was coming together in my head, but I still only had fragments of the pieces I needed. I pulled the paper from my pocket and flattened it out, studying the glyph. It had been designed to keep people out . . . but it could just as easily be used to keep people in.

"Tell me what you've discovered so far about this transformation spell, Rynn . . ."

SIX HOURS LATER, Rynn and I had a long list of notes with whole passages scratched out, plus additional writing on the side. It was messy and had some gaps we had to fill in, but my insane plan was starting to feel more like a real possibility.

We had two main enemies—Carmilla and Erendriel. The Seelie King was trying to court me to his side; I had no doubt he'd be returning tonight to speak with me. I didn't want an all-out war with Carmilla, even if I did have the Houses of Devereux, Salvatore, and likely Tepes at my back. Probably a good chunk of House Harker too.

But a war amongst the Moroi Houses would be the death of our realm. So many of us would die. Not to mention Carmilla wouldn't need to lift a finger—she'd just need to use the crown to steal the will of some key players.

It would be a bloodbath.

I didn't want more Moroi to die in a desperate attempt to

stop Carmilla. Wraiths though? Yeah . . . not going to shed any tears over them.

My plan was actually quite simple. Lure Carmilla to the temple, let Erendriel and his wraiths deal with her, secure the crown, and betray Erendriel.

Honor was for suckers.

I'd lie my ass off to save my people.

The problem—or rather one of the problems—was that you had to word things very carefully with the Fae. Draven had explained as much as he could before his head had damn near exploded from whatever magic was still forcing him to hold his tongue.

A bargain with the Fae had power, so I needed to craft my lie carefully.

If I pulled it off, I'd be able to boast that this gorgeous, twenty-three-year-old ass had outsmarted a centuries-old Fae who had stolen her throne.

If that wasn't motivation, I didn't know what was.

Yes, I ran on spite. No, I was not the least bit apologetic about it.

Kieran and Alaric had come and gone several times as they continued to negotiate Rynn's return to the Alpha Pack. Kieran, bless him, had tried to put in a stipulation that Rynn must be allowed to visit the Moroi realm whenever she wanted. Bastian had pushed back on that, so we'd settled on once-a-month visits with exceptions for emergencies.

Those emergencies were explicitly listed because Alaric lived for the small details.

Vail was exploring the temple to better learn the layout, and Draven had gone to join him after answering as many of our questions as he could. We'd also been looking for a way to break whatever magic was forcing him to hold his tongue, but so far, I hadn't come across any explanations. Granted, we'd only begun to scratch the surface of the knowledge this place stored.

If we survived everything with Carmilla and Erendriel, we might finally be able to learn how everything in Lunaria had come to be.

Cali breezed in at one point, saw Rynn and me conspiring over all the open texts, and promptly turned on her heel and walked back out. She mumbled something about seeing what "that treacherous asshole" was up to.

I assumed she meant Vail and yelled after her to not kill him.

She let out a string of curses, but I was confident that she wouldn't, because if that had truly been her intention, she wouldn't have said anything—and I was *mostly* confident she wouldn't pick a fight with him either. Though they could both stand to burn off some extra energy, so a brawl wouldn't be the worst thing to happen right now.

"This is still a problem." Rynn pointed to one of my notes that had several words boldly circled. *Spell requires permission.*

The transformation spell to turn one thing into another was complicated, and most of it was out of our league, given our basic understanding of magic. But several texts alluded to the spell being far simpler if whoever it was being performed on gave permission.

The soul crown wasn't a person . . . but it wasn't just an object either. I'd conversed with it and had felt its emotions. What if the soul crown wasn't just named that because it could bind the will of others? What if the Fae had actually bestowed a soul into it?

My plan hinged on performing the transformation spell. If the crown could give us permission to turn it into something else, then that would drastically simplify things. Unfortunately, that created a new problem—how could I speak with the crown beforehand to determine if this was possible?

Because if we waited until the plan was in motion, there was a very real chance I'd end up dead.

Not my preferred outcome.

We were also running out of time. While we were relatively safe here in the temple, our allies were not. Once Carmilla had a plan in place to deal with Cali, she'd figure a way to lure me out. I knew she wanted to limit the loss of Moroi lives, but I also knew she could be a ruthless bitch when she wanted to be.

What if she found Alaric's parents? Or used any of my friends from House Harker?

I needed to control the information about where I was, making sure it was leaked at just the right time in just the right way so she wouldn't question it.

"Wait." Rynn suddenly sat up straighter, drawing me out of my ponderings. "'While the Unseelie are adept at spying with their shadows, the Seelie have crafted a way to counterspy,'" she quoted. "'By mindwalking through the minds of sentient but simpleminded creatures, they can easily put themselves in the same rooms as their completely unaware enemies. This is why we have put defensive measures in place . . .'" She trailed off, skimming the page before flipping the book to look at the cover. "I have no idea who wrote this, but it clearly wasn't the Fae. It's like a history of them . . . before they came to Lunaria."

I glanced at the page, a frown forming on my lips. "It's written in Seelie though."

"Maybe it was translated?" We both stared at the book before looking around the room and its floor-to-ceiling shelves. "What in the fuck is this place?" Rynn murmured.

"We'll just have to survive long enough to figure it out." I grabbed the book and started scanning the pages until I found what I was looking for—a glyph. I read the words below it, which were simple enough. Focus and intention were key. I could do this.

"Should we wait until the others get back?" Rynn asked hesitantly.

"No, they'll just distract me." I rose from the table, taking the book with me, and sat on the floor, crossing my legs. Then I set the book slightly to my right and bit my wrist until I tasted blood. "Besides, when I checked on Roth an hour ago, they were close to cracking how that barrier spell works, and we're going to need that."

"Fine," she grumbled. "Just don't get yourself stuck in a mouse or something, okay? I can't be friends with you if you're food."

I rolled my eyes as I dipped my fingers in the blood flowing from my wrist and drew the glyph on the floor. "Noted."

Rynn moved to sit beside me. For all her concern, I could feel the excitement practically rolling off her. This was a new spell, unlike anything we'd ever done before.

Following the instructions from the text, I rested my fingertips on the blood of the outer circle of the glyph that vaguely resembled an eye. Then I closed my eyes and focused on my intention, feeling it wrap around the magic that flowed through my veins before pushing it into the glyph.

Sometimes, when I'm sleeping soundly, I jerk awake with the intense feeling of falling.

This was exactly like that.

When my eyes flew open seconds later, they were not my eyes . . . and I couldn't even close them.

Well, this was weird.

My body wrapped around a vine and continued its upward climb along a stone wall. There was a quick tongue flick, and suddenly, I was processing a bunch of different scents from the air. The blooming flowers, the dust that collected in the cracks of the stones, and the delicious bird perched somewhere above me.

Moons fucking damn me.

I was sharing the mind of a snake. With a careful, gentle nudge, I requested that it turn its head so I could look at myself. A flicker of annoyance brushed against my mind, but then the world tilted and I was looking down at a long, scaled body with an iridescent sheen, rainbows dancing across my scales with every movement.

Well, at least I was a pretty snake.

Umm, sorry about this? I thought loudly. *Promise you'll get that tasty snack of a bird later. I just need to borrow you for a few minutes.*

More annoyance.

Apparently, snakes had a one-track mind when it came to food.

I didn't exactly take over control of the snake's body, it was more like I prodded it into doing what I wanted. We continued climbing up the vine for another few feet and then slid through a window, curling our tail around the bars and dangling into the room.

When I'd formed my intention for the spell, I'd focused on getting as close to the crown as possible. Despite Rynn's joke about me not taking over a mouse . . . I'd totally thought I was going to end up in a mouse. They were everywhere, so it had seemed like a logical assumption.

Rynn had a thing about snakes though, so I'd have to lie to her about this.

I looked through the serpent's eyes at the room we were hanging in. It didn't see colors the way I was used to. The blues and greens felt so much more vivid, and its depth perception was different than mine. Despite the differences, I was able to make everything out just fine.

We were high up in a small space; the ground was almost twenty feet below us and the walls were circular. A turret, maybe? Probably one close to the top of the Sovereign House? Because that's definitely where we were. I'd recognized enough of the landscape when we'd been outside to confirm our whereabouts.

There was nothing else in the room besides the table in the center. It was made of the same stone as the floor and walls, and resting on its smooth surface was the soul crown.

Samara? a familiar voice tentatively asked.

Yes? I had no idea why I'd answered the crown's question with one of my own. If I had hands, I would have been slapping my own face right now.

Why do you feel . . . strange?

Probably because I'm sharing the mind of a snake. It's my first time doing this, so I'm still figuring out the quirks.

The snake started to curve back towards the bars as I felt its interest in the bird renew. Gently, I tugged back.

Stay. Just a little longer, I promised.

A chuckle rumbled through my mind, and the snake's head turned back towards the crown. *Of course this is the beast you would choose.*

It wasn't a choice, actually, I admitted. *This slithery friend just happened to be the creature closest to you.*

No. The crown's amusement danced through my mind. Our mind? I wasn't exactly sure if the snake understood amusement. *Your bloodline has long been associated with* slithery friends. *The last true Seelie King—your grandfather—was known as The Serpent King before he was banished to Lunaria.*

Oh. It was strange to think of a grandfather in general, let alone one that had been Fae—and the Seelie King at that. There weren't a lot of multigenerational families in Lunaria. I was a fifth generation Moroi, and it wasn't until the fourth generation that the Moroi themselves had stabilized and stopped turning Strigoi every time something looked at them the wrong way.

You came back, the crown whispered.

I told you I would.

I know those . . . rangers, I believe you call them . . . were your friends. You begged me to help, but I . . . There was nothing I could do.

The crown had thought I'd completely abandoned them because of what had happened with Adrienne, Emil, and Nyx, but I'd heard their sorrow that day—felt it. The crown had monstrous magic . . . but they didn't want to be a monster.

Talis, I thought softly.

I . . . I do not know this word.

When I was growing up, my parents were often busy, but we had one tradition. Once a month, we would sneak up onto one of the rooftops at House Harker to watch the stars. I actually knew most of the constellations because a friend taught me, but I never told them that.

For a second, I felt my connection to the snake waver, as if the emotions were too much for it. Vail had been the one to point out and name every star in the night sky. His parents had been just as busy as mine. For a long time, it had just been the two of us. Before life had torn us apart.

But I still listened with rapt attention as my father pointed out his favorite star every time, I continued. The crown didn't say anything but I could feel their presence. *It wasn't the brightest star in the sky. Some nights, it was so dim, you could barely see it. Most of the constellations have Fae names, but this one had been named in the common tongue by the humans who had lived here. Talis. Their word for hope.*

Talis, the crown said slowly, as if tasting the word. *I like it.*

Good. Because I think it would be a good name for you.

Another beat of silence. *I have existed for a long time . . . belonged to your family for generations. Nobody has ever thought to gift me with a name.*

It's a new dawn, Talis. Perhaps it's time we change things.

I then told Talis my plan and what I would be asking of them. What they would have to sacrifice.

Yes, they said immediately once I was done. *But I have one request . . .*

CHAPTER TWENTY-SEVEN

—

Vail

"Rynn, calm down," I tried again.

"You calm down!" the lycan screamed from where she stood on top of the table.

"Little help?" I growled at Draven, who was leaning against a table on the opposite side of the room with a curious look on his face as he stared at Samara—who was very much still out of it—and the three-foot badlands viper coiled up in her lap.

The serpent had a thick body and a triangular head. Its scales were a mix of white and a light tawny brown that allowed it to blend in well with the badlands' arid surface.

It was also highly venomous. Not enough to kill us, but enough to make us hate our lives for a few hours.

I hadn't attempted to tear the thing out of her lap because it seemed very calm, and I was worried about startling it.

"It doesn't mean her any harm." Draven waved a hand towards Samara and her new scaly friend. "This isn't normal behavior for a viper; they're ambush predators. It was probably coiled up somewhere in the temple and the magic of whatever spell she's working drew it towards her."

"I don't care!" A low, panicked whine underpinned Rynn's

words. "Nowhere in that fucking book did it mention *anything* about fucking snakes crawling out of the fucking walls!" The viper raised its head from where it had been resting on Samara's knee and flicked a tongue in Rynn's direction. "Fuck!" she shrieked and backed up farther on the table.

"Rynn, if you scream one more time, I'm going to strangle you." Roth stomped into the room, their deep red hair looking a little messy, like they'd been running their hands through it. "I can hear you all the way downstairs. What are you going on about—oh." They looked at the badlands viper. "Huh. I guess Sam has an affinity with serpents. Or maybe it's all reptiles. The strikers really like her, and they're more reptile than bird anyway."

"Affinity?" Draven glanced at Roth.

They pointed at the stack of discarded books on a nearby table, the ones that didn't contain information useful for our current problems. "One of those books talks about it. I think it's a Seelie thing, which makes sense, I guess, since their magic is earth-based. Normally, they are drawn to one type of animal, and those animals are also drawn to them. Maybe the more in touch Samara gets with her Fae magic, the more weird shit like this will happen."

"You use Fae magic." I looked at Draven. "This ever happen to you?"

He frowned and started to shake his head, but then his eyes widened. "Weasels. The bold little things often come up to me when I'm camping in the woods. I thought maybe they just smelled my food and wanted to steal it. They've never shown an ounce of fear."

The Moroi Prince was friends with quite possibly the only animals that could be considered adorable in Lunaria.

"If somebody doesn't—" Rynn growled, only to be cut off when Samara let out a long exhale and said, "Well, that was fucking weird."

Her beautiful purple eyes glanced down at her lap, and a perplexed expression spread across her face. "Okay. Not what I was expecting. Umm . . . shoo?"

"How are you so calm about a snake in your lap!" Rynn glared at her best friend.

Samara grinned at Draven. "Too bad Kieran isn't here. He'd have so many jokes."

"Is that a snake in your dress, or are you just happy to see me?" Draven asked with a completely straight face.

"My snake's bigger than yours." Samara impersonated Kieran's smooth voice.

"Sam!" Rynn barked.

"Oh, fine." Samara rolled her eyes and gently lifted the viper off her lap like it couldn't knock her ass out with one bite and wrack her body with seizures for hours until it burned off the venom. "I was just in the mind of a snake—southern tree boa, I think—so my tolerance for strange shit has gone up a bit."

"Really?" Roth perked up. "What was that like? Did you completely take over its body? Or was it more of a shared consciousness thing?"

"The latter. It was kind of grumpy about the whole affair to be honest." Samara held the viper up with one hand, letting its body curl around her forearm. "You're not grumpy though, are you?" she cooed, and then to Rynn's horror—and mine too, if I was being honest—Samara booped the thing on the nose with her finger. "I can *feel* how content you are right now. Who's the cutest little viper there ever was? You are!"

Another boop.

"Samara," Rynn whined pitifully.

"Alright, alright." She smoothly rolled to her feet. "Just let me go set this pretty girl outside. I think she's digesting a meal or something. She just wants to find somewhere warm to curl up and rest."

"Sure. Fine. Whatever." Rynn pointed to the exit. "Just get it out of here!"

Samara practically flounced out of the room, and only when her footsteps faded did Rynn hop down from the table, grumbling something about smothering Samara in her sleep.

"Where's the book that has the exact spell?" Roth asked, looking at the glyph on the floor where Samara had been sitting.

Rynn grabbed it off the table and tossed it to them.

"Careful." Roth snatched the book out of the air and turned to glare at Rynn, eyes flashing orange in warning. "You damage any of these books, and you'll be the one getting smothered in your sleep."

The mirror rippled in the corner, and a second later, Alaric and Kieran stepped into the room before freezing.

"Why do I smell Samara's blood?" Alaric gave me an accusing glare.

"Because Samara decided to use a Fae spell nobody has ever heard of that resulted in her sharing a mind with a snake and talking to a crown that apparently has a soul," I deadpanned.

Roth snorted. "Succinct but accurate."

"Bonus points for an excellent delivery," Draven added.

"Right." Alaric rubbed his forehead with one hand and held out some documents with the other. "Look this over, Rynn. I believe we have everything covered. Kieran and I have both reviewed it twice. All it needs is your signature."

Rynn swallowed before striding towards Alaric and taking the contract from him. "Thanks. Be back in a bit."

Without another word, she left the room. A moment later, the sound of Samara coming down the stairs echoed through the hall outside, followed by soft murmurings between her and Rynn. When Samara joined us again, any hint of amusement was gone from her face. Cali was right behind her with an equally grim expression.

"What happened?" I looked between the two of them.

"I'll get to that." Samara sat on one of the tables, and everyone else took a seat. I remained standing against the wall with my arms crossed, feeling too anxious to sit.

Whatever had happened must have been bad because Cali didn't sneer at me once.

"First, the crown has agreed to go along with the transformation spell. So that will make that portion of the plan easier." Her dire expression softened for a moment. "Also . . . I gave them a name. Talis."

The recognition hit me instantly. Samara's parents had often taken her stargazing, and if my parents had been away—which they often had—they'd invite me to join them. The star named after hope had been her dad's favorite.

"It's a good name," I said softly. "He would approve."

Samara looked at me and saw the understanding in my eyes. "I think so too." She smiled back before swallowing and growing serious once more. "Tell them, Cali."

"A striker just delivered a message from a courtier at House Corvinus." The Furie's gaze flicked to Kieran. "Your friend, actually—Riah."

Kieran blinked in surprise. "Is she okay? What did she say?"

"Tamsen defected from House Corvinus. She left in the middle of the night with Riah and a handful of others; they took shelter at a small outpost close to the Velesian border." Cali's fisted hand shook before she tossed the crumbled-up message onto the table. "Carmilla sent three squads of rangers after them. The people in the outpost refused to grant them entry. They said Carmilla was a false queen."

Samara sat perfectly still, but her eyes had turned a solid black.

"What happened?" I asked when silence reigned.

"The rangers . . ." Cali trailed off, clenching her jaw hard enough that I could see the muscles feathering along her jawline.

"They burned the outpost down," Samara cut in. "With the people inside. Tamsen, Riah, and less than a dozen people made it out alive."

Rangers swore an oath to serve not only their House but all of the Moroi. Either those rangers had disregarded that oath of their own volition . . . or Carmilla had stripped them of their free will and forced them to carry out a heinous act that would likely haunt them forever.

A mixture of disgust and rage rolled through me, and I could feel the same sentiments echoed by everyone in the room.

"We have to stop her," I rasped, drawing Samara's dark gaze. "Whatever it takes."

"We will," she swore.

"Where is Tamsen now?" Draven asked.

"The group split up after escaping," Cali said. "According to Riah, the Corvinus Heir refused to risk any more lives protecting hers. Tamsen traveled with them to another outpost but then ordered Riah and the others to keep their heads down and deny any involvement with her before leaving. She told Riah she was heading towards House Devereux."

"Shit," Roth swore. "I can't express how bad of an idea that is. They won't trust her—not a Corvinus. My family made an exception for Nyx because they turned their back on their House and have proven themself over the years, but Tamsen is the bloody Heir. There's a solid chance they'll kill her on sight with how high their paranoia probably is right now."

"This all happened several days ago—probably at the same time we were leaving House Salvatore. Riah lucked out and found an outpost where another of Kieran's friends was—one who just happened to have a striker that could track Kieran's scent," Cali continued.

"Jasi, probably," Kieran grunted. "I pulled some strings to get him out of a tight spot with House Tepes a few years back, and he's one of my best informants now. Lives in an outpost on one of the main trade routes—hears all kinds of gossip."

"Which one?" I asked.

"Morningwell."

I started calculating the distance in my head and the possible paths Tamsen could have taken. The Morningwell outpost was southwest of House Corvinus, towards the middle of the realm. The main road went directly east and west from it, but Tamsen likely hadn't taken that. It might have been safer, but the road would be heavily patrolled. If she were desperate enough—and it seemed like she was—the rogue Heir had likely cut straight through the wilds.

Which meant she was either dead . . . or was a couple of days away from House Devereux, maybe a little less if she lucked out and didn't run into any trouble.

Hesitation fluttered through my thoughts, but I realized it wasn't mine; I'd been staring at the floor, unseeing, while contemplating all the possibilities. When I looked up, I found Samara's heavy gaze on me, then that flicker of doubt rolled through me again.

"You might as well tell me what you're thinking." I laid my hand flat against my chest, over my heart. "Because I can already feel it, *mate*."

Her gaze dropped to my hand before returning to my eyes. She didn't deny that we were mates or say something caustic to me, so I considered that a win.

"In order to set the plan in motion, we need to let Carmilla discover where we are." Samara held my stare, even as Cali grumbled something about hating this plan. I didn't blame her. If things went the way we expected, as soon as Carmilla learned our whereabouts, she'd enact her strategy to remove Cali as a player.

And we were going to let her do it—as long as the Furie's life wasn't in danger. Samara's plan would only work if Carmilla believed she was winning.

I would have been pissed too if my friends were going to enact an absolutely insane plan that could fall apart in so many ways and I wouldn't be there to help them.

Cali had been the one to read that message first though, so she knew what was at stake. We couldn't let more innocent people die. This plan might have been crazy, but if we pulled it off, it would also limit the bloodshed.

Samara let her words hang in the air, then opened her mouth to speak before closing it again and looking away from me. Fear echoed down the bond before suddenly being cut off. She was walling off her emotions from me, trying to hide.

I knew what she wanted to ask me. To find Tamsen, if she was still alive, and get her to safety. It wasn't hard to figure out because, of those gathered here, I was best suited for the task. Traveling through the Lunarian wilds was literally my job. Draven could probably do it, but he was needed here, as Erendriel would no doubt show up again, and even with the magic binding his tongue, the prince's knowledge of his father would be useful.

But still, Samara didn't ask. Frustrated rage swirled inside my gut, and based on the way she flinched, I knew she felt it.

She believed I would betray her. Even now, after everything I'd done, Samara didn't trust me to do this.

"Roth," I said evenly. "Write a note to your family asking them to protect Tamsen—even if they throw her ass into the dungeon. As long as they don't lop her head off because she looks at them funny."

"Vail—" Samara took a step towards me.

"It'll likely take me at least four days to find her," I cut her off and stalked towards the table with the Fae weapons. On the off chance I ran into some wraiths, these could be useful. "Maybe up to a week depending on how well she's covering her tracks."

Kieran quietly snuck out of the room. Everyone else remained silent, eyes bouncing back and forth between me and Samara.

"Vail." Samara closed the distance between us until she stood next to me at the table.

I ignored her.

"Carmilla is likely watching House Devereux, so I can't just walk Tamsen up to the front gate—that would be too obvious —but I'll make sure she gets there and then double back a bit." I grabbed a second sword harness and strapped it on before sliding a Fae sword next to my regular one. Then I swapped the daggers on my thighs for Fae ones. "Carmilla will only send out her best rangers looking for us. I'll leave just enough of a trail that they can find it but make it look like I was trying to cover my tracks."

"*Marshal*," Samara said more firmly.

I wanted to look at her but also knew doing so might weaken my resolve—because I didn't want to leave. But it had to be me. If Tamsen had truly defected, we couldn't leave her to the wolves. Plus, Samara's plan to deal with her aunt would only work if Carmilla didn't know she was walking into a trap.

"Here." Roth held up a folded-up letter. "She probably won't get the best treatment, but they won't kill her."

"Good enough." I walked over and took the letter from them just as Kieran strode back into the room, holding a bag.

"We're getting low on food, but I packed what we could spare and some water. You'll probably have to restock somewhere."

"Once I get out of the badlands, there are ranger stashes I can use."

Kieran nodded as I took the bag from him, then I headed towards the door without a backwards glance.

"Stubborn fucking asshole," I heard Samara growl, but I kept walking. My long strides were eating up the distance as I went up the stairwell and then stalked through the temple. Whatever it took to prove my loyalty to her, I'd do it—even if I was pissed that she didn't even seem willing to give me a chance.

Yes. I'd fucked up. Massively.

But I'd also helped get her out of that dungeon. I'd done everything I could to keep her alive while we'd been on the run. Cali was clearly teetering on losing it, but I hadn't said one damn word about it. And I wasn't bitching about the fact that I'd have to share my mate with four others—part of me was actually relieved by that because it meant there were four other people in this world who would love and protect her as much as I would.

None of it mattered though, because apparently, she still believed I was one breath away from betraying her again.

The heat of the late summer afternoon hit me like a runaway horse as soon as I stepped outside the temple. This was going to be a brutal run across the badlands.

My best bet was straight east to avoid the trapper spiders. Once I made it to the forests, I'd angle south a bit and then—

"Oof!"

A pair of bright purple eyes brimming with fury looked up at me from where Samara had slammed me against the wall of the temple.

"Something you need, my queen?" I asked in a flat, bored tone, doing my best to keep my emotions from rolling down the bond.

"I wasn't done talking to you." Her hands gripped the fabric of my shirt as she crowded my space. It should have been absurd. I had over a foot of height on her and could easily outmuscle her, but some small part of me had enough self-preservation to not try.

Samara liked to fight dirty, and I'd prefer to keep all my bits attached.

"Oh?" I tilted my head in a way that I knew would annoy her. Black flashed across her eyes, and I smiled. "You don't have to say anything. I can feel it, remember?" I tapped the back of her hand that was covering my heart. "If there were anyone else you could have asked to do this, you would have because you don't trust me. I felt it all. Your hesitation. Fear."

"Vail," she ground out.

"Yes, my queen?"

She stood on her tiptoes to get a little closer. "You are a fucking idiot."

I blinked. "What—"

Samara let go of my shirt to yank my head down. Then her mouth claimed mine, and for a second, I stood there rigidly, not completely sure this was happening.

I felt her lips curve into a smile against mine before she whispered, "This is the part where you kiss me back."

"So bossy." I smiled before doing just that, sliding my tongue into her mouth, reveling in the way she tasted.

Then I flipped us around so she was pinned against the wall and broke our kiss. Samara panted before going still as I wrapped my left hand around her throat and planted my right hand against the wall.

"You're so fucking frustrating," I growled.

"Yeah," she rasped. "You're a real fucking peach yourself."

I chuckled and squeezed her throat a little harder, and she let out a low moan that went straight to my dick.

"What do you want from me, Sam?" I brushed my thumb against her rapidly beating pulse, and she arched her back at the touch.

"Everything," she breathed out. "I want everything from you."

"You have it." I leaned my forehead against hers. "You are mine, and I am yours. I will never betray you again, and I will spend the rest of my life making up for it."

"I know," she whispered, and I eased my grip on her throat a little but didn't remove my hand.

"Why?" I closed my eyes as I breathed in her scent. "Why did you hesitate in asking me to do this? I felt your fear."

"Because if you get captured, Carmilla will make an example out of you." Her throat bobbed as she swallowed. "I'm not saying all of our bullshit is resolved, but I want to have the chance to fix it—to fix us. You still piss me off half the time you open your mouth, your bullish attitude is incredibly frustrating, and Draven is right, you suck at apologizing, but none of that changes the fact that I love you beyond reason."

"Fuck." I yanked her to me and kissed her hard, pouring every ounce of what I felt for her into it even as I practically screamed it down our bond. I'd never been good with words the way that Kieran and Draven were, and apparently I was even worse than Alaric and Roth at expressing how I felt. I'd just have to make damn sure she knew from my actions that I fucking loved her beyond reason too.

My tongue slid across one of her fangs, and she groaned as my blood filled her mouth. Then I slid my hand down until I cupped her breast and squeezed. She sucked on my tongue as her soft body pushed into me more. Suddenly, I was very desperate to know how wet she was.

I tore my hand away from her breast and roughly dragged up her dress until I felt bare skin. Then my fingers dove underneath her panties.

It was my turn to groan as I found the hot slickness waiting for me. I slid two fingers through her wetness, and Samara moaned, finally breaking our kiss as she tilted her head back against the wall.

"More," she demanded.

I didn't have it in me to tease her right now or go slow. Instead, I just shoved two fingers as deep into her cunt as they could go and started fucking her roughly with them.

"Is that what you want?" I growled as she writhed on my hand.

"Yes!" She looked at me with solid black eyes before tilting her head. "Drink."

My fangs were buried in her throat a second later as I continued to pump my fingers in and out while I rubbed her clit with my thumb. Her intoxicatingly rich blood filled my mouth, and I swallowed it down as she came undone on my hand.

She tasted even better than I'd remembered, but I didn't want to take too much. I started to pull my fangs out, but she pushed hard against the back of my head and held me in place. "More," she panted. "Drink more."

I bit down harder and added a third finger, fucking her faster and rougher as I drank her down. Her pussy tightened around my fingers as she came again. Only when she was finished and I felt her trembling with ecstasy did I pull away from her neck.

Slowly, I pulled my fingers out as well, and Samara watched as I swiped her blood off my lips before sucking each finger clean.

"Come back to me, Vail," she said through heavy breaths.

"There is nothing that will keep me from you." I laid my hand against her rapidly beating heart; the bond that had felt so frayed now felt so much more solid. "I love you too, Samara."

CHAPTER TWENTY-EIGHT

—

Samara

Erendriel did return that evening, an hour after sunset, but he didn't come alone.

"Serril." I nodded in greeting. "Pleasure to see you again in the flesh." An apologetic smile graced my lips. "Forgive me, I mean shadow."

He chuckled, and wisps of darkness rolled off his shoulders as his shadow form strolled towards me. Like the night I'd first met him, he'd chosen to appear in a Fae form rather than something monstrous. He halted a foot away from the archway, where the boundary between us was.

"Feeling bold this evening, are we?" A hand of inky black shadows stretched towards the invisible wall, and he mimed tapping against it.

"It's easy to be bold when you're young and naive of the world around you," Erendriel said evenly.

"Still . . ." Serril pondered me. "I like her more than Velika. Too much human in that one, not enough Seelie."

The question I'd been about to ask died on my lips. "Velika had Seelie blood too?"

Erendriel snorted dismissively. "Haven't figured it out yet, have you? I would have thought with all the tomes at your disposal that you would have by now." He gave me an appraising look. "Perhaps you're not as clever as I thought."

"Oh, come now." Serril's voice held a mocking quality to it. "Let's not judge her too harshly. She's so young, and the only ones who have been able to teach her are other Moroi. It's the ignorant leading the ignorant. That never bodes well."

"I suppose you have a point." Erendriel remained in the center of the small landing with his hands clasped behind his back. It reminded me of the way the old scholars would stand when they launched into a lecture. The false Seelie King might be my enemy, but I'd be a fool to turn down any knowledge. I'd just have to cross-reference whatever he told me with the books to unravel any lies he might have slipped into the truth.

Serril's hand moved away from the boundary to tap a long finger against his chin. "Have you ever wondered what determined who became Moroi, Velesian, or Furie when your human ancestors cast that original spell?"

Disappointment hit me. I did know, and it wasn't particularly interesting. "They chose their symbols." I pointed to the crescent moon on the left side of my neck. "Everyone chose where to paint the symbol. Left for Moroi, right for Velesian, and the front of the neck for Furies."

"'We will give our lives for the blood. We will yield our fates in the wild. We will lose our souls to the fury,'" Serril recited.

They were the original words spoken for the spellcasting. I was a little surprised he knew them, but then again, the wraiths had been raiding the old human settlements to collect the obsidian stones, which had been used in the original ritual. He'd probably stumbled upon copies of the spell they'd used.

"Your point?" I arched a dark brow.

"Just like you, your ancestors tampered with something they couldn't begin to comprehend." Serril held his hand up again, letting talons form at his fingertips. Then he grinned widely, and I was able to make out large fangs. "The spell was already in motion when they began painting those symbols. They did not choose what symbols to carve into their skin; the magic did."

The disappointment I'd been feeling vanished. In all my readings, I'd never come across that distinction. We'd assumed they'd decided who became Moroi, Velesian, or Furie—likely just divided things up evenly—but if Serril was telling the truth, they hadn't chosen . . .

"How did the magic decide?" I asked slowly.

Apparently, Serril didn't like to just give answers. "I think you know. Only the Furies can use shadow magic, some more than others, like your gifted friend. The Moroi can use Seelie magic. And the Velesians, well, they cannot directly use either type of magic, but if a Moroi were to give them an enchanted bracelet of Seelie magic . . . they could use that. Just as they could use something enchanted with Unseelie magic. The Velesians are magic-neutral."

It was like gears started turning in my mind as I took it all into account. How had I never realized this before? It seemed so damn obvious.

"Some of the humans had Fae blood," I whispered. "The ones with Seelie blood became Moroi, Unseelie became Furies, and the pure humans turned Velesian."

Serril whirled to face Erendriel. "See? So much potential in this one. She just needs a little knowledge, that's all."

I was so blindsided by this revelation that I only had a brief flicker of annoyance at his patronizing tone. Was this what made the House bloodlines different? We had higher amounts of Seelie blood, and that gave us the ability to control our bloodlust better?

If Serril was telling the truth, and my gut told me he was, this pointed us in a whole new direction to explore. But first, we had to survive.

As much as I wanted to pepper Serril with more questions, I needed to keep my focus on the goal of this conversation.

"Thank you for sharing your knowledge with me," I told Serril politely. "It gives me hope for a future alliance between us. Speaking of which . . ." My gaze slid to Erendriel. "What are you offering if I choose to ally with you? And what would you require of me?" I raised my chin. "Marriage is off the table. I will not leave my mates."

I'd been preparing for this conversation since Vail had left. Draven agreed with me that his father would be suspicious if I suddenly became open to discussing marriage after being so adamantly against it before. This had to be played just right.

The Seelie King studied me. "As long as your aunt bears that crown, you cannot defeat her. You need me far more than I need you."

"I've made it this far." I crossed my arms. "I'll figure something out."

"Before or after she burns down another outpost?" Serril drawled as he sauntered back over to stand near the archway. "How many more of your precious people do you think she'll kill before you accept that you're in over your head, my pretty little queen?"

"Not your queen," I said coldly before turning my attention back to Erendriel in a clear dismissal.

Serril chuckled again.

"Still feisty." The corners of Erendriel's mouth turned up in a small, amused smile. "I see why Draven likes you. A little bit of light for his dark thoughts."

"I do miss making the half-blood scream," Serril reminisced wistfully.

Rage burned through me, and I let it show on my face briefly before masking my emotions. It wasn't my words that were going to make this part of the plan successful. It was my body language. Those little tells that Erendriel and Serril were no doubt cataloguing.

Young and inexperienced. Overwhelmed by the world falling apart. Angry at my aunt. These were the things I let them see.

But as Rynn always said, an injured and cornered wolf still had fangs. I just couldn't snarl with mine yet.

"Draven is not to be harmed," I said evenly. "Nor are any of my other mates. This will be a business arrangement between us and nothing more."

"Of course." Erendriel gave me a placating nod. "A mate bond would be preferred, as that would almost certainly grant me access to places like this . . ." His eyes left mine for a moment to peer at the stairs behind me. Whatever he was thinking, I couldn't read it in his expression. Then his gaze returned to me. "But there are other things we can do. Until then, you will answer my call and be my eyes and ears for the other hidden areas throughout Lunaria."

"How many are there? And where?"

"That is not knowledge you need right now."

If I had to guess, they were in the mountains above the Velesian realm. Draven said Erendriel spent most of his time there. Whatever he was searching for had to be in those mountains.

"Anything else?" I looked over my shoulder and down the stairs quickly.

"Expecting someone?" Serril asked, and my gaze snapped back to him. "Or did you not tell your mates the deal you were seeking to make this evening?"

I stiffened. "I am queen. It's my decision."

Erendriel's smile widened, as if he could already see the cracks of descension forming that he could exploit later. I had no doubt that he still planned to pursue me as queen or at least a mate bond. He wanted to get into those hidden rooms, and he likely suspected that some things might be locked down further to my blood. He wanted access—I was that access.

"And what is it you seek?" Erendriel's gaze lifted to the top of my head. "Perhaps the crown that is yours by right?"

"Yes, actually." I straightened. "I have no intention of using it to bind the wills of my people, but it is an object of power that I will not allow to fall into the hands of another."

"Of course," he answered in that placating way of his that was really starting to irritate me. I kept that off my face though and instead let a hint of insecurity flash through my eyes.

"I don't trust you," I said tightly. "I'm not some foolish young girl for you to manipulate. You're still set on trying to make me your mate, but I will never do that." My inflection wavered a bit towards the end, and I halted my words a little too harshly. I stood up a little straighter, as if I were encouraging myself, and stared straight into Erendriel's ancient eyes. "Help me get back my birthright. As long as the crown sits on my head—as long as I possess it—I will not act against you and will assist you in searching these spaces."

"I find this acceptable."

My heart raced a little faster, and I let more uncertainty settle into my features. "I . . ." I trailed off and glanced behind me again. "I can go fetch something so we can hammer out the contra—"

"No need," Erendriel cut me off. "You are part Fae. Let us bargain like Fae."

"How do we do that?" I shifted slightly on my feet before killing the movement.

Erendriel smiled wider. "Simply step across the boundary. Skin-to-skin contact is necessary."

I swallowed.

"Come now, little queen," Serril mocked. "Don't lose that wonderful bravado now."

I cut him a sharp glance before deliberately stepping

forward—over the boundary. My heart was beating so hard for a second that I swore it was all I could hear. Draven had warned me that this was likely what Erendriel would ask for. None of us liked it, but we needed Erendriel's help, and he clearly needed mine.

The risk wasn't that he would kill me; it was that he'd simply take me and try to force me to obey him, but I'd thought about the story Draven had told me a night or two ago —about that test Erendriel had put his son through at the outpost. Erendriel would prefer me to ally with him willingly, even if I were doing so reluctantly, because it would make me easier to manipulate in his eyes.

If I ended up defying him like Draven, then he'd fall back on a different plan. He'd learn more about me in the meantime though, so he'd have plenty of weaknesses to exploit.

I closed the distance between me and Erendriel, who just continued to stare at me like a moon devil watching a rabbit hop closer. The hairs on the back of my neck rose as I sensed Serril move to stand at my back.

Erendriel was even taller than Vail, so I had to tilt my head back to look him in the eye, and I could have sworn I saw shadows swirling in his deep blue eyes for a moment.

He held out his hand. "Let's make a bargain, *kilfid min tros.*" Little blood queen.

I slid my hand into his and squeezed.

CHAPTER TWENTY-NINE

—

Samara

FOUR DAYS LATER, I was still feeling the rush of my encounter with the Seelie King. It wasn't just that I had bargained with him—it was that I'd outsmarted him.

Or at least, I was fairly confident I had.

When I'd walked down the stairs after he'd left, I'd practically fallen into Draven's arms as the adrenaline had worn off. My wicked prince had cooed praises at me for doing well while whispering promises of all the things he would do to me as soon as he had me alone.

Because in that moment, we had very much not been alone. Everyone had been hiding in the stairwell just out of Erendriel's sight so they could listen in, and Rynn had taken notes.

We all agreed that the words spoken in the bargain would work with our plan. I'd been very careful to only refer to Talis as "the crown" in my wording. Erendriel had added stipulations so that it wasn't simply the crown resting on my head but being in my possession—and that allowing my mates to hold on to it still counted as "in my possession," as they were an extension of me in Fae eyes.

I'd conversed with Talis twice more since then—both times borrowing the body of the same serpent, who seemed to live in the vines growing up the Sovereign House. The viper was grumpy each time, but it was getting easier to control his body. I always thanked him, but I don't think he cared. I'd have to make sure he had a nice supply of mice or something when I made it back to the Sovereign House in person.

Each time I'd woken up, there had been a snake in my lap. Rynn was not happy about that.

I was also beginning to notice that I could sense any snakes in the area. My Fae magic definitely seemed to be stirring more. And I was fairly certain I could summon the serpents to me if I wanted, like if I just tugged on that thread which connected me to them, they would answer.

In addition to my new scaly friends, I'd also been able to do small things like coax some flowers on a cactus into blooming and stifle my footsteps like Draven so I could move about silently.

It was something I'd been practicing by sneaking up on Rynn and scaring the shit out of her. I'd tried to do the same to Cali, but the bitch had *stabbed* me. When I'd shrieked that it was just me, she'd snorted and said, "I know. Why do you think it's just a flesh wound?" And then she'd pulled the dagger out from between my ribs.

In fairness, she had missed my vital organs and I'd healed within minutes. Still, a bit of an overreaction, in my opinion.

Two days ago, Ary and Aniela had shown up looking beat to shit. Apparently, all of the Moroi realm was crawling with rangers who reported only to Carmilla, and the Heirs hadn't been sure if they'd make it to House Devereux, so they'd opted to come here instead. It was actually a boon for us because part of our plan required blood—a lot of blood.

Once we'd told them what we'd been plotting, the two of them had been more than willing to open up a vein and donate to the cause. They'd given quite a bit and were currently passed out downstairs . . . in the same bed.

Something had clearly happened between the two, but I'd have to get the full story later.

We hadn't heard anything from Vail during all this time, and I was trying very hard not to dwell on that fact. Thanks to our mate bond, I could feel him, but it was definitely fainter the farther he went. Our bond was stronger than it had been—it no longer felt like it was crumbling—but, clearly, distance had an impact.

Roth had found a couple of books that mentioned Fae mate bonds. From what we could tell, the bonds formed in one of two ways. Naturally, which only occurred when the people forming the bond were genuinely in love with each other and declared their devotion, or through spell castings. It seemed the Fae had been fans of arranged political marriages, and mate bonds were used in those cases as well.

I hadn't come across anything about them being possible to break like Erendriel had claimed, but the books hadn't had a ton of information. It didn't matter though, because I was keeping my mates, and I'd kill anyone who tried to take them from me—the Seelie King included.

To keep myself from going insane, I'd started limiting how often I checked the bond between me and Vail. Otherwise, I'd just obsess over it, and I was worried that I might tug on it or send some of my emotions barreling down the bond and distract Vail at the worst possible moment.

My imagination had run wild with Vail fighting against monsters or some of Carmilla's rangers, only to miss a step because I'd practically screamed my growing panic through our mate bond.

So I'd diverted my obsessive mind into fine-tuning the transformation spell and going over the plan with everyone repeatedly.

Which apparently was starting to get on everyone's nerves.

Kieran, of all people, had threatened to find a spell to seal my lips shut if I attempted to run through everything again, which had everyone grunting in agreement. According to Talis, I had perfected the transformation spell. Granted, I was pretty sure they'd been only half listening the last time we'd spoken.

I'd managed to bore an ancient Fae crown. Go me.

Logically, it made sense that Vail hadn't sent any messages of his progress. Strikers were our main form of communication, and they were trained to either follow specific routes or track people down. The temple wasn't on any normal routes, and while every House had strikers trained to find me, Vail couldn't exactly stop by and ask to borrow one.

I knew all of this, yet it did nothing to keep me from freaking out. Vail had been gone for five days now. He'd said it might take longer than that to return, but all I could think about were the worst-case scenarios. We'd also been holed up in this temple for a week now, so everyone's nerves were a little frayed.

Erendriel had promised to return when I needed him and gave me a coin to summon him. I didn't understand how he was moving around so quickly, because he definitely wasn't in the temple during the day, and there wasn't much around here. Draven didn't know how he did it either, only that he could go from one end of the continent to the other in the same day— the same hour, even.

Now that I knew about the mirrors, it didn't seem so impossible, but it wasn't like he was lugging an eight-foot mirror around with him.

There had been no sign of Serril or any other wraiths either, but it was still suspicious that Erendriel hadn't left someone behind to keep an eye on us.

We'd been careful about setting up the rest of our plans— only working on the temple during the day and only after

Draven did a thorough pass-through to make sure no wraiths had found a dark corner to lurk in. Everything was coming together—we just needed Vail to come back.

I needed Vail to come back.

"Have we accounted for—"

"*Yes!*" Roth, Alaric, and Rynn all said at once.

I stopped where I'd been pacing in the middle of the room and glared at the three of them. "You don't even know what I was going to say," I accused.

"You no doubt thought of yet another variation of how things could go wrong." Alaric closed the book he'd been reading and selected a new one from the piles in front of him.

"Even though we've already come up with multiple contingency plans at this point." Roth's ropes snapped out to steal the book Alaric had chosen and tossed a different one to him.

"It's impossible to plan for all scenarios—that way lies madness—and we've covered all the major ones," Rynn added, not even looking up from the scroll her eyes were glued to.

"Sure, but what if—"

"For the love of the moon, shut up!" Cali growled from where she'd been resting her eyes on her folded-up arms at the weapons table.

"Why don't you go for a walk?" Kieran offered. "Maybe practice your magic a bit?"

"Don't go far though." Draven glanced up from the sword he'd been admiring. "And please don't bring any more snakes inside. I don't think I can listen to Rynn scream again."

"Oh, don't start," Rynn sneered, finally looking away from the text she'd been absorbed in. "I've been listening to all of you make Samara scream for days now. My ears are bleeding, and I'm honestly worried for my best friend's pussy at this point."

"Yeah, exactly how much pounding can that thing take?"

Cali twisted her head so she could stare at me—well, a certain part of me anyway.

"Oh, we haven't just been playing with that perfect little pussy," Kieran said cheerfully. "We've als—"

"I'm going to go for a walk now!" I announced loudly and beat a hasty retreat. Rynn was already in a foul mood, and Kieran reciting the many ways I'd been fucked over the last four days would not make her any more pleasant to be around.

The clock was ticking on our plan, which meant time was also running out before Rynn had to return to the Alpha Pack.

I went up the stairs, passing through the ward, and then turned left to head towards the temple entrance. My eyes flitted about the large, open chamber. This was where we'd been sneakily laying all the glyphs the past few days. The even larger room further in the temple would have been better, but that was also where the entrance to the secret level was, and the ceiling was broken in places. We'd needed a room that was entirely contained, so this had been the only option.

The white marble that made up every inch of the room, from the ceilings to the floors and the columns that spiraled up between them, didn't show even a hint of what we'd spent the last three days doing after Roth had perfected the spell.

Or at least, we were hoping that was what they'd done. We couldn't exactly test it beforehand.

If it failed . . . we'd just have to run fast. Real fucking fast.

Maybe I should check them again . . .

My hand flew to my chest at the same moment I inhaled sharply. Then I was sprinting towards the temple entrance and flinging myself into the arms of the approaching man.

"Vail," I breathed out as I clung to him before inhaling that scent I had missed so much.

"Miss me, Sam?" Vail held me tightly against him.

"Only a little," I lied.

He laughed, burying his face into the crook of my neck.

We stayed like that for a long moment, just holding each other. Safe. He was safe . . . and he'd come back to me. The bond thrummed happily between us.

"What's that smell?" I wrinkled my nose after taking another deep breath, then stepped back enough to look him over.

"Well, I have been traveling basically nonstop for the past few days," he said dryly.

"Not that." My gaze fell to the bag he must have dropped when I'd thrown myself at him. The brown canvas was stained dark red in places. Blood. Decay. "Are you carrying body parts?" I looked at him, wide-eyed. "Tell me you didn't kill Tamsen!? That was not the plan, Vail!"

"I didn't kill Tamsen." His silver eyes were alight with amusement. "She is safe in the loving and not at all crazy embrace of House Devereux. I brought you a present."

"A present?" I gave the bag and then him a skeptical look. "You know how Draven tried to explain how apologies work? Maybe you should talk to him about how gifts work. See, rotting body parts aren't really—"

"Grigor's dead."

I blinked. "The sleazy guard from the Sovereign House? The handsy one?"

Vail grinned widely. "He's a little less handsy now."

"You didn't," I said with a choked laugh before glancing back down at the bag. It *was* basically the perfect size for two hands . . .

"I saw the way he kept coming up with reasons to touch you," Vail said in a low, dangerous tone. "He volunteered to be on one of the teams to track Tamsen down. Apparently, he is —was—a good tracker. After I got her to safety, I doubled back and took him out."

"How?" I prodded the bag with my toe.

"Lured a pack of howlers to where he was, cut off his hands, and let the pack tear him apart."

"Let's leave them out here—they smell, and it's the thought that counts." I grabbed Vail's hand and started pulling him into the temple.

"So you like my gift then?"

I glanced over my shoulder. "Oh, yes, but we need to get you cleaned up so I can show you just how much."

Vail's hand slipped from mine, and the next thing I knew, I was being thrown over his shoulder. I laughed as Vail jogged down to the secret levels. He paused at the first level, but when I tried to turn to see why, he just slapped my ass.

"Vail!" I shouted and wiggled to get free. Another slap.

"I take it things went well then?" Draven drawled. I couldn't see him, but I could practically hear the smile in his voice.

"Tamsen is safe. At least two of the rangers picked up my trail. They're keeping their distance, but I doubled back a few times to check on them—they're definitely following me." A hand gripped my ass and squeezed. "Also, I killed that prick of a guard I told you about."

"The handsy one?" Draven asked.

"Less handsy now," I laughed while repeating Vail's words.

Draven chuckled. "Do us a favor and keep her busy for a few hours? Everyone is feeling a little stir-crazy, and our devious little Blood Queen has been rather antsy."

First, Vail and Draven had been chatting about the guard, and now Roth was sharing their nickname for me. I kind of liked that all my mates were getting along. Although I wasn't going to let Draven's comment about my antsiness slide.

"It's rude to talk about me like I'm not here," I said in a mockingly stern tone. "And it's not for you both to decide where I go. As you said, I am your queen, so—" I yelped when

Vail raised the hand that had been kneading my ass and slapped it again—hard.

There was no way I wasn't going to have a bruise.

"At least two people should be on lookout from now on." Vail started down the stairs again.

"I'll see to it." Draven blew me a kiss when we passed him. I blew one back because apparently I was sappy as shit now that I had five mates.

Plus, I was about to get railed for several hours. That was an instant good-mood maker right there.

Vail went straight to the room he'd claimed on the second level and put me down. The layout of this one was different from mine. A large bed took up the back left corner, its sheets still askew from when Vail had last been in it, and the opposite corner on the back wall had a little alcove built into it. The Fae had taken the time to create a waterfall mural in it using different types of stones and gems.

They really had put a lot of effort into making these hidden layers feel like a home. Once again, I was curious about who had built it and why they weren't here enjoying the fruits of their labor.

All those thoughts fled the second Vail pulled his shirt over his head before tugging off his pants and boots a second later.

"Strip," he ordered before activating the glyph that had been cleverly worked into the waterfall mural. Water started to fall in a controlled spray of fine droplets from the alcove's ceiling.

I briefly thought about saying no just to be contrary, but then I made the mistake of looking at Vail's thick, hard cock, and my mouth watered.

I could always be bratty later.

Vail smirked, as if he'd seen my momentary inner struggle and was amused by it. Then a groan slipped from his lips when I shucked my dress off, revealing I wasn't wearing any undergarments—Alaric had torn my last pair yesterday. It was my turn to smirk at him.

"See something you like, Marshal?" I sauntered past him to duck under the warm water, letting it plaster my long, black hair to my breasts and over my soft belly.

Vail's gaze darkened. "I see something I want to devour."

Fuck. Me.

"Clean first." I curled a finger, and he joined me under the water. "You're covered in dirt, blood, and only the moon knows what else."

Vail stood there quietly while I took my time getting him clean, running my fingers across his broad chest before tangling them in his hair. The more I touched him, the more his dark grey eyes shifted to silver until that was all I could see. His patience finally snapped when I reached down and dragged my fingers up the bottom of his hard length.

One second, I was debating dropping to my knees and teasing him a little more, and the next, I was six feet off the ground with my back against the cool wall and my legs over Vail's shoulders.

"Oh, fuck!" I screamed. There was no teasing. No light little licks. Vail just gripped my ass with his hands and buried his entire face in my pussy. Instantly, my thighs clamped around his head, but he didn't seem to mind. If anything, it only spurred him on.

Arching my back as much as I could and trusting him not to let me fall, I let myself slip into bliss while Vail devoured my cunt. His tongue speared my core, and I ground against his mouth. I didn't even attempt to be quiet as I moaned with every lick and thrust of his tongue, and when he switched to sucking on my clit, I came so hard, I was surprised I didn't pass out.

Hot breath tickled my inner thigh as Vail pulled back. "You still with me, Sam?"

"Mm-hmm," I breathed out as tremors ran through my body.

"I promised Draven I'd keep you distracted for hours. Don't tell me I've already worn you out?"

"Not even close." I leaned my head forward from where it had been resting against the wall and almost groaned when I saw Vail grinning, the evidence of my arousal glistening in his short beard. "That was just a bit of stress relief."

"Oh?" Vail's hands slid up to my lower back, holding me in place as he stepped out of the alcove, taking me with him. I squeaked at my precarious position, which just made him laugh as he carried us towards the bed. "And what were you so worried about?"

I scowled down at him. "You were gone for five days, Vail! Any number of things could have gone wrong, and it's all I could think about."

"Funny. You said you only missed me a little bit." He carefully lowered me to the bed as if I weighed nothing. I should have probably cared about the fact that we were both still wet and soaking the bed, but my eyes were glued to Vail's impressive chest and abs.

Which I would argue were more important from a priority standpoint.

"Okay, maybe I missed you a moderate amount."

Vail's silver gaze bored down on me, the back of my legs still resting loosely against his body. "A moderate amount?" He grinned and jerked my legs so that my butt was closer to the edge of the bed. I inhaled sharply when I felt his cock notch against my entrance. Vail chuckled and leaned down, pushing my legs so that the tops of my thighs were almost touching my breasts. "Is that your final answer?"

I bit my lip and acted like I was thinking about it before nodding. "Yep. Definitely a middling amou—" A scream tore from my throat as Vail buried his cock balls-deep inside me.

"I felt you," he growled. "Every fucking day. You missed me. Desperately. Like your soul had been fractured." Vail pulled his hips away, only to thrust roughly back inside me again, drawing out another moan as my pussy stretched around his hard length. "I felt it too. It was fucking torture to be away from you that long."

"Show me," I breathed out. "Show me how much you missed me, Vail."

"Fuck," Vail ground out, then slammed into me one more time before pulling out. I hissed my disapproval at his cock no longer being inside me, and the bastard just chuckled as he flipped me over until I was on my hands and knees. With one smooth motion, he gripped my hips and thrust back into me.

I screamed and clenched the silky fabric of the bedspread as I did my best to push back against Vail's brutal pace. "Fuck me harder! I want to feel every inch of you."

I felt the second his nails shifted to claws and tore through my flesh. My pussy clenched at the mixture of pain and pleasure, and Vail groaned in response. "You are so fucking perfect." He pounded harder against me until all I could hear was the sound of flesh slapping flesh. "You like me stretching out your tight little pussy, don't you? "

"I do," I panted. "Fill me up, Vail. I want to feel you dripping between my thighs . . . and then I want you to fuck me again."

"Gods, I love that filthy mouth of yours." One hand ripped away from my thigh to push down on my back until my forehead was against the bed. Then both hands were on me again as Vail rutted roughly into me. "You're going to take every inch of me in this perfect fucking pussy until you can't take anymore, and then I'm going to come down your throat before fucking this glorious ass. You're going to be feeling me for days. Is that what you want, Sam?"

"Yes!" I let out a half-strangled scream.

After that, all I could do was moan as Vail pounded into me until he let out a low groan. He gave me a couple of minutes to recover before flipping me over and spearing me with his fingers. Then I whimpered when he pulled them free and admired how soaked they were before he swirled them around my clit. "Tell me again how much you missed me, *mate*."

"Make me," I said a little breathlessly before giving him a wicked grin, "mate."

CHAPTER THIRTY

Samara

I was dreaming about the hot springs and being worshipped by all of my mates. Kier was doing amazing things to my clit with that tongue of his while Draven thrust his fingers into my aching cunt. Vail was fucking my ass, and Alaric and Roth were teasing my breasts.

It was a glorious dream . . . which was completely destroyed by someone pounding on the door.

"Fuck off," Vail rumbled when I started to jerk upright, only to be stopped by his arm tightening around my stomach and chest. My back was to his chest and I could feel his erection pressed against the curve of my ass.

All kinds of ideas popped into my head. I hadn't meant to fall asleep, but Vail had been very . . . demanding. Between the mind-blowing sex and lack of sleep the last few days, I'd passed out shortly after he'd made me come for at least the dozenth time in three hours.

Vail's bossiness might have driven me insane most of the time, but damn did I like it when he was ordering me to come all over his cock while bruising my thighs with his grip.

The knocking increased.

"The Furies are here," Rynn growled from the other side of the door. "They've come for Cali."

All sexy thoughts instantly vanished.

"Shit." I scrambled out of bed and grabbed my dress off the floor, only to remember Vail had shredded it.

"Here." Vail tossed me his shirt, and I tugged it on. It fell to mid-thigh. Good enough.

I yanked the door open and practically collided with Rynn, who was gripping both sides of the doorframe like she needed something to ground her. "How'd they get here so fast?"

We'd suspected Carmilla would put her plans to remove Cali from the picture in motion as soon as she figured out where we were, but we'd assumed it would be tomorrow at the earliest. The Furie stronghold was on the southwestern coast of Lunaria. Even if Carmilla had sent a striker to them right away, they wouldn't have received the message until this evening.

Rynn dropped her arms, grabbed my hand, and tugged me towards the stairs. "I have no idea, but if we don't calm Cali down, she's going to kill him, and then our best-laid plans are going to be absolutely fucked."

"Who?" I ran a little faster to keep up with Rynn's long stride. "Fuck, it's Malachi, isn't it?"

"Of course it is," Rynn answered tightly. "We should have killed that fucker years ago. I told you he was nothing but trouble."

"You said the same thing about Vail," I pointed out.

"Yeah, and I stand by that," she hissed over her shoulder.

"Exactly how long are you going to be mad at me for, Rynn?" Vail asked from where he kept pace behind us.

Rynn slammed to a halt, and I bounced off her, only to be caught by Vail, who steadied me on my feet. My friend turned to glare at Vail, who was only wearing a pair of pants that he hadn't even bothered to button up all the way. "You knocked me out and stole the crown, which I had basically promised Samara I would keep safe."

"Fair enough," Vail replied evenly. "I regret my actions that day, and while Samara and I have already worked out our differences—" I snorted, and he corrected himself. "I am in the process of apologizing to the love of my life and will do so with many, many orgasms. But since I can't offer that to you, I will offer you my sword. Whatever you need from me in the future, it's yours. Want me to kill the Alpha Pack? I'll figure it out. Want to wipe out the Pack that essentially sold you to them? Also done. Whatever you want, Rynn. I'll make right by you."

I bit my tongue, not wanting to get between my best friend and my mate—even if I was literally standing between them at the moment—but I did make sure the gratitude I was feeling made its way down the bond. Vail and I might have had our issues, but they were just that—ours. Rynn had trusted him, and he had betrayed that trust. I couldn't fix that between them, but I loved him for recognizing he'd fucked up and attempting to fix it.

"Alright," Rynn said slowly, her mismatched eyes staring at Vail. "I'll hold you to that."

He nodded deeply, but any further conversation was thwarted by angry shouting coming from somewhere above us. The three of us took off running again and quickly made it up the stairwell and through the temple until we were outside in the hot afternoon sun.

Roth, Alaric, Kieran, and Draven stood just in front of the temple columns, watching the two Furies face off. Alaric and Draven observed with tight expressions, whereas Roth and Kieran were looking at Cali in concern.

I didn't blame them. Outside of us, if Cali had a weak spot, it was Malachi.

Rynn was right. We should have killed the prick and spared Cali a world of heartache. The only thing that had stopped me from pursuing such a path was the fact that I very much suspected my wild and untamed best friend was in love with the bastard.

Even though that love might get her killed one day.

Cali had never admitted to such a thing, and I was pretty sure Rynn just thought of him as someone Cali had a passing fancy for, but I remembered what Cali had been like after Malachi had ended things. She'd been so . . . broken.

That kind of pain was only caused by love. I would know.

Rynn skidded to a stop ten feet from the temple, and Vail and I stopped with her. A short distance away, Cali squared off against a dark-gold-haired Furie, who was a few inches taller than Vail and just as bulky.

My mind had trouble accepting that someone as large as Malachi could move as nimbly as he did. But when Cali thrust her sword at his gut, he easily twisted around the blow, his dark, leathery wings tucked in tight against his back.

Cali matched his movements, her dark red hair lit up by the sun, making it flow around her like living flames. Her golden brown eyes came alive in the way they always did when she was fighting. If Cali was fire incarnate, Malachi was the darkness that wanted to swallow her whole.

"Is that all you got?" Cali sneered, backing up a step with her sword raised, blood dripping from it.

"Don't make me hurt you, Rayne." Malachi's black eyes were bottomless pits as he stared at her, not even bothering to acknowledge the rest of us. My eyes were normally a deep purple and only turned black when my bloodlust rose, but Malachi's eyes were always a solid black.

If Cali was the most powerful Furie, he was a close second. I'd always suspected that was at least part of the reason the Elders had forbidden them from being together. On their own, Cali and Malachi were terrifying. But together? They would be unstoppable.

And the Furie Elders didn't like anything they couldn't control.

"What do you want, Mal?" Cali's sword might have been stained with the other Furie's blood, but she'd taken plenty of hits too. Based on the careful way she was standing with more of her weight on her left foot, I suspected the prick had injured her right knee.

Cali had been attacked by wraiths years ago. She'd survived—obviously—but it'd been closer than any of us liked to think about. Her right leg in particular had been badly mangled, and no amount of healing had seemed to fix her knee. It was her weak spot in a fight.

That type of knowledge wasn't something most knew. Malachi clearly did—and he'd used it against her.

Rage at his callousness had my nails shifting to claws. I wouldn't fuck up our plan . . . I'd just make him hurt a little. My Fae magic stirred, and I tried to focus on the ground beneath the asshole's feet.

A crack formed in the dry, compact dirt of the badlands. I pushed a little more—

"No!" Cali snarled, but not at Malachi—at me.

I lost my focus, and the magic slipped from me.

Fuck. We'd all agreed that it was best to keep my abilities and Draven's as much of a secret as possible. House Devereux wouldn't tell anyone, and I'd have to decide if and when I wanted to tell the other Houses once Carmilla was dealt with, but with how tense things were with the Velesians and how unreliable the Furies were, it was better to keep them in the dark on this.

We'd need all the advantages we could get in case we really did go to war one day.

That was fine. I still had my daggers.

Malachi seized Cali's moment of distraction to lunge

forward, his sword aiming for Cali's thigh, right above her weak knee.

He was fast—I was faster.

The Furie roared as my blood daggers bit into his flesh. He sensed them just in time to turn so the one I'd aimed for his throat hit his shoulder instead. And the one that had been flying towards his groin sank two inches to the left.

Pity.

His black eyes focused on me. I tugged on the magic within the daggers, and both of them tore free from his body and flew back towards me. I licked the blood off the blades. Not as tasty as my mates', but Furie blood did pack one hell of a punch. It practically sizzled across my tongue.

I pointed one of my now-clean blades at him. "Don't fuck with my friend, Malachi."

"What are you going to do about it, Moroi trash?" he growled. "You seriously think you can take me on with your two little knives?"

"Of course not, silly." I bared my fangs at him. "I'm the distraction."

Four-hundred pounds of pissed-off lycanthrope slammed into the Furie. To his credit, Malachi didn't panic. He just let them fall before twisting at the last second, forcing Rynn to either jump off his back or risk getting pinned beneath him— she bailed.

In an instant, Malachi was on his feet, but I was already sliding behind him. "How do you like my two little knives now?" I pushed the one at his throat in enough to draw a little blood while tapping the other one over his groin that I'd sadly missed earlier. Hard to miss at this distance though, which was something he seemed to understand because the Furie had gone perfectly still.

Cali walked over to us, her expression tight and a slight limp to her step. I dug my blades in a little deeper—both of them. Malachi didn't seem to care. I couldn't see his face from where I stood, but I could tell that all of his attention was on my friend.

"You ever call my friend trash again"—her hand snapped out to grip his chin—"and I'll rip out your tongue. Now, once again, why are you here?"

"Aiofe is in the pit." He kept his voice even, but I could have sworn I heard a hint of despair in it. Who was Aiofe? His new lover? I swear to fuck, if he came to beg Cali to help him rescue his new love, I'd slit his throat. Plan be damned.

Cali released her hold on him and took a step back, as if she needed the space between them. "Why is your little sister in that godsforsaken place?"

"Because of you and your refusal to obey." Malachi twisted his head slightly towards me, not even caring about the blood dribbling down his neck. "Either slit my throat or get the fuck away from me."

"I vote to slit his throat!" Kieran called out.

"Same!" Alaric and Roth chimed in.

I glanced at Cali, and she shook her head. Reluctantly, I pulled my blades away—making sure to open up some nice cuts on the way out—and stepped back. As if by magic, Draven and Vail appeared on either side of me.

Malachi instantly spun to face me, his expression filled with rage and a dagger in his hand.

"I wouldn't," Vail warned.

"Oh please do," Draven purred. "I've always wanted to taste Furie blood."

"Here." I held up one of my daggers, and Draven leaned forward, his tongue darting out to lick the flat side.

"Mmm." He took another swipe. "Tasty."

Malachi's mouth twisted in disgust, and he took another step towards us, only to stop when Rynn growled behind him.

"Focus, Mal," Cali ordered, "or I'll let my friends tear you apart, and I promise, I won't shed a single tear over it."

Something flickered in those glittering black eyes of his, there and gone in an instant. Regret, I thought. Maybe guilt.

Whatever it was, I didn't care. Malachi had hurt my friend deeply, and he seemed intent on continuing to do so. I had to let the events of today play out, but sooner or later, I was going to bury my blades in his flesh again, and next time, he wouldn't be walking away.

Malachi slid his dagger back into the sheath on his thigh and turned to face Cali.

"The Furie Elders have decreed that they will not be involved in the petty squabbles of the Moroi," he said evenly.

I snorted. Apparently the slaughter of our previous Sovereign and the brutal rise of another was just a *petty squabble.*

Malachi ignored me and kept going. "All Furies have been ordered to return. You've been ignoring their commands for weeks, so they told me to handle you. Aiofe is my incentive to be successful."

"I don't know why they bothered." Cali shrugged. "We both know you would have done it anyway. Always the good little soldier."

The muscles in Malachi's jaw flexed. "Some of us have people we care about—who care about us. We don't get to just flutter about Lunaria doing whatever the hells we want."

"Listen here, you piece of shit—" I took a step towards him.

"I'll go," Cali cut me off. Her tone was harsh, but her look at me was pointed. This had always been the plan. We just had to make it believable in case Carmilla had someone watching. If Cali went without a fight, it would be suspicious. "Let me just get my thi—"

"Now," Malachi interrupted. "We leave now. Aiofe's

already been in the pit for two weeks. I've been flying around looking for you this whole time and just happened to stumble across some of the new queen's rangers this morning, who told me where *that one* had been spotted." He pointed at Vail before glancing at me. "Your own people were quick to sell you out to a Furie, by the way."

"Yeah, we're a treacherous lot," I deadpanned.

Malachi narrowed his eyes.

"Let's get this over with." Cali sighed before stomping over to me. "I'll be back as soon as I can. Don't do anything stupid while I'm gone, okay?"

"I don't like this," I said with a tightness that I wasn't faking.

"I know." Cali gave me a sad smile. "But sometimes we just have to deal with the hand we're dealt. I'll see you soon, I promise." Then she took a step back and launched herself into the sky. Black wings snapped open, and she waved a hand at Rynn and the others before flying off.

"She can't keep doing this," Malachi said, a dangerous edge to his voice, his eyes tracking Cali's movements before turning to me. "Her friendship with you is causing her more harm than you can possibly imagine. Stop being selfish and let her go."

I took a step forward, away from Vail and Draven, and let the Furie see the predator in my eyes—ones that were now as black as his. "You were wrong earlier when you implied she didn't have anyone she cared about—or who cared about her." Rynn moved to stand next to me, her lips pulled back in a silent snarl. "She has us—she always will."

"Let's hope that's enough," he said so quietly, I almost thought I misheard him before he leapt into the sky.

"Have you summoned him?" Draven asked, his gaze locked on the silver coin I was flipping back and forth across the top of my knuckles. It was a habit I'd picked up from my father. I still remembered him teaching me how to do it. He'd even made me a smaller coin so that it was easier for my child-sized hands.

I'd stopped doing it the day he'd died.

As soon as Cali had been gone from sight, I'd retrieved the coin from the lower levels of the temple. I'd been sitting in the large room in the main entrance—the unwarded part—playing with the coin in the same way my father had once done.

I wondered what he would have said about my plan. About who his daughter had grown up to be.

The coin stopped, balanced on my middle knuckle. For all the secrets he and my mother had kept, I had no doubt that they'd loved me. In keeping my grief locked away, I'd also prevented myself from remembering all the good times. Maybe it was time to change that. Accept the past once and for all so I could truly focus on the future.

I rolled the coin towards my thumb and flicked it up before snatching it out of the air. "No. But I'm about to." Then I rose from where I'd been sitting on one of the long benches and closed the distance between me and Draven, who was leaning against one of the pillars. "You don't need to stay," I said softly. "You can join the others downstairs."

Everyone except Rynn and Vail had retreated back to the first underground level. We had everything in place for our plan, but keeping busy seemed to help everyone deal with the anxiety of what we were about to do. Plus, the knowledge contained in those secret rooms was truly astounding. We'd learned more in the last week than we had in our entire lives. Hells, we'd probably learned more than all of the Moroi had in our collective existence.

Things that could change life in Lunaria as we knew it.

Assuming we all survived what came next. If Carmilla was in charge of the information, I didn't have faith in her to let others know.

Knowledge was power, and my aunt had already demonstrated just how far she was willing to go to claim it.

"You're going to kill your aunt," Draven said wryly as he tucked a strand of loose hair behind my ear. "Least I can do is have a face-to-face with dear old dad."

"Someday we'll figure out a way to kill him too," I promised. "He doesn't get to live after everything he's done to you."

"Agreed." Vail strolled into the temple, sweat plastering his hair to the sides of his face. It was a blistering hot day in the badlands, and even in the shade, it was warm and stuffy. "Rynn's scouting a little farther out, but so far, we haven't seen any signs of Carmilla. I doubt she would risk traveling at night, so we likely won't see her until at least tomorrow."

I nodded. Now that Cali was gone, my aunt would come for me. It was unlikely she knew I'd been speaking with Erendriel and had wraiths backing me up, but I agreed with Vail. All kinds of nasty things roamed Lunaria at night, so Carmilla would likely launch her attack during daylight.

"Alright." I held the coin up between two fingers. "Time to get this over with." Erendriel had told me all I'd have to do was think about him and push a small amount of magic into the coin. I wasn't sure if that would be enough or if I'd need my blood to make it work, but I figured I'd try without it first.

For a few seconds, nothing happened, then the coin started to pulse with a soft glow.

"Guess that means it worked?" We all looked around, as if the Seelie King was just going to pop into existence.

He did not.

"Come on." Draven grabbed my hand. "I have a hunch."

I tucked the coin into the pocket of the dress I'd changed

into and held my hand out to Vail. He intertwined his fingers with mine, and the three of us headed farther into the temple.

"My father has kept most of his abilities a mystery. Some I know but can't talk about." He winced. So far, in all our readings, we hadn't come across anything to explain how Erendriel had spelled Draven to be unable to tell us things, but I was still hopeful we'd find something. "How he travels around Lunaria is something I don't understand, but I've noticed on a few occasions that if he does it during the day, he always comes from somewhere dark."

"You think he needs shadows to do it," Vail guessed.

"I think so."

Draven stopped, and I did the same, Vail halting next to me. We were in the back of the temple now. Only two rooms were left, and both had a narrow hall that led to them. The last time I'd been in one of those rooms, wraiths had attacked Nyx and hurt them badly. I also hadn't been faring particularly well.

"Let's wait out here." I squeezed their hands. "I'd rather not be in a tight space with Erendriel, even if he is our ally."

"That's a shame," a deep voice called out from the dark passageway, "because I'd very much enjoy being in a tight space with you."

Erendriel strolled out of the hall on the left before stopping a few feet away from us. His hands were tucked into the pockets of his black pants, and the dark tunic he wore was practically molded to his upper body. Apparently, he was still hoping to tempt me into marrying him.

"You'll just have to dream about it." I shrugged. "I'm a happily mated woman—four times over." *Soon to be five once Kieran gets his party.*

Erendriel gave Vail a dismissive glance before looking at his son. "You managed to hide just how strong your magic was from me all this time and get yourself mated to a rising power.

I suppose you're not a total disappointment after all, unlike your brother."

Draven's fingers tightened around mine, but he remained silent.

The Seelie King chuckled. "She won't be able to keep you safe from me forever, boy."

"And the deal you have with our queen won't protect you forever either," Vail drawled.

"How about we all play nice so everyone walks away with what they want?" I cut in and gave Erendriel a polite smile, ignoring the way being so close to him without the safety of the ward had my instincts screaming at me to run. Very fast. "It's time to set our plan into motion. Carmilla will be coming for me, very likely tomorrow."

"Of course." Erendriel gave me a deep nod. "Once night falls, I will summon the wraiths here as we discussed." He offered me his hand, and after hesitating for only a moment, I took it and allowed him to tug me away from Vail and Draven, both of whom growled.

Erendriel ignored them as he guided me back towards the front room, one of his hands resting on my lower back. "Now, have you been practicing closing the door as I instructed? I'd love to see what progress you have made with your magic. There is so much I could teach you if you'd only let me . . ."

CHAPTER THIRTY-ONE

—

Samara

"SHE'S ALMOST HERE."

Irritation simmered beneath the mask of apprehension I'd fixed my features into. I'd been switching back and forth between that and one of shaky confidence. Erendriel had barely left my side since arriving yesterday, and while part of me enjoyed the thrill of outsmarting the Seelie King, I was more than a little exhausted from wearing all these different masks.

Honestly, I didn't know how Kieran did it. I hadn't been able to roll my eyes *once* in over twelve hours.

The only reprieve I'd gotten had been when night had fallen and he'd summoned the wraiths to him. For hours, they had poured into the temple. It had been an eerie experience, to say the least. My entire life, wraiths had been something to fear—and they still were—but now, I was relying on them. I tried not to think about the fact that some of these wraiths could have been the same ones that had killed my parents.

Nothing good would come from dwelling on that, and if all went according to plan, we'd only be allies for a little while longer.

To my disappointment, Serril hadn't been amongst the wraiths to answer Erendriel's call. I would have loved to have him caught up in all of this, but for whatever reason, Erendriel had not summoned him. And I didn't want to risk raising suspicion by asking about him. He would almost certainly be a problem when the dust settled, but not much we could do about that now. As my mother used to say, *"No point in asking tomorrow for its problems when you still had to deal with today's bullshit."*

"Just remember what you promised, Erendriel." I glanced to my right, where the Seelie King stood next to me, gazing out into the badlands. "The rangers are not to be harmed."

He gave me a patronizing smile. "Of course, my young queen."

I started to clench my jaw but killed the motion immediately, instead keeping my mask of apprehension and fear on. For just a little while longer, I needed to play the role of eager but inexperienced queen. It was a tightrope to walk, and part of me was thankful that it was coming to an end, but another part dreaded my showdown with Carmilla.

She had to be stopped, I knew this, but it didn't mean I could just turn off my feelings for her. I knew Vail was struggling as well. We had both loved Carmilla as a stand-in parent. Her betrayal had left deep wounds in us both. At least now we had each other to lean on. Another person to talk to who understood exactly what the other felt.

Currently, Vail stood with Draven inside the temple, and everyone else waited in the first underground level until Carmilla was secured.

"Can you feel them approaching?" He gave me a curious look.

We'd been practicing for most of the time he'd been here. By which I meant I'd made pathetic attempts at using my Seelie earth magic and he'd played the role of patient teacher. I'd been mostly honest about my magic capabilities since I already had to balance so many other lies. Plus, I was never one to waste resources, and while I didn't trust everything Erendriel said, that didn't mean he wasn't a fountain of knowledge. One just had to wade through his bullshit.

Although, the scholars at Drudonia had never laid a hand on my lower back while giving instructions or found reasons to brush against my skin.

Vail and Draven hadn't been fans of that but also hadn't interfered—trusting me to handle the situation. They'd just glowered from where they'd been leaning against the wall, watching us.

I wasn't blind—Erendriel was truly stunning, but he was also an arrogant asshole.

I already had plenty of those and wasn't in the market for another.

Plus he didn't understand the concept of no. Sooner or later, he'd meet the same fate as Demetri and that prick guard Vail had so kindly taken care of.

Maybe we could host a celebration once a year in their honor? Like a mock funeral of sorts. *Here lie a bunch of handsy fuckers who got what they had coming. Rest in pieces, assholes.*

"Samara?" Erendriel arched a dark golden brow at me.

"Apologies. It's been a long day." I gave him a tired smile and hoped that covered up the amused one I'd been sporting a second ago. "I can feel . . . something." I looked away from him out into the badlands, and a crease formed between my brows as I concentrated. "But I can't tell what it is exactly. Either it's large or there are lots of somethings, and I get the sense that it's moving this way, but it's more a feeling than anything else."

There was also the fact that I already knew Carmilla and her rangers were out there, courtesy of Rynn's scouting, so my magic had something to go on. I wasn't sure, if I'd had no knowledge of the situation, I would have been able to sense her.

"You're actually doing quite well for someone who is so new to their magic," he said encouragingly. "You'll get better with time and practice, and of course I can teach you to speed things up a bit."

A shriek came from deep within the temple.

"It seems your wraiths need to learn what it means to be quiet." I glanced back towards the only room that was dark enough for the wraiths to gather during daylight.

"They do have a tendency to get excited," he explained. "This temple is where we conducted most of the rituals to make them whole again. The ones who are still shadows are clamoring for the chance to be what they once were."

"There will be no more rituals," I reiterated firmly. "No more spilling of Moroi blood for your wraiths."

"Hold up your end of the bargain, my young queen, and we won't need to. Once we find the Unseelie Princes, their blood will be the answer to everything I seek."

I very much wanted to find these Unseelie Princes, but I sure as shit wouldn't be giving their location to Erendriel. Maybe they wouldn't be assholes like him. I almost snorted. Of course they would be. I was rapidly coming to the realization that all Fae were assholes.

Maybe they were dead and we were all chasing ghosts. That would certainly be annoying. Although, as much as I wanted to find these princes, part of me wondered if it was for the good of Lunaria that they stayed lost.

More loud wailing came from the back of the temple, and a hint of annoyance flickered across Erendriel's face. "I will see to my people," he conceded and gave me a nod. "Make sure you get that door closed so that they can move around easier. They cannot walk in the light as I do and there are only so many shadows for them to hide in."

"Of course." I nodded back, keeping my tone respectful. He smiled at me before striding into the temple. I watched him go, keeping a close eye on his posture to see if he suspected any hint of deception, but I saw nothing.

As soon as he left, Vail and Draven appeared at my side. I sighed contentedly as I breathed in their scents.

"Everyone ready?" I asked quietly.

Draven leaned in to kiss my neck before whispering in my ear, "Of course, my love. Although Rynn is extra grouchy today. Damn near took my hand off."

"You did call her a bad dog," Vail pointed out.

"She growled at Kier," Draven said coolly.

"Don't antagonize Rynn. You know why she's on edge." I leaned against him while holding a hand out to Vail, who took it, intertwining his fingers with mine. "Our guests are doing well?"

"Woke up an hour ago." Draven wrapped an arm around my waist and tucked me further into his side. "They still look like death but will probably come up for the fun part."

"Good." I watched as shapes started to appear on the horizon. "It's just a waiting game now."

We fell silent as Carmilla and her rangers drew closer. Rynn had to keep her distance while scouting, but we knew Carmilla had at least a hundred rangers with her. Maybe closer to two hundred. She clearly wasn't fucking around this time.

When Carmilla was less than a quarter mile away, I stepped back. "Let's get into position."

The three of us retreated back inside the temple, which was as silent as a tomb. Erendriel had gotten the wraiths under control. Good. The last thing we needed was to tip Carmilla off. I tried not to think about all the moving pieces of this plan and how many ways it could fail.

If I stumbled now, it wasn't just my life on the line—it was the lives of all of all those I loved.

I would not falter.

We walked towards the archway that led further into the temple but stopped just short of it. On either side of us, pillars of white stone spiraled from the ceiling to the floor. Only the spirals and a few tables with benches made of the same stone decorated this room.

Standing in the center of the archway was a pedestal that Draven and I had dragged over from a small room in the back. Erendriel had barely glanced at the large shallow bowl full of blood that was resting on it. I'd explained this morning that it was part of the ceremony I would invoke to challenge Carmilla. He'd made some backhanded compliment about me cleverly using the *ridiculous* Moroi customs to my advantage. Clearly, in his eyes, I was more Fae than Moroi.

Draven and Vail moved to stand on either side of the pedestal, facing the temple entrance, while I stood directly in front of it. A few minutes later, I heard the telltale sound of hooves pounding into the hard surface of the badlands.

I took a deep breath and let it out.

"We've got your back, Sam," Vail said solemnly, and I felt Draven's agreement through our mating bond.

Not a flicker of doubt crossed my mind. Vail was every bit mine as I was his, and Draven had been mine for longer than I'd known.

"And I've got yours." I smiled over my shoulder at each of them.

Our attention snapped forward as Carmilla and the rangers flooded the temple.

"So this is where you've been hiding." My aunt walked confidently towards me as the rangers lined the walls. She'd traded her typical refined dress for black pants and a deep purple tunic that matched her eyes perfectly. The soul crown rested on her head, making her look every inch the queen she was—or would be for a few more minutes anyway.

Doing okay, Talis? I asked.

I'll be doing better once you get me off this psychopath's head. Kind of worried that you're related to her, if I'm being honest.

Soon, my friend, I promised. *Soon.*

Only half of the rangers here are bound, by the way. The others have enthusiastically followed her.

That's unfortunate, but we'll deal with that later. I'd made a promise to Vail about how the rangers that came today would be treated, and I wouldn't be breaking that.

"I felt it had a certain amount of charm." I waved a hand flippantly through the air. "Could do with a bit more color though. All this white stone feels a bit ostentatious."

"How fortunate for you that you'll be returning to your cell soon." She smiled.

"No." I shook my head and moved to the side so she could see the bowl behind me. "I don't think I will."

I saw the moment my aunt realized what I intended. "The Claiming?" she scoffed. "My dear, there hasn't been a Claiming in over a century."

"Not since the Tepes bloodline overtook House Stoker," I agreed.

It was a bit of a throwback tradition. The Houses had been stable for some time now, but that hadn't always been the case. Sometimes, a Moroi bloodline had emerged to challenge one of the existing Houses, and that was where the Claiming came in.

A fight to the death between two Moroi. No weapons. No submissions. You fought until one was dead.

Few attempted it, because if they failed, not only would they die but their entire line would be wiped out by the House they challenged. And once a Claiming was invoked, it had to be answered.

Of course, usually it was invoked in a public manner so that if the challenged House didn't answer, they would look weak to the other Houses. One never wanted to be perceived as *weak* in Lunaria.

Carmilla studied the bowl for a long moment before shrugging. "Cute attempt, niece, but I have no interest in fighting you."

"Scared?" I bared my fangs at her.

She laughed. "We both know hand-to-hand combat was never one of your strengths, and the Claiming is just that. Tooth and claw only." A smile stretched across her lips, one that didn't meet her eyes. "I regularly trained with your mother when she was still alive . . . and bested her on more than one occasion, I might add. You cannot beat me, and I'd prefer to take you alive."

"You cannot reject the Claiming once it's been extended," Draven drawled.

Carmilla's temper snapped. "I can do whatever I damn well please, and I think our first order of business when we return to the Sovereign House will be to hold a public execution for the bastard prince." Then her dark gaze slid to Vail. "And for the traitor."

"How fortunate for us," I echoed her previous words, "that you won't be leaving this temple alive."

Her eyes flicked back to me before she waved a hand towards us. "Bind them, then search the rest of this place for anyone else." My aunt stared at me for a long moment. "If the wolf is here, kill it. My niece could use a reminder on obedience."

As one, the rangers stepped forward from the walls, splitting into groups, with some angling towards me and others towards Vail and Draven.

"Last chance," I warned, even as I started to summon my earth magic. "Honor the Claiming, Carmilla Harker."

At the temple entrance, the two large, flat stones on either side of it started to silently move inward.

"It's an outdated ritual," my aunt hissed.

I pushed, and the stone pieces clicked together, cutting off the only way in or out of the temple—and the sunlight that had been beaming in.

Darkness fell, only for the Fae lanterns to flicker to life, their soft blue flames casting an eerie light across the room.

"On that, we agree." Erendriel strolled past Vail and Draven to stand at my side. "A fight to the death without weapons or magic?" He shook his head in disgust. "Honestly, I don't know how you all have survived this long."

Carmilla stared at the Seelie King in horror before glaring at me. "What have you done?"

"What I had to," I said calmly.

Before my aunt could open her mouth again, wraiths streamed into the room, and the rangers immediately backed up. True to Erendriel's word, the wraiths didn't attack. Instead of taking a specific shape, they all joined together until a ring of writhing shadows wrapped around the space with the rangers on the outside and the five of us on the inside.

The only break was in front of the pedestal, allowing a path to it. Now that this part of the plan had been enacted, the others joined us. Kieran, Roth, and Alaric walked up to stand behind the pedestal while Rynn, Ary, and Aniela stood behind them and a little off to the right.

A few rangers tried to step forward, only for the wraiths to turn solid for just long enough to shove them back. One overzealous ranger tried to run through, only to be flung into the wall—hard. A crack formed as he slid down, but he was still moving, and a fellow ranger was already drawing a healing glyph on him.

"So, now what? You're just going to have the Seelie King do your bidding?" Carmilla sneered. "The Moroi will *never* follow you."

"To be fair, they're not exactly willingly following you

either." My eyes flicked pointedly to the crown. "The wraiths are only here to ensure you play fair." I looked away from my aunt to address the rangers standing on the outskirts of the room. "You will not be harmed. You are only here to bear witness to the Claiming."

"We'll never follow Fae trash," a ranger called out. "You're not even a true Moroi."

"Technically, we all have Fae blood running in our veins." I smiled in the direction of the ranger who'd spoken. "Surprise. It's true that I have a little more than most, but make no mistake, we're all part Fae. Also"—I pointed at my aunt—"she's wearing a Fae crown, and you seem inclined to follow her. Assuming you're not one of the ones who had their will stripped away."

Several faces tightened at that before wincing in pain.

Roughly half of the rangers here were under the crown's compulsion, but the others had voluntarily come. If I truly wanted to unite all the Moroi, I needed them to respect me.

If I couldn't have their respect, I would take their fear. Despite what Erendriel thought of me, I wasn't some naive upstart. My goal was to be a good leader for all of the Moroi, but that didn't mean I'd allow people to walk over me.

The Claiming was my way of proving myself worthy . . . and performing a little trickery. It was Carmilla who had constantly lectured me to work smarter, not harder. That the best strategy was one which could accomplish multiple goals at once. I needed a demonstration, and we needed to buy time for the transformation spell to work its literal magic.

My aunt hadn't been lying about being my mother's regular sparring partner. Carmilla might have spent most of her time behind a desk these days, but that didn't change the fact that she was a lethal fighter. This was going to hurt.

"Your life has turned out to be a waste." Carmilla shook her head. "I suppose it's only fitting that your death should be too." She walked over to the pedestal, giving everyone a cool look before lingering on Roth. "You won't be alive to see it, but know that I'm going to wipe your family and their House out of existence."

Roth held her stare, orange lines bleeding through their hazel eyes like living flames. "You won't be alive to hear it, but know that my family will get a good laugh when I tell them about your ridiculous claim."

My loves and I smiled at Roth's declaration.

For the first time since striding into the temple, a flicker of doubt showed on Carmilla's face before she squashed it. With a dismissive sniff, she turned away from Roth to focus on the three beings standing behind my mates and slightly off to the side.

"Surprised the Alpha Pack has let you off the chain for so long, Rynn," she drawled. "You never did know your place."

Rynn growled, and her hackles rose. Talis had claimed being in her animal form would protect Rynn from the crown's magic; the last thing we needed was my aunt taking away Rynn's free will and using the Velesian as a weapon. Flanking her on either side were Ary and Aniela, both still looking a little pale, but thanks to taking a long drink from me earlier, they had a little more color in their cheeks, and more importantly, they were protected from the crown.

Them showing up hadn't been part of my original plan, but we were lucky they had. It had taken a lot of blood to pull this off, and having two additional Moroi had helped considerably. It was probably the only reason my mates were standing and not unconscious downstairs.

Erendriel eyed the two Heirs from where he was still standing next to me, several feet in front of the pedestal. They'd spent most of their time sequestered in the hidden levels below and hadn't emerged once since I'd summoned Erendriel. I could have come up with some reason for their presence, but it'd been simpler to just keep them out of his sight. We hadn't wanted to give him even the slightest hint of underhandedness, and the more lies one told, the harder it became to keep them all straight.

The only reason they were above ground now was because I wanted them to bear witness to the Claiming so they could attest to what happened here today.

When the Seelie King's gaze fell on me, I explained quietly, "It is tradition as part of the Claiming for other Houses to be present. Apologies. I should have introduced you sooner."

"Any other change of plans you care to share?"

I gave him a close-lipped smile. "Everything else is according to plan. No other changes."

He stared at me for a long moment, those ancient eyes searching for a hint of deception. "Shall we begin? You and I have things to do." Without another word, he walked to the front of the temple to stand with his back towards the mass of darkness that were his wraiths before clasping his hands behind his back.

I suspected that if he truly thought I was going to lose, he would intervene. After all, he didn't actually give a shit about the Moroi or my leadership of them. All Erendriel wanted was a way to get into all these secret rooms—and he needed me alive for that.

Turning away from the Seelie King, I moved to stand on the other side of the pedestal, facing Carmilla. "I, Samara Harker, Heir of House Harker and beloved daughter of Kasem and Mariona, issue a challenge of the Claiming. For not only House Harker, but also for the soul crown and the Sovereign House."

Carmilla reached up and removed the crown from her head. Part of the tradition was to place something of significance from the party being challenged into the blood of the challenger. I'd had several plans in place if she'd tried to use something other than the crown, but since she hadn't been prepared for this, she likely had nothing else on her that would work, and she knew it.

"I, Carmilla Harker, the reigning Moroi Queen and Head of both the Sovereign House and House Harker, answer the Claiming." Slowly, she lowered the crown into the bowl of blood that was just deep enough to cover the Fae artifact.

You okay, Talis?

The blood is cold. You could have at least warmed it.

Duly noted that you prefer warm blood baths. Let me know when it's done.

Of course, young queen.

Unlike with Erendriel, there was no hint of mockery with that title. More like a term of endearment from an old friend.

I dipped my fingers into the bowl and pulled them out to smear streaks down my cheeks. Carmilla did the same before returning to the center of the room. I glanced at each of the people I loved more than anything. They remained lined up a few feet behind the pedestal, all wearing matching tight expressions.

They knew what was about to happen and that they could not intervene. We needed time for the transformation spell to work on Talis, and that time would be bought with my pain.

Despite their tense faces, I felt nothing but love, strength, and confidence down the bonds. My mates were concerned for me and not looking forward to what was coming, but their faith in me was absolute.

I love you all. I pushed the sentiment down the bonds, knowing they wouldn't hear the exact words but would feel what was behind them. Kieran met my stare, and even though we didn't have that bond yet, we didn't need it to know what each other felt. He was already my mate in my heart, and once we survived this, he'd be it in my soul too.

Then I squared my shoulders and moved to the center of

the room. Without looking, I knew Erendriel watched me closely. His gaze felt like a heated brand, but it was the dark-haired woman with eyes that matched my own who took all of my attention.

I watched as Carmilla let her bloodlust rise until her purple irises turned a solid black, then her lips parted enough to display her fangs, and her usually well-trimmed nails shifted to sharp claws. The blood dripping from her cheeks was meant to show that, even with her bloodlust riding high, she was still in control of herself and not lost to our baser need to consume.

My own bloodlust had been simmering just beneath the surface, and with half a thought, I let it out all the way. I felt the instant my muscles strengthened, my body became that much faster, and the sweet coppery tang of the blood rolling down my face became even more intense.

Around us, the wraiths kept up their endless circling, ensuring Carmilla's rangers couldn't interfere. Silence fell across the temple. The only thing I could hear was the solid beat of her heart—and the split second it quickened.

I leaned back just as Carmilla's razor-sharp nails grazed my throat, a small bead of blood forming along the shallow cut. There was no time to dwell on how close I'd just come to having my jugular ruptured, because Carmilla followed it up with a vicious punch to my solar plexus.

"This is going to be over faster than I thought." She bared her fangs at me before licking my blood off her claws. "It was a deliberate choice on my part, you know."

I twisted to the side as she struck at my ribs, only to let out a hiss of pain when she sliced through the top of my hip.

"What was?" I ground out, stepping back to create more space between us.

"Nudging you to not worry too much about learning how to fight or defend yourself."

She lunged to my right, and I spun away, only to scream as

she slammed her fist hard against my side, cracking several ribs. I took several sharp inhales, one hand wrapped around my midsection as I tried to breathe through the pain.

"You were easy to manipulate," she continued. "Although I was a little worried about your obsessions with the bow and then the throwing daggers, but those won't save you now."

Carmilla stalked towards me. Fortifying myself, I tried to push aside the fiery pain along my ribs and held my ground as she launched another assault. I managed to block her first punch and turn my hip enough to take her follow-up kick on the side of my leg instead of on the wound she'd been aiming for, but I raised my arm a second too slow for her third hit.

I turned my head in just enough time to take the punch on my jaw instead of my nose and stumbled back several feet.

"Pathetic," Carmilla sneered.

We fought across the temple floor—me desperately trying to keep space between us, and her closing that distance to land hit after hit. Sometimes, I managed to block or at least deflect them, but not often. Ten minutes later, I could tell she was getting bored of playing with me—because she *was absolutely* toying with me.

Which was exactly what I'd been hoping for.

Tell me it's almost done, Talis? Even in my head, my voice had a pained edge to it. Carmilla had landed a solid kick to my ribs a minute ago, and I was pretty sure a bone shard was poking into my lung right now.

Almost, their voice strained. *One. More. Minute.*

Thank fuck.

"Is this the queen some of you would choose to follow, given the choice?" Carmilla looked around at the rangers as she pointed a bloody claw at me. "You may not like how I rule, but at least I'm strong enough to do it. She is nothing." Cruel eyes turned back to me. "This ends now."

I hastily stepped back like I was trying to flee, and Carmilla's eyes lit up, a predator closing in on its prey. Just like with her opening move, she struck for my throat.

This time though, I didn't dampen my speed like I had been doing this entire fight.

My feet slid to the side, and my right hand shot out to grab her wrist, using her own forward momentum against her. She'd been so committed to the move and overconfident that she hadn't been prepared for me to twist her arm back until it was fully extended with her elbow pointing upward.

It was Carmilla's turn to scream as I slammed my own elbow down on the back of her arm, forcing the joint to bend the wrong way.

I leapt back as she twisted and struck at my face, trying to blind me.

"You're right," I panted, doing my best to keep my weight off my injured leg. "I didn't spend much time learning to fight growing up or at Drudonia, but I did spend some time traveling with rangers these past few months. Nyx taught me that move. You remember them, right? The ranger who devoted themself to House Harker? The one whose mind you *shredded*?"

Growls sounded from some of the rangers lining the walls. These ones might belong to the Sovereign House, but it was common for rangers to feel just as much loyalty to each other as to whichever House they served.

Carmilla glared at me, her left arm dangling uselessly at her side. She couldn't heal it until it was pushed back into place —and I'd be on her the second she tried it.

I wasn't foolish enough to think she was defeated yet. Wounded predators could still kill. And buying time had cost me. Warm blood coated my leg; another minute, and it'd give out completely.

Something that didn't get past my aunt, because that was the leg she targeted with a forward kick.

Knowing there was no way to avoid it without falling, I

bellowed as her foot connected with my thigh and bone cracked. I went down hard, but I took her with me.

My fingers wrapped around her calf, and I didn't let go when she tried to yank her leg free. Then I sank my claws deeper until I felt bone. Carmilla shrieked as she slammed to the ground a second after me. With a pained grunt, I flung myself on top of her. Agony ricocheted down my left side, and I had to practically drag my leg with me, but I made it.

Carmilla went completely still as my left hand closed around her throat. I was straddling her, with both of her arms pinned beneath my knees. If she bucked up with her hips, she had a solid chance of dislodging me, but not before I ripped out her throat.

I had her. We both knew it.

It's done, Talis whispered through my mind.

"It was Emil who taught me that sometimes you have to take the pain to win the fight." I pushed my claws into the soft flesh of her throat a little more. "And it was Adrienne—someone so bold and fearless that we both know her bloodline could have founded a House—who told me that if you ever get the chance"—my right arm snapped back before plunging down—"go for the heart."

The Head of House Harker and the reigning Moroi Queen gasped as I shoved my hand through her chest. Then Carmilla's eyes locked onto mine, and I watched the light go out in them as I tore out her still-beating heart.

CHAPTER THIRTY-TWO

—

Samara

I STARED at the heart in my grasp. It beat a few more times before going still. Carmilla's blood was warm on my hand, and I was trying not to dwell on that. The time to process would come later—there was still a Seelie King to betray.

Through the mate bonds, I conveyed that I needed some assistance. In an instant, Vail and Draven were there, helping me to my feet. Roth knelt in front of me, and I felt them draw a healing glyph over my thigh and then over my ribs while Alaric offered me his wrist. My fangs sank into his flesh, and I drank deeply as my body burned with healing magic.

Once I was confident that I could stand without my leg collapsing under me, I walked towards the pedestal, my mates falling into step behind me. There was one last thing to do before enacting the final part of the plan. Making good on the promise I'd made to Vail.

I briefly made eye contact with Erendriel and he gave me a shallow nod. Through some wordless command, the wraiths pulled back until they were flat against the walls, coating the white marble in shadows.

"Rangers of the Sovereign House, your new queen

requests that you wait outside while I finish my business here." I casually tossed my aunt's heart onto the floor like it was nothing as I summoned my earth magic and pulled the doors of the temple open just enough for them to slip out and only allowing only a sliver of sunlight in.

For a few tense seconds, none of them moved. Then a tall ranger with ashen blond hair made eye contact with me for a long moment before giving me a shallow bow. "You heard our queen. Move out!"

Relief flickered through me. If they hadn't listened, I would've had to ask Erendriel to use his wraiths to force them out, and that would have increased the chance of some of the rangers being hurt or killed. I moved to stand behind the pedestal, the bowl resting right in front of me. Silently, my lovers moved to join me until we created a half circle around it. Ary, Aniela, and Rynn didn't move from their spot behind us.

When the last of the rangers walked out, I closed the doors, and the wraiths flowed down from the walls to gather around Erendriel.

"Well . . ." Erendriel kicked my aunt's heart across the floor, and I tried not to wince at the wet, plopping sound it made when it landed. "Your aunt is dead. You have your crown. It's time to honor what you promised, young queen."

This time, I did allow myself to roll my eyes.

"About that . . ." I drawled, letting my fingers slip into the bowl of blood. Behind me, I knew Aniela and Ary were now kneeling, activating the glyphs we'd painstakingly carved around the perimeter of the room. Most of them were hidden, thanks to Draven and me using our earth magic to bury them slightly beneath the surface, but they were all connected.

"A Fae bargain cannot be broken without dire consequences." Erendriel continued strolling towards us. The wraiths fell in behind him. Some took Fae forms, others chose the shapes of monsters. "You can act like a Moroi all you want, but enough Fae blood is running through your veins that the magic will tear you apart."

"Oh I know." I grinned wickedly. "We found quite a few books on bargains that were *most* helpful. One thing they pointed out over and over again was how carefully words had to be chosen—to prevent loopholes."

"There are no *loopholes* in our bargain," Erendriel growled. "I am six hundred years old. You've barely seen two decades. Did you seriously think you could outsmart me?"

"You think of me as a Fae tainted with Moroi blood." I raised my chin a little higher. "But you have it backwards. I am a Moroi . . . tainted with Fae blood." My grin widened. "And you are nothing but an arrogant old king who should have remained in the shadows."

"Enough of this." Erendriel snapped as he strode closer to where we were gathered at the pedestal—only to slam into an invisible wall.

"Oops," Kieran deadpanned.

Draven chuckled. "What's the matter, Father? Feeling a little trapped?"

Erendriel's eyes widened as he looked down at his feet. The stone floor split apart, revealing a thin channel of blood flowing beneath it.

"It flows around the entire room," I told him. "We had a run-in with some trapper spiders recently, and it got me thinking about all the dangerous things that can lurk right under our feet without us even knowing."

"And you walked straight into our trap." Draven strolled up to the barrier so he could look his father directly in the eyes. "Kalias and I used to think you were untouchable. That there was no one stronger or smarter." My vicious prince grinned. "But from where I'm standing, you seem rather *disappointing.*"

"I'm going to break every bone in your body and then give you to Serril to play with." Erendriel's cruel gaze slid to me.

"After you watch that whore die a slow, agonizing death as the magic tears her apart for breaking the fucking bargain."

"I haven't broken a thing." I shrugged. To my left, Roth, Vail, and Alaric slid their hands into the bowl. Kieran and Draven returned to stand to my right and did the same.

"You were very thorough in your wording for the bargain, and as someone who has reviewed a lot of contracts, I respect that. But I thought the Fae were known for being clever with their words—that's what all the books say. And you, my friend" —I let my voice drip with condescension—"were far from clever."

"Don't be too harsh on him, Sam," Alaric drawled. "You heard him. He's seen six centuries come and go. Maybe he's just not as sharp as he used to be."

Roth smirked. "That would explain why he never once caught on to the fact that you very specifically referred to the Fae artifact as *the crown*—and only the crown—in the bargain."

"I did, didn't I?" I chuckled. "Look at that . . . a loophole."

Erendriel slammed a fist against the barrier, and the boom echoed across the room, but it held fast. The wraiths scattered in streaks of darkness as they tried to find a way out.

My fingers moved through the cold blood until they touched something solid and considerably smaller than a crown. I felt the ripples in the liquid as my mates continued their own searching.

Erendriel glared at me furiously from the other side of the invisible barrier—the one we'd created based on the spell that had been used here and in the secret room beneath the Alpha House. It hadn't been hard to figure out how it worked . . . and then to adjust it so it could keep something *in* instead of *out*.

"No more queens. No more kings." My voice boomed across the temple, and I slipped the band onto my finger. "No more crowns."

Magic sparked within the bowl, and I felt the echo of it

through the mating bond. As one, we all raised our left hands, blood dripping to reveal the rings we all wore on our index fingers—the one that had a direct line to our hearts.

Each ring was made of three woven bands. Gold, silver, and a deep ruby red.

Home. Talis hummed happily.

I bared my fangs at the Seelie King. "Welcome to the dawn of the Blood Sovereign."

"WHEN DO you think he'll stop ranting?" Aniela stared up at the ceiling from where we were all gathered on the first hidden level.

"Probably not for at least a few more hours." Draven snorted.

"A silencing spell might be necessary." I wrinkled my nose, drawing a chuckle out of Kieran.

Vail and Ary were outside, speaking with the rangers. Thanks to Erendriel and the wraiths being trapped in the front room, the only way in or out was to climb out of the hole in the ceiling in the large room directly above us. Neither Draven nor I were confident enough in our earth magic to attempt to make a hole in the wall and risk structural damage to the temple.

I had no idea what would happen to our spell if the temple collapsed around it. Sooner or later, Erendriel would find a way out. We'd been confident—mostly—that the barrier spell would work, but there were definitely nuances to it that we hadn't had time to fully grasp. I had no doubt Erendriel, or maybe Serril, would find a way to exploit those and get out.

And then I'd have a very pissed-off and powerful Fae coming after me. My eyes flicked to the table full of weapons.

How fortunate that we found ourselves in possession of weapons that could harm them. Maybe even kill them.

"So, what's the plan now?" Aniela asked. "Now that you all have those fancy rings?"

I am quite fancy, Talis said excitedly.

Roth frowned. "This is going to take some getting used to."

"What is?" Aniela glanced at them in confusion.

"Talis—that's the name of the crown—now the rings," I corrected myself, "can speak in our heads."

Aniela's green eyes darted between our bands. "While I'm envious of being able to see people's true intentions, not sure I'd be willing to sign up for an ancient Fae artifact to live in my head. No offense, Talis."

Tell her none taken. Not everyone can handle how amazing I am.

Kieran laughed. Something told me he and Talis were going to get along very well.

"They're not offended," I assured Aniela. "And Talis has been through a lot. It's the least we could do."

In truth, we'd discussed it for quite some time. What it would mean for our lives to be forever bound to the rings. Talis had sacrificed the part of their magic that allowed them to control the will of others, but they could still read a soul and reveal the truth of a person. In exchange for their cooperation, they'd asked to never be alone again.

Vail and Alaric hadn't been thrilled about it. I'd been surprised Roth was fine with it, but then I'd realized it was because they now had an ancient artifact they could constantly ask questions. Talis might have been locked away for a long time, but there was still so much they could tell us.

"We need to go to House Devereux first. We won't stay there long, but I need to check on Tamsen . . . and Nyx. Then we'll travel to the Sovereign House to assess things there."

I tried not to look at the silver box that held Carmilla's heart. When Erendriel had kicked it, the organ had landed on the other side of the barrier. I didn't know exactly what had possessed me to pick it up and put it into the box. Nobody had said anything while I'd done it, and it'd been sitting on the table since we'd come down here.

I directed my attention to Aniela. "You should go to the Sovereign House ahead of us to meet Dominique. According to Talis, all the bindings ended during the transformation spell, so her mind is her own once more."

"Alright." Aniela nodded. "When you get to House Devereux, please let my people know they can return home." She swiveled from where she was sitting on the table to fully face Roth, who was seated at the end. "And thank you, Roth—and your family—for taking them in. We are in your debt."

"What kind of debt exactl—" Roth winced, and I got the distinct impression that Alaric had just kicked them under the table. They gave Aniela a curt nod before grumbling, "There is no debt between us. Happy to help and all that."

The discussion moved to what we would do about House Harker—something I didn't have an answer for yet and wasn't in the mood to discuss with my aunt's corpse still lying above us.

I left them to discuss the options for that while I went in search of Rynn.

I let my feet carry me to where I suspected she'd gone—down the stairs to the bottom level. Sure enough, when I walked into the cavern of hot springs, Rynn sat on the ledge of one of the pools, her back to me, legs dangling in the water.

"There isn't anything like this near the Alpha House," she said. "Nothing I've found anyway. Just lakes of ice-cold water."

"Might be nice in the summer." I sat down next to her, hiking my dress up to my thighs so I could slip my legs into the warm water too. "You hate the heat."

We sat there for a few minutes while sadness rolled off Rynn. It was a quiet, defeated kind that made me furious.

"Tell me you don't want to go back," I said when I couldn't take it anymore. "Just say the fucking word, Rynn."

She leaned her head on my shoulder. "I love you, Sam. That's why I'm going back. You would go to war for me—you are absolutely that crazy—and Cali would too. But we have all of our people to think about. You need to get the Moroi Houses in order, and I need to accept my fate with the Alpha Pack. Cade is tolerable most of the time. I can do some good there, I know it. I just need to not let the others get under my skin."

I thought about it. "What if we just kill one or two of them? Maybe the mouthy wolf and Warrick? Have I told you how much I don't like him?"

"You might have mentioned it a few times," she said wryly. "No killing anyone . . . for now. Just sit with me for a bit longer?"

I wrapped an arm around her shoulders. "As long as you want."

CHAPTER THIRTY-THREE

—

Samara

"Welcome back, child," the Head of House Devereux greeted Roth before nodding to the rest of us as we strode through the main gate of Roth's birth House three days later. Thessalia's long, deep red hair had been pulled back into a tight bun, and her shirt clung to her sweat-soaked skin. The guard who had escorted us inside took the sword from her when she held it out to him, and she murmured her thanks.

Gods, had she been voluntarily sparring in this weather? I was wearing one of Vail's shirts over a pair of pants that were also too big for me. Both were soaked from my own sweat because the sun was doing its best to burn everything out of existence today and we'd been walking all morning. On the surface, Thessalia might appear as fierce as the rest of the Devereax clan but clearly she was just as unhinged about training as the rest of them.

The only thing that could make me run in heat like this was a swarm of trappers. And I had no plans of repeating that experience. Ever.

Fuck. Spiders.

"I'm twenty-two years old," Roth grumbled as their aunt messed with their short hair that was the same shade of red.

"You can be a hundred and twenty-two, my dear." Thessalia smiled as she dropped her hand. "You'll still be that scrawny whelp hiding under my desk to avoid practicing your sword skills with your brothers."

"Speaking of . . ." Roth glanced around the small entry courtyard. "Where are the banes of my existence?"

"You can admit that you missed them, you know," their aunt said wryly.

Roth scowled.

Thessalia's bright hazel eyes danced with amusement. "Your parents are currently in the back courtyard, planning your wedding. I believe your brothers are being their helpful selves and encouraging them to make it a big one. Probably in hopes that it will further take off the pressure of them settling down with someone"—she looked at me and then all my mates —"or several someones."

A torrent of curse words in multiple languages flowed from Roth's lips before they gave me a hasty kiss on the cheek. "I need to go wrangle my parents and probably choke my brothers." Their ropes started to unwind from their forearms. "You going to be okay, babe?"

"Yes." I laughed. "Go."

Roth practically sprinted out of the courtyard. They must have been seriously freaked out if they voluntarily ran without something chasing them. It made me wonder if I should be more concerned about what exactly a Devereux-style wedding entailed . . .

"I'm gonna see how Rothie Bear's parents feel about doing a double celebration." Kieran planted a kiss on my cheek before chasing after Roth.

My wicked prince chuckled as he watched his mate—and my soon-to-be mate—go and stepped closer to me.

"Drav . . ." I rose onto my tiptoes so I could kiss him on the cheek. "Please go and make sure Kier doesn't get carried away and that Roth doesn't have a heart attack."

"I will do my best, my love." His dark brows furrowed. "But honestly, Roth's parents frighten me, so if they push for something, I'm not inclined to push back."

"Wise boy." Thessalia nodded.

Draven smiled at her before dipping his head in a respectful nod and casually strolling down the path Roth and Kieran had taken. Alaric sidled up to my left and Vail to my right.

Roth's aunt stared after Draven in bemusement. "It's good that he didn't take after either of his parents. Would have been a shame to kill one that pretty."

"I mean—"

Alaric grunted when I elbowed him in the gut and gave him a warning stare.

Be nice, I mouthed. He rolled his eyes.

"Why don't the rest of you come inside so we can discuss the future of things?" Thessalia offered. "You're welcome to get cleaned up first while I have some refreshments brought to my study."

"That is honestly the best thing I've heard all day." I picked at my sweat-soaked shirt in distaste. "I desperately need to get out of these clothes."

Alaric and Vail both cleared their throats.

"And into fresh ones," I amended. "Work first. Play later."

"We've prepared a guest suite for you in the same wing as Roth's room—not that they've used it in years. Your suite has an attached washroom." Thessalia's gaze slid to Alaric and then Vail. "And a silencing glyph for your . . . playtime."

"We thank House Devereux for its hospitality." I grinned. "I'll have to spread the word about how accommodating you are."

"Please don't." Thessalia laughed. "Come on, I'll show you the way."

"If you don't need me, I'd like to go check in with the rangers here," Vail said. "I'll catch up later."

"That's fine."

Vail gave me a quick kiss before striding off down a different path from the one the other three had taken.

I glanced at Alaric. "Looks like it's just you and me then."

His lips quirked up into a small smile. "I do so enjoy when I get you all to myself."

An hour later, some servants kindly directed us to Thessalia's study. Alaric had been very . . . attentive about helping me get clean in the washroom. Then he'd undone all his hard work by shoving me to my knees when I'd sassed him and fucking my mouth roughly until he'd come all over my face and chest.

He hadn't even let me rinse off. Just carried me to bed and devoured my pussy until I'd begged him to fuck me, which he had.

After cleaning up for the third time, we'd successfully made it out of the room.

"Ah, there you are. I was beginning to worry you'd gotten lost." Thessalia's eyes twinkled, and she rose from her desk to take a seat at one of the four chairs casually set up to face each other in the corner of her study. The room was large, and weapons adorned most of the wall space. I suspected the enormous window behind her desk overlooked the sparring courtyard, based on the faint sounds of yelling and metal striking metal.

On the table between all the chairs was an assortment of bread, cheese, and fruit, along with several glasses of water and ale.

"Alaric was *very* dirty," I said with a completely straight face, even as I tried not to drool over the cheese. "It took a lot of work to get him all squeaky clean again."

"I'm sure." Thessalia grinned.

Alaric sighed and moved towards one of the chairs, pinching my side as he went.

I laughed under my breath and followed. We both chose a chair opposite Thessalia, and she watched as we tore into the food for a few minutes.

"Better?" She arched an eyebrow.

"Mm-hmm," I answered around a mouthful of cheese.

She nodded. "A good fuck and some food will do that for you."

Alaric choked on the bread he'd just swallowed, and Thessalia chuckled before sipping her ale.

Once I finished eating and had picked up my own glass of ale, I proceeded to tell her everything that had transpired since we'd parted ways. Alaric occasionally added more detail, but twenty minutes later, we had it all out there.

"I'm sorry you had to kill your own family," Thessalia said solemnly. "That can't have been easy for you, even knowing that it had to be done, but I do think you handled it tremendously well. We'll need to keep an eye on the rangers who willingly followed her of course, but I doubt they will make a move against you anytime soon."

"Thank you." A flicker of grief at Carmilla's death hit me. It felt strange to mourn her, considering all she'd done. Perhaps it was more accurate to think I was mourning the idea of who I'd thought she'd been. Either way, it was something I'd have to work through. I wouldn't be bottling up my grief and negative emotions any longer.

"We're going to do an assessment of the rangers and advisors of the Sovereign House when we return." Alaric hesitated for a moment, glancing at me and only continuing when I gave him a nod. "We don't want people to feel as though they are being punished, because that will only create further friction. After spending many hours discussing this on the journey here, we think it best to keep the ones most likely to stir up animosity at the Sovereign House, where we can monitor them. The rest, we'd like to send to other Houses—Tepes and Salvatore have already agreed to take some. House Harker can take some as well, and we were hoping House Devereux would be amiable to accept some new rangers too."

Thessalia looked at both of us thoughtfully. "To what purpose?"

Some of the tension that had formed in my shoulders while Alaric had been explaining faded. That wasn't an outright no.

"When the Moroi Houses originally rose, they were united with one purpose—to protect our people. Over the decades, that mantra changed. It was no longer *protect all Moroi* but only those who belonged to one's House."

"Perhaps the Houses were all united once, but that time has long since passed." Thessalia shook her head. "There is no going back."

"No," I agreed. "Nor should we try. The past is there for us to learn from it—not repeat it. Part of what allowed Velika and then Carmilla to seize power the way they did is that none of us could trust each other. I want there to be more collaboration between our Houses. I want us to heal what is broken. And that means giving some of the people who willingly followed Velika or my aunt a chance. Some of them might always be thorns in my side, but others could change their tune when they interact with other Houses more—when they start thinking of Moroi as one united front instead of seven fractures."

I sat back in my chair and waited. If she didn't agree, I wouldn't give up. Just rethink my strategy about how to get her onboard.

"I admit that my immediate inclination is to say no."

Thessalia snorted. "But I also acknowledge that I—and my House—are part of the problem here. We've isolated ourselves quite thoroughly, and while that has worked quite well for us, some of the younger generation are getting a bit antsy."

"It's getting hard to find new bedmates when it feels like you're related to half the people here." A blond-haired man with a charming grin and bright green eyes chuckled as he practically sauntered into the room.

"Zander, what have I told you about eavesdropping?" Thessalia scolded the Moroi, who appeared to be about my age, as he dropped into the remaining empty chair.

His eyes widened a little as he gave her an innocent smile. "To not be so obvious about it, but I would never deign to lie to you, my liege."

She rubbed her forehead. "This pain in the ass is the son of my most trusted advisor."

"Pleased to meet you." I grinned at him. "Eavesdropping on a Devereux is a bold move."

"To be fair, I only do it on Thessalia because she adores me."

Roth's aunt snorted again before dropping her hand to her lap. "And because the one time he tried it on Severen, he found himself tied up tighter than a hog over a spit and hanging from a tree."

"Took me hours to cut myself free." Zander laughed. "Had to dislocate my shoulder and everything."

Alaric stared at him for a long moment before turning to me. "Clearly it's not just the Devereux line that is insane—it's everyone in this House."

"I think you just need to spend a little more quality time with them." I smiled sweetly, and Alaric narrowed his eyes. "How about the three of you discuss this a little further?"

"And where will you be while I'm talking to the heathens?"

"Why do we get the rude one?" Zander muttered. "That blond fella looked much more easygoing."

I patted Alaric on the cheek. "You'll be fine. Just flutter those pretty eyelashes at them and—owww!" I yanked my hand back and sucked on my bleeding finger.

Alaric licked the blood off his lips, turquoise flaring in his eyes . . . and staying. "Go do what you need to, but you're going to get punished for that sass later."

"Can't wait." I winked.

"I can't believe this is what Astaroth is marrying into." Zander stared at the two of us wide-eyed before gleefully smiling. "This wedding is going to be amazing."

Fifteen minutes later, I found myself in a dungeon very similar to the one I'd been locked in beneath the Sovereign House. Thessalia had summoned a guard to escort me, who was now waiting outside the door to give me the illusion of privacy. He hadn't spoken much on our walk here, but he'd borne a wary expression when we'd stopped on this level, which told me that Nyx hadn't magically gotten better after the crown's magic had changed. It had been a small hope that was now extinguished.

"Is Carmilla dead?"

I looked at the woman in the cell on the right; she'd definitely seen better days. Normally, Tamsen's hair was a shiny curtain of dark russet brown that hung to her waist. Now, it was a dull nest of tangles. Even from where I stood, I could smell the dry blood on her clothing.

"Yes," I answered, continuing to study her profile. "Did they not offer you a chance to clean up?"

"House Devereux isn't exactly known for their hospitality," she said tonelessly. "Frankly, I'm impressed they let me see to my needs twice a day instead of just giving me a bucket, and I'm even more surprised they didn't just kill me." Finally, those sky-blue eyes that were the same as their sibling's looked at me. "I take it I have you to thank for that? Given it was your Marshal who saved me and brought me here?"

I walked a little closer to the cell and rested my hand on the bars. The iron bit at me, and I dropped my hand. "I happen to be marrying into the family, so to speak. It comes with perks."

"So you killed your aunt and you're marrying into the most formidable of the Houses from a fighting standpoint." She looked away from me. "Should I also assume that you're here to order my death, considering my House is far from trustworthy?"

I pondered her. Tamsen was . . . tricky. She was loyal to Nyx—of that I had no doubt—but House Corvinus was a problem.

"Why did you run? All this time, you've played the game with your asshole parents. Played the role of dutiful Heir."

Tamsen let out a joyless laugh. "I stayed because I foolishly thought I could just wait it out. That when my parents died, I could fix things. That they could come home." Her voice broke as she spoke.

For the first time since walking into the room, I allowed myself to look at the person huddled in the dark back corner of the cell next to Tamsen's. Nyx was sitting with their knees bent, arms loosely resting on them, while black eyes threaded with blue stared at me.

They didn't say a word.

"My parents quietly issued an order that if Nyx were spotted, they were to be brought back to House Corvinus by any means necessary."

My gaze snapped back to Tamsen. "Why?"

She let out a chilling laugh. "To get to you. They know of your friendship with my younger sibling—and that Carmilla was looking for you. Nyx was the bait for the trap they planned to set."

"So you ran to find Nyx." It wasn't a question.

Tamsen's face twisted in rage and heartache. "You were supposed to keep them safe. I got them out of our wretched House to keep them safe."

Guilt hit me. I didn't think it would ever stop, but I also knew it wasn't rational. While Tamsen *had* done everything she could have to keep Nyx safe, so had I. And so had Adrienne.

My throat tightened.

I was trying not to lock away my emotions the way I had when my parents had died, but that didn't mean I could fall apart here. That wouldn't help Nyx, and I needed Tamsen to get herself together.

"This is Lunaria. Safety is fleeting," I said softly before unlocking her cell. "You're now the Head of House Corvinus. It's on you to make it so Nyx can come home someday. If that's what they want."

Tamsen blinked. "Just like that? What about my parents?"

"According to the reports Thessalia has received, they're gone," I growled. "So is Lucian."

There were likely others we'd find missing as well. People who saw the way the wind was blowing and decided they didn't want to stick around for it. We only had so many resources. Decisions would have to be made about who to hunt down and who to forget about.

I wouldn't be forgetting about Lucian anytime soon though.

Outside came the sound of footsteps and then quiet murmurs before the guard who had escorted me walked in, carrying a familiar silver box.

Tamsen cautiously left her cell, as if she was still expecting a trap, and eyed the box as I took it from the guard, who left without another word. I turned towards Nyx's cell and almost jumped. Tamsen swore harshly when she did the same.

Nyx now stood at the front, just behind the bars, a little more blue in their black eyes.

"I made it hurt," I told them as I stepped closer. "Not enough, but she didn't go quietly."

"Is that a good idea?" Tamsen asked in a strained tone when I unlocked Nyx's cell. "They're not . . . Nyx isn't themself."

I stayed perfectly still as Nyx stepped forward until they stood directly in front of me. "Nyx is my friend, and I'm not going to give my friend a gift through the bars of a cell."

Nyx watched as I opened the lid. I hadn't realized it until later, but some type of preservation spell was laid into the silver. Carmilla's heart rested within it, just as fresh as the day I'd torn it from her chest. The blue vanished from Nyx's eyes until they were nothing but pools of darkness.

But they made no move to hurt me or their sister. Nyx stared at the heart for several seconds, and then, faster than I could track, they snatched it up and tore into it. My heart raced as they swallowed down the chunks while growling faintly.

Do not run, Talis warned. *Their soul teeters on the edge of the abyss.*

Soon, all traces of the heart were gone, and Nyx closed their eyes and tilted their head back, blood and gore smeared all over their face. I could hear Tamsen's heart pounding as rapidly as my own, but like me, she stayed perfectly still. Waiting.

Finally, after what felt like an eternity, Nyx's head dipped down, and they opened their eyes once more. Obsidian eyes with rivers of blue looked at me, and my friend gave me a bloody smile. "You always did bring me the best gifts."

EPILOGUE

—

Samara

"We're not talking about it." Rynn gave my hair a vicious tug and I yelped, then she glared at me through the mirror resting on the wall in front of me. Four months had passed, and we were back at House Devereux for the wedding and mating bond ceremony.

I hadn't anticipated the amount of jitters that would flutter through me all morning. I mean, Roth and I were already mated, and I was eager to form the bond with Kieran. It had been incredibly challenging to hold back from doing it the past few months, but he had been adamant about wanting the whole ceremony thing.

Plus, Roth's parents had been ecstatic over the idea. Apparently, the only thing that excited them more than wholesale slaughter was a wedding. Or in this case, a wedding followed by a mating bond ceremony. We'd all arrived yesterday and collapsed into the large bed of the guest suite that had been set up for us. It wasn't easy to step away from our responsibilities, but we'd been working around the clock until the moment we'd left.

Surprisingly, I'd all slept until late morning. Although when

I woke, Roth and Kieran were already gone, so I had a late breakfast with Vail, Draven, and Alaric. After that, I'd been ushered into this small room.

I'd cackled when I'd walked in to see the weapons on one side and the dress hanging on the other. Clearly, this was just an extra weapons storage space that they had temporarily converted into my dressing room. It was close to where the main event was being held—which, in true Devereux fashion, was the sparring ring.

In their defense, it was the biggest open space within the walls, and many buildings overlooked it.

I'd expected some of the Devereux staff to come help me get ready, but to my surprise, it had been Rynn, Cali, and Nyx who'd walked in. My eyes had misted a little at the latter. Nyx was no longer confined to a dungeon cell, but they still kept their distance from most of the Moroi and really only interacted with me and my mates.

Except Vail. They no longer attacked him on sight, but Nyx had made it clear they had no interest in seeing him. It hurt Vail, but none of us knew how to mend that bridge other than to allow Nyx their space.

We'd set up a small cottage just outside the Sovereign House for them. The ward around it made it safe, but it still worried me that they were out there on their own most of the time.

Several rangers had volunteered to keep an eye on Nyx's new home, not because they were wary of them but because, like me, they were concerned for them. Many of the rangers liked Nyx and wanted to keep them safe. Knowing that helped my stress quite a bit.

I'd invited Nyx to come today, but they'd given me a noncommittal response, so I'd assumed they weren't coming. And while I'd hoped Rynn and Cali would make it, communication with them had been sparse since we'd all parted ways, and they hadn't been able to fully commit either.

"Don't make her cry again," Cali snapped. "Her face will get wrecked." She waved at my eye makeup from where she was perched on several boxes containing crossbows next to me.

Like Rynn, she also refused to talk about her situation. They'd both declared that today was all about me and only happy thoughts were allowed.

Any time I deviated from that, I got my hair pulled or my arm pinched.

I sank into the chair and scowled.

Smack!

"What the fuck, Rynn?" I rubbed the back of my head.

"No frowning!" she barked before staring at the messy braid situation. I'd say it was her fault for smacking me, but honestly, I think that might have improved it. "We might need to find someone to help."

"Or you could just let me do it." I started unraveling some of the braids, which were more knots than anything at this point. Fancy hairstyles were beyond me, but simple and elegant, I could do.

Nyx sighed before pushing off the wall where they'd been leaning since arriving. They hadn't spoken much, but their posture had been relaxed, so I figured they were okay.

"Move," they rasped and hip-checked Rynn out of the way before detangling my hair and sectioning parts of it off. Rynn happily went to sit by Cali, and the two of them started to idly chat about the events today. Mostly placing bets on how long it would take before some of the guests got caught fucking. Or a fight broke out. Or a fight that led to fucking started.

It was . . . nice.

Everything had been mostly nonstop for the past few months. I'd spent most of my time at the Sovereign House, although I had made a quick trip to House Harker just to make sure everything had been in order there. To my delight, our advisors had stepped up and kept everything going without a hitch. They'd quietly admitted to me that they had been uncomfortable with the path Carmilla had chosen.

Nobody was rejoicing in her death; it was more of a bitter acceptance that I'd done what had been necessary and that they were grateful for it. Long-term, I still didn't know what would become of House Harker, but it wasn't something I had to solve right this second.

Which was good because we had a long list of other problems.

Both the Head and Heir of House Laurent were dead, and no suitable candidates had risen to take over yet. With no other choice, Alaric had reluctantly volunteered to step in as a temporary leader—something he absolutely loathed because he had to talk to people on a regular basis. It also meant he had to spend time away from me, but things at House Laurent were improving, and he was confident he'd be able to leave things in the hands of the advisors soon—those we'd borrowed from House Harker and House Salvatore, because I knew all of the Laurent advisors and didn't trust a single one of them. Something Talis backed me up on. They weren't outright evil, so I wanted to give them a chance, but I wouldn't be heart-broken if Vail or Draven made good on their threats involving the advisors having an accident while traveling between Houses.

If the advisors were too stupid to realize insulting me in front of my protective mates wasn't good for their long-term health prospects, then they probably weren't cut out for being a House advisor in the first place.

As much as I wanted all the Houses to play nice with each other, there was no magic fix for that. We were going through a lot of growing pains, but I was hopeful.

Roth had been coordinating with the scholars at Drudonia

in cataloging and documenting all the information contained in the secret rooms beneath the temple. We'd discovered that, much like the room beneath Lake Malov, nothing there could be removed, so the scholars had to travel to the temple.

It wasn't that far of a journey, but the problem was we still had a very pissed off Seelie King and almost a hundred wraiths trapped in the temple. Rangers were always posted there, all carrying the weapons we'd discovered that worked against wraiths. We'd also set up more barrier wards to create more safe zones within the temple. I knew it was only a matter of time before Erendriel and his wraiths got free; the wards we'd put in place were merely to ensure our rangers weren't killed when it happened.

I had contingency plans for my contingency plans. The only time I'd stopped working was when my menstrual cycle had come last month.

All of my mates had dropped what they'd been doing to make sure I'd been as comfortable as I could have been. We'd all done the same for Roth weeks prior when they'd had their cycle.

I'd allowed Roth to keep working in bed, but they'd flat out refused to let me so much as *read* correspondence. I found it extremely unfair, but everyone had sided with Roth and outvoted me.

My anger had lasted all the way until my heat had kicked in. Then I hadn't left my bed for five days . . . but for much more fun reasons.

I'd cut back on my work a little bit after that. Nothing terrible had happened during those eight days, so it was clear I could give myself a little more time off. I had five mates to enjoy, after all.

My brows furrowed. Had I sent that letter to Tamsen replying to some of her ideas for improving travel between the outposts? She'd raised some really good points, and I wanted to implement some of them soon. We co—

"Stop thinking about work, Sam," Nyx growled before stepping back and returning to their spot on the wall.

"Damn," I admired myself in the mirror. "You do good work, Nyx."

Out of the corner of my eye, I saw them shrug. "I used to always do Tamsen's when we were growing up. She's even worse at doing hair than Rynn."

"Hey!" Rynn crossed her arms. "I'm not that bad."

"Yes, you are," Cali and I said at the same time.

Nyx had braided the top half of my hair into multiple braids that twisted into a bun with several loops draping down. The rest of my hair was pinned back away from my face before it fell in a dark wave down my back.

"Thank you." I turned in my chair to beam at them. "It's perfect."

Their expression softened for a moment. "You're welcome, Sam."

"We better get going." Cali hopped off the box. "Celestina was very specific about where we had to stand and when." She grinned at me. "Your future mother-in-law is terrifying in the best kind of way."

"I know," I gave her a dreamy smile.

Rynn laughed, jumping to her feet and walking out the door. Cali followed her, only to pause and glance at Nyx. They caught her look and shook their head. "It's probably best I stay here." The blue lines running through their black eyes flashed in and out of existence. "The hunger . . . it becomes more difficult to control around a lot of people."

"It's fine, Nyx," I told them softly. "I appreciate you coming at all."

Cali stomped forward and grabbed Nyx's arm, ignoring

their hiss, and dragged them towards the door. "Don't worry, I'll keep you in line."

"Cali," I warned as fear raked its claws across my heart. Cali liked to push things—and Nyx wouldn't respond well to that.

"It's been months, Sam," she called over her shoulder. "Quit babying them. I mean, who hasn't lost their mind here or there?" A deranged laugh spilt from her lips.

When Nyx glanced back at me before Cali pulled them through the door, I gave them an encouraging look, and they just rolled their eyes. That little hint of the old Nyx settled my concerns. Cali and Rynn would be with them, and I had no doubt Celestina had thought of Nyx's well-being for this. She'd probably set them up with a good view but slightly apart from the rest of the guests.

I turned back to the mirror. The deep purple dress was made of a smooth, clingy fabric that hugged every single one of my curves. It was perfect, and I couldn't wait for my mates to see how spectacular my ass looked in it.

All I had to do was wait for someone to come fetch me. I bit my bottom lip as a happy grin split my face.

Today, I was marrying Roth and finally forging the bond with Kieran, and the rest of my mates would be here to celebrate. I'd asked if they wanted to do something—like take part in their own ceremony—but Vail and Alaric had made it very clear that they didn't want to be, in their words, a public spectacle. And Draven had said he was content with the role he had secured—whatever that meant.

I took a deep breath and let it out. For today, no problems existed. There was no correspondence I needed to read. No deals to negotiate. No advisors to scrutinize.

Today was just for me and my mates.

My fingers ran across the silky fabric of the dress. It might not have had pockets, but this dress was to die for.

"I'm going to need it to go on record that I didn't step into this room and lock the door behind me."

I whirled to find Draven leaning against the doorframe, his gaze slowly drinking in every inch of me.

"So you like the dress then?" I arched a dark brow.

"I love the dress." He pushed off the doorframe and stalked towards me. "Don't get too attached though. We both know Vail is going to be tearing it off you later."

"Not you?" I smirked.

His fingers toyed with the thick straps that supported the corset-style top half. "Personally, I'd love to see it pooled around your feet while I bent you over the bed so you could suck Kieran down your throat while I feasted on your delicious little pussy."

"Fuck." I clenched my thighs together.

Draven spun me around until I faced the mirror again. Then his hands slid down over the tight bodice, giving my breasts a hard squeeze before continuing to glide over my hips. "Not even a hint of a panty line," he commented before his fingers found the high slit over my right thigh.

"We don't have time," I argued half-heartedly.

"My love, do you really think I didn't plan for this?" he purred as he kissed the side of my neck. "We have exactly enough time for me to fuck you hard and fast . . . and for you to walk down that aisle with my seed dripping down your legs."

His fingers grazed my clit, and I moaned. "Roth will be pissed," I said through panted breaths as he sunk two fingers straight into my aching core.

"Already cleared it with them." Draven grunted and kicked my feet apart as he pumped his fingers in and out. With his other hand, he pushed lightly on my back. "Hands on the wall."

I did as he said, planting my palms on the smooth wood on either side of the mirror. Draven took his hand out from between my thighs, and I watched in the reflection as he flipped my dress up over my ass.

"Don't mess up my hair."

"Wouldn't dream of it," he promised as he unbuttoned his pants and then slammed his cock into me. I let out a strangled scream as he bottomed out before pulling back and doing just as he'd promised—fucking me hard and fast.

I watched my tits bounce in the mirror as the sound of flesh slapping against flesh filled the small room. Draven's fingers sank harder into the soft curve of my hips, but he was careful not to pierce it and risk getting blood on my dress.

I felt the mixture of our combined pleasure dribbling down my leg just as he let out a deep groan. Our eyes connected in the mirror, and Draven smiled at me. "You are fucking perfect. Now let's go get you married and bonded."

Less than two minutes later, we exited the room. Draven hadn't been kidding about me wearing him down the aisle. He'd made sure my dress was okay but hadn't let me clean up further. With every step, I felt more of him slip out.

We turned the corner and almost ran into a familiar russet-haired Moroi.

"There you are!" Zander grabbed my wrist and tugged me along. "You're late."

I glared over my shoulder at Draven. "Told you."

He shrugged unrepentantly. "Worth it."

Zander led us through a few narrow alleyways until we reached the edge of the large courtyard where the sparring area was—or had been. I gasped as I looked at the once dirt-filled ground that was now covered with soft green grass. Flowers of purple, yellow, and white rose on delicate stocks, lining a path for us.

"Do you like it?" Draven asked.

I tore my gaze away from the beautiful garden my

charming prince had created just for me and drank in his appearance. My eyes stayed locked on his. "I love it."

"I love it too." He smiled.

"Yes, you're both gorgeous and sickeningly in love." Zander let go of my wrist and gently nudged me towards Draven. "Save the fireworks for the main event, yeah?"

Draven extended his arm, and I looped mine around his before we approached the large crowd, all wearing happy and wistful expressions. Above us, petals of soft yellow and purple rained down from those spectating in the buildings.

The crowd parted at our approach, and more petals were tossed onto the soft grass as we made our way forward.

They're so happy, Talis said. *I don't remember the last time I was around this many people and they were all so excited and joyous.*

Just wait until they get a few bottles of wine in them, Draven joked. *Then you can add delightfully drunk and rambunctious.*

Amusement danced across my mind before Talis pulled back. We were still figuring out how their magic had changed. Talis had sacrificed the ability to control souls but could still see them in their own way. They relayed what they saw to us, making us walking lie detectors. But we'd also discovered that, while Talis was actively in our minds, we could hear each other's thoughts.

Which was sometimes handy . . . and other times not so much. Because Vail was still Vail, and nobody—myself included—wanted to listen to his grumpy thoughts all the time.

Plus, Kieran had told me I looked beautiful one morning when in fact he was thinking the shade of my dress was hideous and that I'd done my hair strangely.

Talis was getting better about limiting what thoughts we heard. They were also never pushy through our connection, seeming perfectly content to just soak it all in most of the time.

The crowd finally parted, and I got to see the rest of my

mates as well as Roth's family. Vail and Alaric were dressed similarly to Draven in fitted black pants and dark burgundy shirts. Vail had even pulled his hair back into a bun and trimmed his beard, which had become rather unruly lately. Roth's brothers were on either side of them. Both still wore fighting leathers, but the ones they had on today were perfectly clean and a shiny black —not a hint of brain matter or blood in sight. Taivan's hair had been braided neatly back, and Desmond's head was freshly cut.

Standing several feet in front of them were Severen and Celestina. They wore matching beaming smiles. I briefly spotted Cali, Rynn, and Nyx standing off to my right, but it was Roth who commanded all my attention.

I was only vaguely aware of Draven kissing me on the cheek before going to stand between Alaric and Vail.

I practically floated forward, closing the distance between me and Roth. "You look stunning."

Most of the time, Roth wore baggy clothing, which was often smeared with ink. Today, they wore formfitting black pants and a matching button-up shirt, plus a vest that perfectly complemented the purple of my dress.

"Don't get used to it." They grinned wryly.

"Tease." I tried to pout but was smiling too hard for it to work, and based on the snort Rynn let out, my face had contorted into something ridiculous.

"Thank you all so much for joining us today to celebrate the union of our youngest, Astaroth Devereux, to Samara Harker," Celestina announced loudly.

Instantly, my eyes started to tear up, and I had to blink them back. Moons damn it all, why was I such an easy crier? We'd barely even started, for fuck's sake.

"It is the hope of every parent that their child will find someone who loves and respects them. Who makes them happy." Celestina smiled at me and Roth. "I needed only to spend a few minutes with the two of you to know how much you love each other."

A few tears fought their way free and raced down my cheek. *It's okay. You're okay. It's okay.* I chanted over and over in my head. *Your makeup is still fine. You're definitely not leaving blurry black tracks down your cheeks right now.*

Umm . . . is it normal to think to yourself like this?

Not now, Talis!

Roth's lips twitched, as if they could hear every one of my thoughts.

Celestina turned to Roth. "Do you, my sweet and brilliant child, swear to love, protect, and honor Samara Harker for the rest of your days?"

Orange fractures lit up against Roth's hazel eyes. "I do."

"And do you, Samara Harker"—Celestina's intense gaze fell onto me—"swear to cut down any enemy who comes for your beloved, dote on them like the treasure they are, and above all else, love and cherish them for the rest of your life?"

"I do," I croaked as tears streamed down my face, not giving a single shit about my makeup any longer. How could I when Roth was looking at me like I was their entire world?

"Then we welcome you, Samara Harker, into our family as you welcome Roth into yours." Severus stepped forward to join his wife, a long, thin dagger in his hand. "Two souls and two Houses, united to stand strong through the good times and the bad, because there can be no happiness without pain."

Roth raised their hand, palm facing me, a wicked grin on their face. I sniffed and blinked quickly to try to clear my vision before doing the same, connecting my palm with theirs. As we intertwined our fingers, the tears started to dry up as adrenaline kicked in. Roth's parents had explained the ceremony in great detail because, in their words, "We wouldn't want a repeat of Roth's cousin's wedding."

They'd offered no further explanation, and when I'd asked Roth about it, they'd just smiled and strolled away.

While I might not know what had happened there, I knew exactly what was coming next. I kept my eyes locked on Roth's while, in my peripheral vision, I saw Celestina take the knife from her husband and smile at both of us . . . before slamming it through the back of my hand and straight out Roth's.

I'd been prepared for it, so I swallowed my grunt of pain as Roth let out a low, deep chuckle. Fucking House Devereux and their insane wedding nuptials. The crowd cheered as Roth gripped the back of my head with their hand that didn't have a fucking dagger sticking through it and claimed my mouth with their own. They swallowed my hiss as their mother pulled the knife free.

Roth kissed me, demanding but still somehow sweet, and a few more tears leaked from the corners of my eyes. They pulled back enough to laugh breathily. "Such an easy crier."

"I had a dagger shoved through my fucking hand," I whispered adamantly.

"That's not why you're crying, and you know it."

"True," I huffed and kissed them gently again. We leaned our foreheads against each other as Roth's parents wrapped our hands. The knife was enchanted so that it would leave a scar.

"You did so good, babe," Roth praised, and my core instantly tightened. They let out that raspy laugh again that I absolutely adored and leaned forward to whisper in my ear, "And good girls get rewarded."

I whimpered, and they just smirked at me as they took my now-bandaged hand and gently kissed the back of it before cockily strolling over to my other mates, who happily murmured their congratulations.

"And now, for the second part of today's ceremonies."

Severen gestured towards the crowd, and I followed his gaze. Once more, everyone parted, allowing Kieran to pass through.

His golden blond hair gleamed in the sunlight, and unlike the rest of my mates, who'd chosen dark clothing, Kieran wore a crisp white shirt with dark blue pants. He was perfect. And he was mine.

He was also riding my fucking horse.

Zosa pranced as she made her way down the aisle. Some valiant soul had woven white flowers into her silvery mane.

"Brave bastard," Vail muttered.

Light brown eyes that I'd been in love with since the moment I'd seen them laughed at me as Kieran drew Zosa to a stop. He slid off the mare and kissed her on the nose before moving to stand in front of me. Draven gracefully stepped forward to grab Zosa's reins and lead her over to stand with him and the others.

"You are absolutely ridiculous, Kier." I grinned at him.

"I know." He winked.

"I can't believe Zosa let you ride her." Or that she hadn't taken a bite out of Draven.

"This might be hard for you to accept Samara." Kieran gave me a serious look. "But your horse is kind of an attention whore. It's why I get along with her so well."

"Rude." I glanced at Zosa, who just so happened to be standing in a way that made the sunlight capture her dapple grey coat perfectly.

Okay. Maybe he had a point.

"Was this suitably dramatic for you?" I asked, turning back to Kieran.

"Honestly, even if it wasn't, I don't think I could wait another day." He smiled at Celestina and Severen. "Everything is absolutely perfect though. Thank you again for allowing us to do this."

"You're family now too, Kieran Blake." Celestina smiled back at him, and Severen looped his arm around his wife's waist, an identical happy expression on his face.

Kieran looked back at me, his eyes narrowed slightly, and he took a deep breath, then his gaze dipped to the apex of my thighs. "I see Draven did a good job of escorting you," he said slyly, hazel eyes twinkling with amusement.

I kept my face perfectly straight. "He was very gentlemanly about the whole thing. Didn't even mess up my hair at all."

Kieran laughed loudly, and my heart clenched with pure joy. I would never get tired of hearing the beautiful sound.

"I love you so much, Kier."

His laughter faded away before his face morphed into a look of pure adoration. "I love you too, Sam."

"Will you do me the honor of allowing me to forge a mating bond between us? To forever bind our souls?" I placed my hand over his heart but held back my magic as I waited for his answer.

Kieran laid his hand on top of mine. "My soul already belongs to you. It has since the moment I met you."

Tears once again flowed as I did what I'd wanted to do for so long. I stopped denying my magic and let it flow into him, joining us. The mating bond lit up like a bonfire, and his emotions poured into me. So intense, I almost fell to my knees. Only Kieran wrapping his arms around me and kissing me kept me upright.

The crowd erupted once more, and I was vaguely aware of more petals raining down on us. Then Kieran swept me off my feet and carried me back through the cheering crowd. The rest of my mates followed after us as barrels of ale and wine were rolled out.

Roth's brothers stood in front of Zosa, as if they were negotiating with the mare to not bite them.

Good luck.

"Our honored guests are going to change into more comfortable clothing," Celestina announced. "Let us drink and be merry while we wait for their return."

"In an hour!" Severen shouted.

"Ah, give them at least two hours! There's six of 'em!" someone shouted.

"Okay, two hours," Severen amended. "But no more!"

"So three hours then?" Roth called back. Loud laughter broke out and covered whatever Severen's response was.

Kieran trotted us up the stairs and into the main building. Within minutes, we were in our guest suite. A bottle of wine and some snacks had been left for us on the table. And *two* pitchers of water.

I giggled at the thoughtful arrangement and then squealed as Kieran tossed me onto the enormous bed. I'd barely landed before soft, bloodred ropes wrapped around my wrists and pulled my arms over my head, then I felt similar ones wrap around my ankles and tug my legs apart. Roth must have stashed them under the bed earlier in preparation for this.

"Something funny, wife?" Roth stood at the foot of the bed, unbuttoning their vest and tossing it aside.

"Someone is clearly worried about us getting dehydrated." My laugh turned husky when Roth's ropes pulled my legs apart even wider.

"It's a valid concern." Draven strolled over and gathered the fabric of my dress before sweeping it to the side, baring my glistening pussy to Roth.

"Already so messy," they tutted. "That simply won't do." Roth glanced over their shoulder to Kieran. "Clean her up for me, would you?"

"Of course, Roth." Kieran grinned wickedly as he tugged off his shirt and sauntered towards the bed. Anticipation raced through me as he crawled onto it, stopping to lick every inch of my inner thighs before sweeping his tongue straight up my dripping slit.

"Fuck!" My back bowed off the bed, and someone chuckled to my right. I turn my head to find Alaric there, already stripped of his clothes, his magnificent cock in his hand. A whimper slipped from my lips as Kieran continued to suck and lick every bit of Draven's cum out of me while my mouth watered at the thought of tasting Alaric.

"Something you want, Sam?" Alaric stroked himself again, and a bead of precum formed at his tip.

I licked my lips before smirking up at him. "See something *you* want?"

"Somehow, you get brattier when you're tied up." He let out a dark chuckle that had my toes curling. "There is zero chance of your hair making it through this unscathed, just so you know."

"It had a good run," I panted, my thighs desperate to clench around Kieran's head but unable to, thanks to Roth's ropes. Alaric climbed onto the bed and knelt next to me, then he gripped the back of my head, twisting it further towards him, and slowly fed me every inch of his hard length.

Someone tugged at the straps of my dress before I felt cool metal slide between my skin and the fabric. I growled around Alaric's cock as my dress was cut away. I really liked that dress, damn it.

Draven laughed. "Told you Vail would be destroying it."

"She has another one," Vail rumbled before making me jump when he ripped the bodice. Alaric grunted as I sucked harder on his cock and pushed my head farther down until my eyes watered.

For several minutes, Kieran continued to eat me out, taking Roth's command to heart as his tongue dove deep to get out any last traces of Draven. Vail leaned over the bed and played with my breasts. First with his hands and then his tongue.

"Don't let her come yet," Roth growled. "I get the first one."

I whimpered around Alaric's thick length because I was so damn close to coming. Vail laughed, his hot breath dancing across my taut nipple.

Kieran must have sensed how close I was because he pulled back after one final lick. "All yours, Roth."

The bed dipped as they switched places, and then Alaric pulled me off his cock. Turquoise lines bled through his green eyes as he smiled. "As much as I love you screaming around my cock, I think we want to hear just how loud Roth can make you come."

I opened my mouth to say something sassy, but what came out was a scream instead because Roth immediately went for my swollen clit. I'd thought for sure that they would tease me a little first, but they swirled their tongue around the sensitive bundle of flesh as their lips closed around it. Vail sucked on my breast, and I felt his fangs graze me just before he bit down—and Roth did the same.

"Oh, fuck!" I arched off the bed as the climax hit me hard and fast. Vail continued to drink harder from one breast while his hand roughly squeezed the other. Roth drank from my clit and slid two fingers into my cunt, pumping them in time with every one of their swallows.

My eyes rolled to the back of my head as I rode the pleasure Roth continued to draw from me. When I sagged into the mattress minutes later, Roth licked me one more time before resting their head on my thigh. I lifted myself up enough to look at them and trembled a little at seeing the signs of my pleasure smeared all over their face.

"As much as I would love to keep you all to myself for a bit"—they grinned at me—"I did promise to share."

The ropes around my wrists and ankles unwound, and then Vail lifted me up and flipped me over so I was on my hands and knees with my head pointed towards the side of the bed. "I was planning on filling your cunt until it was overflowing." He cut away the rest of my dress and tossed the scraps of fabric onto the floor. "But when I saw your gorgeous ass in that dress, a new plan formed."

I groaned as his slick and lubricated fingers slid between my cheeks and he started playing with my tight hole. "And what," I breathed out, "is everyone else going to be doing?"

Draven and Kieran appeared in front of me, both naked and with their cocks at the ready. "We're going to test your gag reflex while Vail plays with you," Kieran replied, bumping the broad head of his cock against my lips. My tongue darted out to lick the bead of precum off his tip, enjoying the harsh inhale I got from him.

"And then we're going to ruin the excellent job Kier did of cleaning up your pussy by filling you up again with all of our cum," Draven finished.

Yes, please.

"I find this plan acceptable," I tried to say evenly, only to moan towards the end when Vail slipped a finger into my ass.

Kieran seized the opportunity and thrust his cock through my lips, making me gag when he hit the back of my throat.

"Relax your throat, love," Draven ordered.

Tears streamed down my cheeks, but I did as he said. Mostly. Sometimes I still gagged when Kier went especially deep. After a particularly hard thrust, he pulled back and bent down to brush a kiss against my lips. "Good girl."

Then it was Draven's cock in my mouth as Vail added a second finger. "Someone play with her clit," Vail ordered.

I couldn't see if it was Alaric or Roth, but somebody dragged their fingers through my pussy and then swirled them teasingly around my clit. A strangled sound leaked from my lips as Draven continued to roughly fuck my mouth.

Alaric let out a dark chuckle. "You love taking all of us, don't you?" Fingers pinched my clit, and I choked on a scream as Draven shoved his cock deeper.

"Fuck," Draven groaned deeply before spilling his seed down my throat.

As soon as he finished and pulled out, Vail withdrew his fingers and lifted me by the hips. He maneuvered us until he was sitting on the bed with his legs dangling off the end and me kneeling next to him.

I hungrily looked at his cock and started to lean towards it, only for Alaric to grab me by the waist and tug me towards him. His mouth slammed against mine, and I kissed him deeply as he raised me up until I was straddling Vail's legs. I felt Vail lean forward more, his chest brushing against my back. Alaric sucked on my bottom lip as he lowered me down slowly, and I felt Vail's cock at my ass.

Alaric swallowed my moan as Vail tugged me down, fully seating himself inside me. Then Roth's ropes wrapped around my thighs and pulled them wide as I leaned back against Vail's chest, breaking my kiss with Alaric.

"Fuck, I'll never get tired of this view." Alaric admired me before notching his cock at my entrance.

His bright eyes, a mix of turquoise and green, were locked on mine as he slowly slid himself into me. Vail groaned deeply as I was pushed further onto him. Once Alaric was all the way in, Vail started to lift his hips, and it was my turn to moan as they both found their rhythm.

My gaze went to Roth, who leaned against the bedpost, watching me get thoroughly fucked. "Strip," I ordered a little breathlessly. "I want to feel your cunt on my fingers."

"Oh, and you think you give the orders around here?"

They arched a brow, and the ropes around my thighs tightened.

I gave them a sultry smile. "You said I did *good* earlier and that I'd be rewarded."

They smirked at me. "That I did."

Roth proceeded to slowly strip off their clothing and crawled onto the bed next to me, then knelt as some of their ropes wound their way across the top of the bed's canopy frame before dangling down directly above them.

They reached up and gripped the rope with both hands. "*Ik dov kov fùshuv sarbà.*" Fuck me into oblivion, Heir.

"*Qà hom gaha rùdmàb.*" As my love desires.

My fingers parted their slick heat, and Roth ground down on my hand as my thumb started to circle their clit.

Kieran let out a low groan that instantly had my eyes snapping to where he and Draven stood at the end of the bed, each of them stroking their cocks as they watched me play with Roth.

Kieran caught me staring and laughed. "Two cocks already buried inside you and you still want more. So fucking greedy."

"That party is going to rage all afternoon and into the night. We have to go out there for at least a little bit."

I gasped when Alaric hit a particularly good spot. He grinned and did it again, scattering my thoughts for a moment.

"And I want"—another breathy moan—"everyone"—Vail's hips jerked sharply up, and I let out a strangled scream before finishing—"to smell all of you on me. To know I am yours."

"And we are yours," Alaric grunted as he fucked me harder and faster. Roth's ropes pulled my thighs even wider as Alaric poured himself into me.

After a few more thrusts, he stepped back, and Kieran

immediately took his spot, slamming into me and causing some of Alaric's seed to gush out.

"Fuck," Vail ground out, and I felt his nails shift to claws before digging into my skin. "Little warning would have been nice."

"You're the one who wanted that spot." Kieran grinned over my head at Vail. "This is going to be rough and brutal because I have been fucking aching to fuck this pussy all morning—and that only got worse when I smelled Draven's cum dripping down her thighs earlier."

My pussy clenched around his cock, and Kieran swore as he did exactly what he'd warned. He hammered into me over and over again, driving Vail's thick length farther into my ass. Draven reached around Kieran to rub my clit, and I practically combusted.

Kieran fucked me through the orgasm as Vail jerked his hips up harder, and wet heat coated my fingers as I curled them in Roth's tight cunt before rubbing them roughly across their clit. They screamed and writhed over my hand as their own orgasm ripped through them.

Somewhere in my haze, Kieran let out a deep groan as he found his own climax. My mind was still scattered as he slid out and Draven sank into my pussy, making an obscene sound as he pushed through both Alaric's and Kieran's releases.

"I love fucking you when you're messy like this," Draven admitted as he slowly pumped in and out, causing more warm liquid to trail down my thighs.

"We can't have that." Kieran reached around and pushed it back into my aching cunt—right beside Draven's dick.

"Fuck," Draven groaned and started fucking me a little faster as Kieran continued to slide his fingers in. "Next time, you're fucking this sweet little pussy with me, Kier."

I whimpered at the idea of the two of them stretching me

out at the same time, while also loving that we still had so many new things to try—and a lifetime to find more.

Kieran bent lower and started kissing the inside of my thigh. To my surprise, Alaric did the same on my other thigh—and he also shoved his fingers into my pussy. Draven's eyes turned almost a solid bloodred as his thrusts became more frantic.

Despite just coming a few minutes ago, I could feel another one building. When Alaric and Kieran bit down and started drinking from my thighs, I let out something between a moan and scream at the intensity of all of it. Roth's ropes tightened further on my legs as they leaned over to sink their fangs into the top of my right breast.

I threw my head back hard against Vail's chest, loving that I was getting throughly fucked and bitten by all of my mates. Tremors still raced through my body, the echoes of that last mindfuck of an orgasm. A litany of curses fell from Draven's lips as he came, and Vail bellowed his own release a moment later.

Roth released my breast and gently moved my hand from between their thighs so they could plop down on the bed next to me. Alaric kissed my thigh one more time before moving to lie down on my left while Kieran and Draven shared a passionate kiss, my blood dripping down Kier's chin.

The ropes binding my legs loosened and fell to the bed, and I practically melted on top of Vail, who was still buried in my ass. Draven pulled out so that he and Kieran could collapse at the foot of the bed, but they reached across my thighs to hold hands, letting them rest on top of me.

A deep sigh of contentment flowed from my lips, not only because of the afterglow of so many orgasms, but at being here with my mates and just enjoying the moment.

There were still so many things I wanted to do—secrets to

uncover and problems to solve—but I wouldn't be doing any of it alone.

"You better not be thinking about work," Alaric grumbled.

"We clearly have to fuck it out of her more." Vail sighed.

"Definitely a tragic burden we all must share," Kieran chimed in.

"I hate all of you." I smiled.

"Today is for us to celebrate." Draven kissed the top of my thigh. "Tomorrow, we'll go back to being the Blood Sovereign."

I settled further into the embrace of my mates. "I can live with that."

Want to see some NSFW art and read more spicy scenes?

Signup for the Alex Frost newsletter at <u>alexfrostauthor.com</u> to read some of the emotional and spicy scenes from an alternative character's point of view and get all the NSFW artwork delivered to your inbox!

Author's Note

Thank you so much for reading *A Throne of Blood and Vengeance!*

I know I left y'all with a brutal cliffhanger ending in book two. My original plan was to make Vail gravel—because I love me a good grovel—the problem is that Vail isn't really the type to grovel, lol.

So instead I had a ton of fun writing him stumble through apologizing and making up for his massively bad decision. Vail was definitely a bit of a surprise for me in this book, including his sort of friendship with Draven. That hadn't exactly been a plan but as soon as I wrote their first scene together, I knew that if anyone understood what Vail was feeling, it was Draven.

Other characters behaved themselves. (Looking at you Kieran and Alaric) and then we had the ever so delightful Roth. If you've read my other series, you know I write queer normative worlds so I didn't want the reason for Roth being distanced from their family to be related to them being nonbinary. That was kind of the only plan going in…then I just thought it would be hilarious if Roth's family were a bunch of paranoid, unhinged, and kill happy vampires…who were also huggers.

So I giggled my way through every scene with Roth's fam.

It was bittersweet to write Samara's last book, but we'll still be seeing plenty of Samara and her mates in the remaining six books of the series.

Rynn's first book will come out in early 2026 and it's going to be a wild ride. Samara had a history with all of her love interests, both good and bad. But Rynn doesn't really have that. And obviously there is a bit of…tension…between Rynn and the Alpha Pack in A Throne of Blood and Vengeance.

Poor Rynn. She's not going to be a happy wolf for a bit.

If you enjoyed reading this book, it would be incredibly appreciated if you could leave an honest review on Goodreads or whichever platform you prefer. Reviews are super important for authors and we really appreciate it when y'all take the time to leave one! Plus it helps other readers find us :)

Guide to the Characters and Places of Lunaria

THE MOROI

Broken up into six Houses, each controlled by the bloodline the House is named after. All six Houses are ruled by the Sovereign House.

Sovereign House

Queen Velika Nacht - Ruler of Sovereign House and all of the Moroi realm.
Consort Lucian - Velika's plaything for the last few decades. Must be very talented with certain body parts.
Prince Draven Nacht - Son of Velika. Suspected father is Lucian but never been confirmed. Sure that won't be relevant later.

House Harker

HEAD OF HOUSE | Carmilla Harker - Samara's aunt.

Raised Samara after the death of her parents; Samara's mom was Carmilla's sister.

HEIR OF HOUSE | Samara Harker - Raised in House Harker before moving to House Laurent for an arranged marriage with Demetri Laurent. Only lasted three years on account of him being a tool. Beloved niece of Carmilla.

Kieran Blake - Courtier of House Harker. Childhood friends with Alaric and Samara. Still besties with Alaric. In love with Samara. Has a complicated ex-lover. Originally from House Corvinus.

Alaric Lockwood - Grew up with Kieran and Samara. Besties with Kieran. Rivals with Samara. Also totes in love with her but won't even admit that to himself. Following in his parents footsteps of being an advisor to House Harker.

Roth Devereux - Librarian. Hot nonbinary librarian. Oh you need more? Hot nonbinary librarian who has magical ribbons they keep wrapped around their forearms. Met Samara while studying at Drudonia. Their aunt runs House Devereux.

Vail Ferenc - Marshal of House Harker. Very devoted to Carmilla who raised him after his parents were killed. Has a complicated history with Samara. Might have tried to kill her once. It's complicated.

Nyx Corvinus - Ranger for House Harker and a part of Vail's unit. They met Samara at Drudonia but left their studies to become a ranger. Their parents run House Corvinus and their sister is Heir. Have a complicated history with their original House on account of their parents being assholes.

Adrienne - Ranger for House Harker and a part of Vail's unit. Very protective of Nyx and view them as a younger sibling.

Emil - Ranger for House Harker and a part of Vail's unit. The oldest of the group but still manages to kick everyone's ass and look hot while doing it. Major "Yes, chef!" vibes.

House Laurent

HEAD OF HOUSE | Marvina Laurent - Massive snob with no plans on handing the House over to her son anytime soon. Rumored that she killed her husband, Demetri's father, shortly after her son was born.

HEIR OF HOUSE | Demetri Laurent - Marvina's son. Was in an arranged marriage with Samara until he fucked it all up and she realized she could do better.

House Corvinus

HEAD OF HOUSE | Mora & Darius Corvinus - Both wicked shady and obsessed with gaining more political power.

HEIR OF HOUSE | Tamsen Corvinus - Nyx's older sister. On the surface she seems crafty and shady like her parents, but she's also done everything she could to protect Nyx, including encouraging them to get the fuck out and join House Harker.

House Devereux

HEAD OF HOUSE | Thessalia Devereux - Warrior and a scholar. Incredibly paranoid, especially against the Sovereign House for currently unknown reasons. Has no marital partner or children which is why she named her nephew as the Heir.

HEIR OF HOUSE | Taivan Devereux - The most quiet and mysterious of all the Heirs. Not much is known about him at this time. Obviously he's wicked hot though.

Severen & Celestina Devereux - Severen is Thessalia's brother. He has three children with his wife, Celestina: Taivan, Desmond, and Roth.

Desmond Devereux - Middle sibling between Taivan and Roth. Perpetually involved in relationship drama.

House Tepes

HEAD OF HOUSE | Raoul and Sylar Tepes - more concerned with hunting monsters than in their words, "bullshit Moroi politics". Raoul is Ary's biological father but both men raised him.

HEIR OF HOUSE | Ary Tepes - Takes after his fathers in that he'd rather be out in the wilds killing shit than dealing with politics. However, he is more adept at it than they are. Him and Anniela have hated fucked.

House Salvatore

HEAD OF HOUSE | Dominque Salvatore - Head of House Salvatore; youngest of all the House rulers on account of her parents and older sister getting killed.

HEAD OF HOUSE | Anniela Salvatore - Dominque's cousin and Heir of House Salvatore. Her and Ary have hate fucked.

THE VELESIANS

Lycanthropes - shift into wolves. In human form their eyes are typically blue, but it's also common for them to have mismatched eye color.

Ailuranthrope - shift into panthers. In human form, their eyes are always green with vertical pupils.

Ursanthrope - shift into bears. In human form their eyes are always brown.

Aetanthrope - shift into eagles. In human form their eyes are alway some variation of yellow.

Broken up into three Orders—Narchis, Avala, and Fervis—each one consists of multiple Packs. Hierarchy and dominance is a big deal with Velesians. Currently the Alpha Pack of the Avala order oversees everyone.

Not everyone is happy about that and they're constantly battling to maintain their position of authority.

Rynn Valatieri - Best friends with Samara and Cali. Born into the Order of Narchis. Her aunt and uncle run the Valatieri Pack which is at the top of the Narchis hierarchy. Because of her high-ranking status, Rynn was promised to the Alpha Pack to cement the alliance between them and Narchis. Rynn is less than pleased by this.

Alpha Pack

Cade - Leader of the Alpha Pack. Calm and steady. Until he isn't. Ursanthrope.

Bastian - Second in command of the Alpha Pack. Charming face with a ruthless personality. Ailuranthrope.

Ryker - Youngest member of the Alpha Pack, close to Rynn's age, hot-tempered and usually serves as a scout. Lycanthrope.

THE FURIES

The Furies mostly keep to themselves and will appear more in the later books. Most of the badlands are in their realm.

Calypso Rayne- most powerful Furie of the current generation, possibly ever. Best friends with Samara and Rynn. Capable of wielding shadow magic with far more skill than anyone else. Her friends think she is keeping a secret from them… she absolutely is.

If you enjoy fantasy romance with morally grey characters and slow burn angst you may like this series...

Lost Legacies

A Shift in Darkness*

A Shift in Shadows

A Shift in Fate

A Shift in Fortune

A Shift in Ashes

A Shift in Wings

A Shift in Death

*A Shift in Darkness is available for free download at maddoxgreyauthor.com.

About the Author

Alex Frost is… actually Maddox Grey. Dun dun duuuuun!

Okay probably not that dramatic of a reveal since it isn't exactly a closely guarded secret. The pen name Alex Frost was created to publish the spicier fantasy series that fall under the "Why Choose" genre.

Why Alex Frost? Because Maddox is a freaking nerd. After being trained by local baristas to respond to the name "Alex" instead of Maddox, it seemed like the perfect pen name. Half of it anyway.

Since Maddox already shares their last name with Jean Grey of the X-Men, it seemed fitting to borrow Emma Frost's last name for their other persona. If you know, you know. (insert smirking face)

To get regular email updates about new releases and other announcements, be sure to sign up for the newsletter on alexfrostauthor.com

facebook.com/alexfrost.author

instagram.com/alexfrost.author

tiktok.com/@greymalkinpress